STAR KNIGHTS

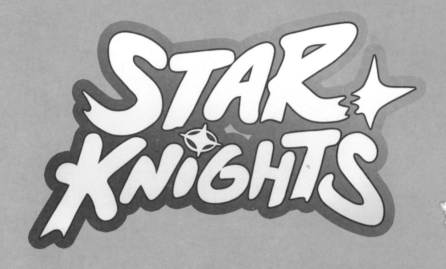

KAY DAVAULT

RH
GRAPHIC

NEW YORK

Star Knights was illustrated digitally with the help of Clip Studio Paint and Photoshop.

Text, cover art, and interior illustrations copyright © 2022 by Kay Davault

All rights reserved. Published in the United States by RH Graphic, an imprint of Random House Children's Books, a division of Penguin Random House LLC, New York.

RH Graphic with the book design is a trademark of Penguin Random House LLC.

Visit us on the web! RHKidsGraphic.com • @RHKidsGraphic

Educators and librarians, for a variety of teaching tools, visit us at RHTeachersLibrarians.com

Library of Congress Cataloging-in-Publication Data is available upon request.
ISBN 978-0-593-30365-8 (hardcover) — ISBN 978-0-593-30364-1 (paperback)
ISBN 978-0-593-30366-5 (lib. bdg.) — ISBN 978-0-593-30367-2 (ebook)

Designed by Patrick Crotty

MANUFACTURED IN CHINA
10 9 8 7 6 5 4 3 2 1
First Edition

A comic on every bookshelf.

To anyone who has ever made a wish

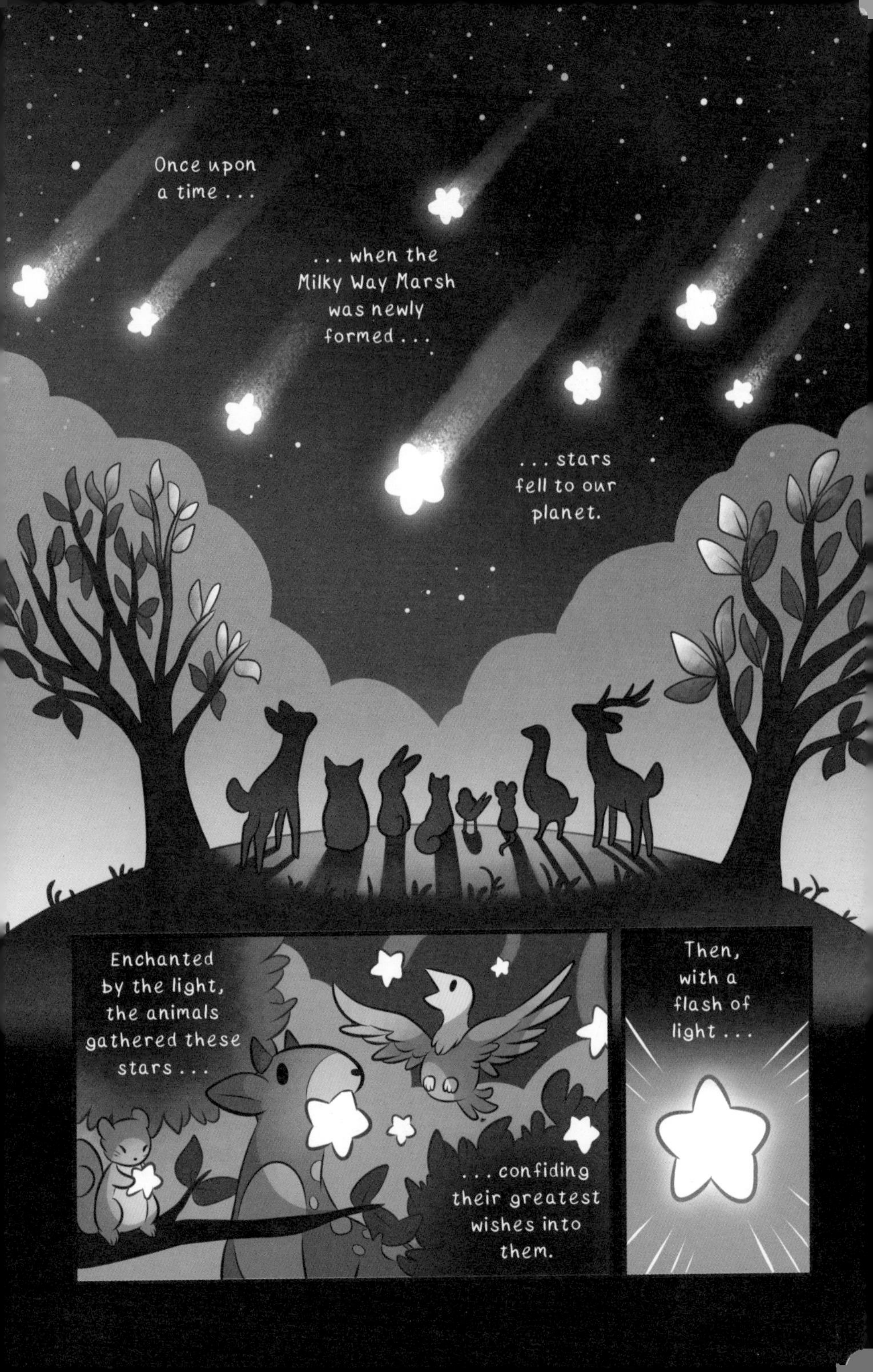

Once upon a time . . .
. . . when the Milky Way Marsh was newly formed . . .
. . . stars fell to our planet.
Enchanted by the light, the animals gathered these stars . . .
. . . confiding their greatest wishes into them.
Then, with a flash of light . . .

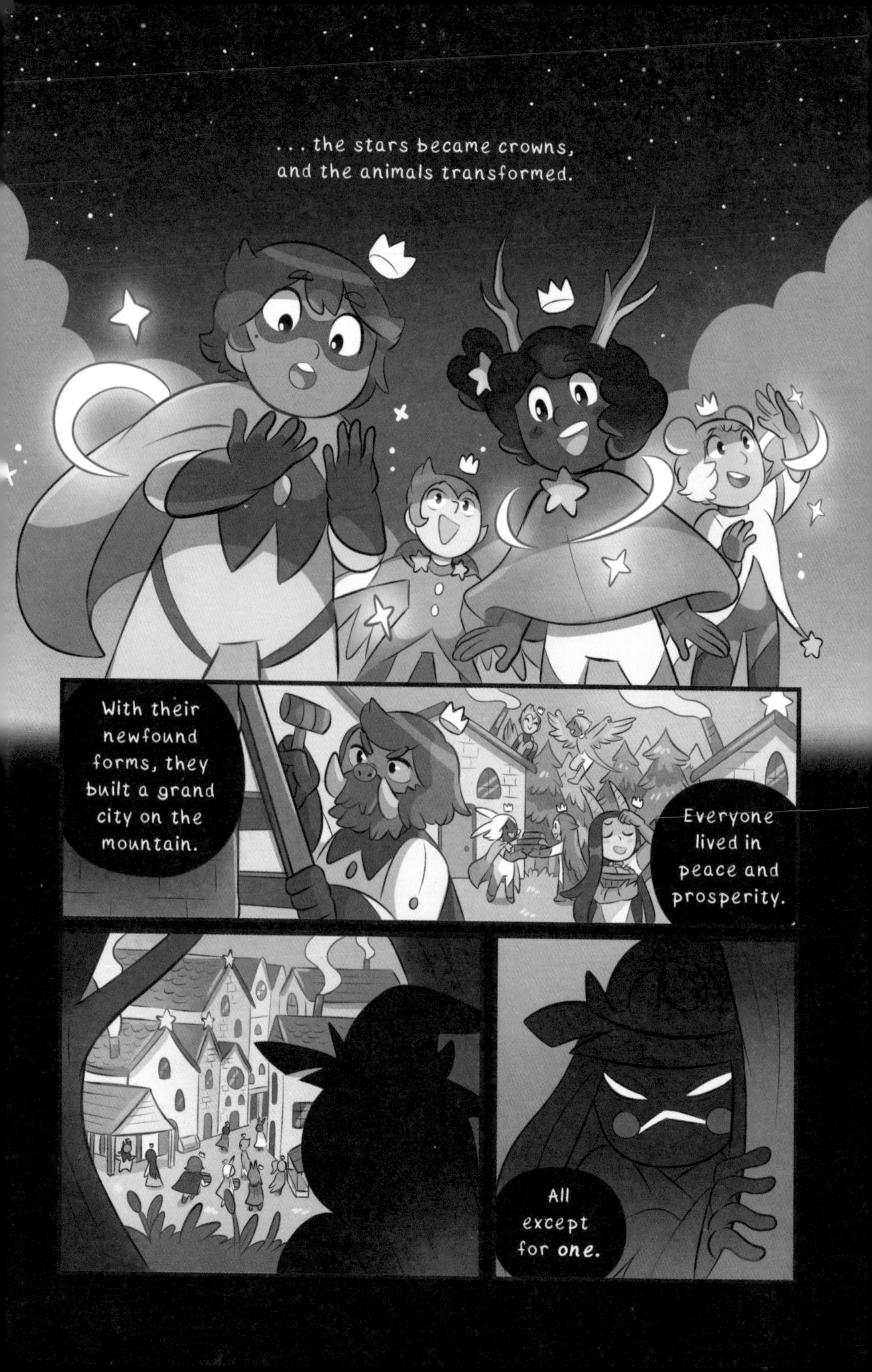
. . . the stars became crowns, and the animals transformed.
With their newfound forms, they built a grand city on the mountain.
Everyone lived in peace and prosperity.
All except for one.

The ugly **Marsh Witch**, wielder of dark magic, unleashed her slimy minions upon the marsh.
CROOAK
Cloaked in mud, they attacked the city, looking to steal the powerful stars.
But the star holders would not back down.
They fought the witch's army with magic of their own!

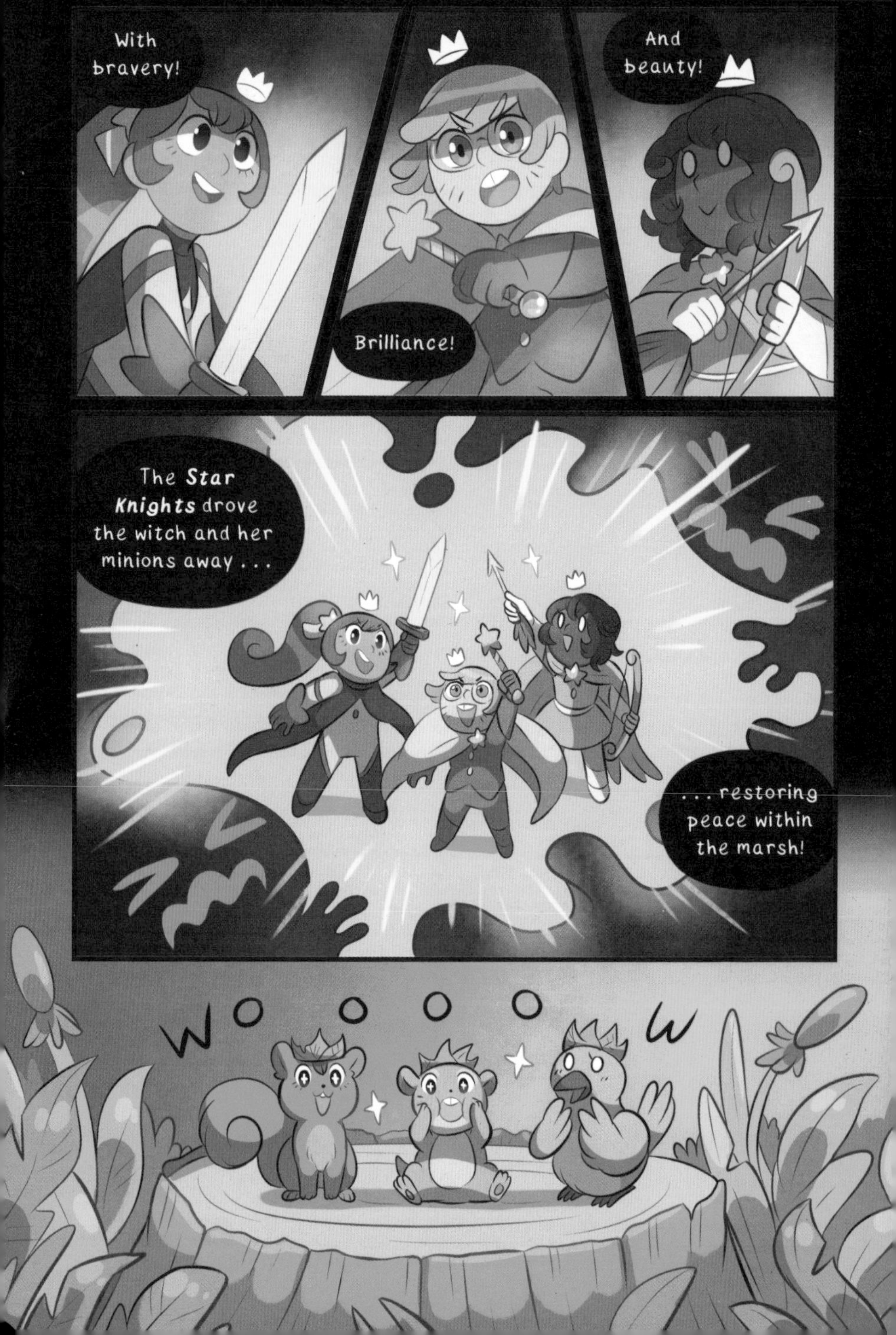
With bravery!
Brilliance!
And beauty!
The **Star Knights** drove the witch and her minions away . . .
. . . restoring peace within the marsh!
WOOOOW

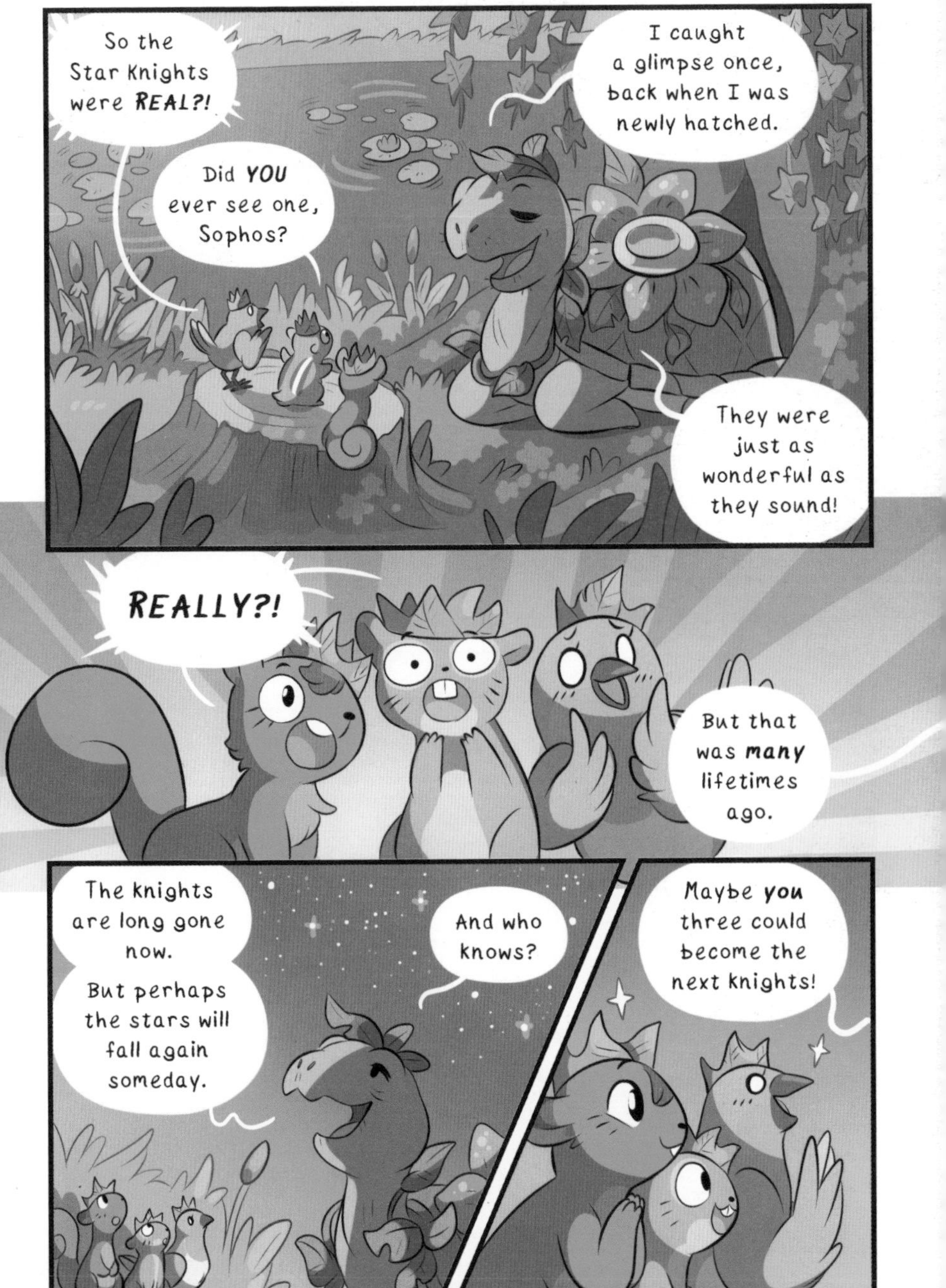
So the Star Knights were **REAL?!**
Did **YOU** ever see one, Sophos?
I caught a glimpse once, back when I was newly hatched.
They were just as wonderful as they sound!
REALLY?!
But that was **many** lifetimes ago.
The knights are long gone now.
But perhaps the stars will fall again someday.
And who knows?
Maybe **you** three could become the next knights!

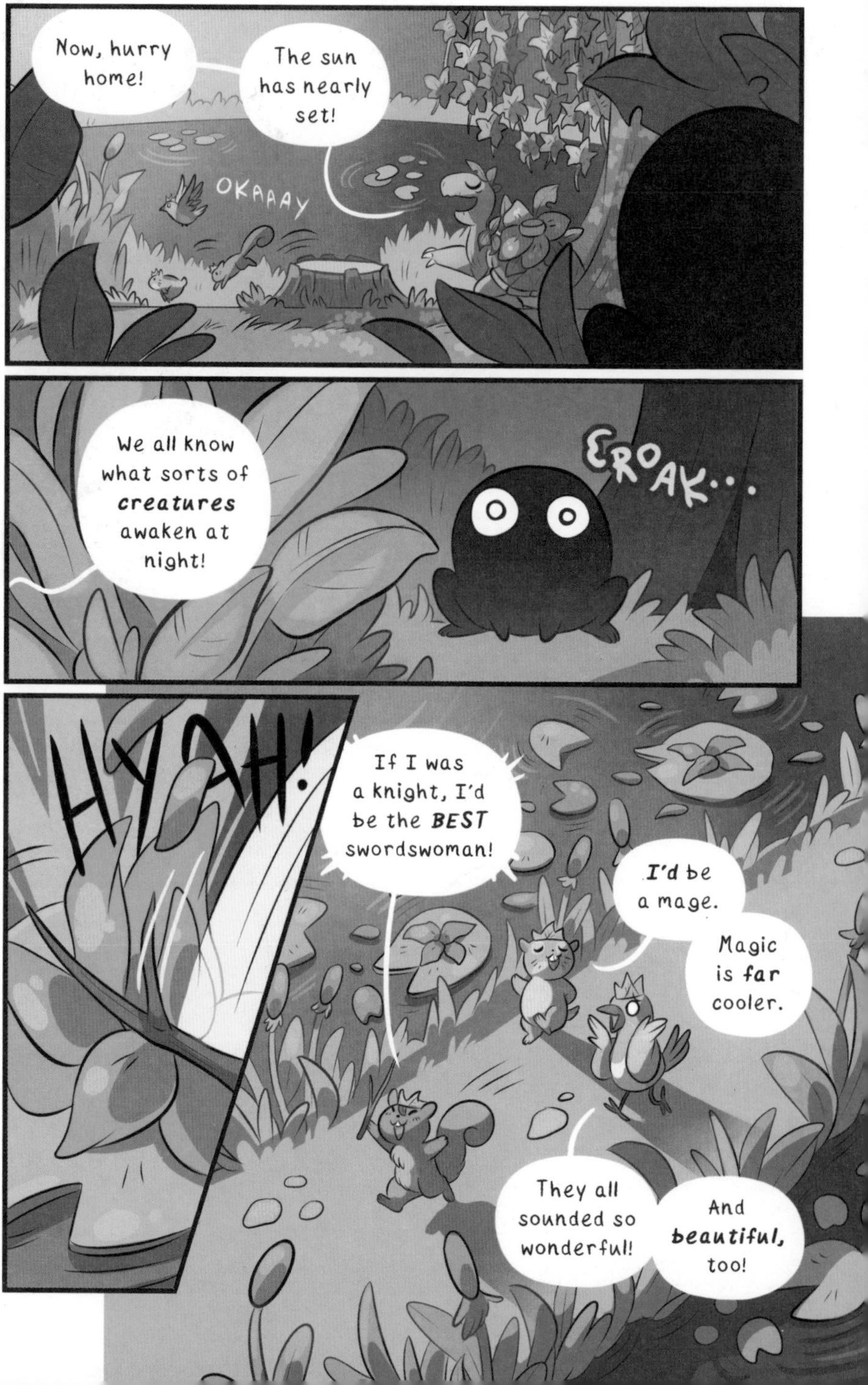
Now, hurry home!
The sun has nearly set!
OKAAAY
We all know what sorts of **creatures** awaken at night!
CROAK...
HYAH!
If I was a knight, I'd be the **BEST** swordswoman!
I'd be a mage.
Magic is **far** cooler.
They all sounded so wonderful!
And **beautiful,** too!

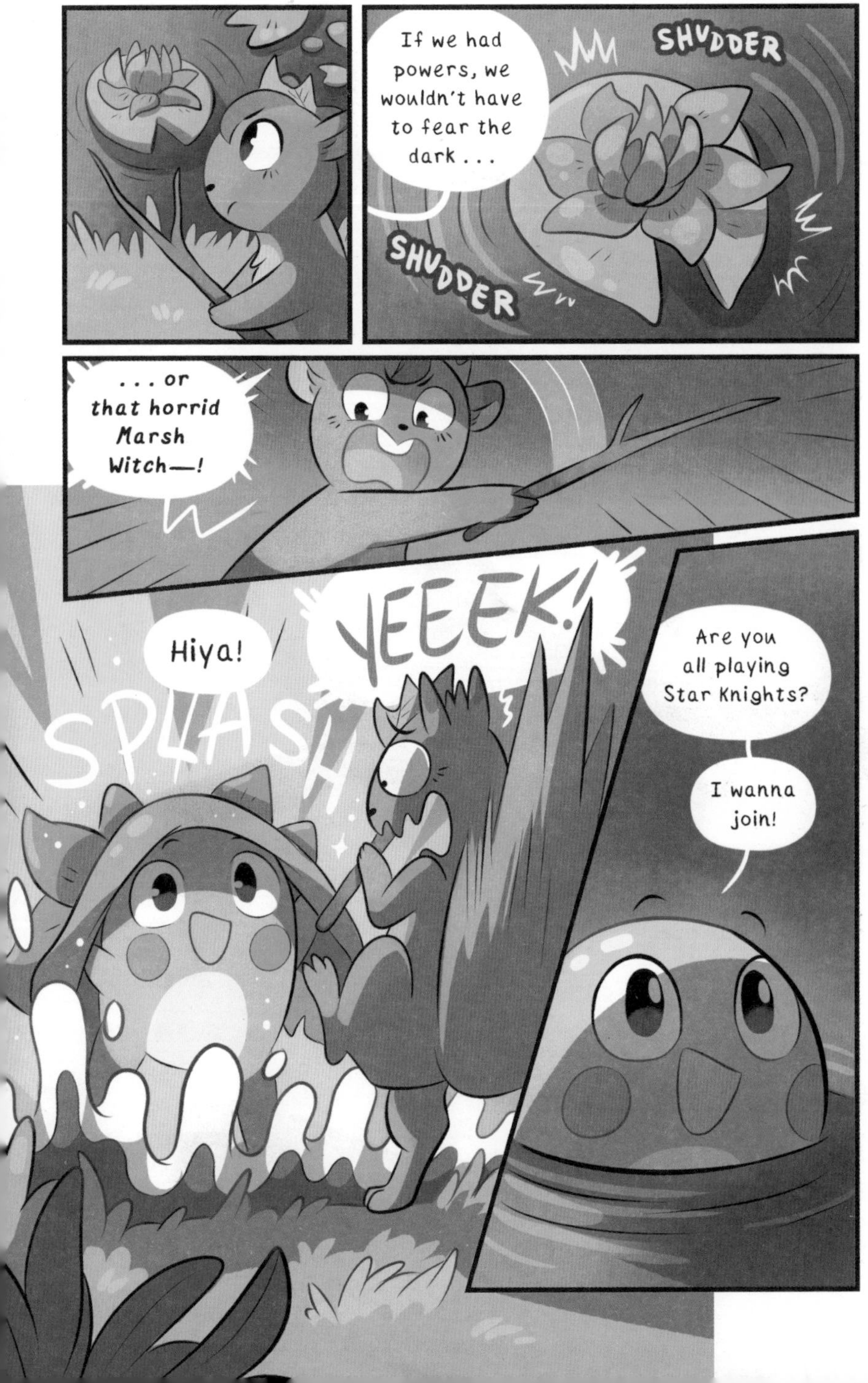
If we had powers, we wouldn't have to fear the dark . . .
SHUDDER
SHUDDER
. . . or that horrid Marsh Witch—!
Hiya!
SPLASH
YEEEK!
Are you all playing Star Knights?
I wanna join!

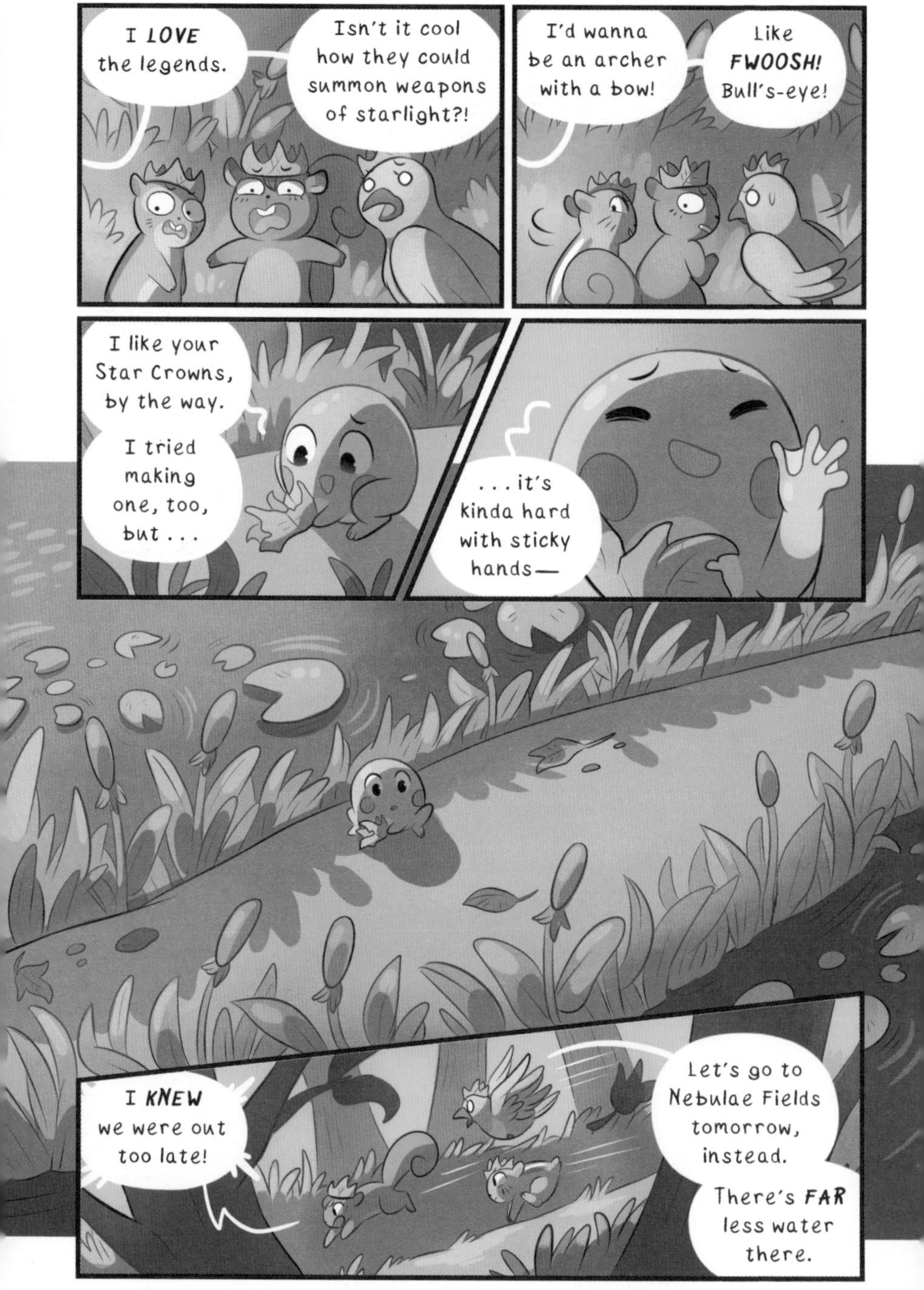
I LOVE the legends.
Isn't it cool how they could summon weapons of starlight?!
I'd wanna be an archer with a bow!
Like FWOOSH! Bull's-eye!
I like your Star Crowns, by the way.
I tried making one, too, but . . .
. . . it's kinda hard with sticky hands—
I KNEW we were out too late!
Let's go to Nebulae Fields tomorrow, instead.
There's FAR less water there.

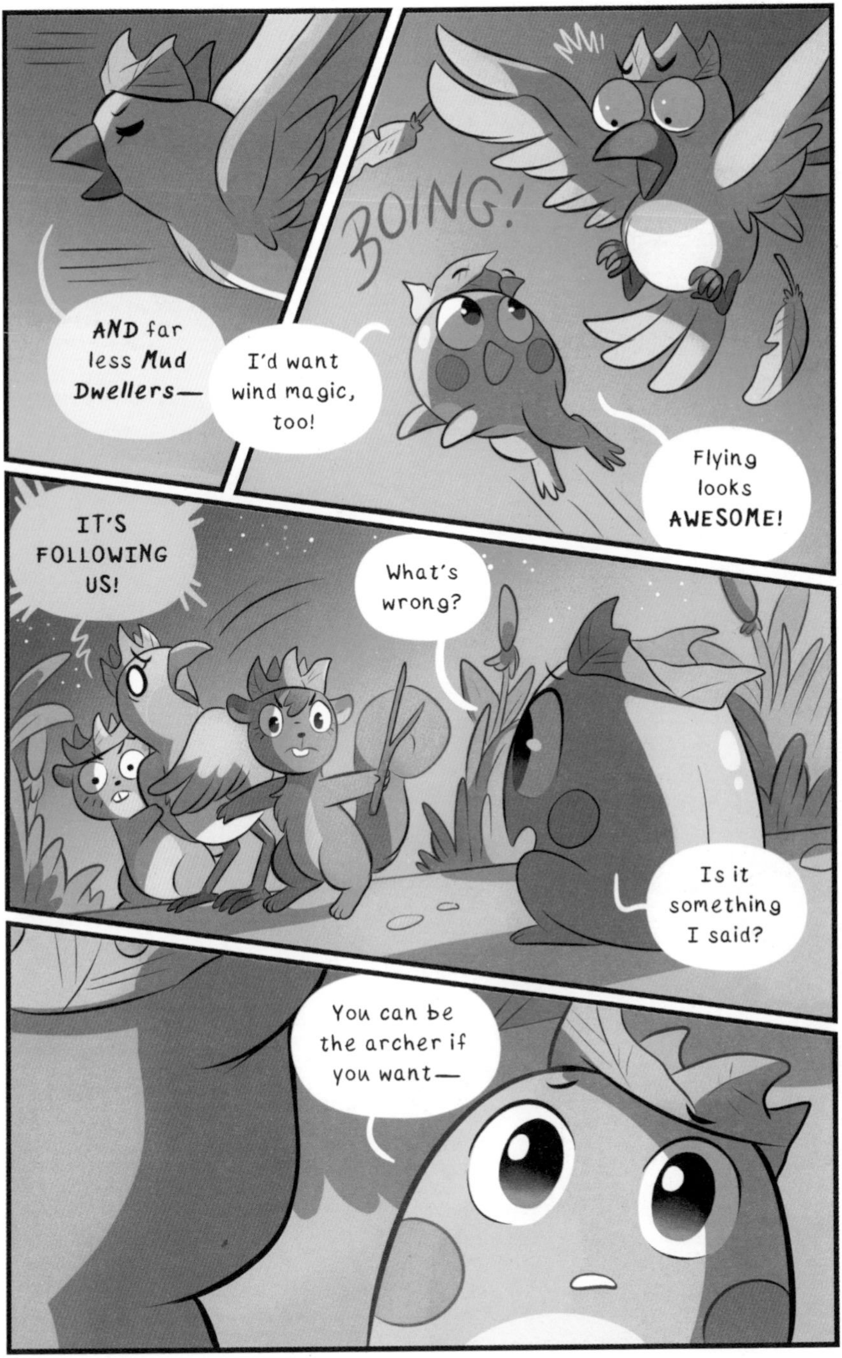
AND far less Mud Dwellers—
I'd want wind magic, too!
BOING!
Flying looks AWESOME!
IT'S FOLLOWING US!
What's wrong?
Is it something I said?
You can be the archer if you want—

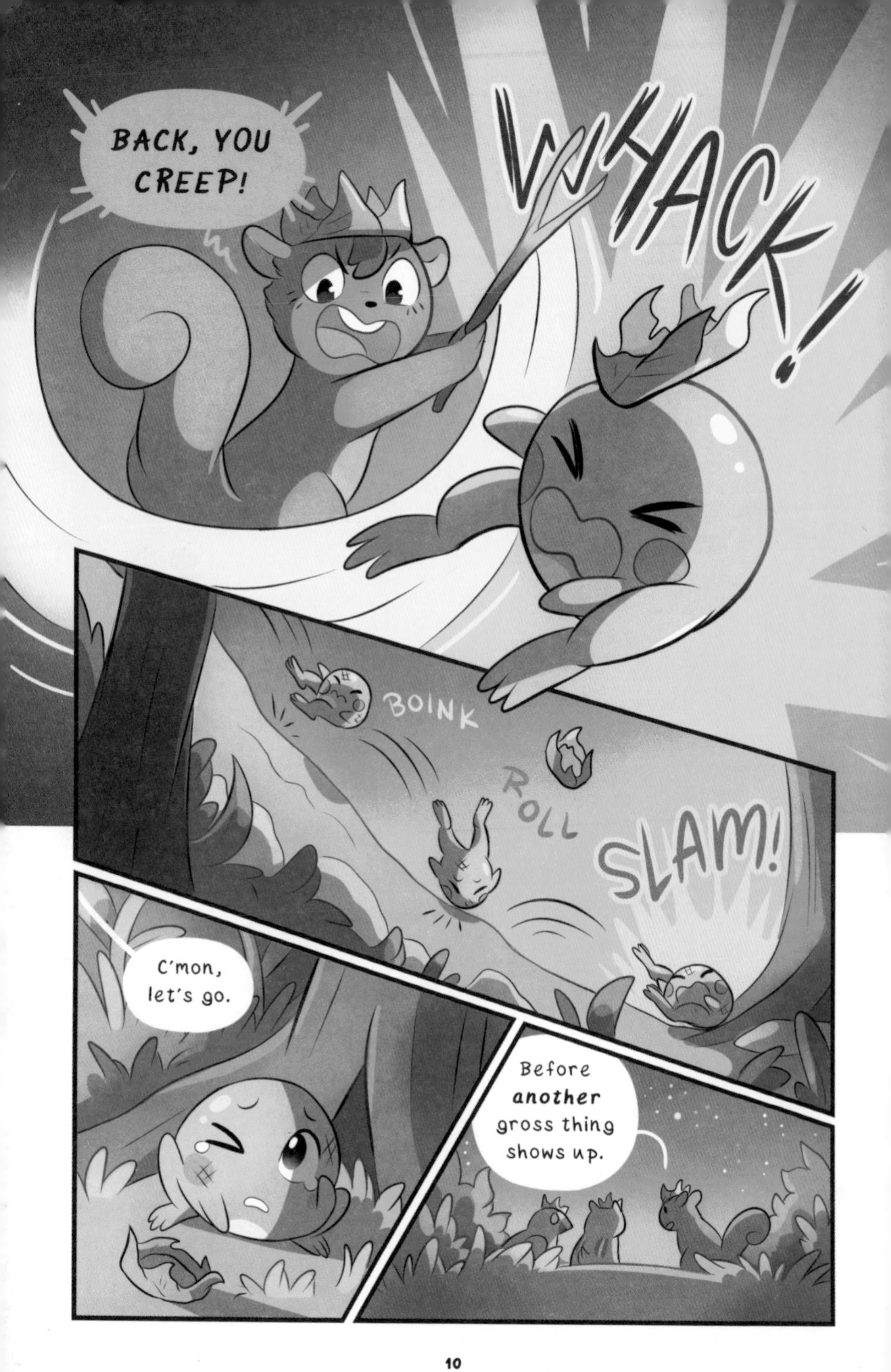
BACK, YOU CREEP!
WHACK!
BOINK
ROLL
SLAM!
C'mon, let's go.
Before **another** gross thing shows up.

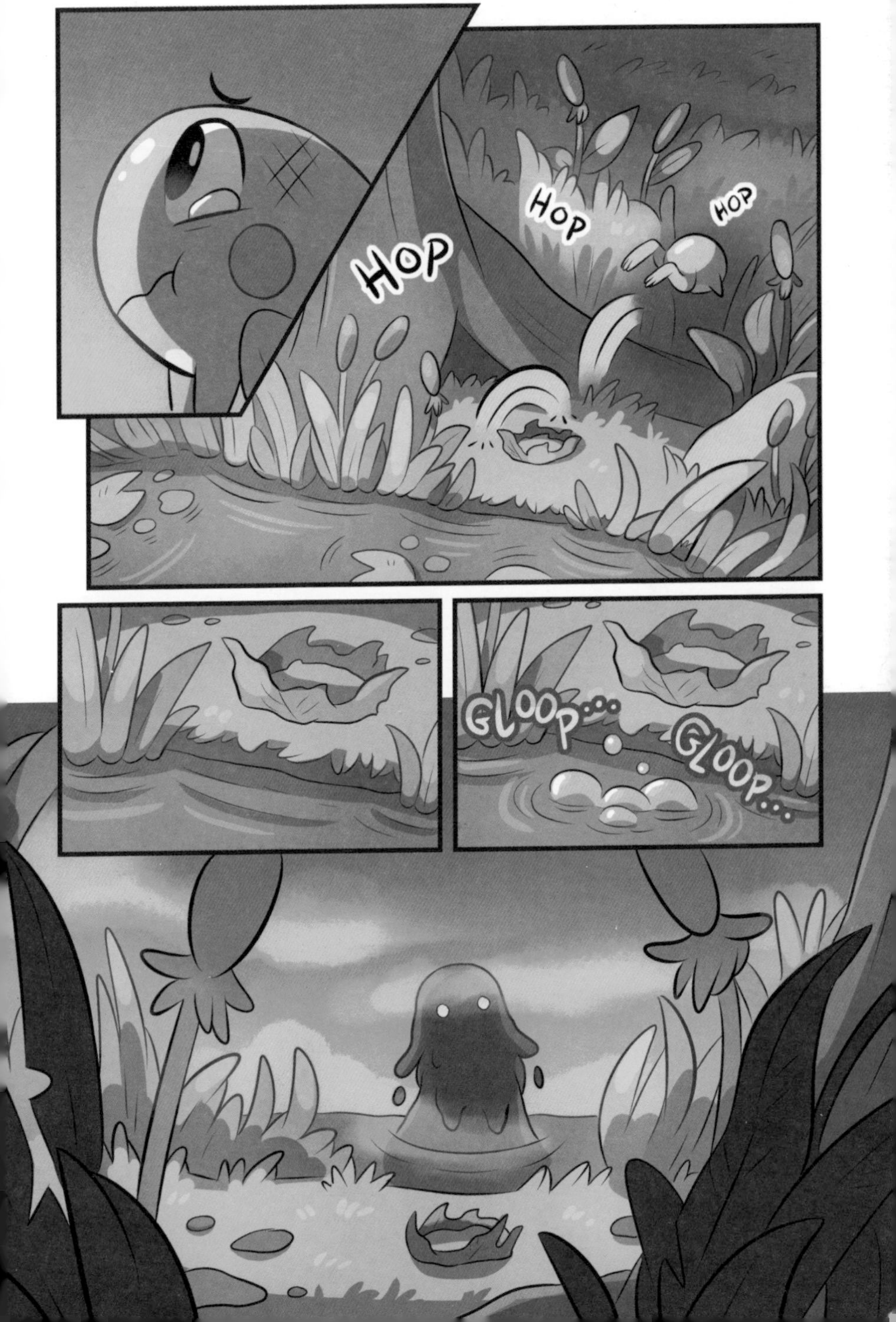
HOP
HOP
HOP
GLOOP...
GLOOP...

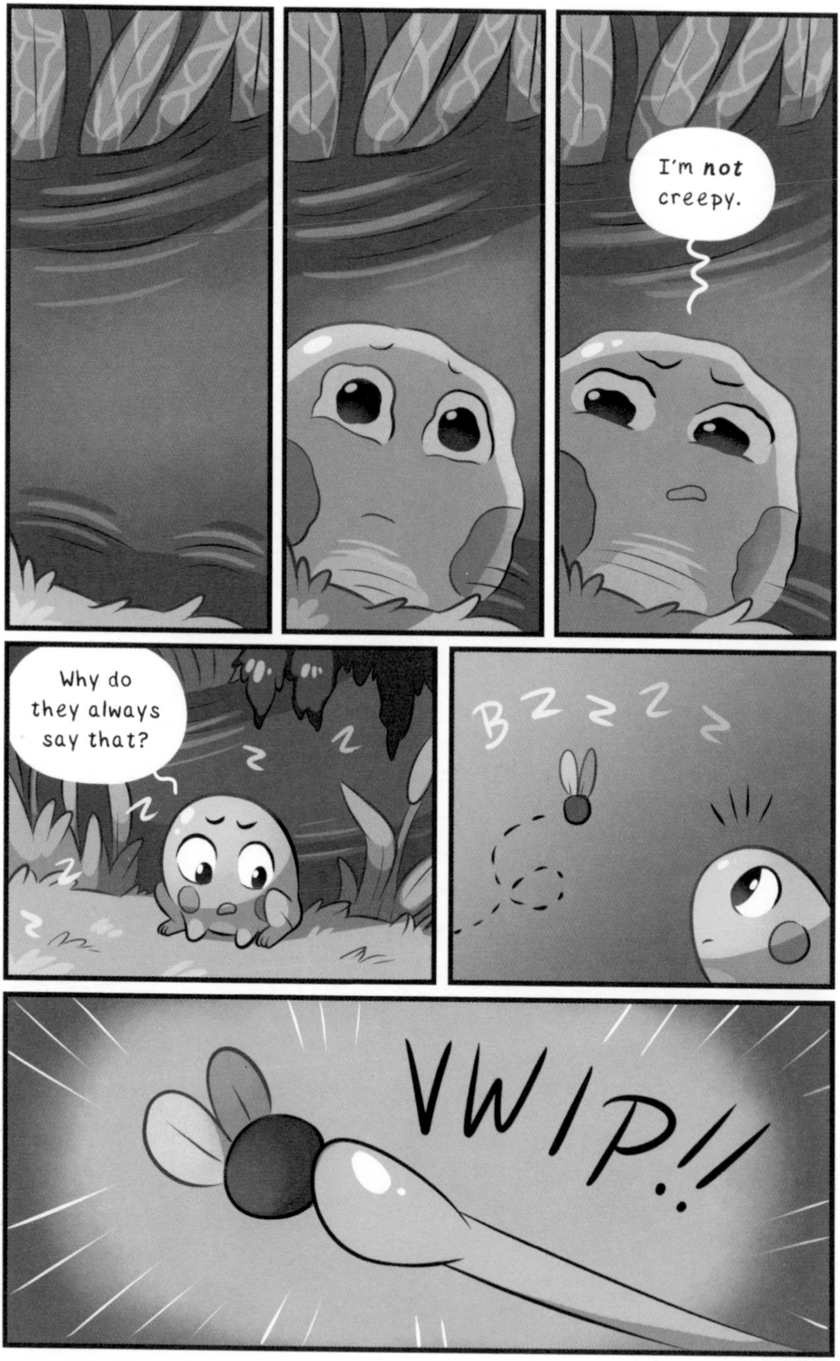
I'm **not** creepy.
Why do they always say that?
BZZZZ
VWIP!!

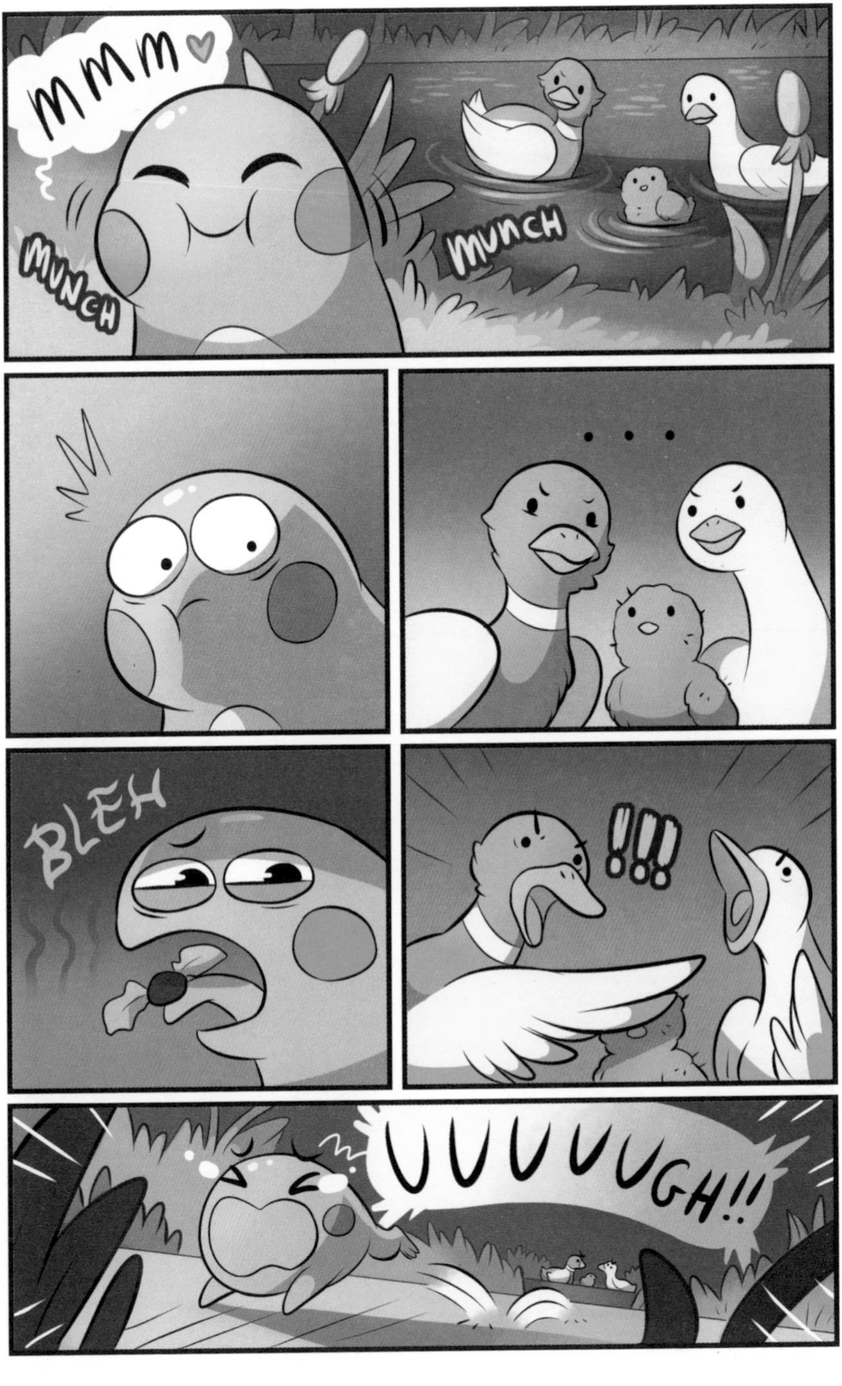
MMM
MUNCH
MUNCH
...
BLEH
!!!
UUUUUUGH!!

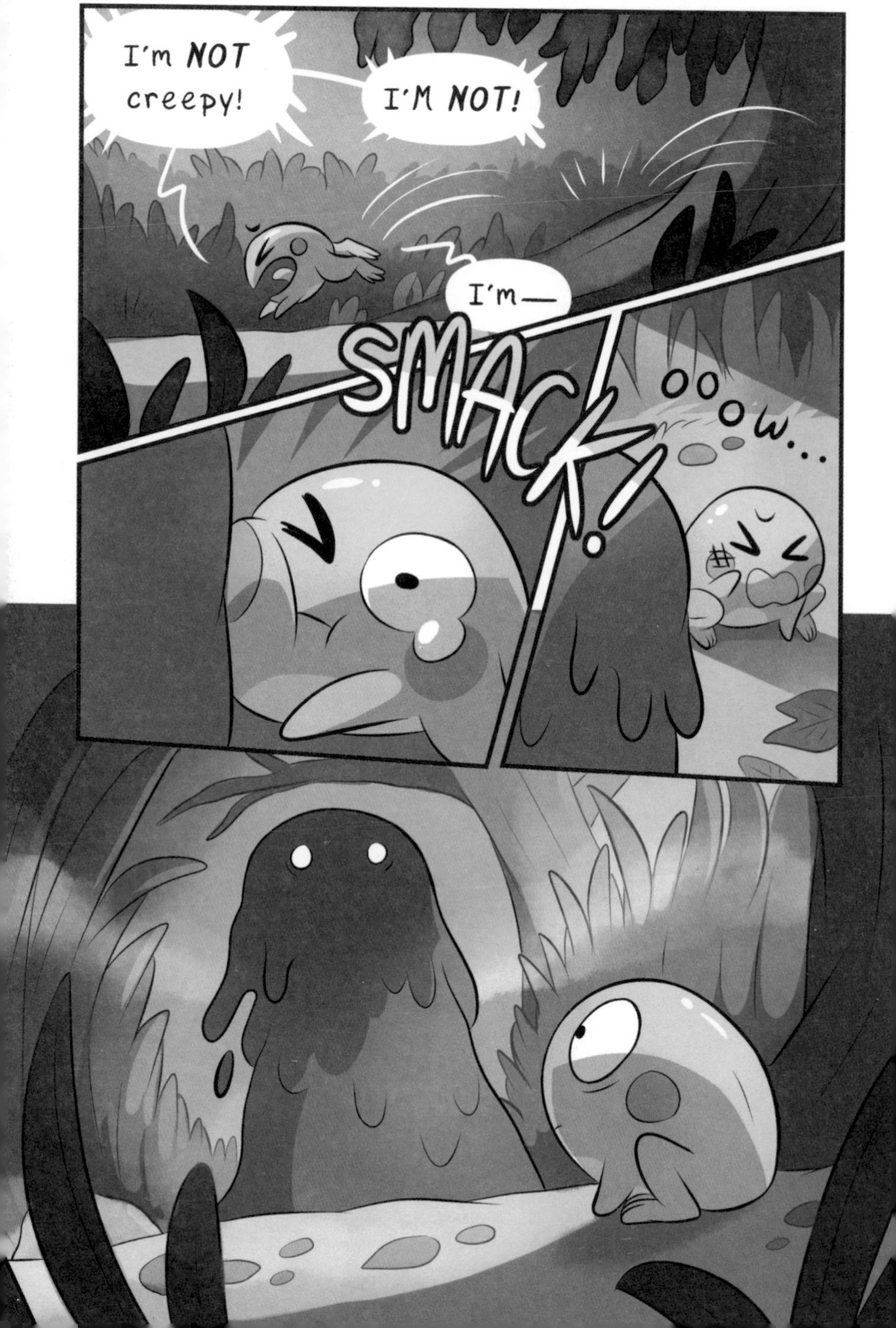
I'm NOT creepy!
I'M NOT!
I'm—
SMACK!
Ooow...

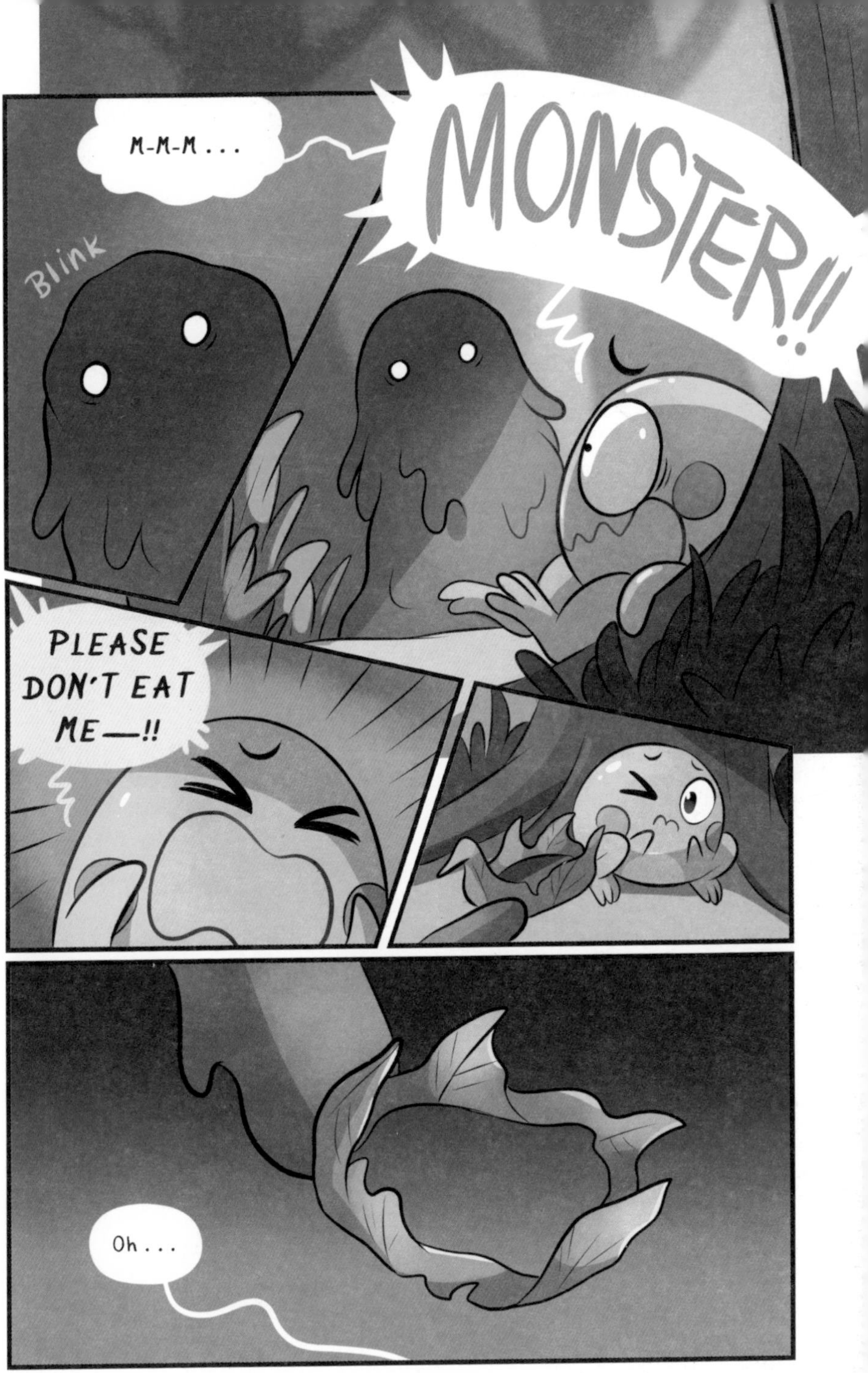
M-M-M . . .
MONSTER!!
Bliink
PLEASE DON'T EAT ME—!!
Oh . . .

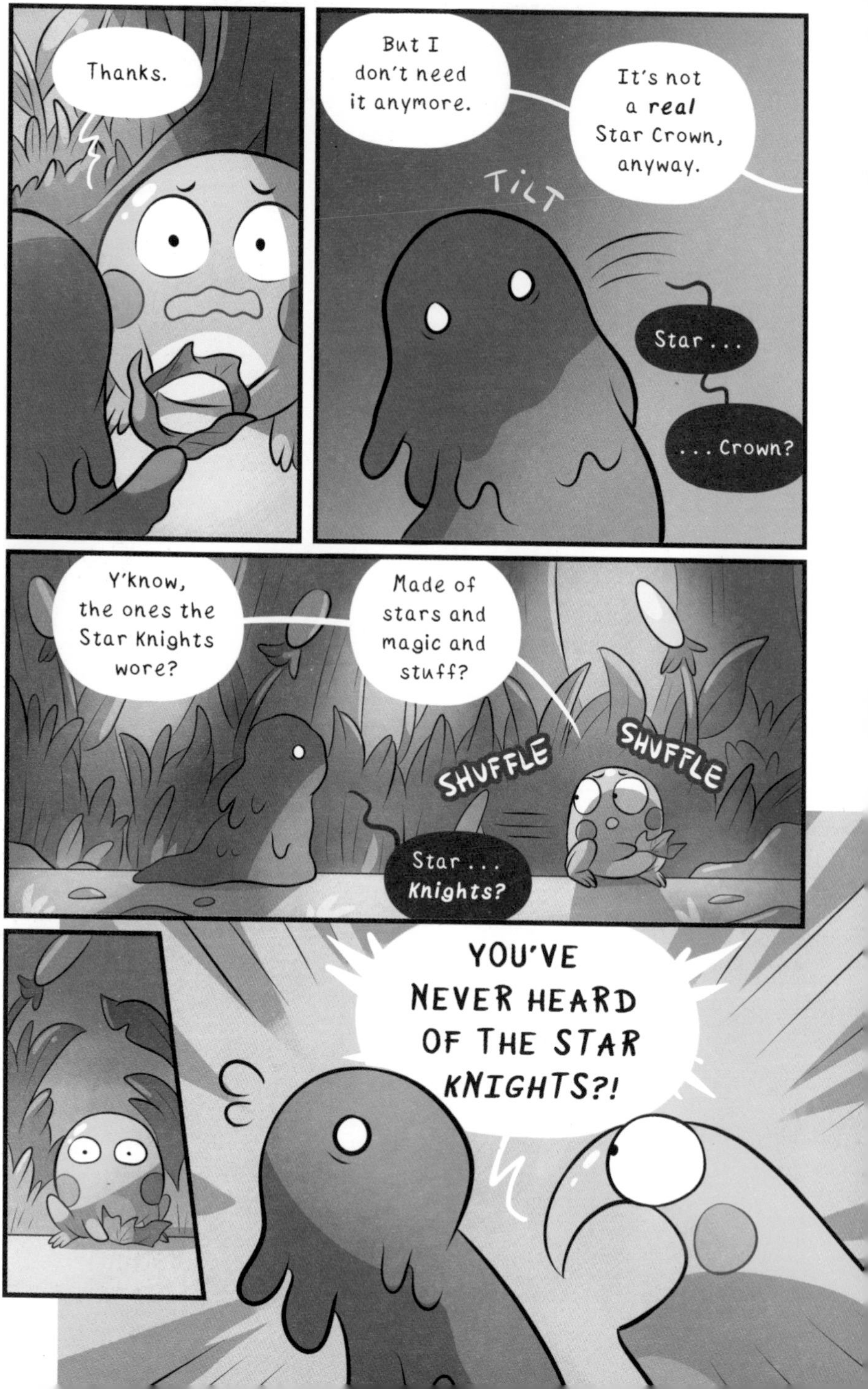
Thanks.
But I don't need it anymore.
It's not a **real** Star Crown, anyway.
TILT
Star...
...Crown?
Y'know, the ones the Star Knights wore?
Made of stars and magic and stuff?
SHUFFLE
SHUFFLE
Star... **Knights?**
YOU'VE NEVER HEARD OF THE STAR *KNIGHTS?!*

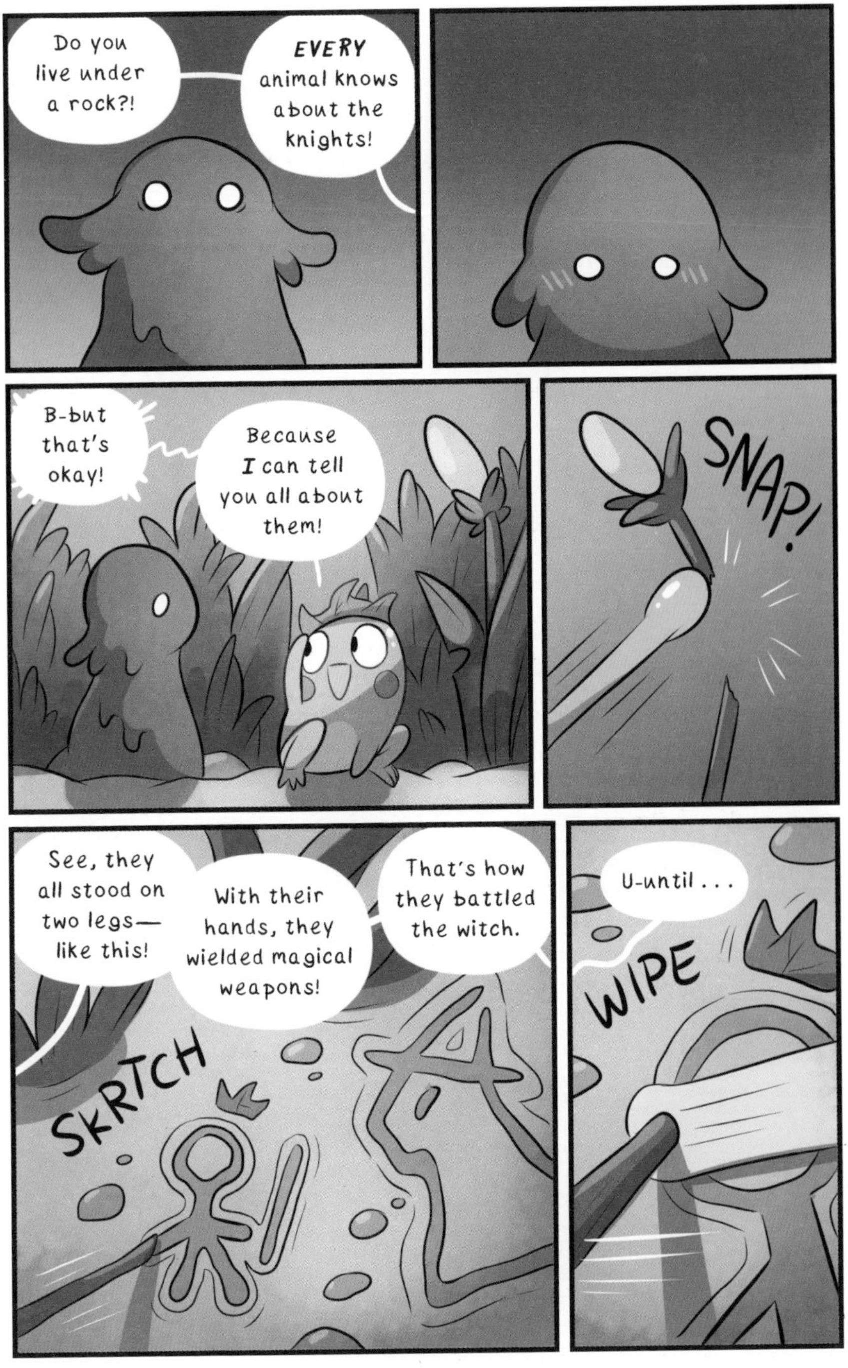
Do you live under a rock?!
EVERY animal knows about the knights!
B-but that's okay!
Because I can tell you all about them!
SNAP!
See, they all stood on two legs— like this!
With their hands, they wielded magical weapons!
That's how they battled the witch.
SKRTCH
U-until . . .
WIPE

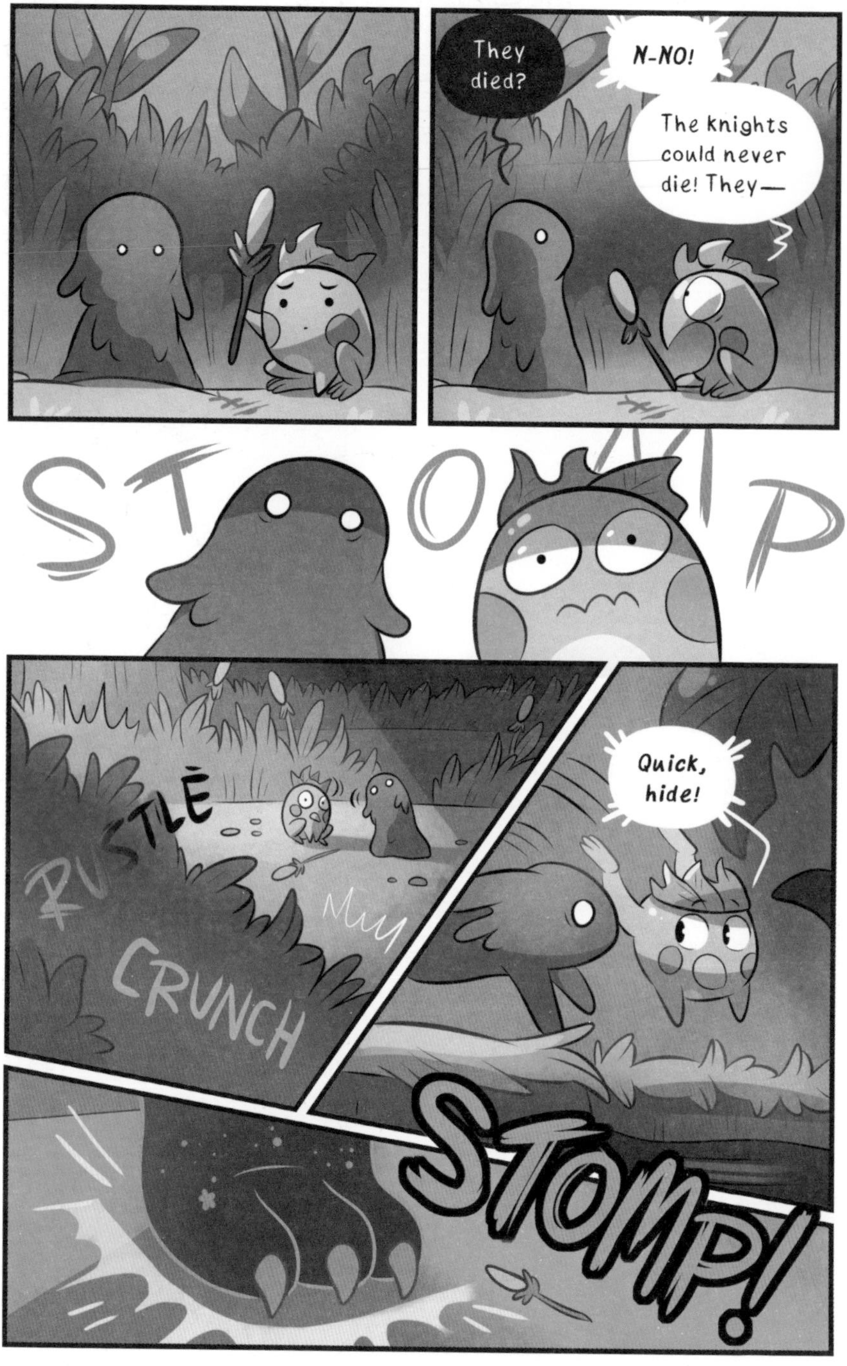
They died?
N-NO!
The knights could never die! They—
STOMP
RUSTLE
CRUNCH
Quick, hide!
STOMP!

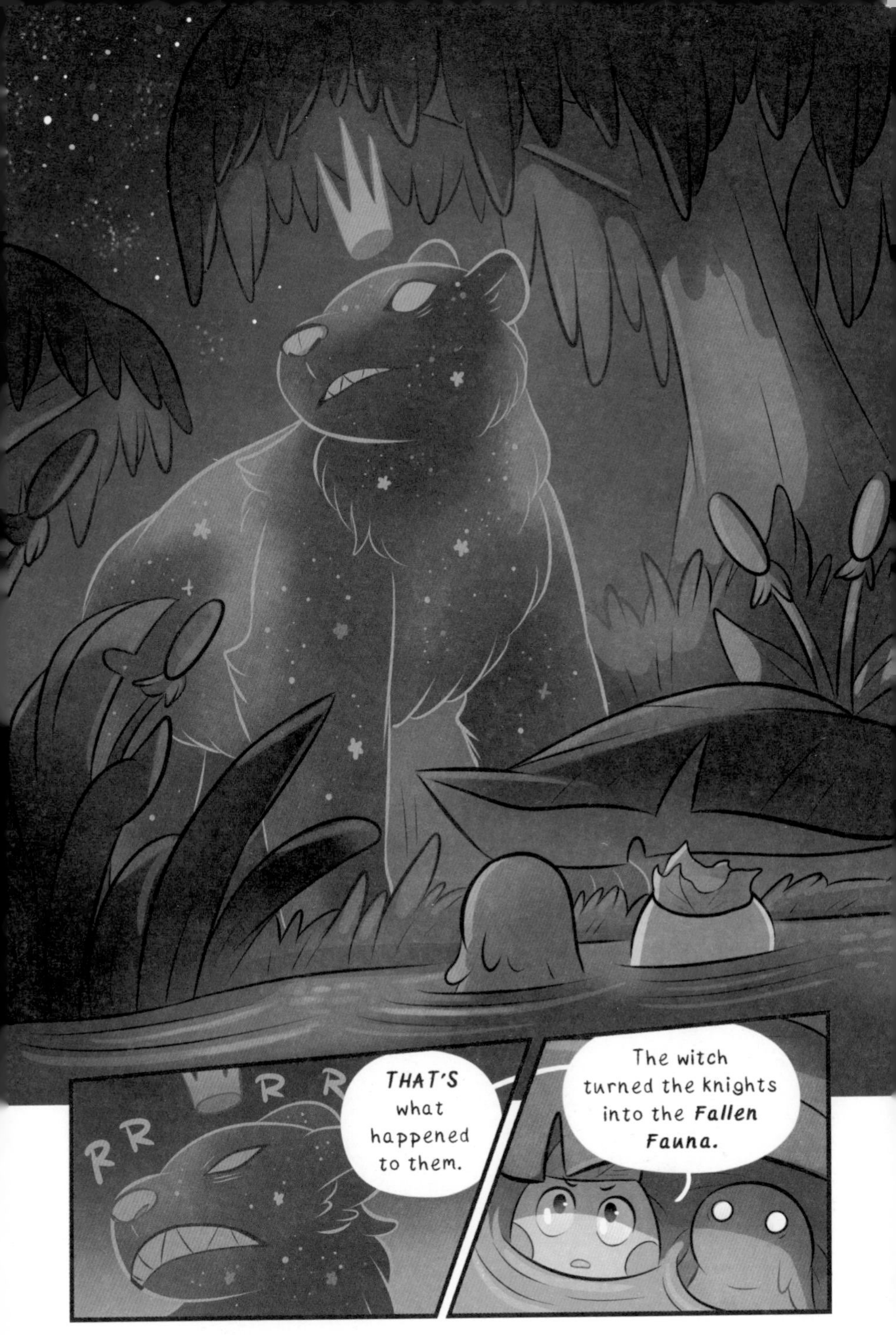
RR
R R
THAT'S what happened to them.
The witch turned the knights into the Fallen Fauna.

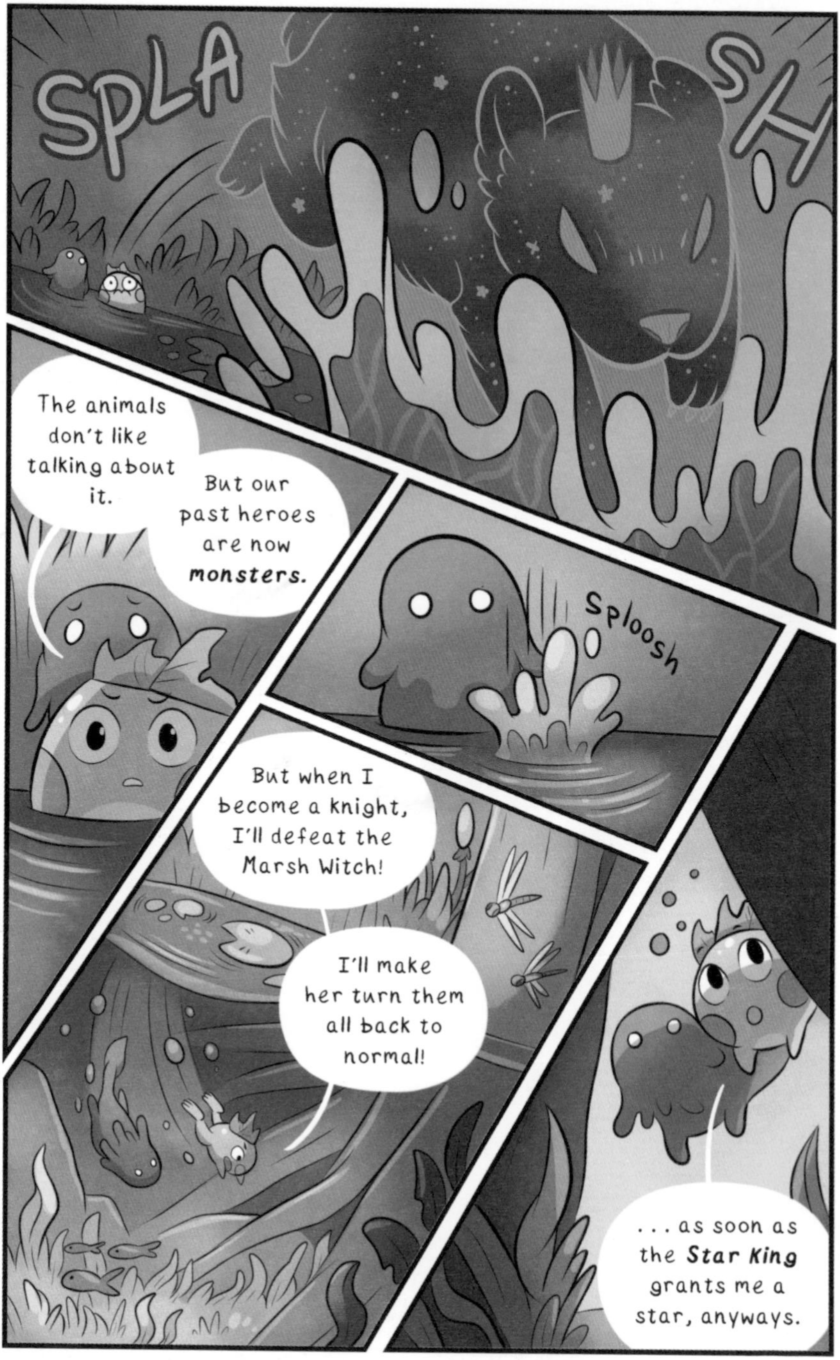
SPLASH
The animals don't like talking about it.
But our past heroes are now **monsters.**
Sploosh
But when I become a knight, I'll defeat the Marsh Witch!
I'll make her turn them all back to normal!
. . . as soon as the **Star King** grants me a star, anyways.

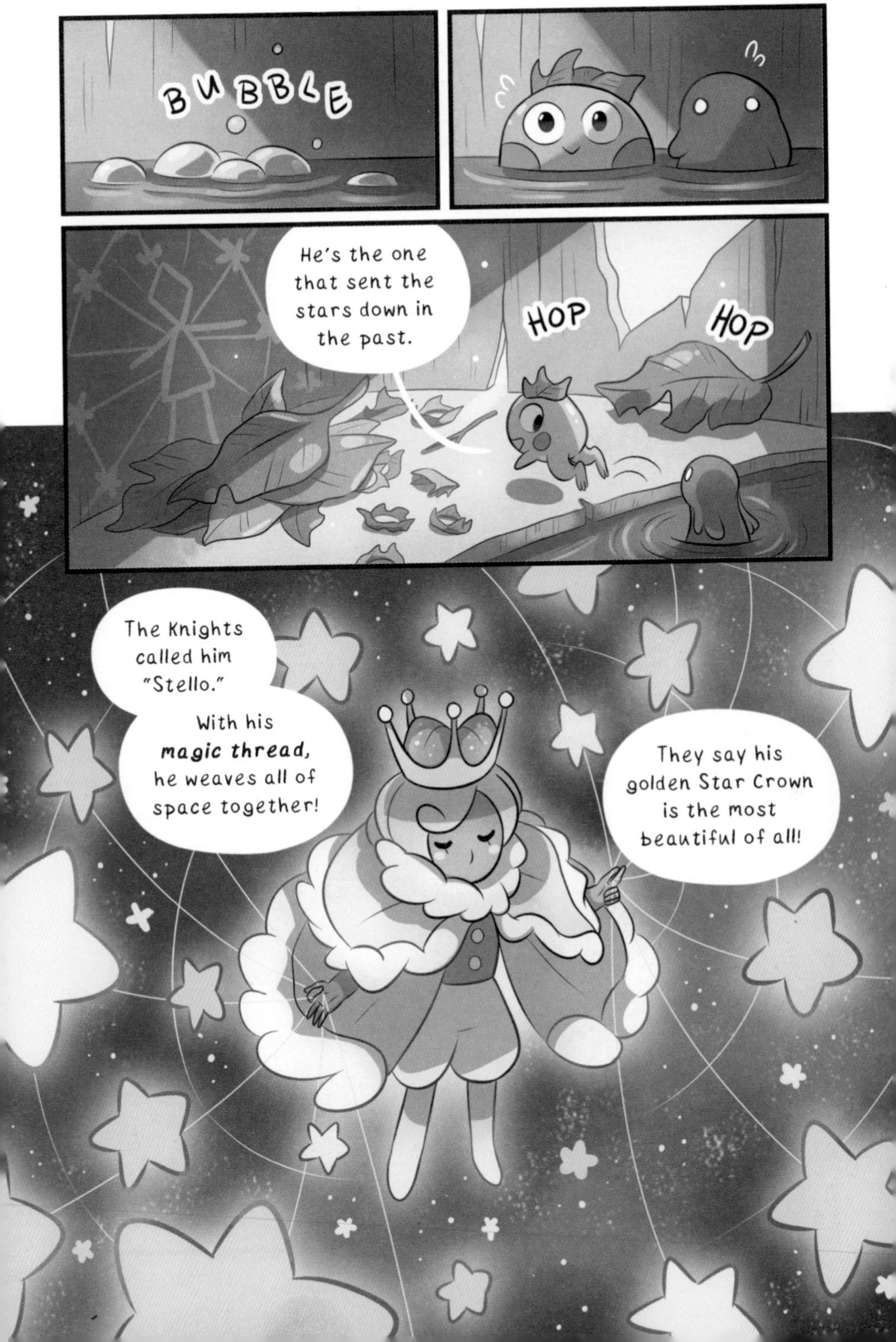
BUBBLE
He's the one that sent the stars down in the past.
HOP
HOP
The Knights called him "Stello."
With his **magic thread,** he weaves all of space together!
They say his golden Star Crown is the most beautiful of all!

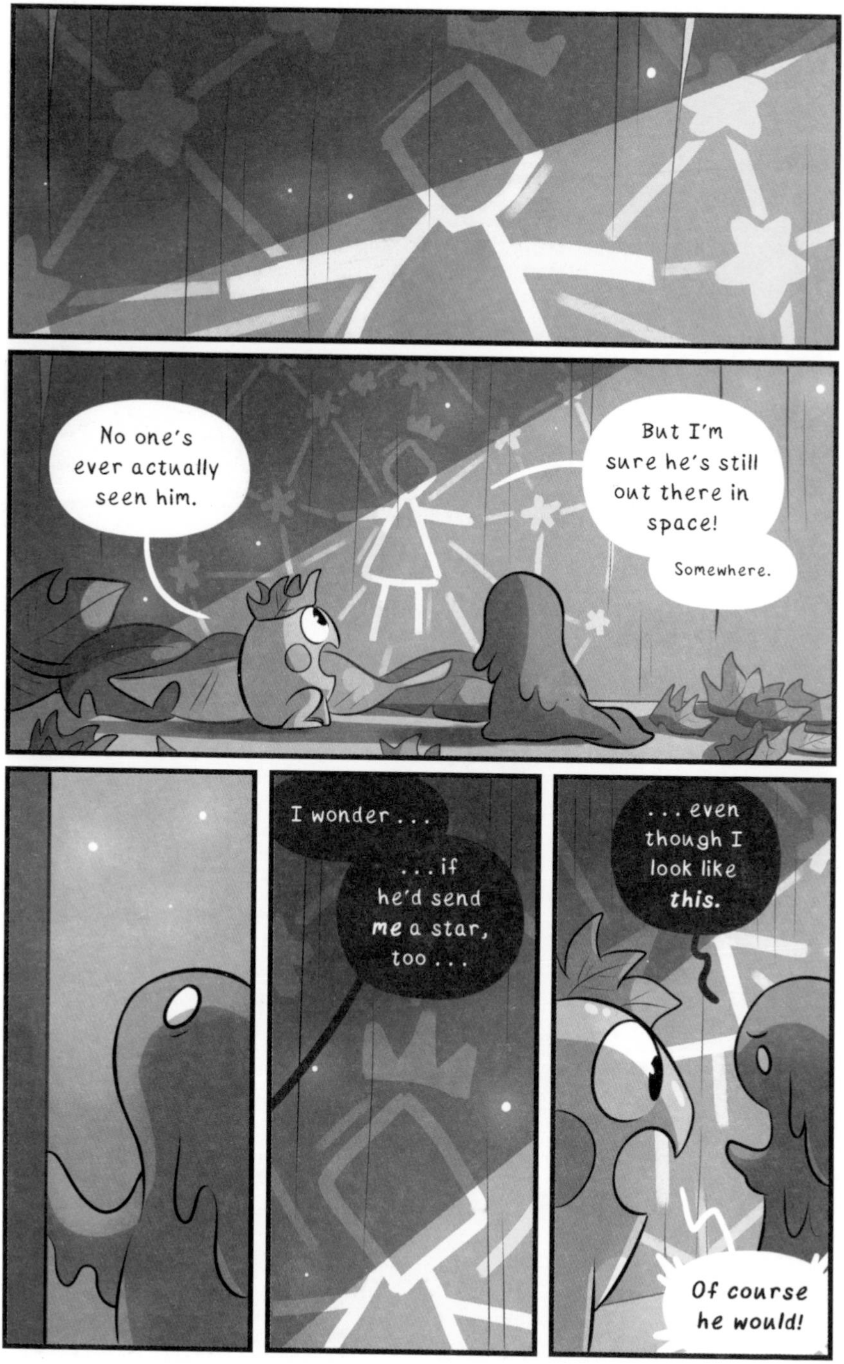
No one's ever actually seen him.
But I'm sure he's still out there in space!
Somewhere.
I wonder . . .
. . . if he'd send **me** a star, too . . .
. . . even though I look like **this.**
Of course he would!

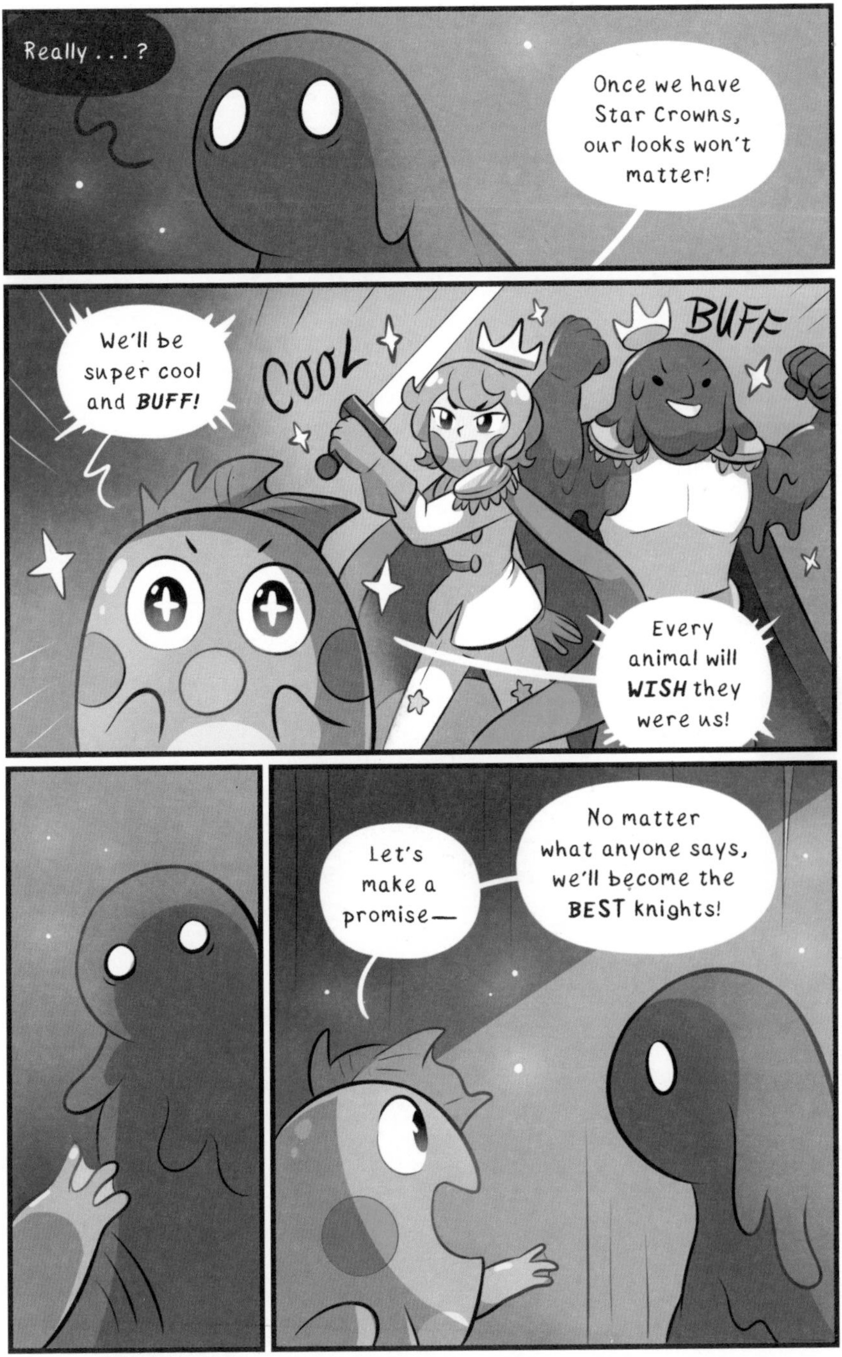
Really . . . ?
Once we have Star Crowns, our looks won't matter!
We'll be super cool and BUFF!
COOL
BUFF
Every animal will WISH they were us!
Let's make a promise—
No matter what anyone says, we'll become the BEST knights!

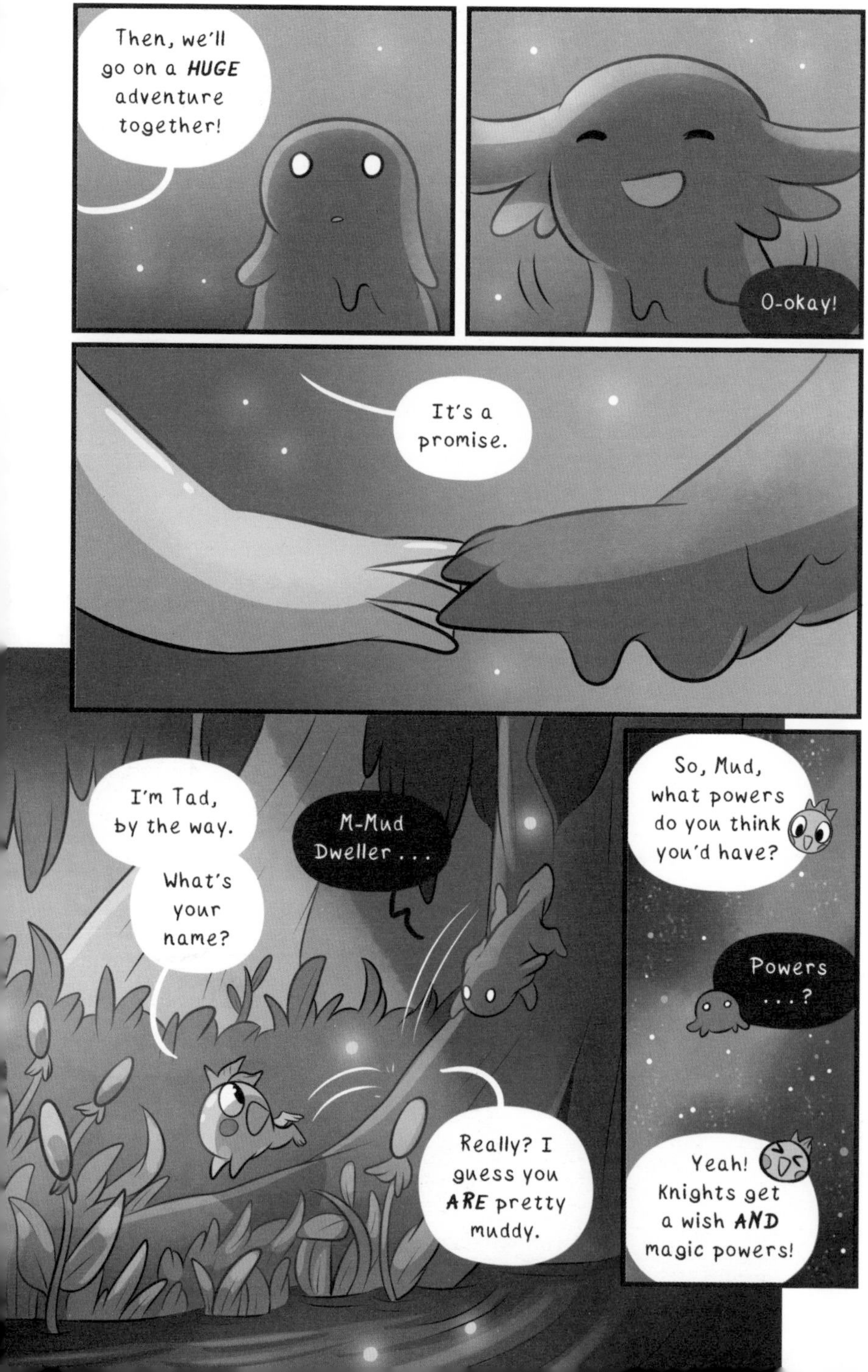
Then, we'll go on a HUGE adventure together!
O-okay!
It's a promise.
I'm Tad, by the way.
What's your name?
M-Mud Dweller . . .
Really? I guess you ARE pretty muddy.
So, Mud, what powers do you think you'd have?
Powers . . . ?
Yeah! Knights get a wish AND magic powers!

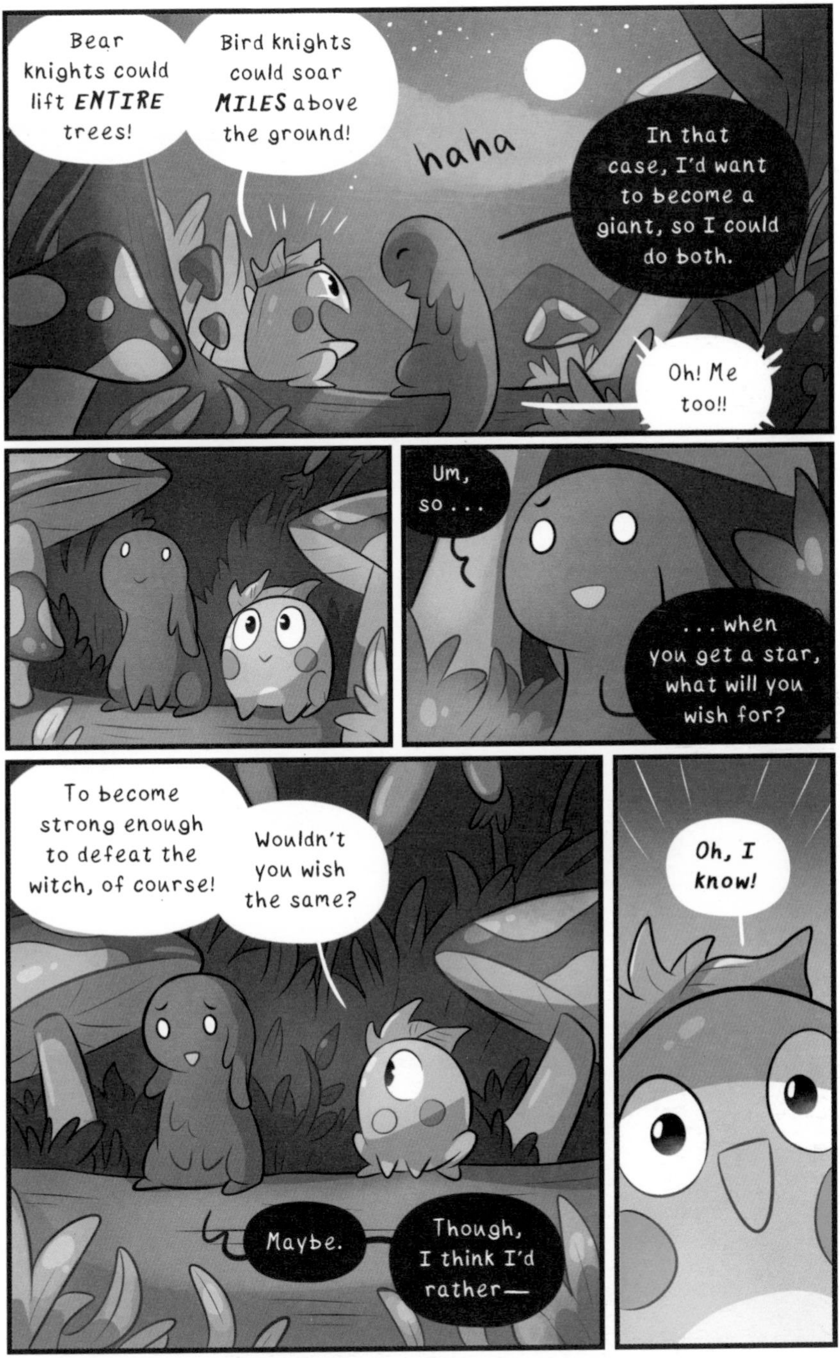
Bear knights could lift ENTIRE trees!
Bird knights could soar MILES above the ground!
haha
In that case, I'd want to become a giant, so I could do both.
Oh! Me too!!
Um, so . . .
. . . when you get a star, what will you wish for?
To become strong enough to defeat the witch, of course!
Wouldn't you wish the same?
Maybe.
Though, I think I'd rather—
Oh, I know!

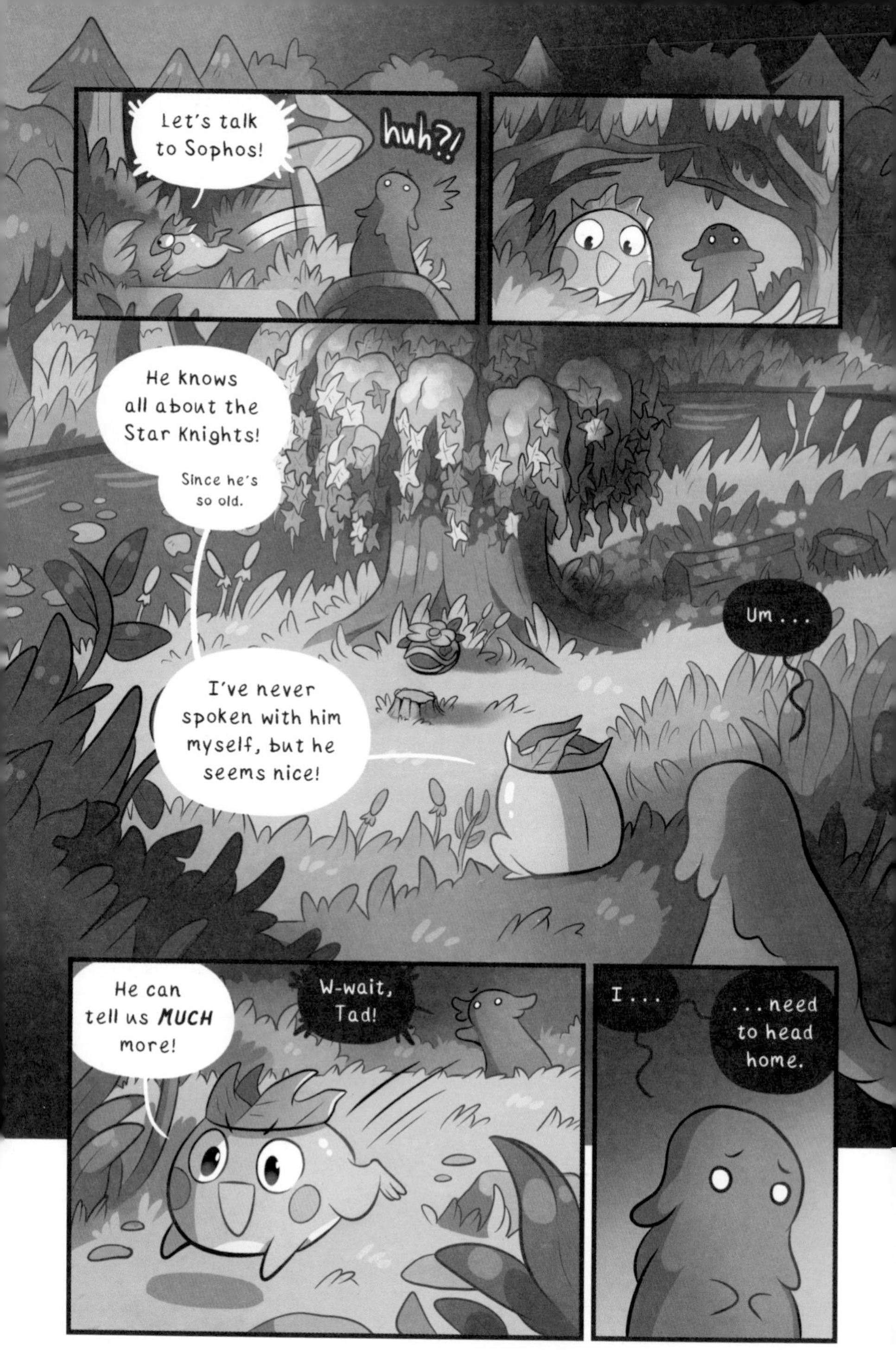
Let's talk to Sophos!
huh?!
He knows all about the Star Knights!
Since he's so old.
I've never spoken with him myself, but he seems nice!
Um . . .
He can tell us MUCH more!
W-wait, Tad!
I . . .
. . . need to head home.

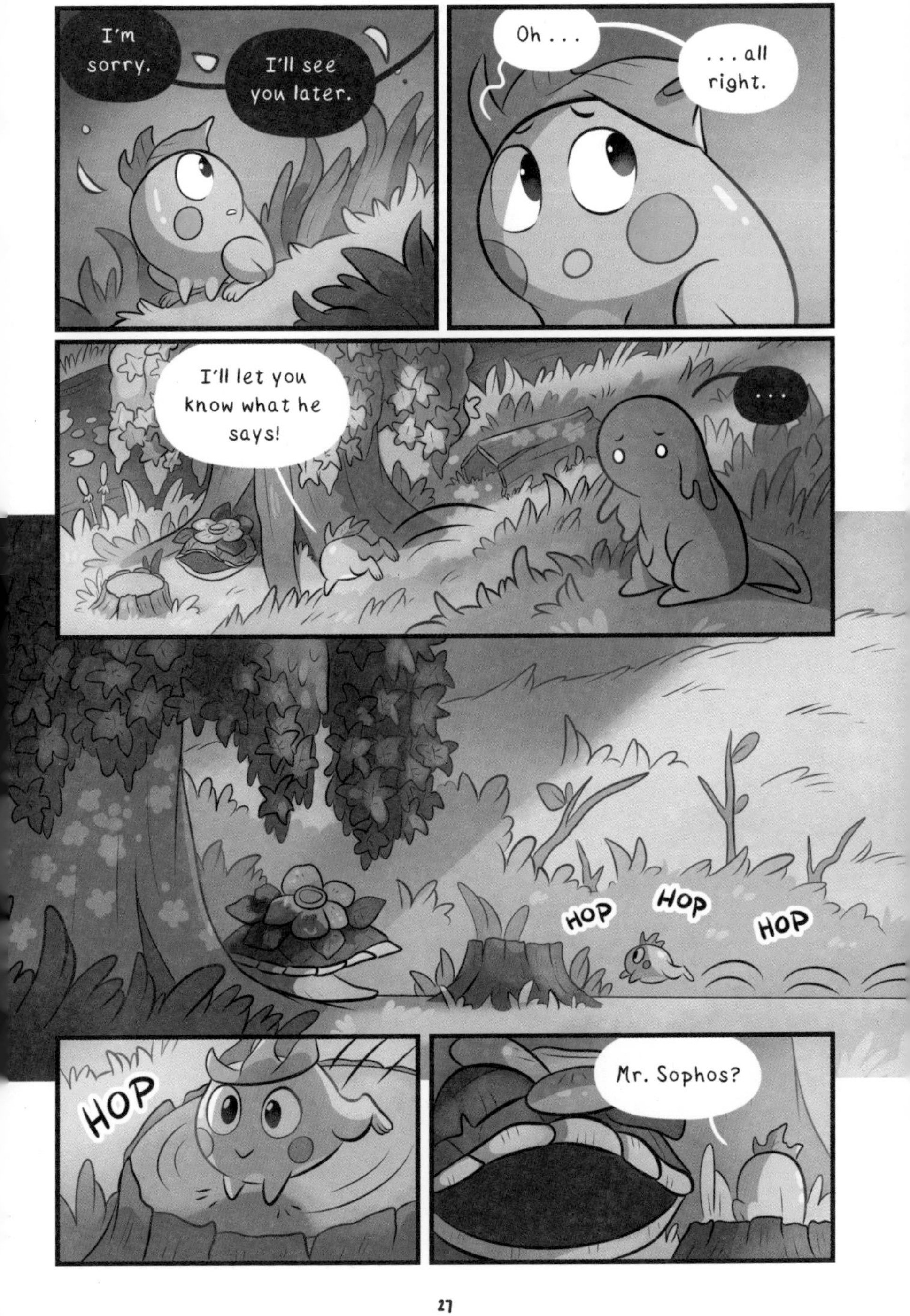
I'm sorry.
I'll see you later.
Oh . . .
. . . all right.
I'll let you know what he says!
. . .
HOP
HOP
HOP
HOP
Mr. Sophos?

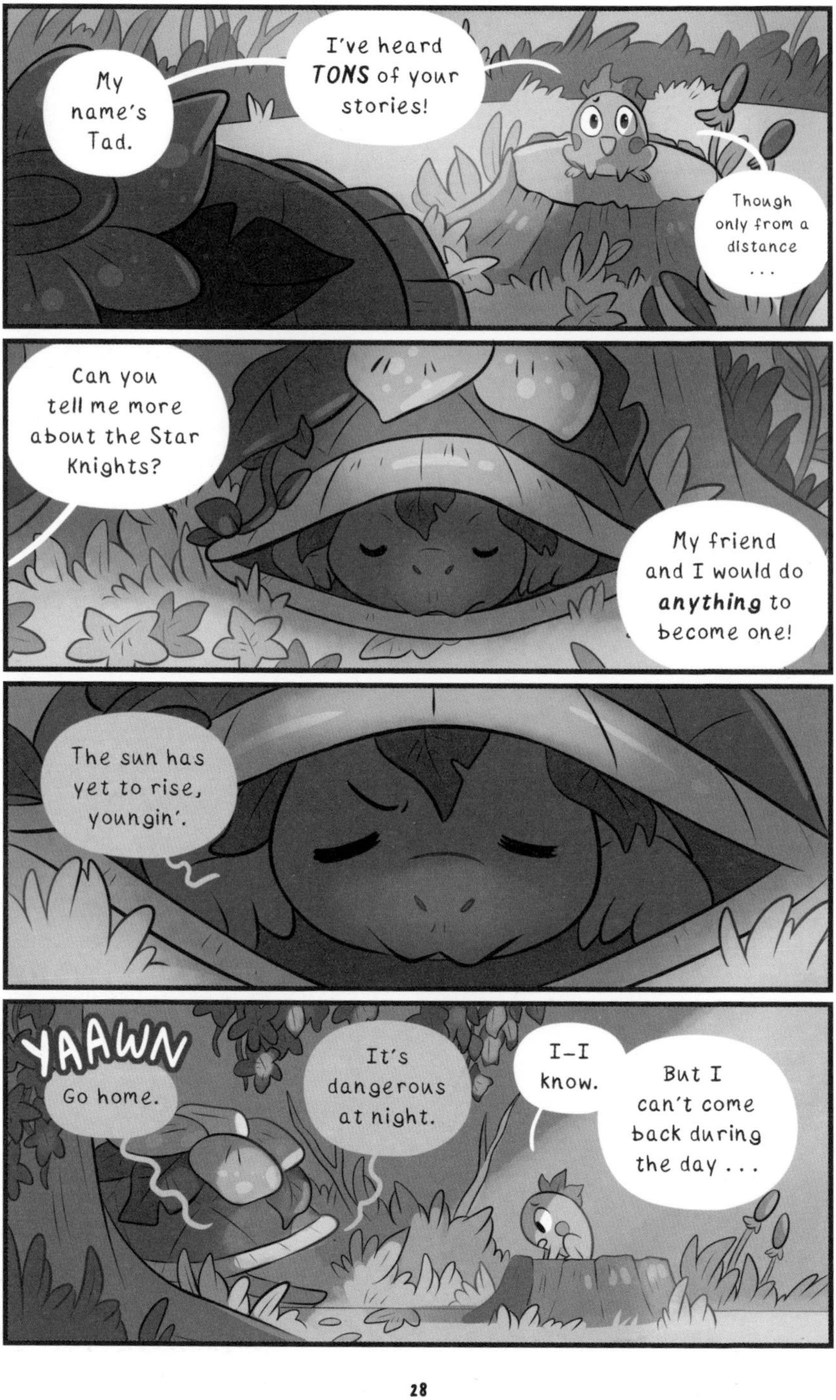

My name's Tad.
I've heard TONS of your stories!
Though only from a distance . . .
Can you tell me more about the Star Knights?
My friend and I would do anything to become one!
The sun has yet to rise, youngin'.
YAAWN
Go home.
It's dangerous at night.
I-I know.
But I can't come back during the day . . .

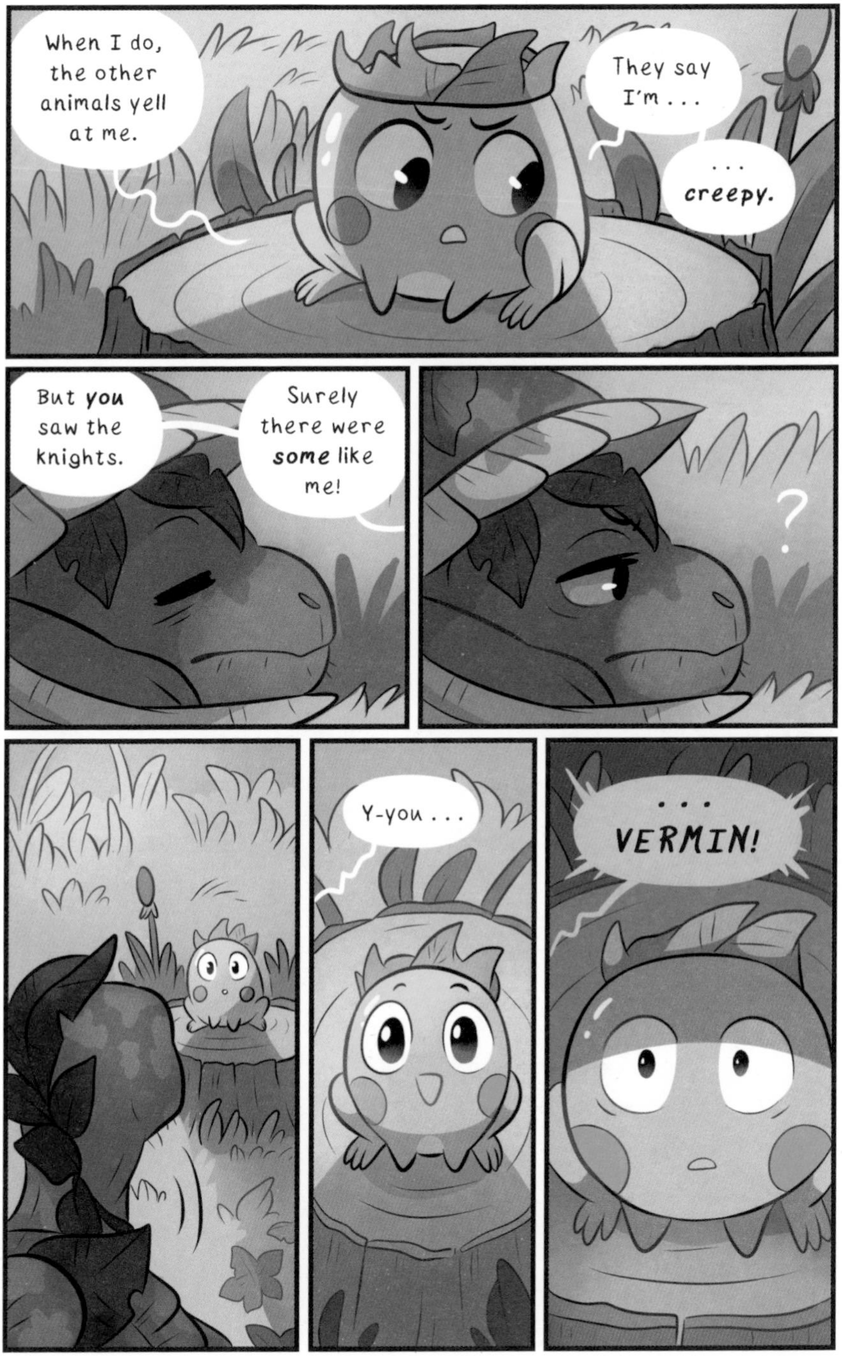
When I do, the other animals yell at me.
They say I'm . . .
. . . creepy.
But you saw the knights.
Surely there were some like me!
?
Y-you . . .
. . . VERMIN!

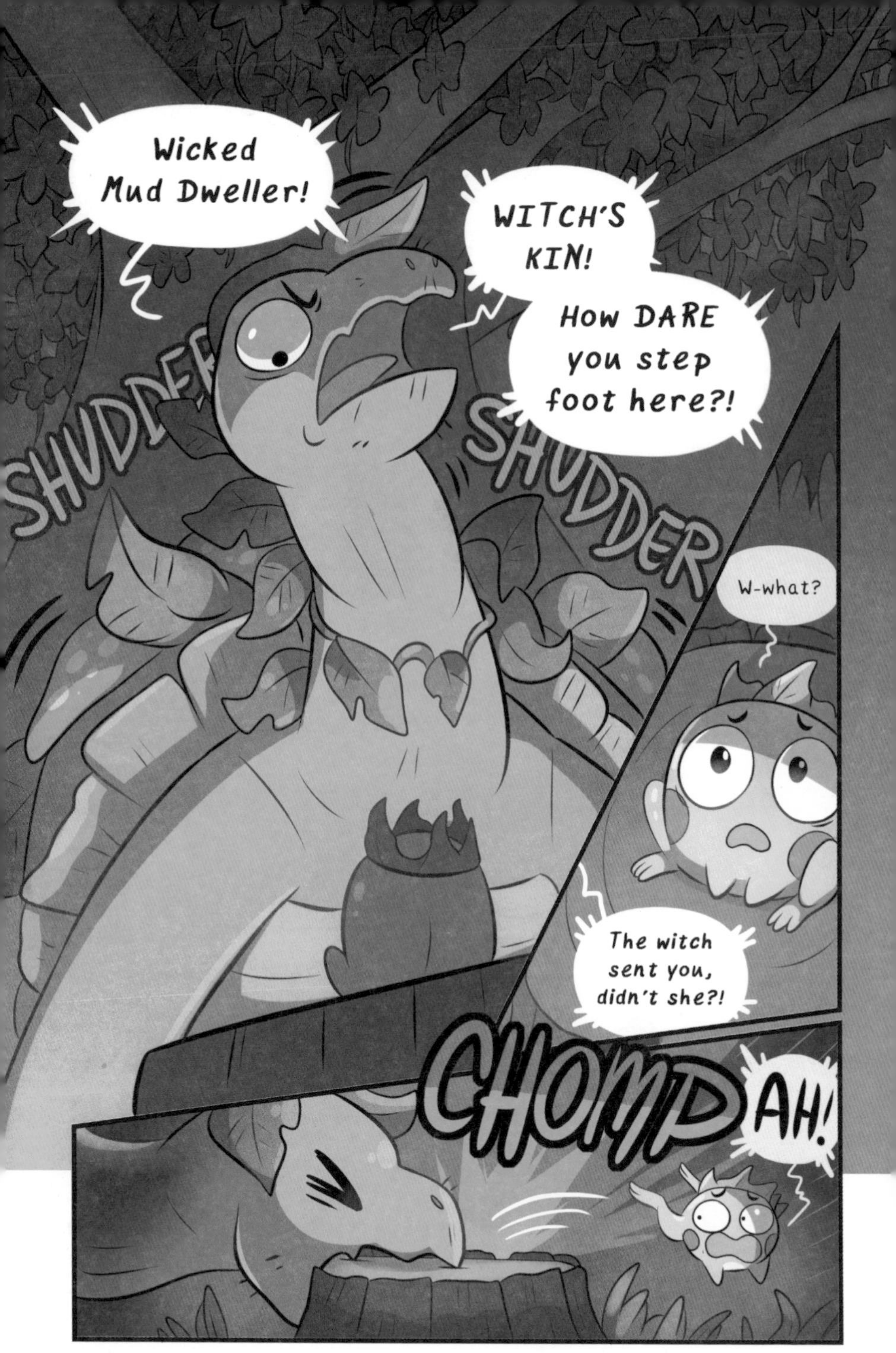
Wicked Mud Dweller!
WITCH'S KIN!
How DARE you step foot here?!
SHUDDER
SHUDDER
W-what?
The witch sent you, didn't she?!
CHOMP
AH!

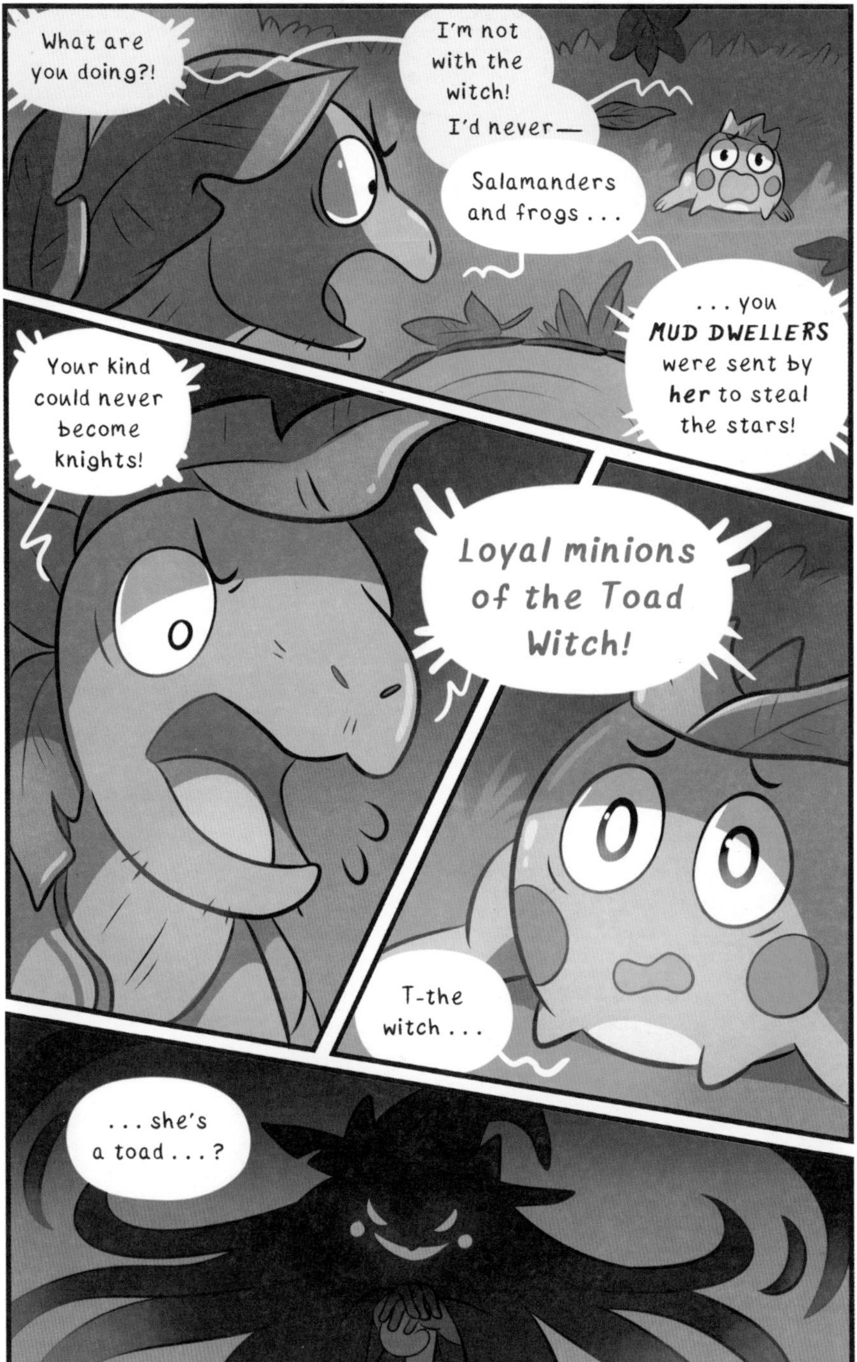
What are you doing?!
I'm not with the witch!
I'd never—
Salamanders and frogs . . .
. . . you **MUD DWELLERS** were sent by **her** to steal the stars!
Your kind could never become knights!
Loyal minions of the Toad Witch!
T-the witch . . .
. . . she's a toad . . . ?

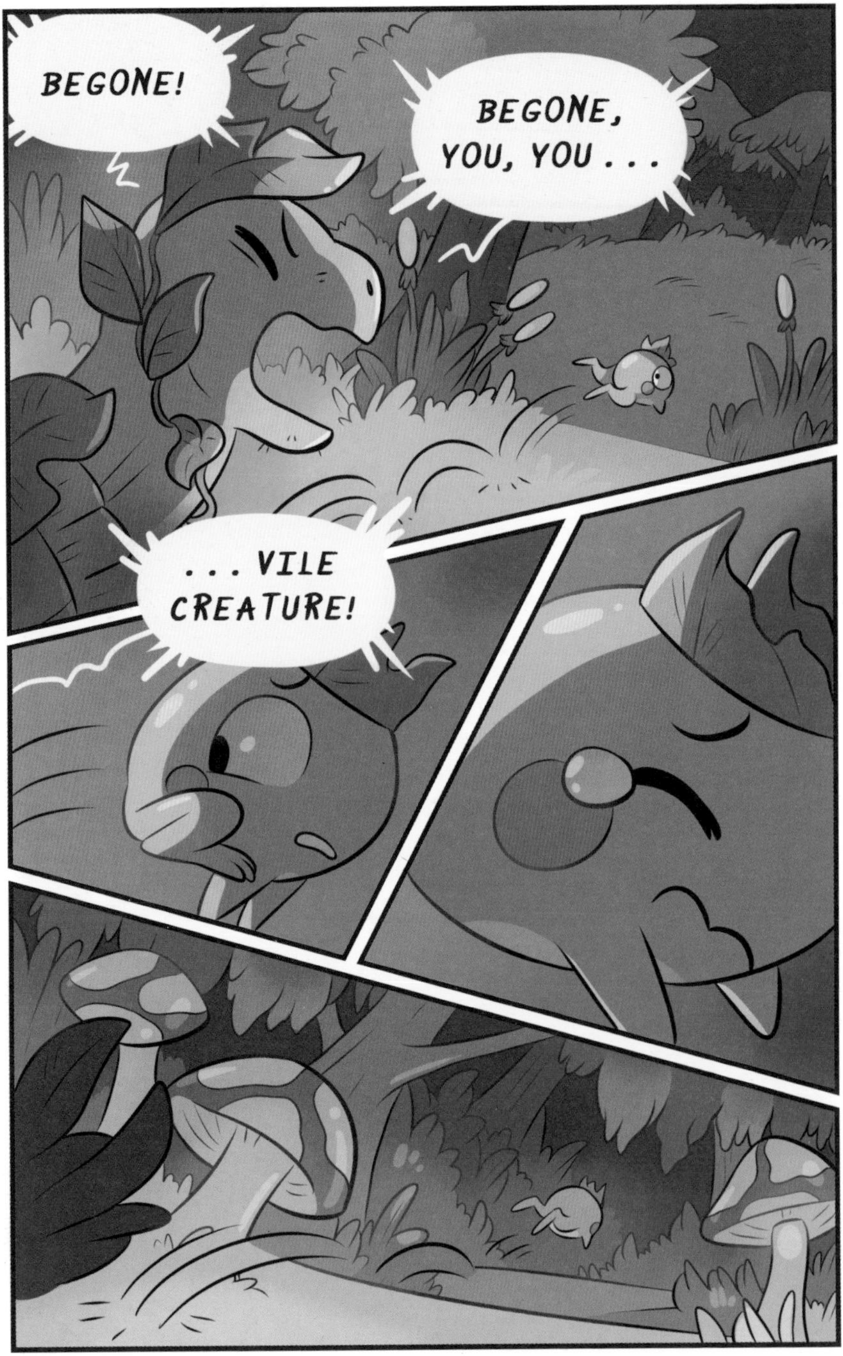
BEGONE!
BEGONE, YOU, YOU . . .
. . . VILE CREATURE!

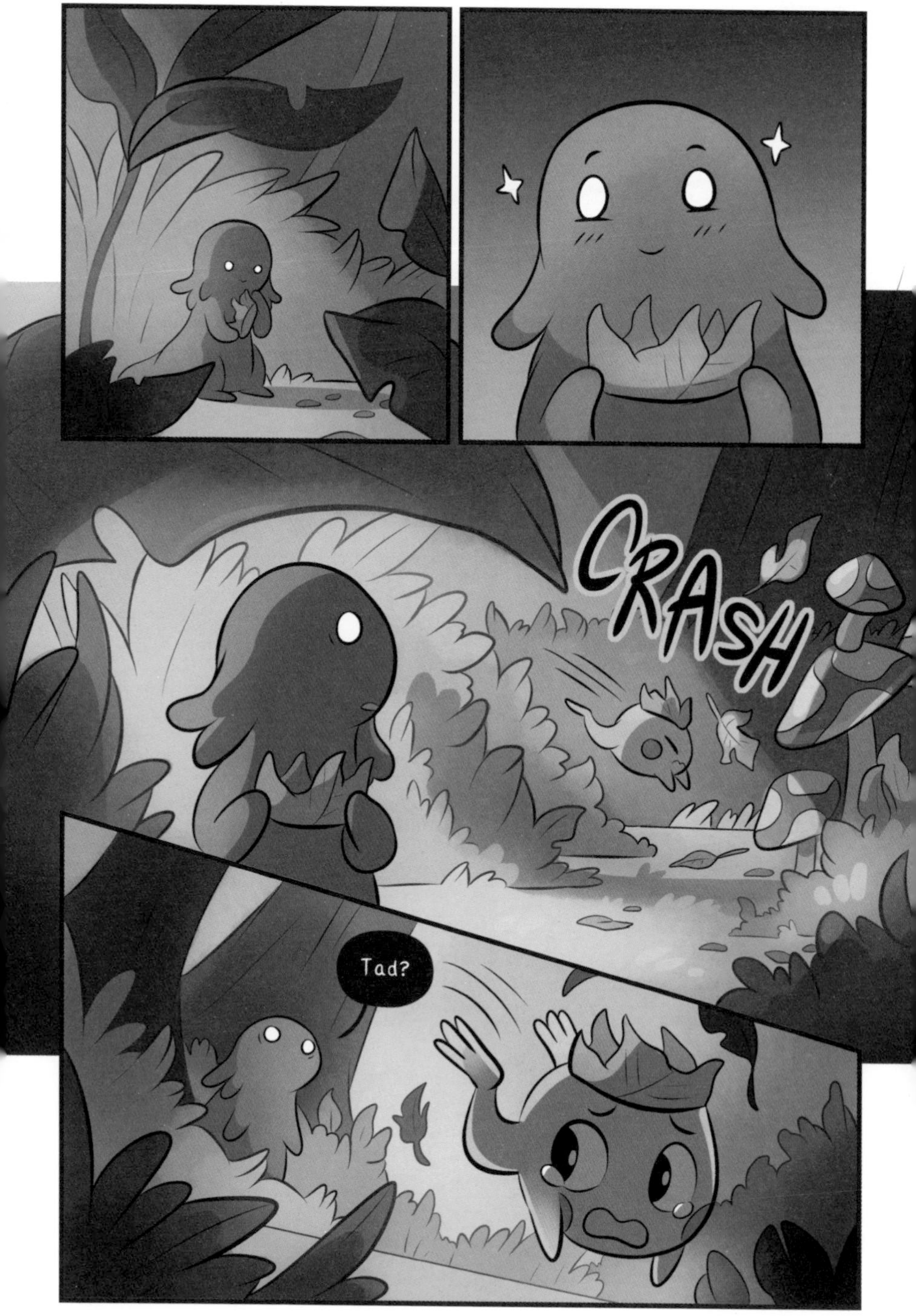
CRASH
Tad?

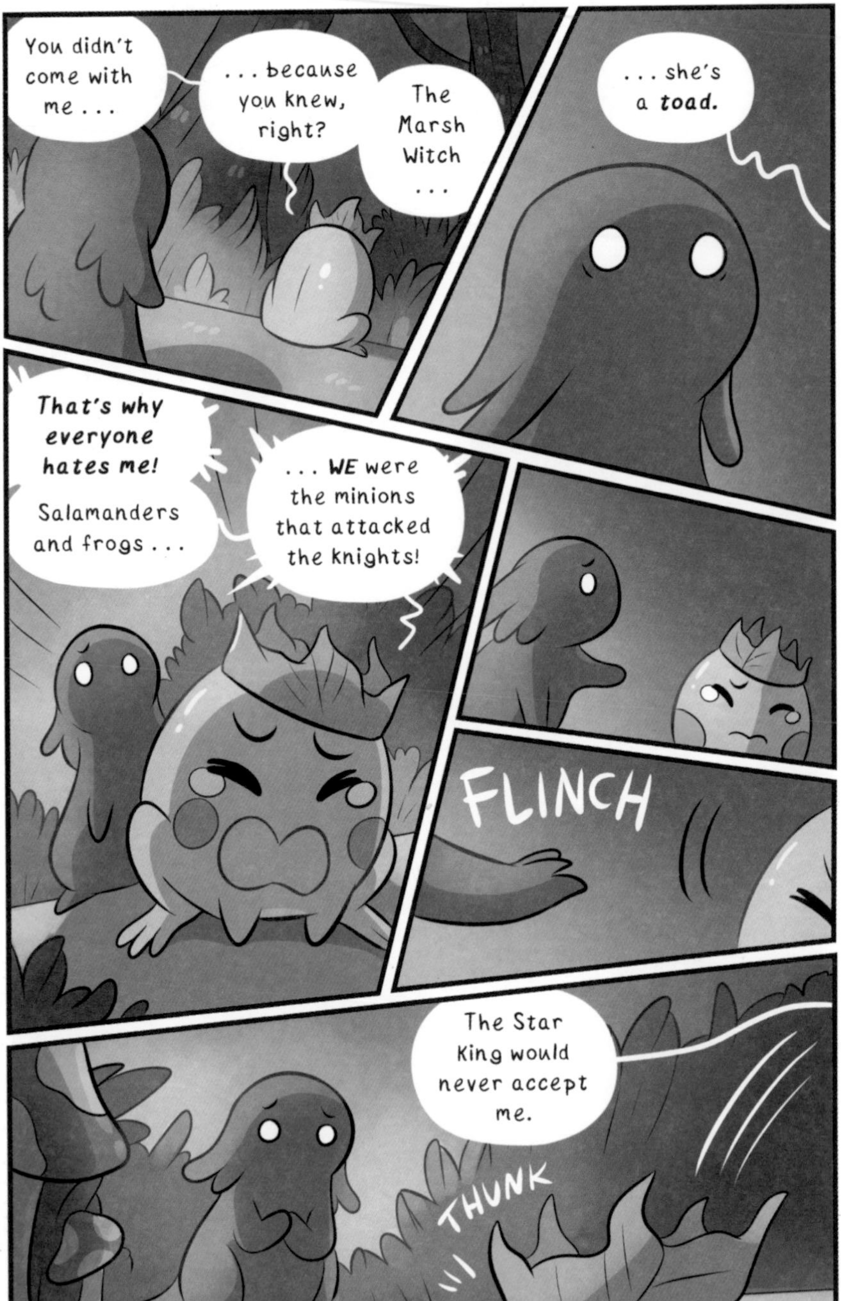

You didn't come with me . . .
. . . because you knew, right?
The Marsh Witch . . .
. . . she's a *toad.*
That's why everyone hates me!
Salamanders and frogs . . .
. . . **WE** were the minions that attacked the knights!
FLINCH
The Star King would never accept me.
THUNK

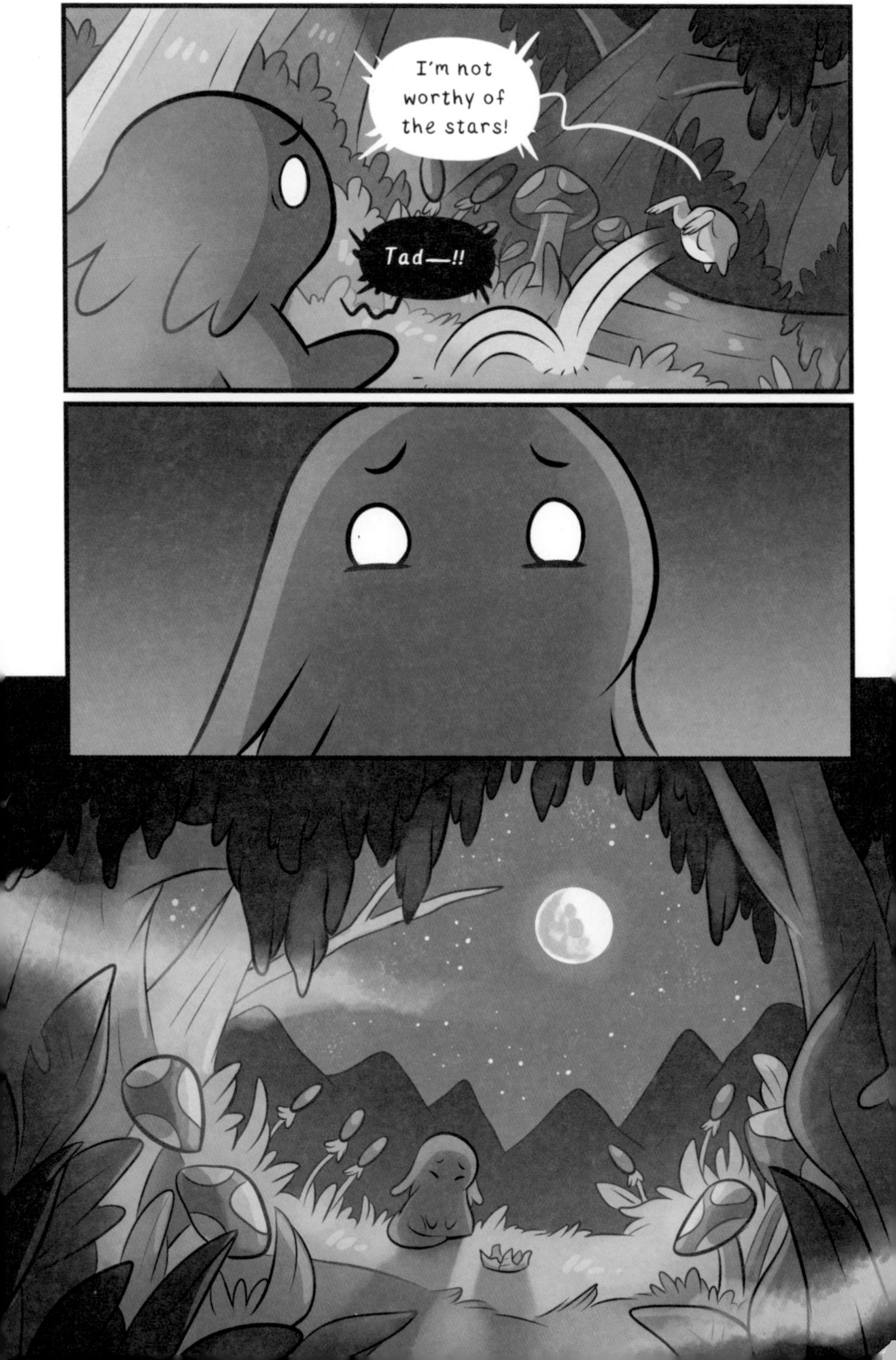
I'm not worthy of the stars!
Tad—!!

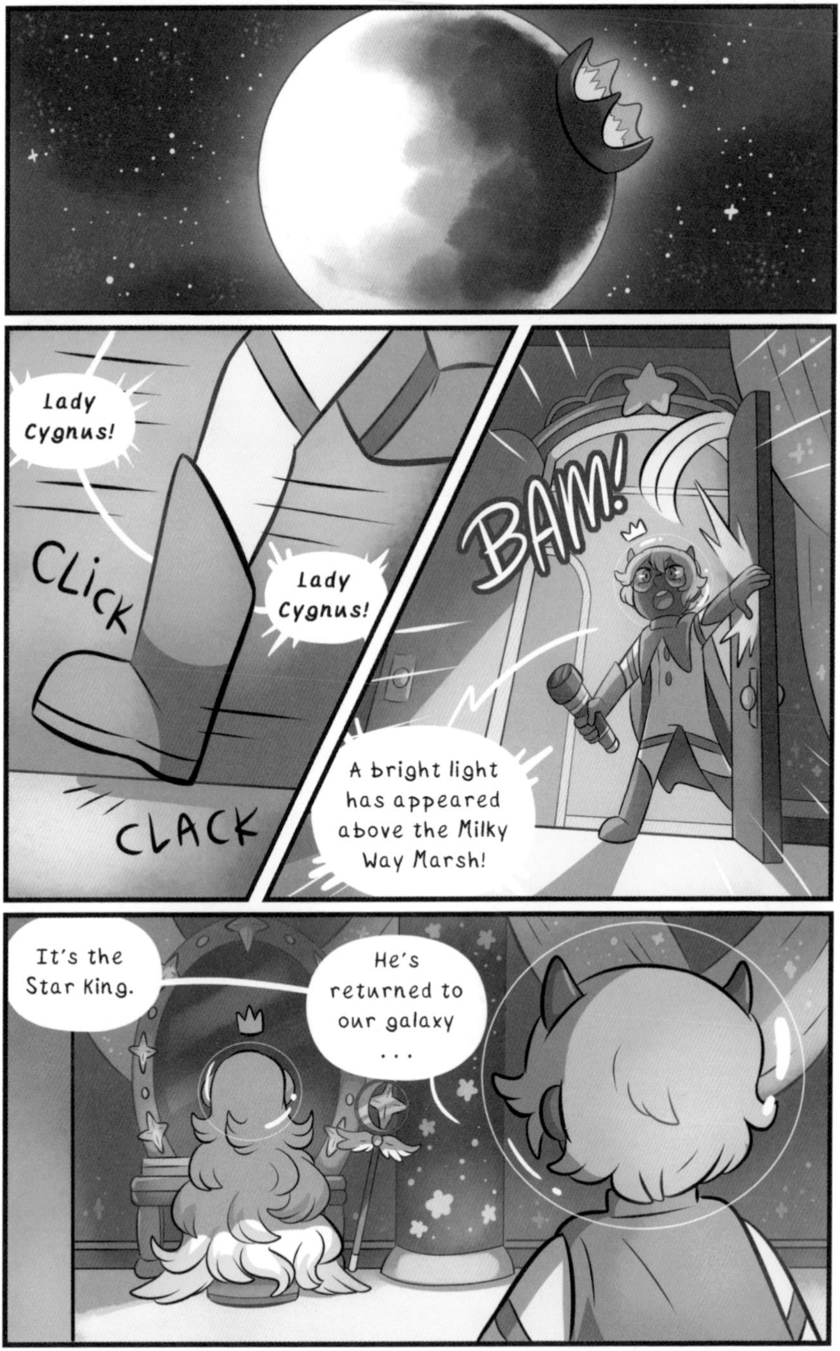
Lady Cygnus!
CLICK
Lady Cygnus!
CLACK
BAM!
A bright light has appeared above the Milky Way Marsh!
It's the Star King.
He's returned to our galaxy . . .

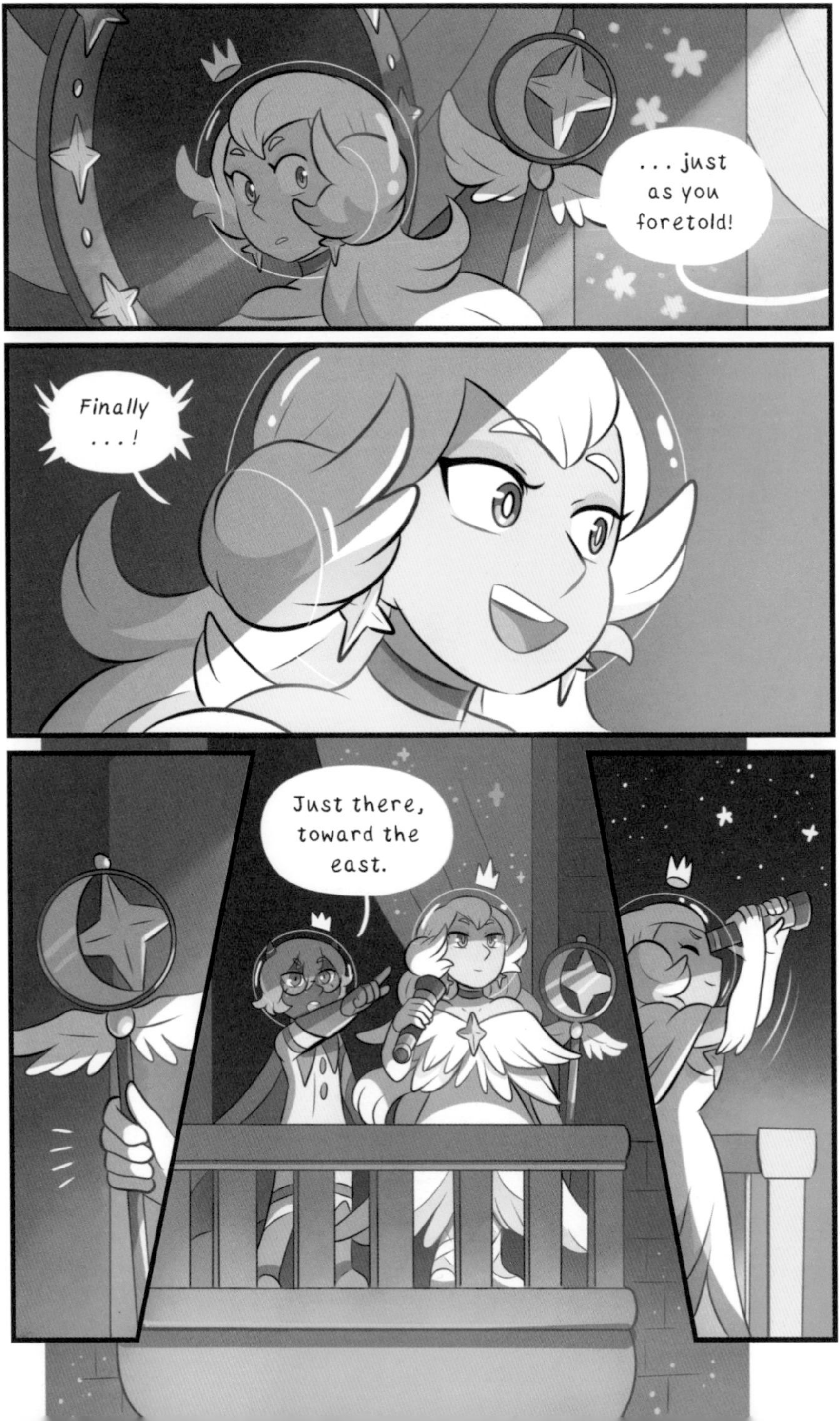
. . . just as you foretold!
Finally . . . !
Just there, toward the east.

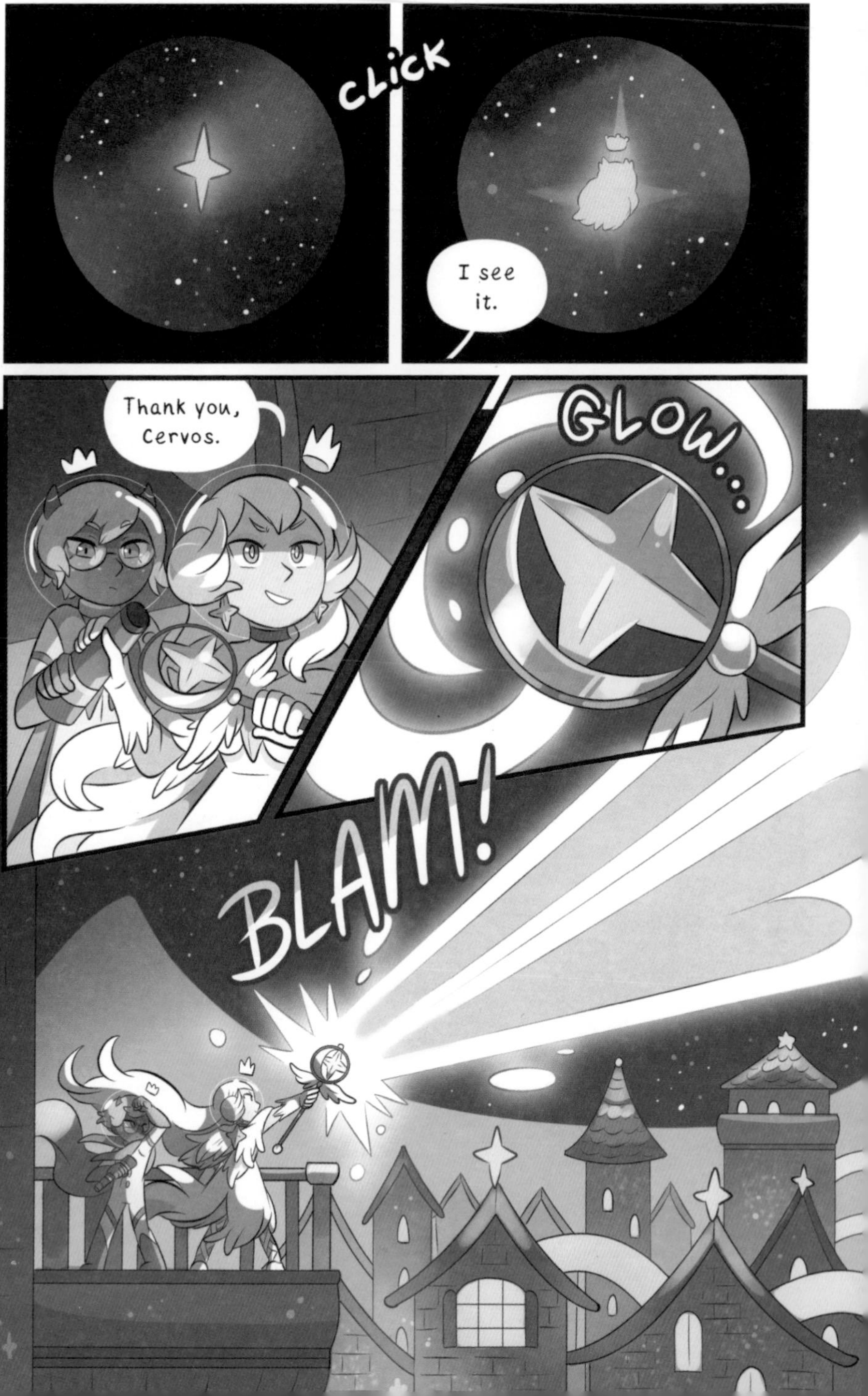

CLICK
I see it.
Thank you, Cervos.
GLOW...
BLAM!

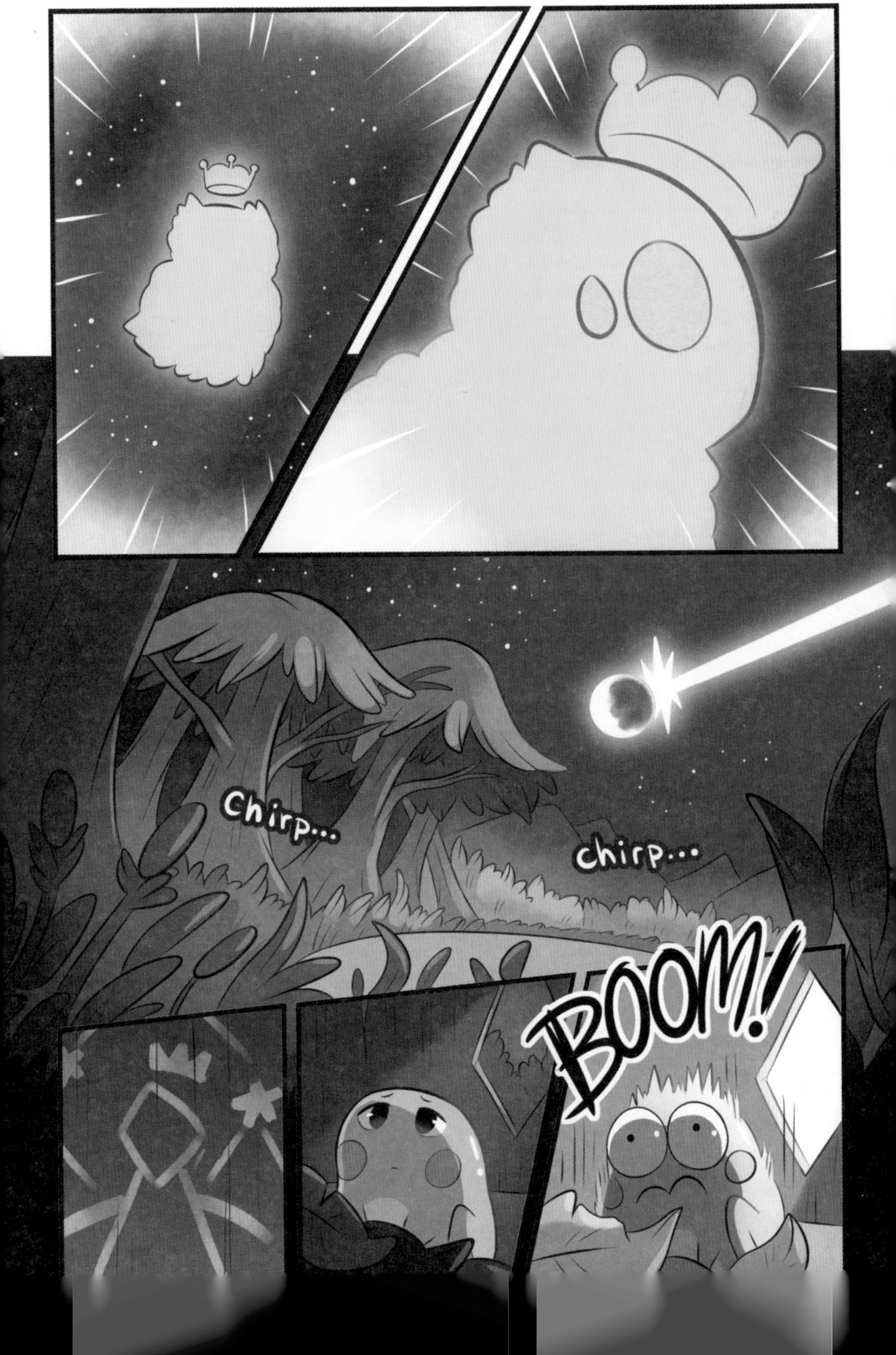
Chirp...
chirp...
BOOM!

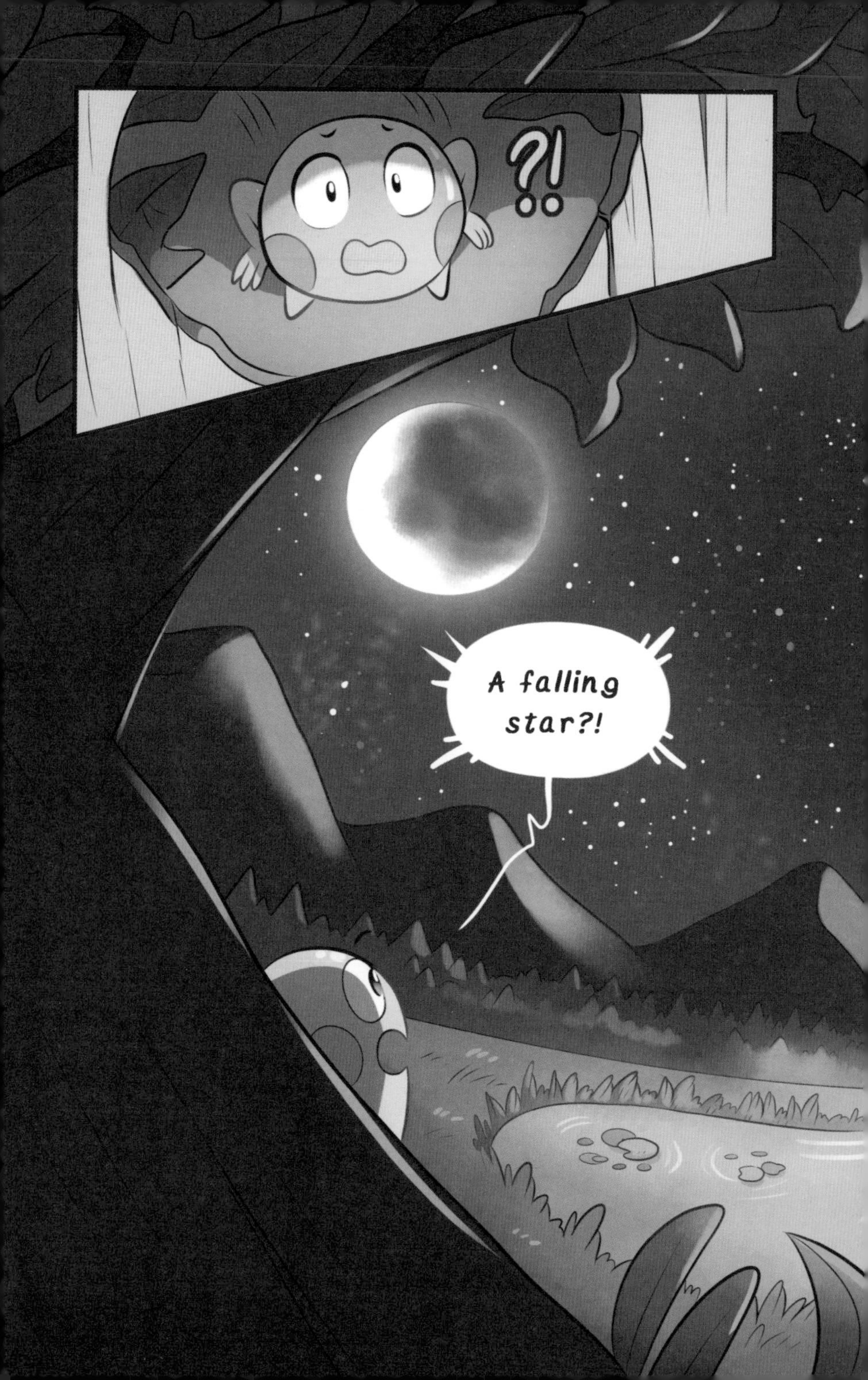
?!
A falling star?!

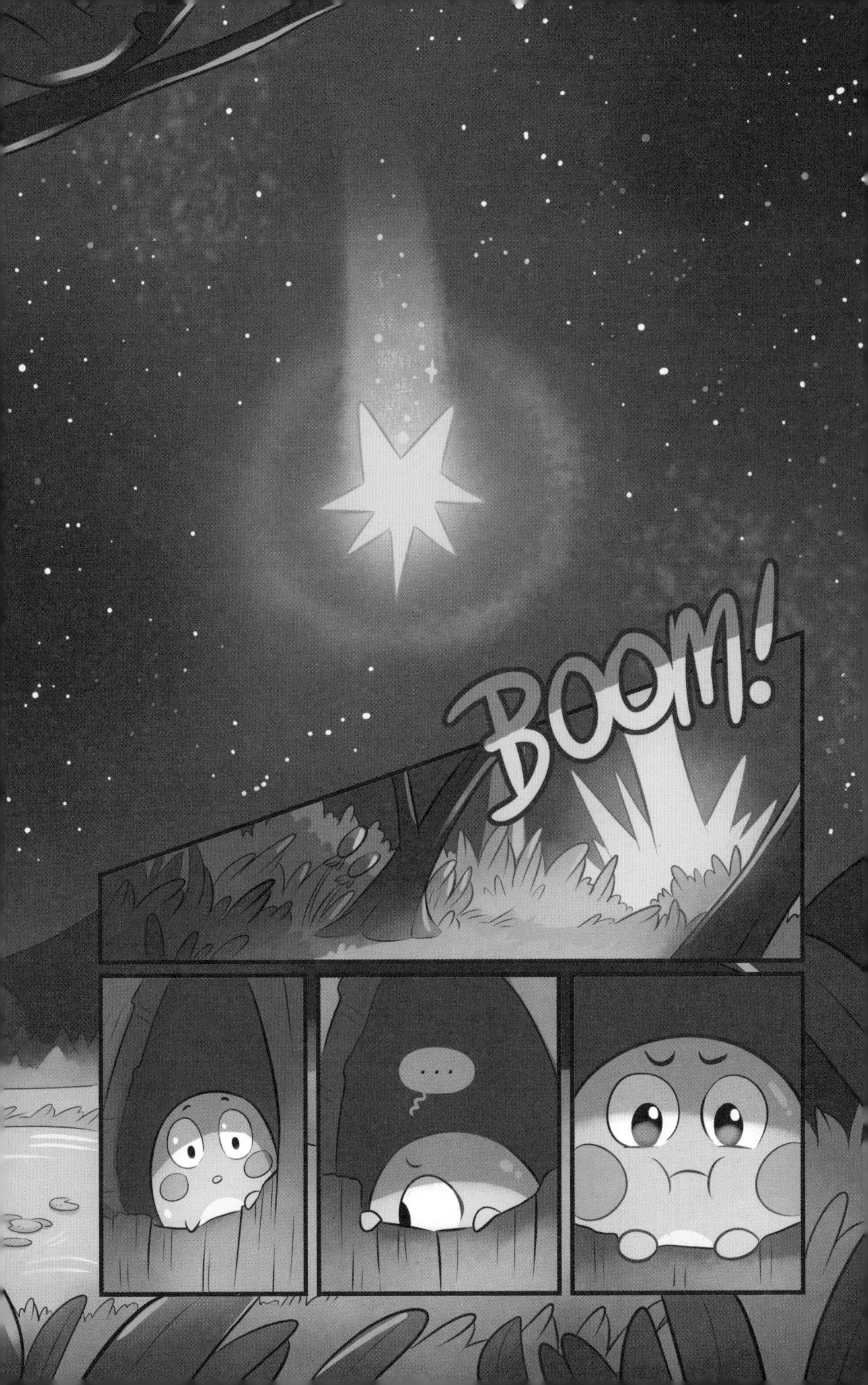
BOOM!
...

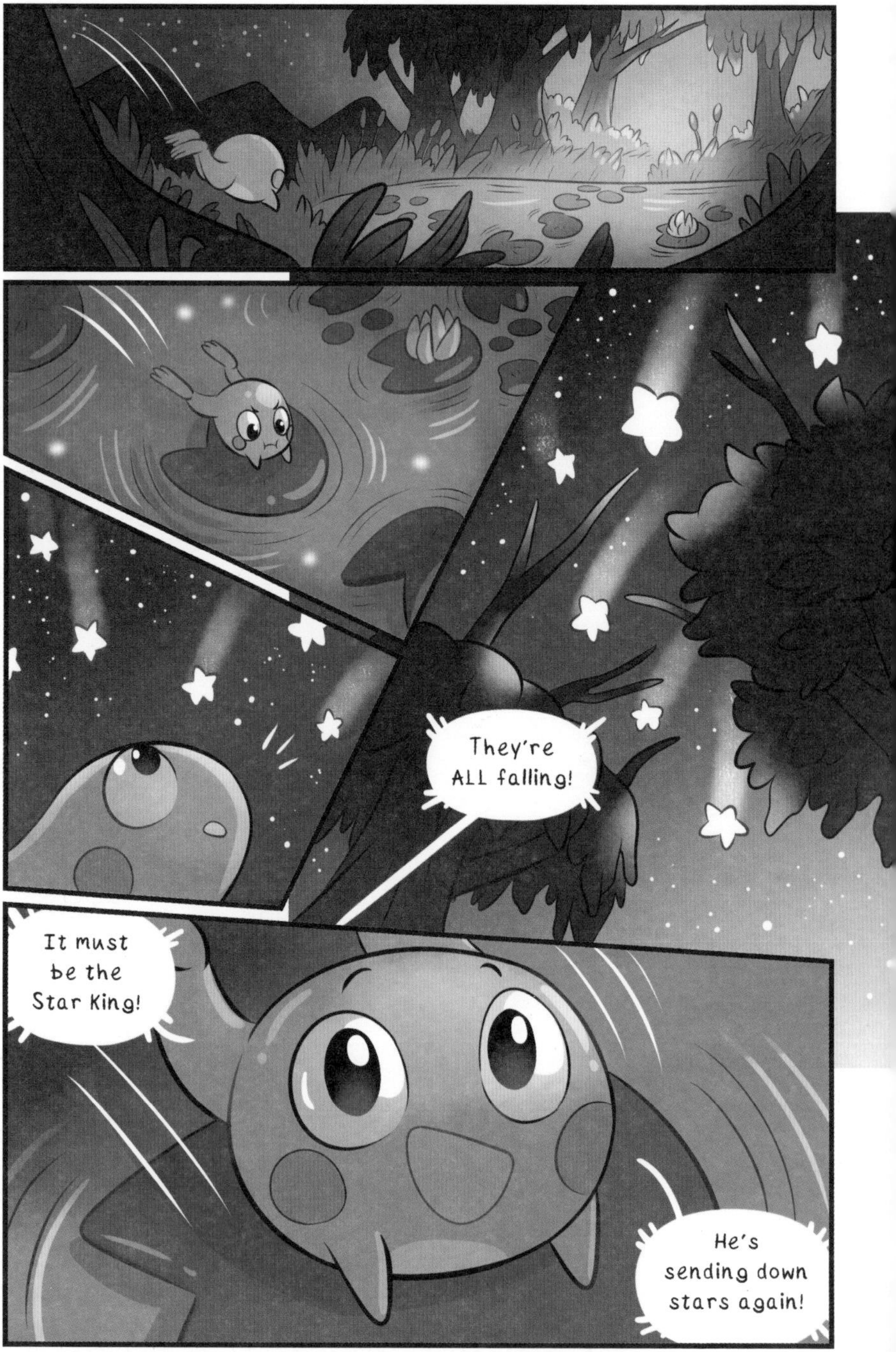
They're ALL falling!
It must be the Star King!
He's sending down stars again!

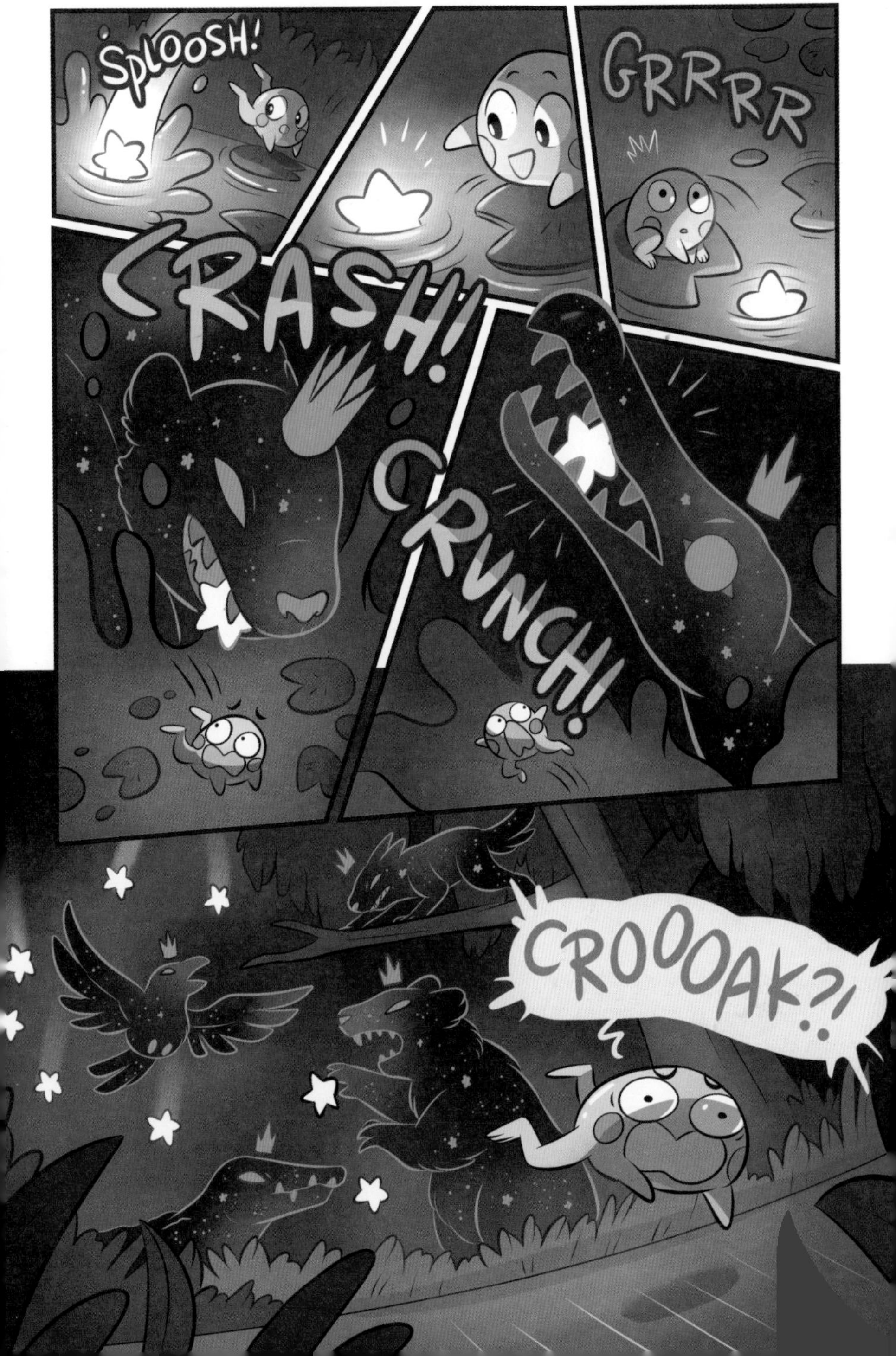
SPLOOSH!
GRRRRR
CRASH!
CRUNCH!
CROOOAK?!

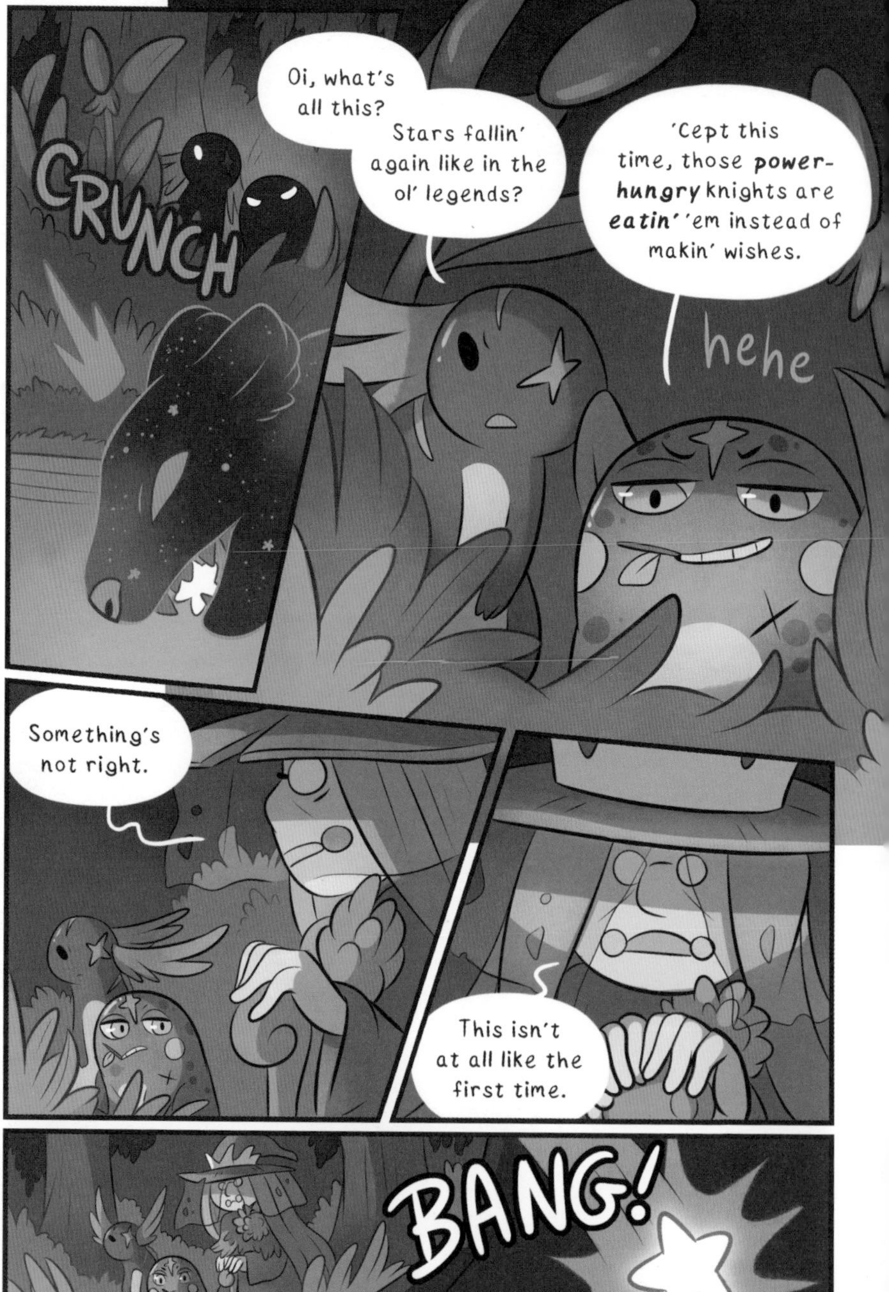
CRUNCH
Oi, what's all this?
Stars fallin' again like in the ol' legends?
'Cept this time, those **power-hungry** knights are **eatin'** 'em instead of makin' wishes.
hehe
Something's not right.
This isn't at all like the first time.
BANG!

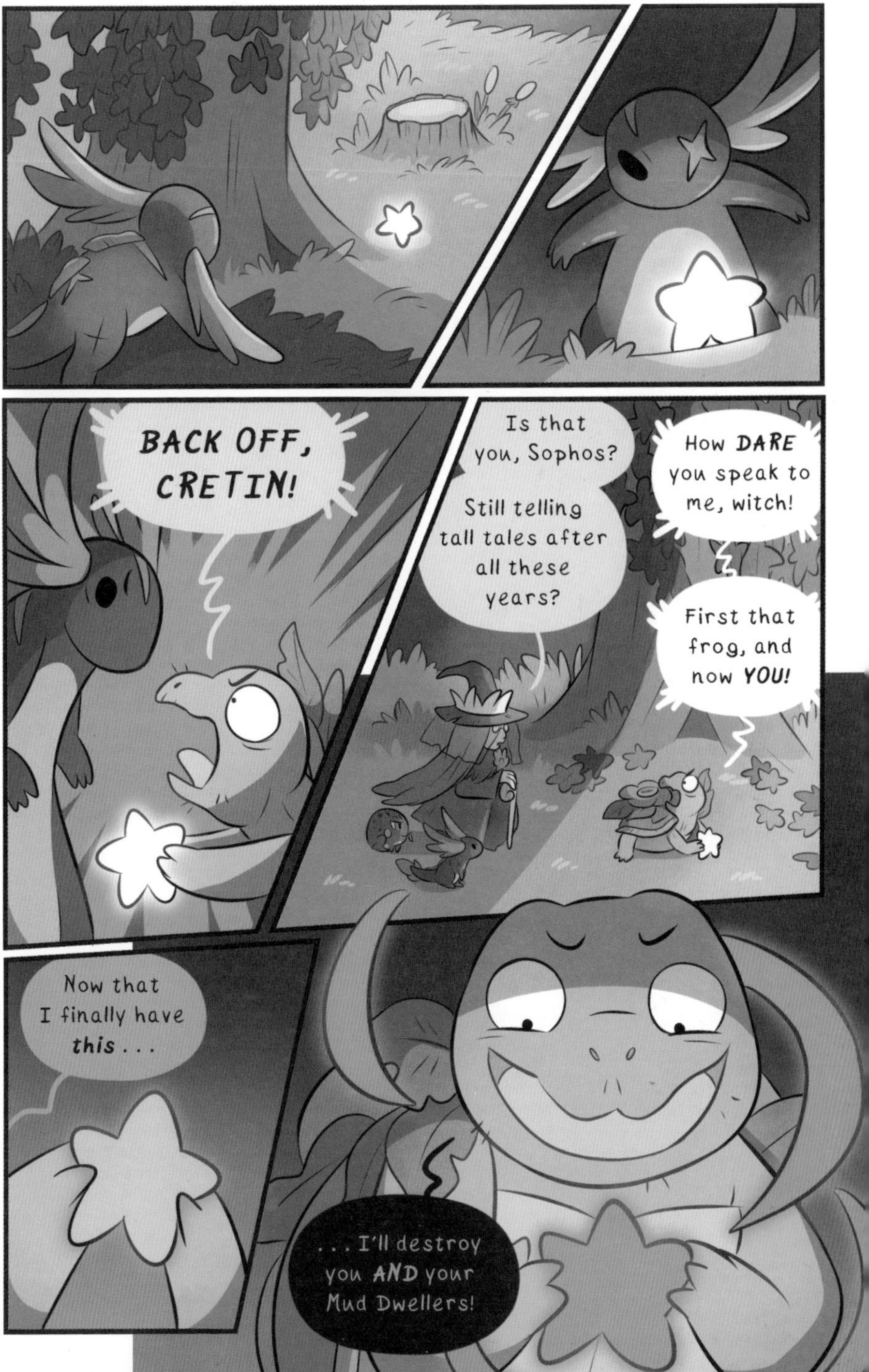
BACK OFF, CRETIN!
Is that you, Sophos?
Still telling tall tales after all these years?
How DARE you speak to me, witch!
First that frog, and now YOU!
Now that I finally have this . . .
. . . I'll destroy you AND your Mud Dwellers!

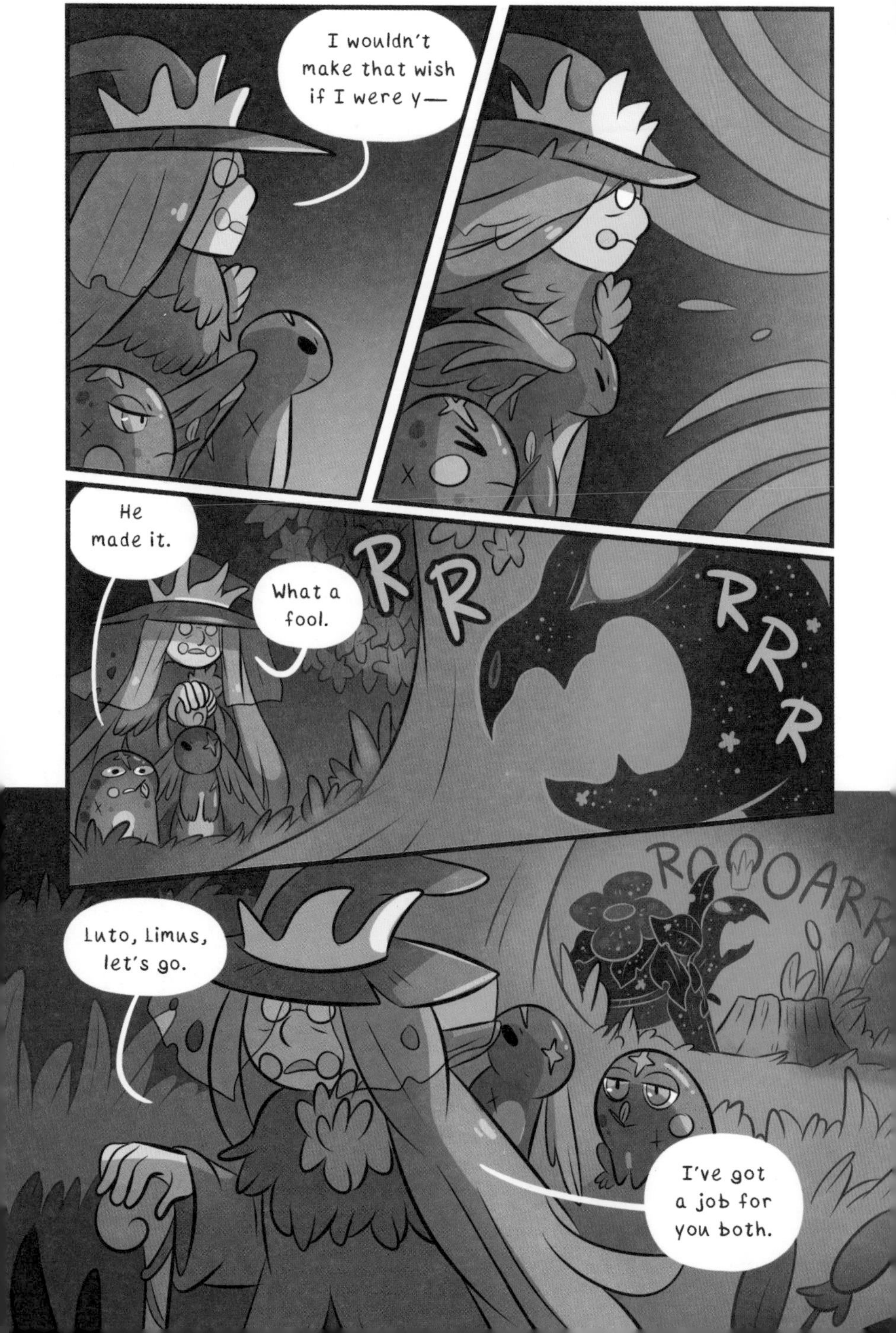

I wouldn't make that wish if I were y—
He made it.
What a fool.
RR
RRRR
ROOOARR
Luto, Limus, let's go.
I've got a job for you both.

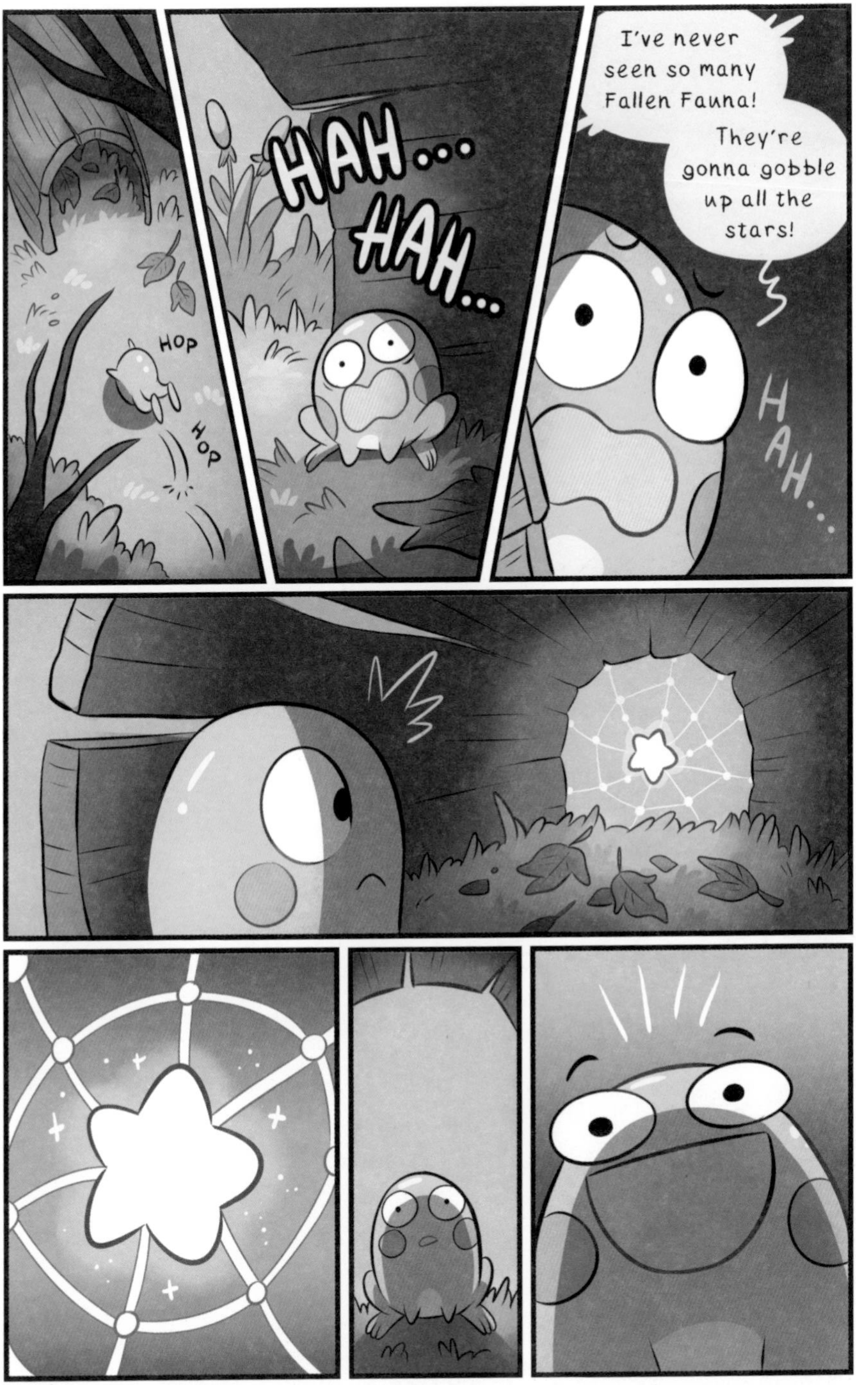
HOP
HOP
HAH...
HAH...
I've never seen so many Fallen Fauna!
They're gonna gobble up all the stars!
HAH...

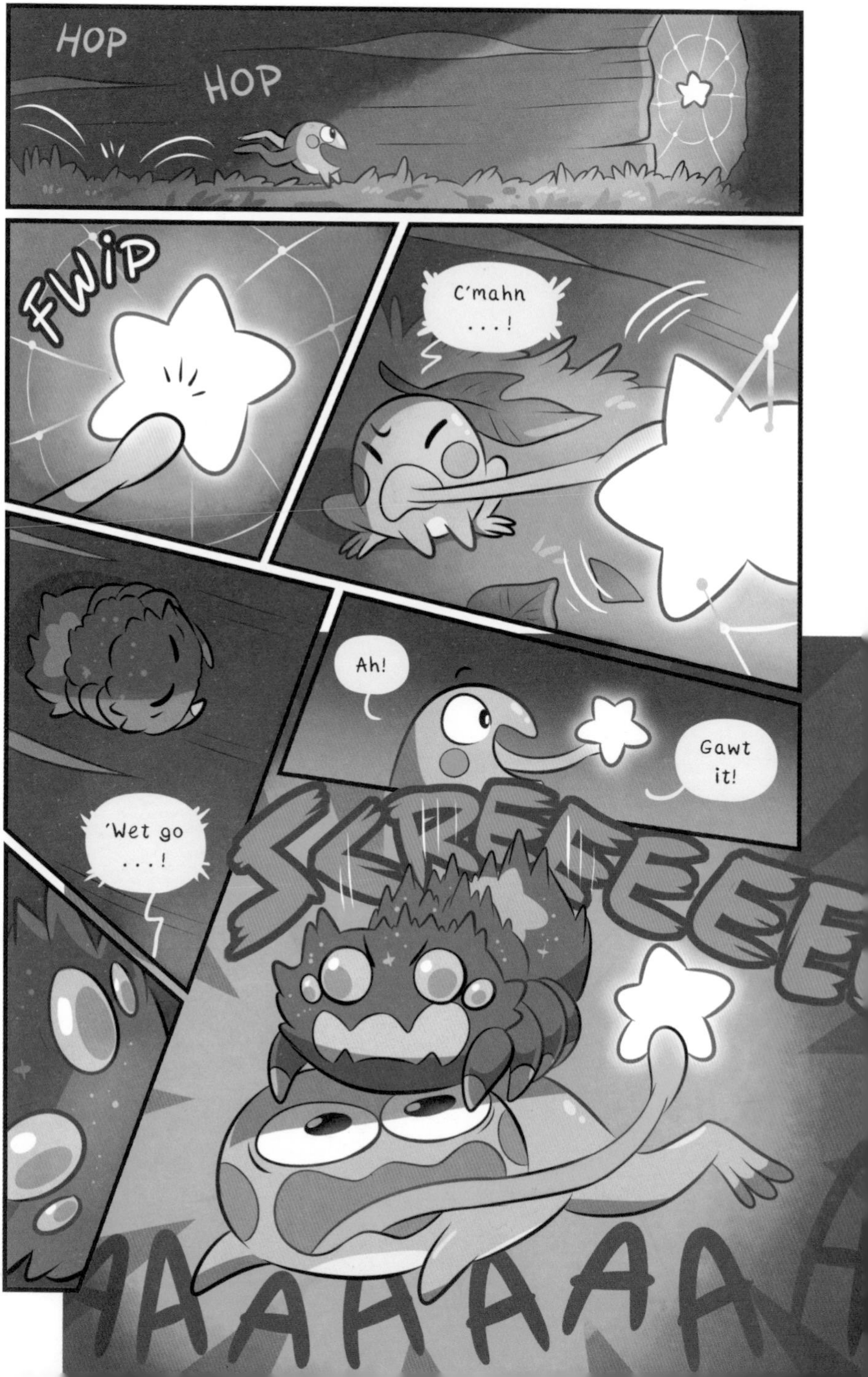
HOP
HOP
FWIP
C'mahn . . . !
Ah!
Gawt it!
'Wet go . . . !
AAAAAA

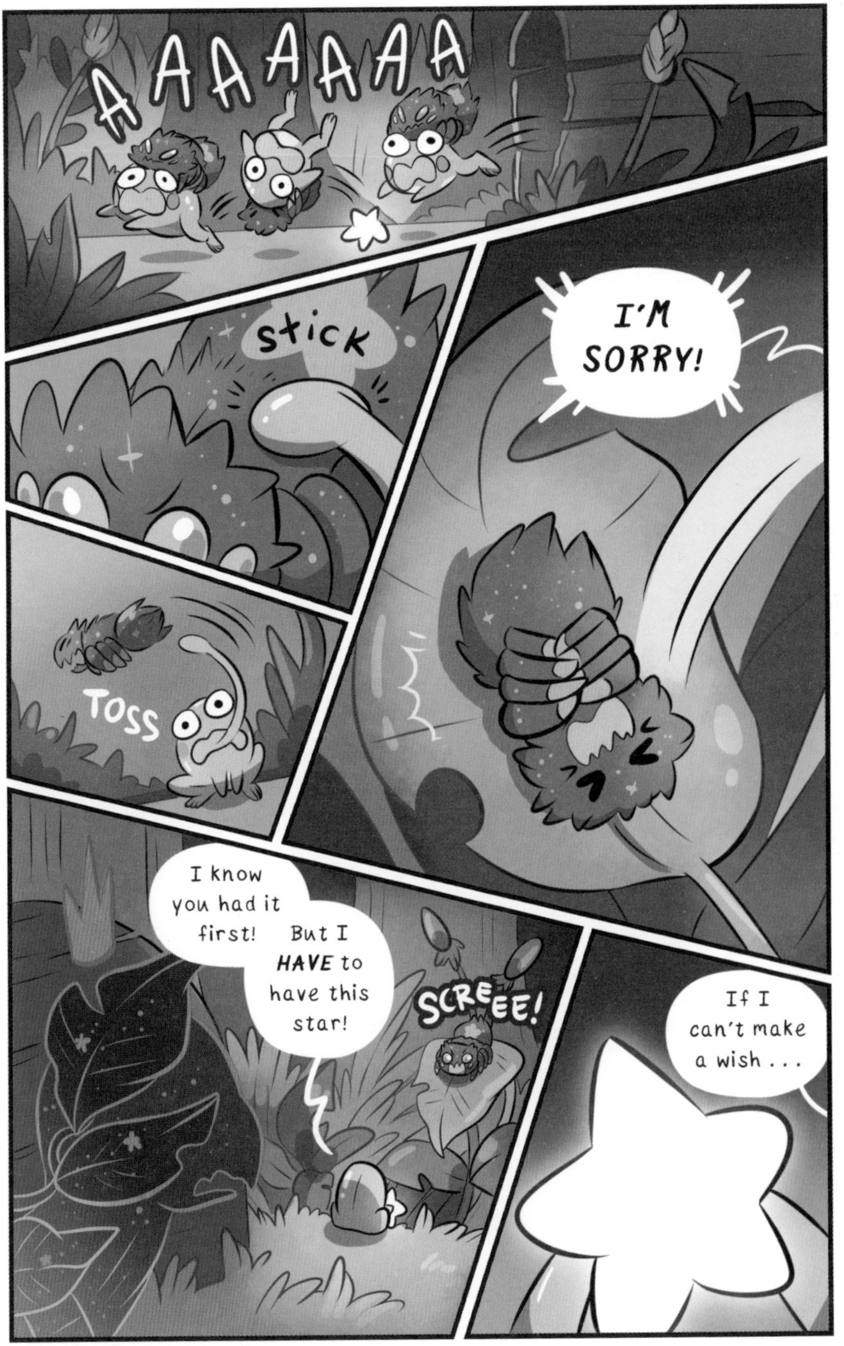
AAAAAAA
stick
I'M SORRY!
TOSS
I know you had it first!
But I HAVE to have this star!
SCREEE!
If I can't make a wish . . .

. . . I'LL NEVER BE ANYTHING BUT A CREEPY FROG!
Mud Dweller...
...what are you doing...
... with that star...?
M-mister Sophos?
SCREEE!
WATCH OUT!
DUCK!

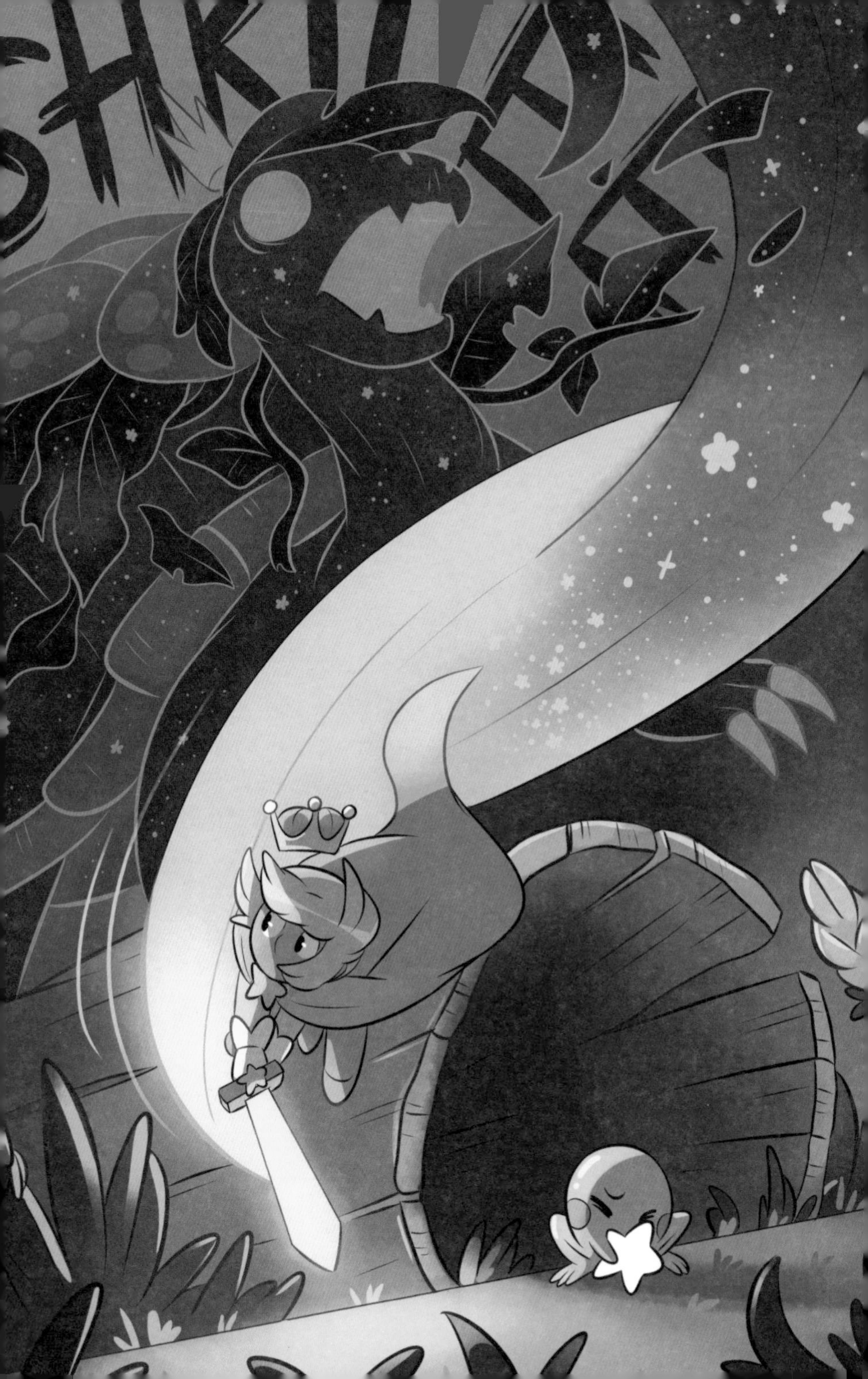

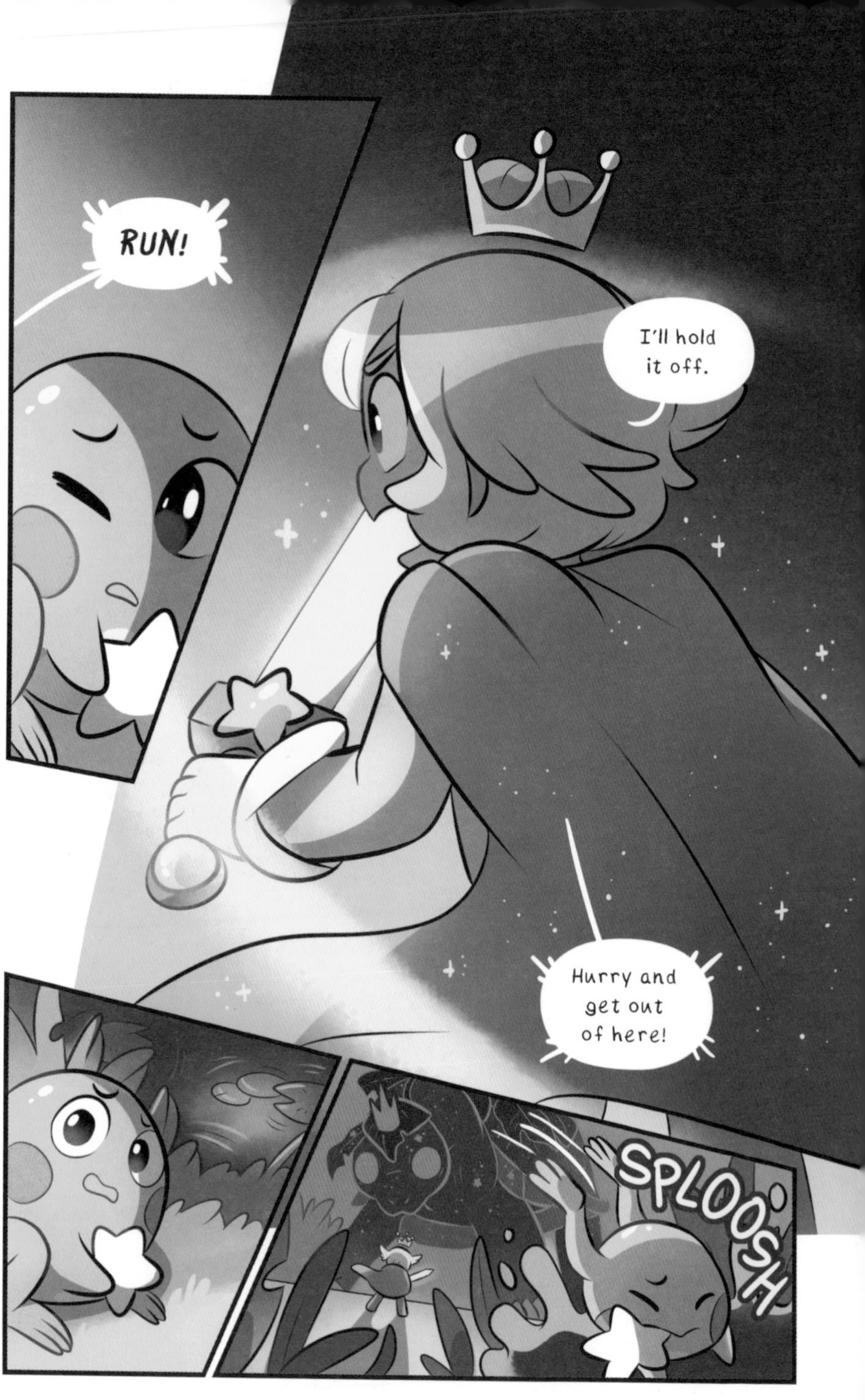
RUN!
I'll hold it off.
Hurry and get out of here!
SPLOOSH

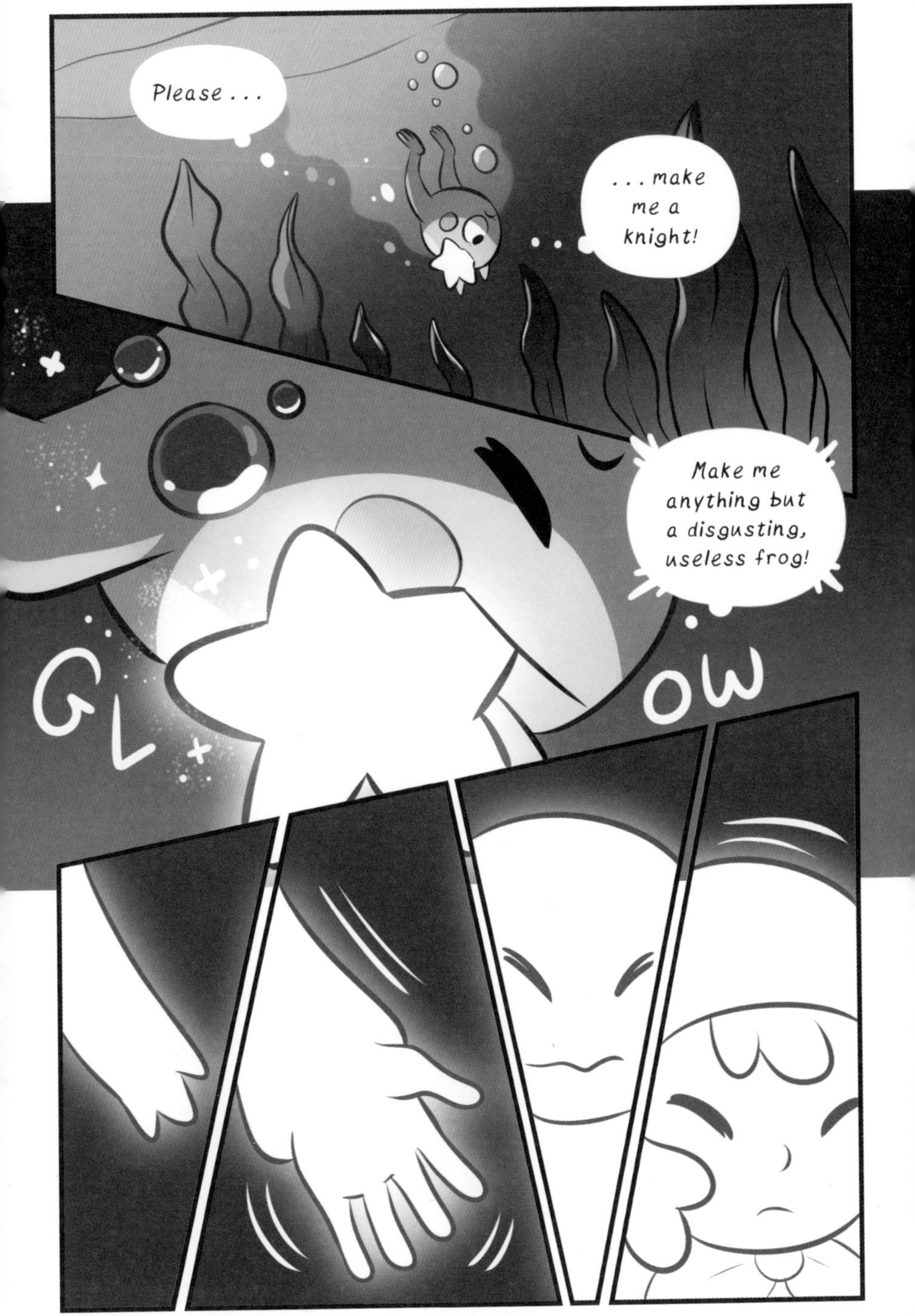
Please . . .
. . . make me a knight!
Make me anything but a disgusting, useless frog!
GLOW

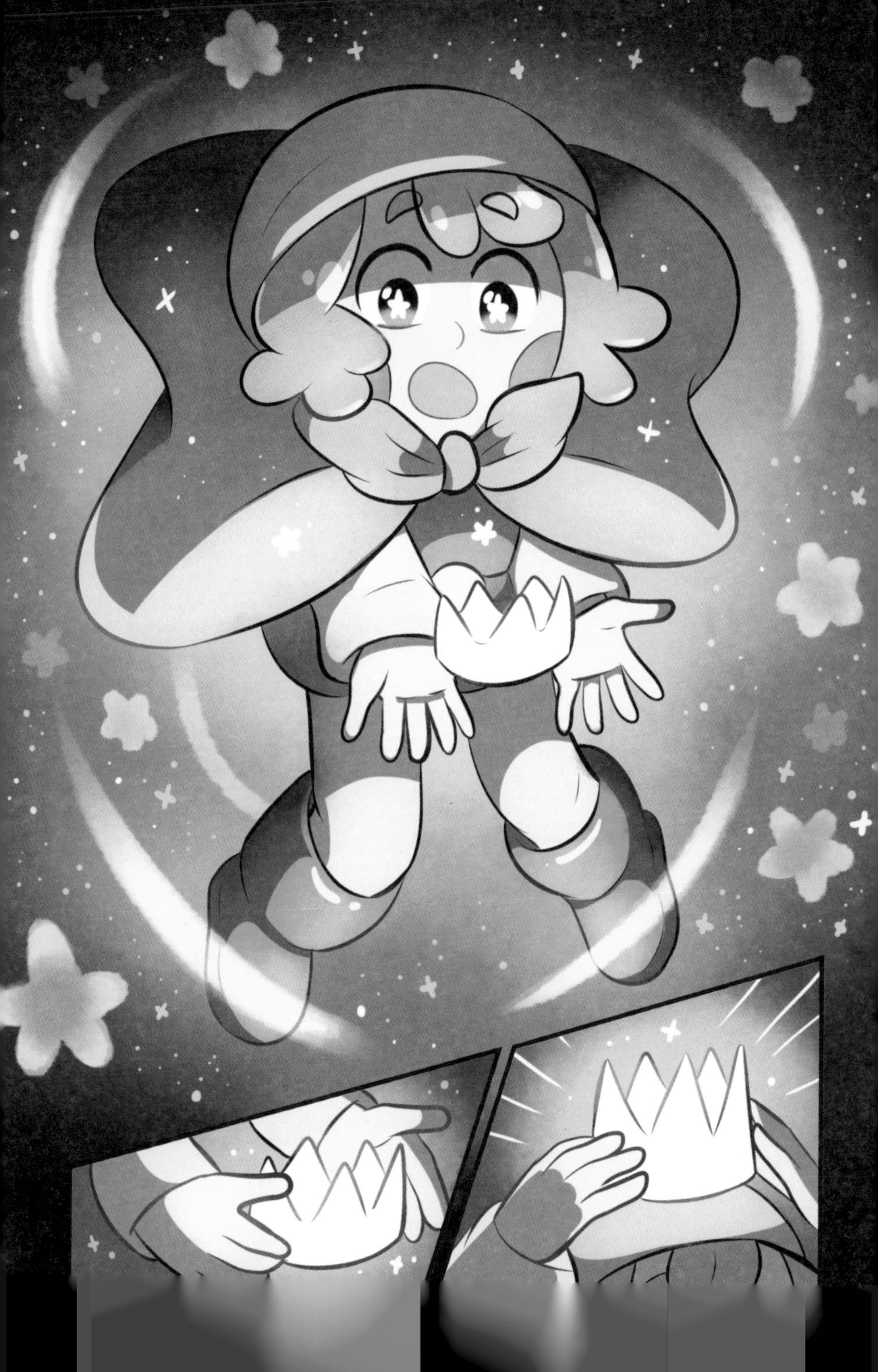

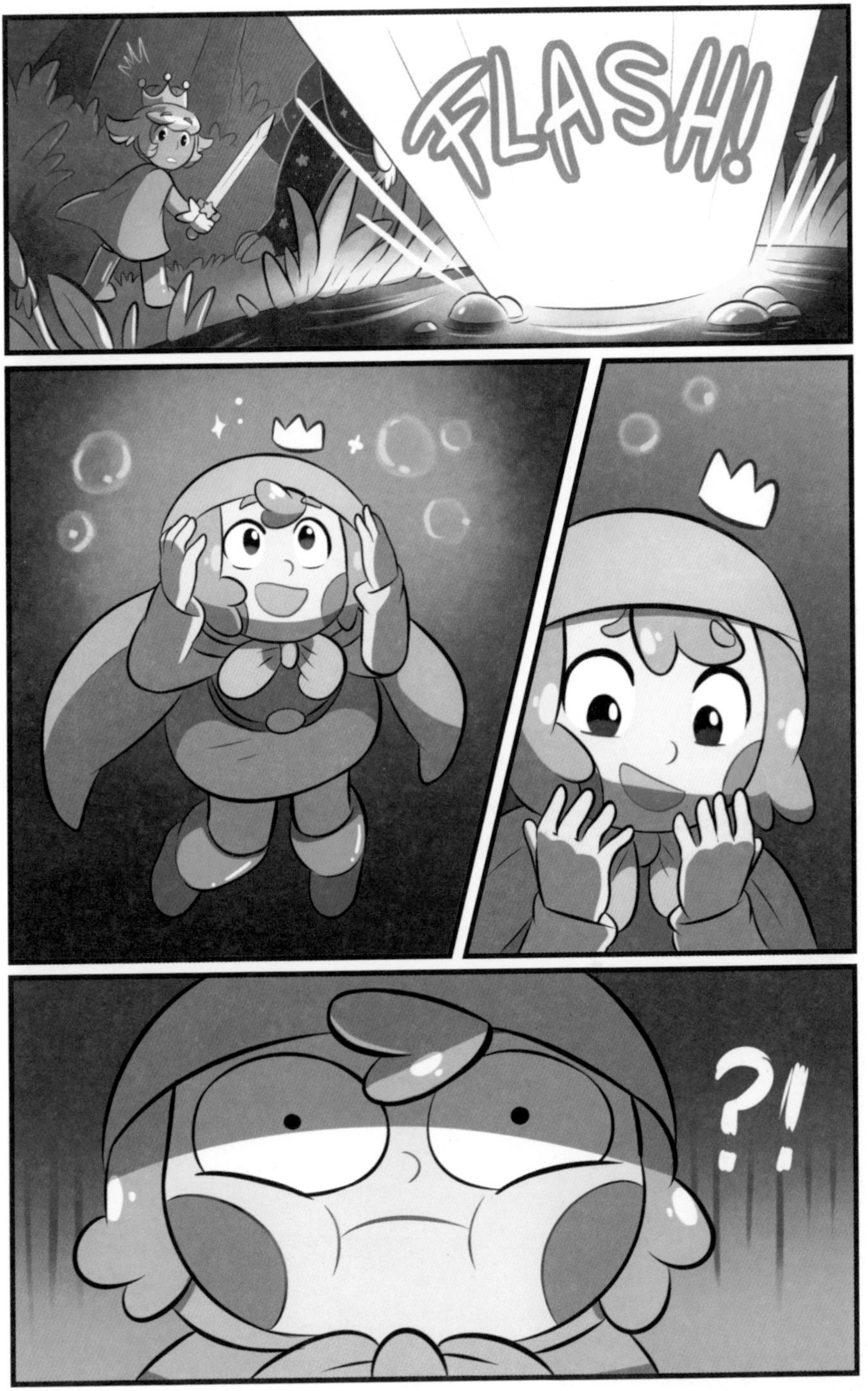
FLASH!
?!
!!

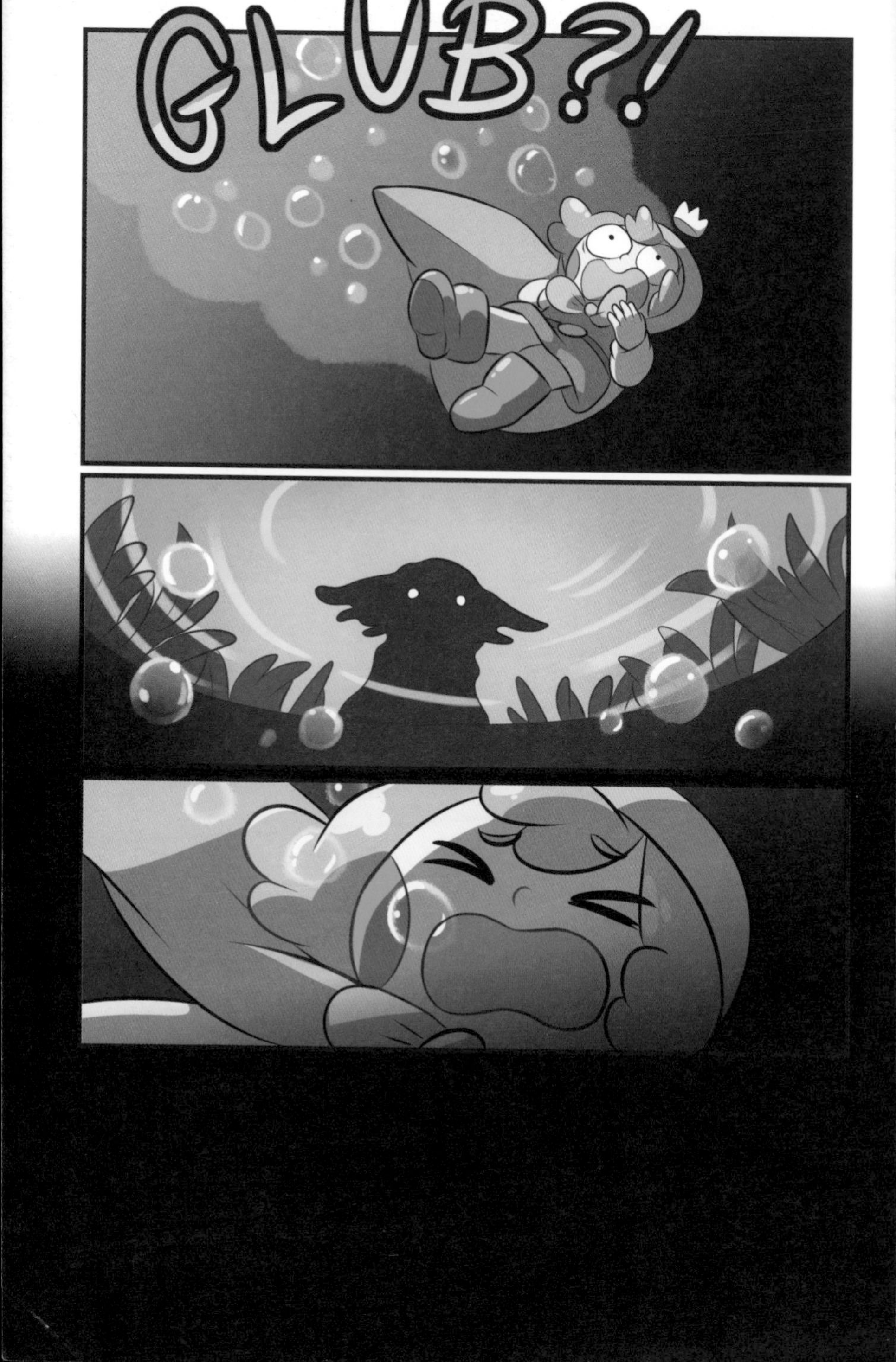
GLUB?!

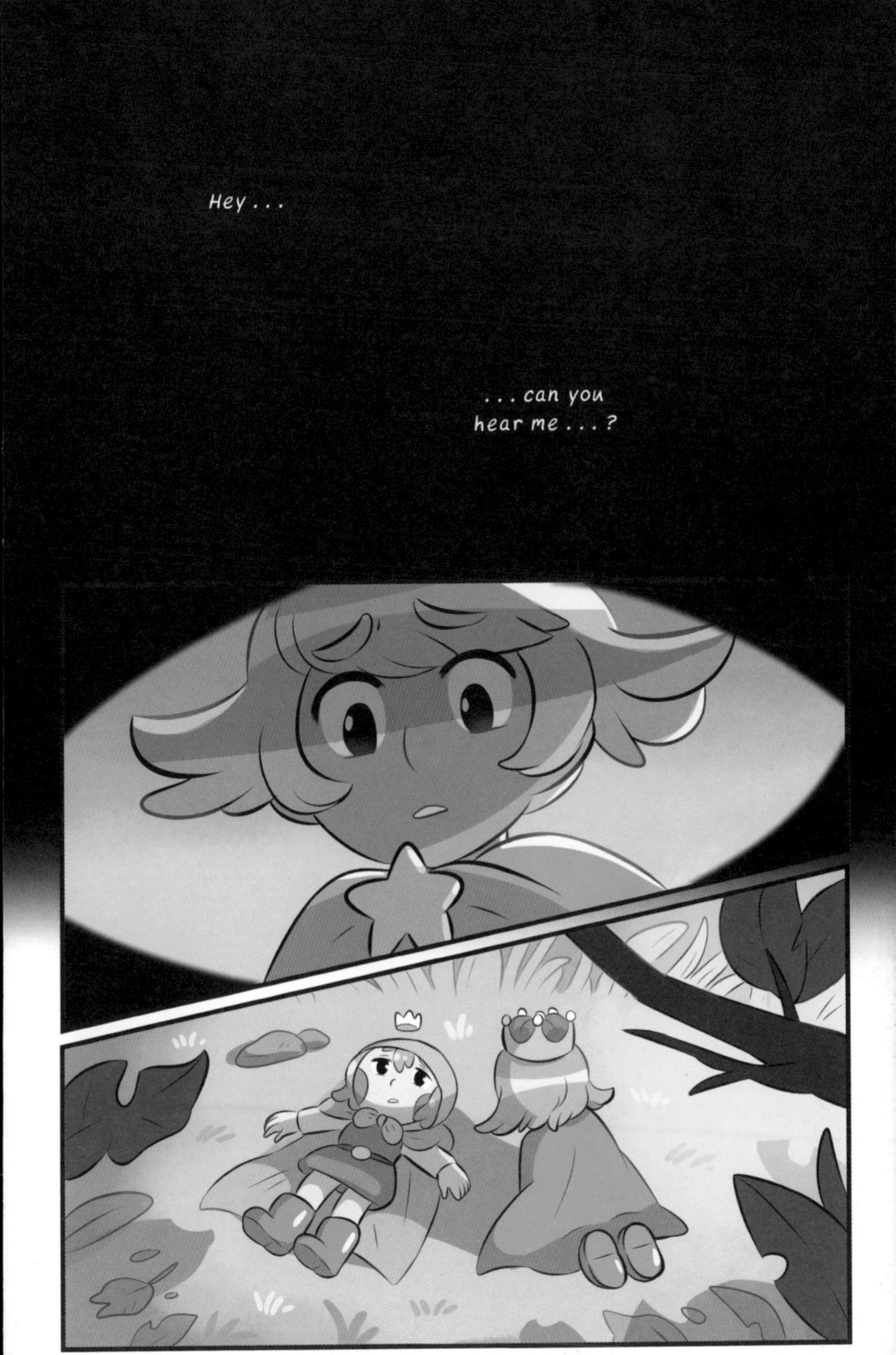
Hey . . .
. . . can you hear me . . . ?

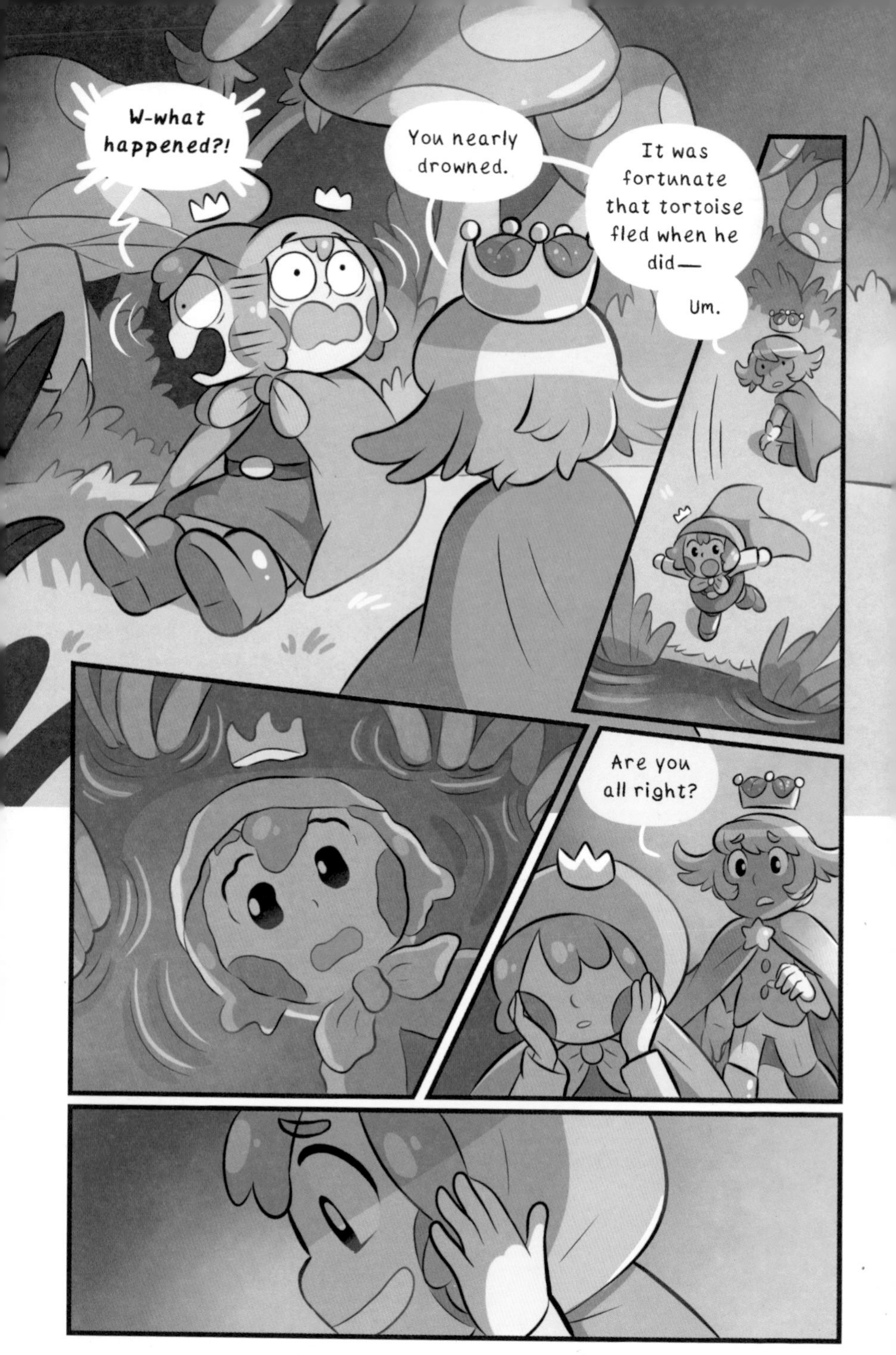
W-what happened?!
You nearly drowned.
It was fortunate that tortoise fled when he did—
Um.
Are you all right?

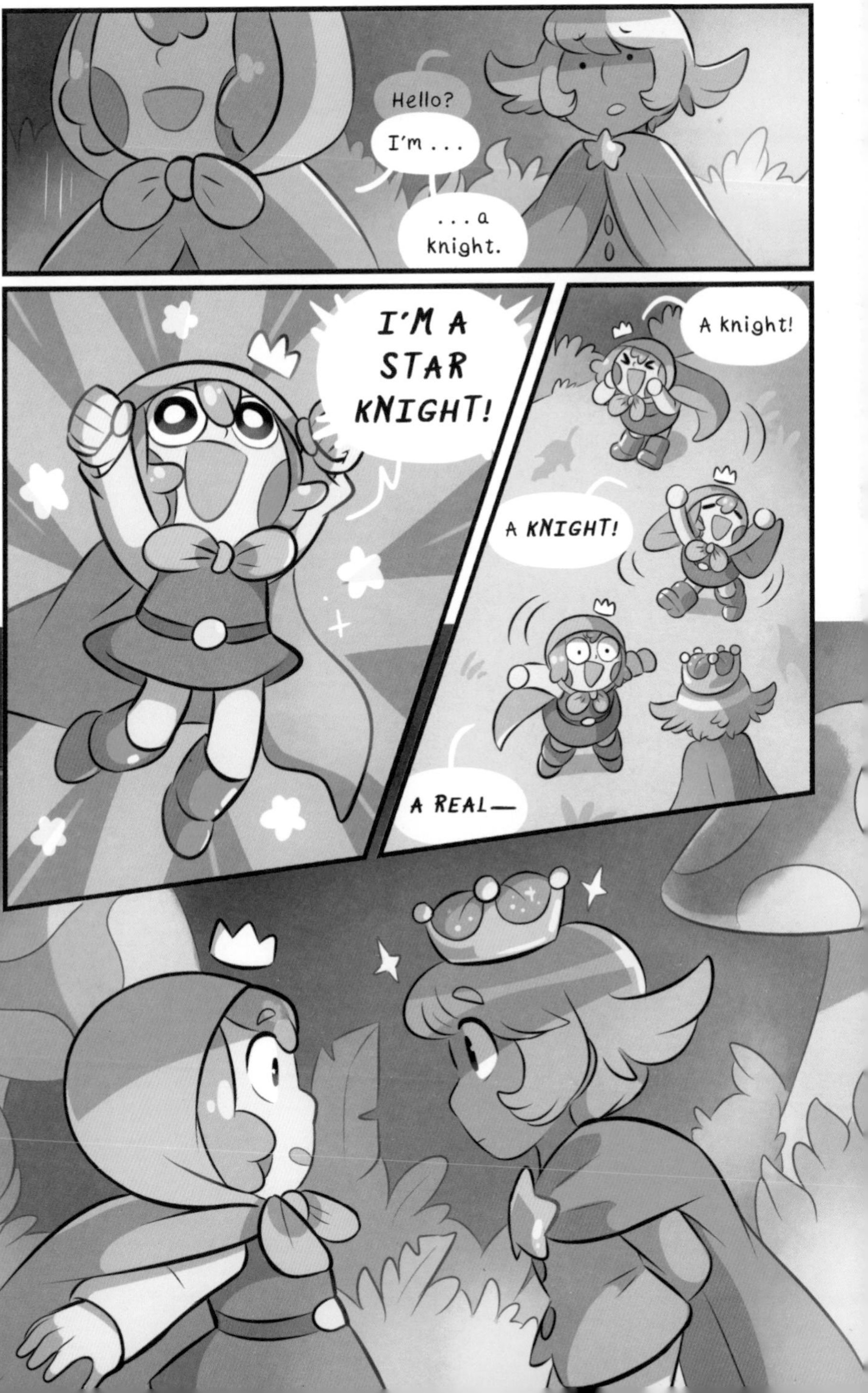
Hello?
I'm . . .
. . . a knight.
I'M A STAR KNIGHT!
A knight!
A KNIGHT!
A REAL—

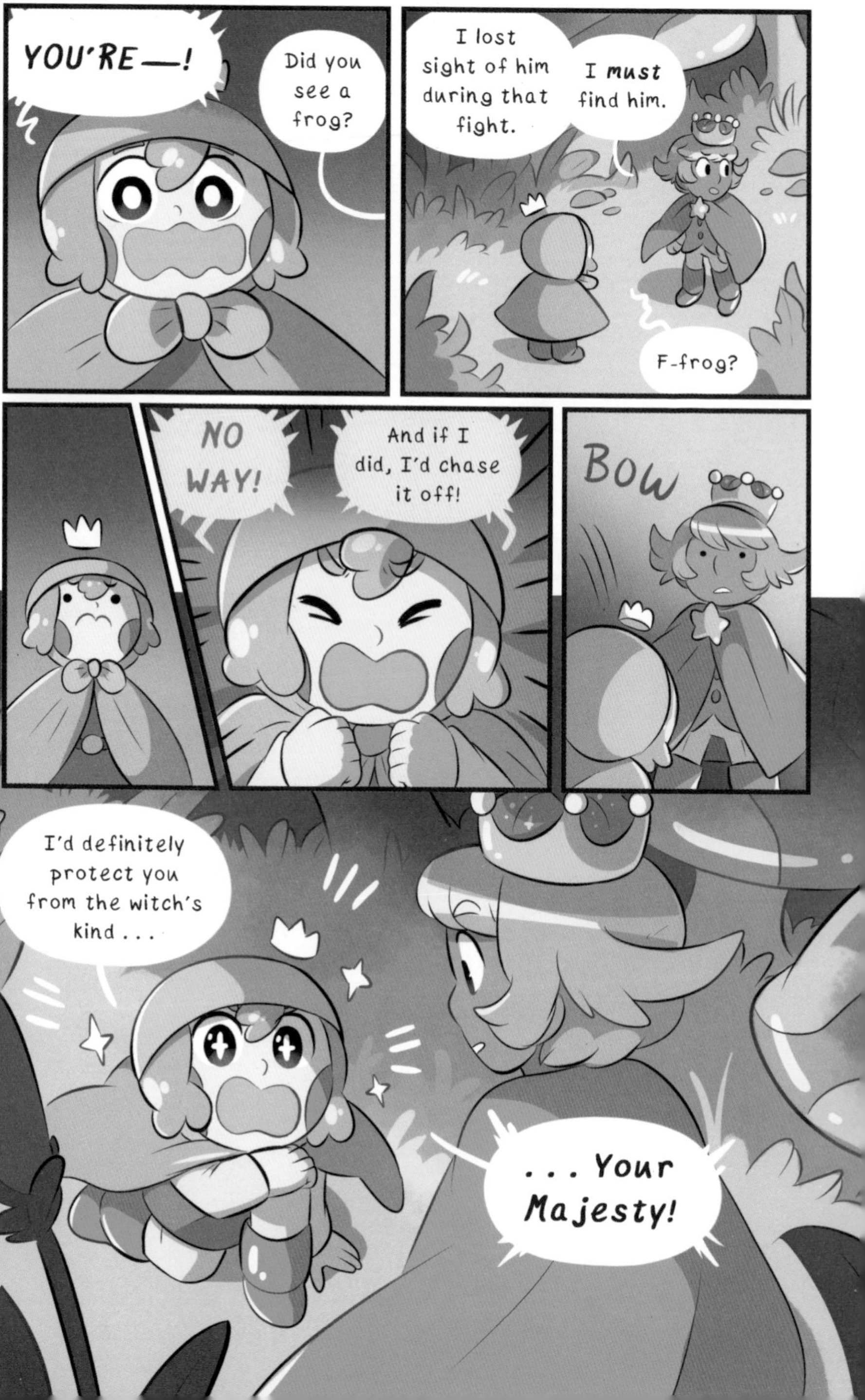

YOU'RE—!
Did you see a frog?
I lost sight of him during that fight.
I must find him.
F-frog?
NO WAY!
And if I did, I'd chase it off!
BOW
I'd definitely protect you from the witch's kind . . .
. . . Your Majesty!

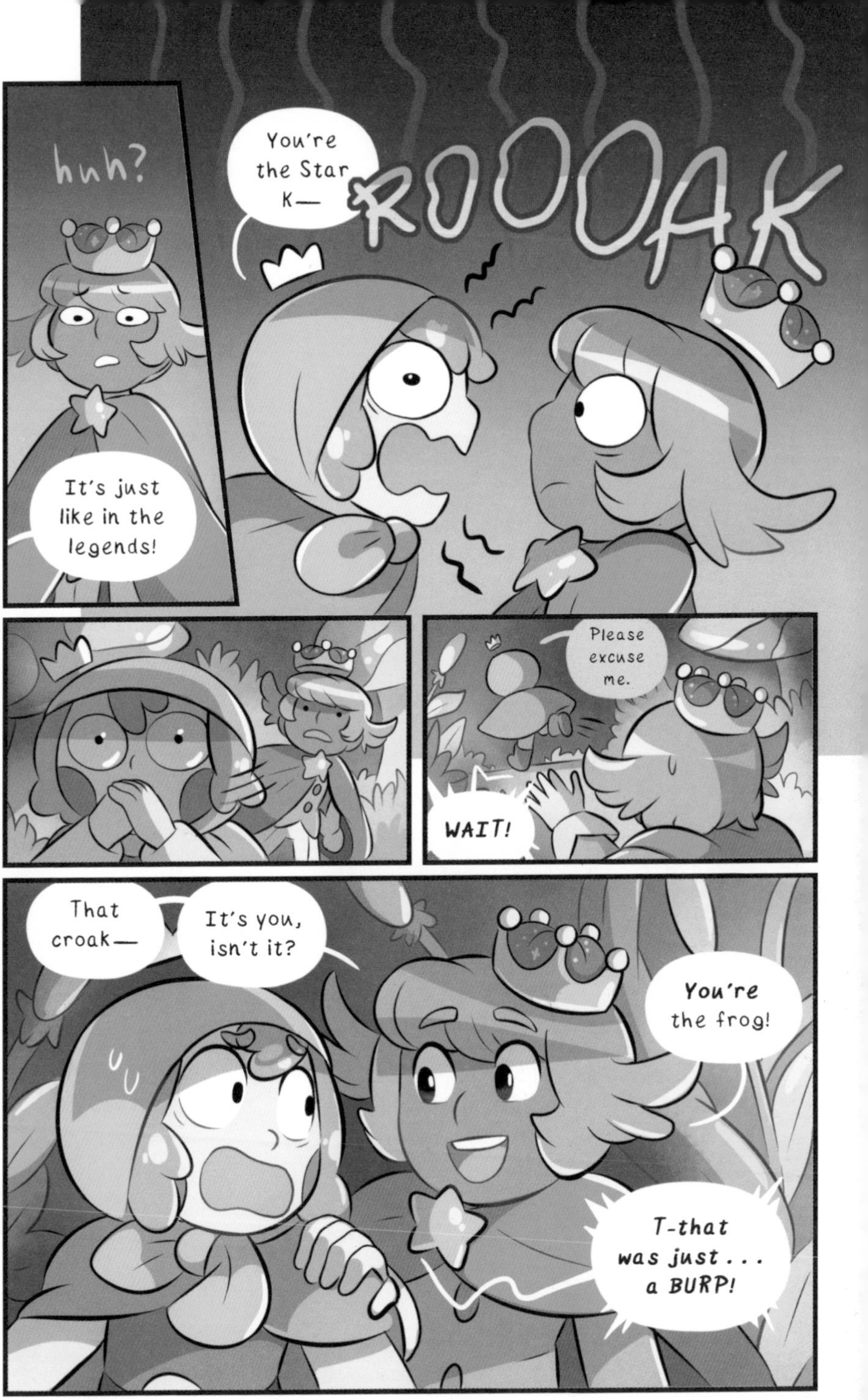
huh?
You're the Star K—
ROOOAK
It's just like in the legends!
Please excuse me.
WAIT!
That croak—
It's you, isn't it?
You're the frog!
T-that was just . . . a BURP!

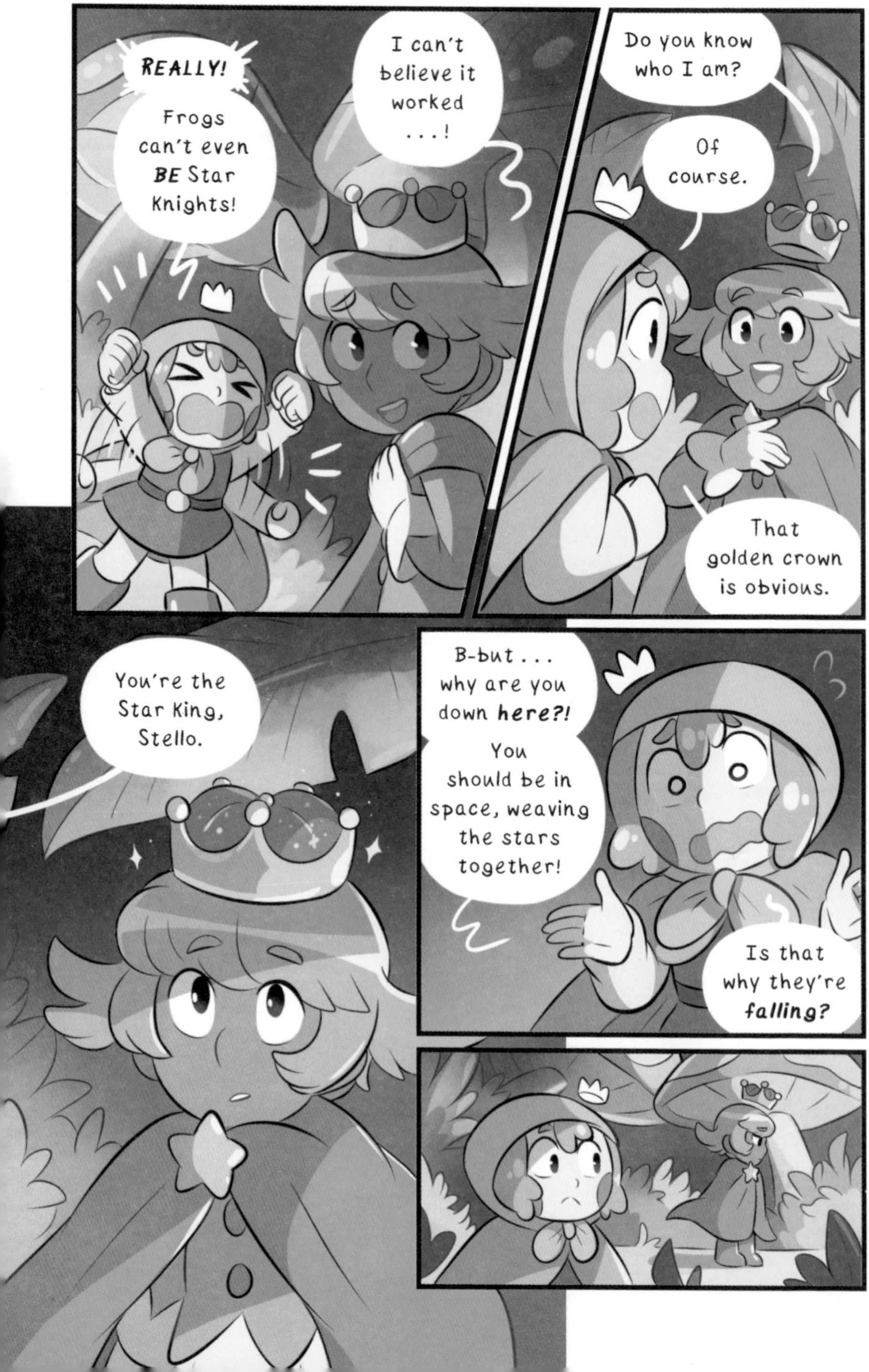
REALLY!
Frogs can't even BE Star Knights!
I can't believe it worked . . . !
Do you know who I am?
Of course.
That golden crown is obvious.
You're the Star King, Stello.
B-but . . . why are you down here?!
You should be in space, weaving the stars together!
Is that why they're falling?

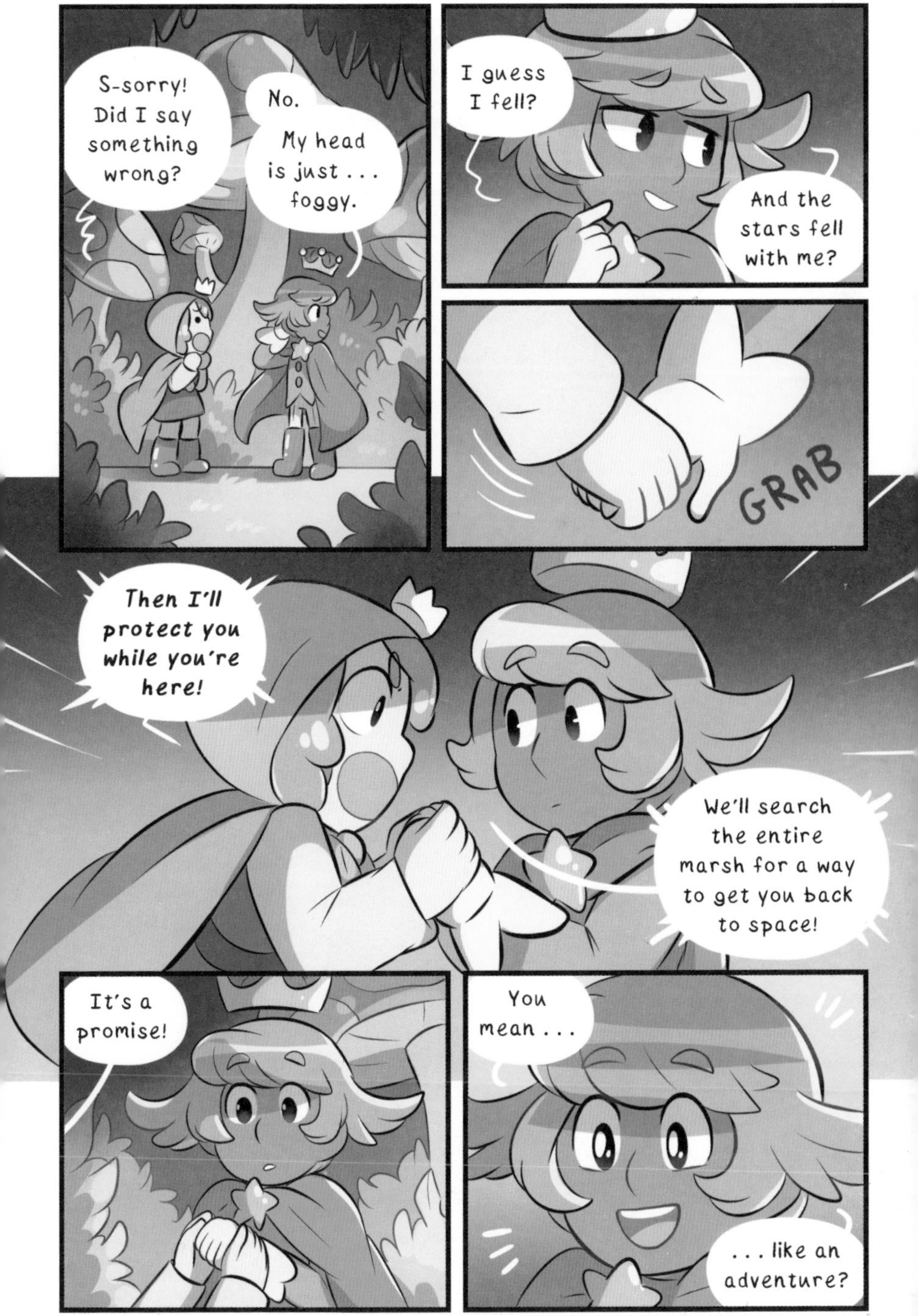
S-sorry! Did I say something wrong?
No.
My head is just . . . foggy.
I guess I fell?
And the stars fell with me?
GRAB
Then I'll protect you while you're here!
We'll search the entire marsh for a way to get you back to space!
It's a promise!
You mean . . .
. . . like an adventure?

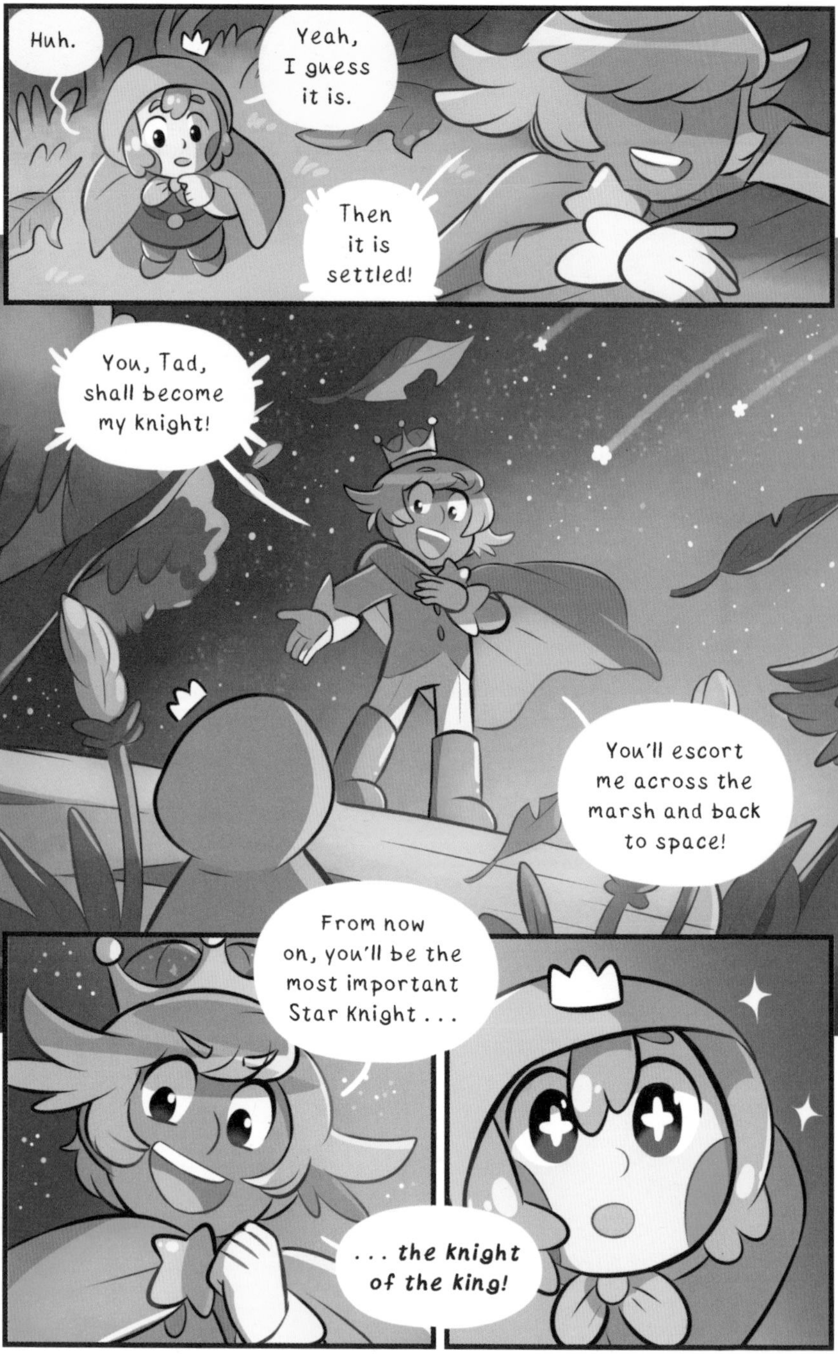

Huh.
Yeah, I guess it is.
Then it is settled!
You, Tad, shall become my knight!
You'll escort me across the marsh and back to space!
From now on, you'll be the most important Star Knight . . .
. . . *the knight of the king!*

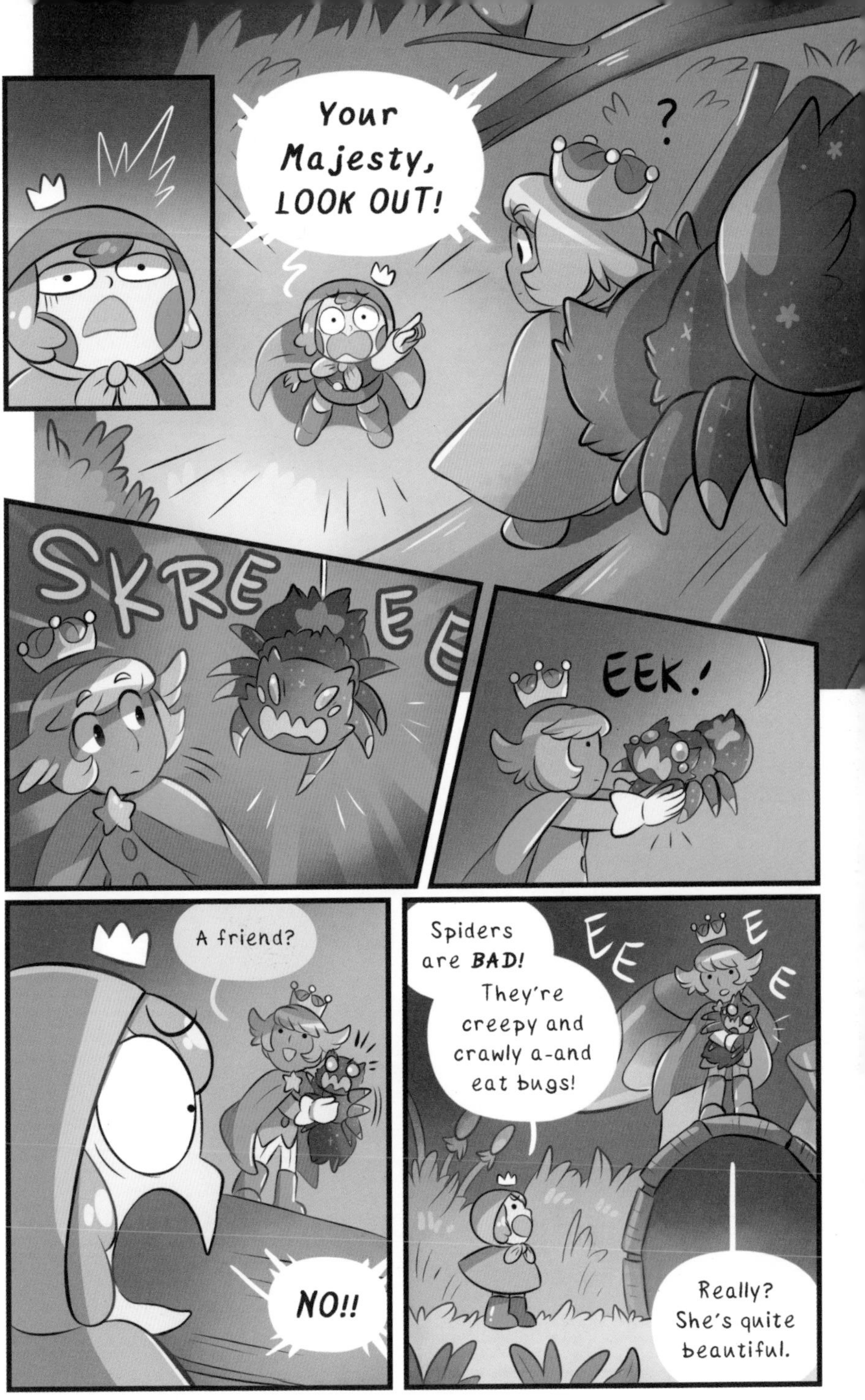
Your Majesty, LOOK OUT!
?
SKREEE
EEK!
A friend?
NO!!
Spiders are BAD! They're creepy and crawly a-and eat bugs!
EEE
Really? She's quite beautiful.

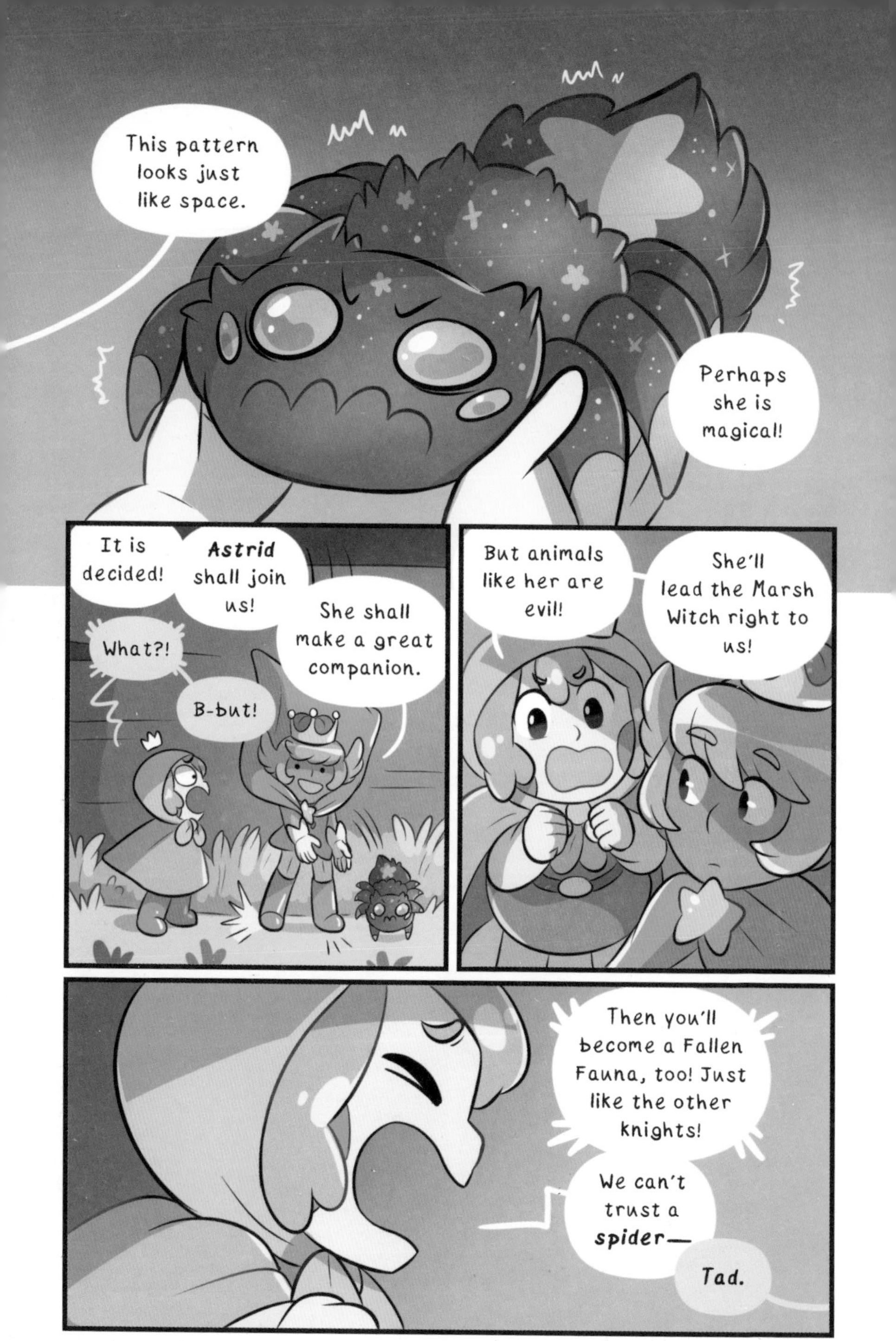
This pattern looks just like space.
Perhaps she is magical!
It is decided!
Astrid shall join us!
She shall make a great companion.
What?!
B-but!
But animals like her are evil!
She'll lead the Marsh Witch right to us!
Then you'll become a Fallen Fauna, too! Just like the other knights!
We can't trust a **spider**—
Tad.

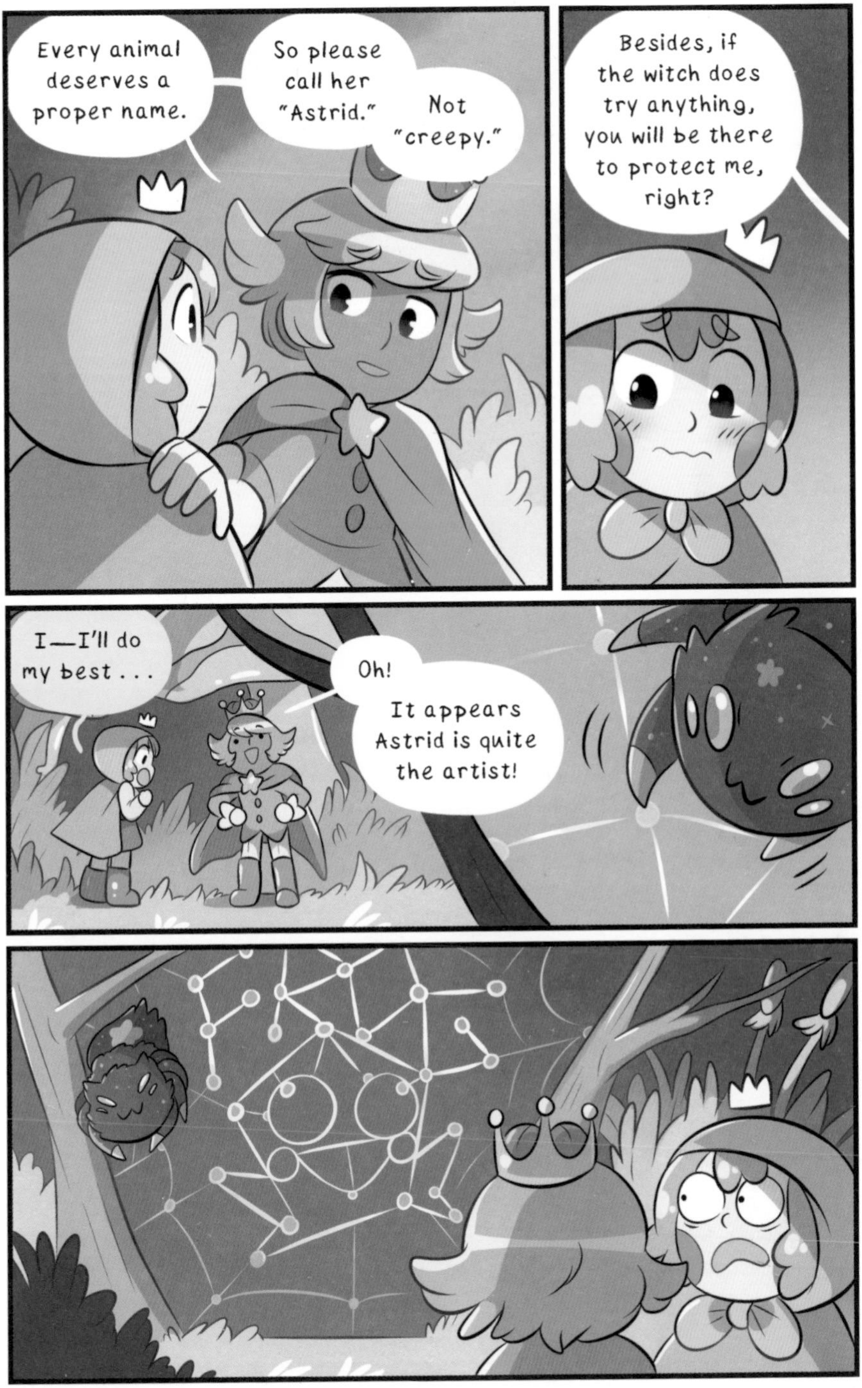
Every animal deserves a proper name.
So please call her "Astrid."
Not "creepy."
Besides, if the witch does try anything, you will be there to protect me, right?
I—I'll do my best . . .
Oh!
It appears Astrid is quite the artist!

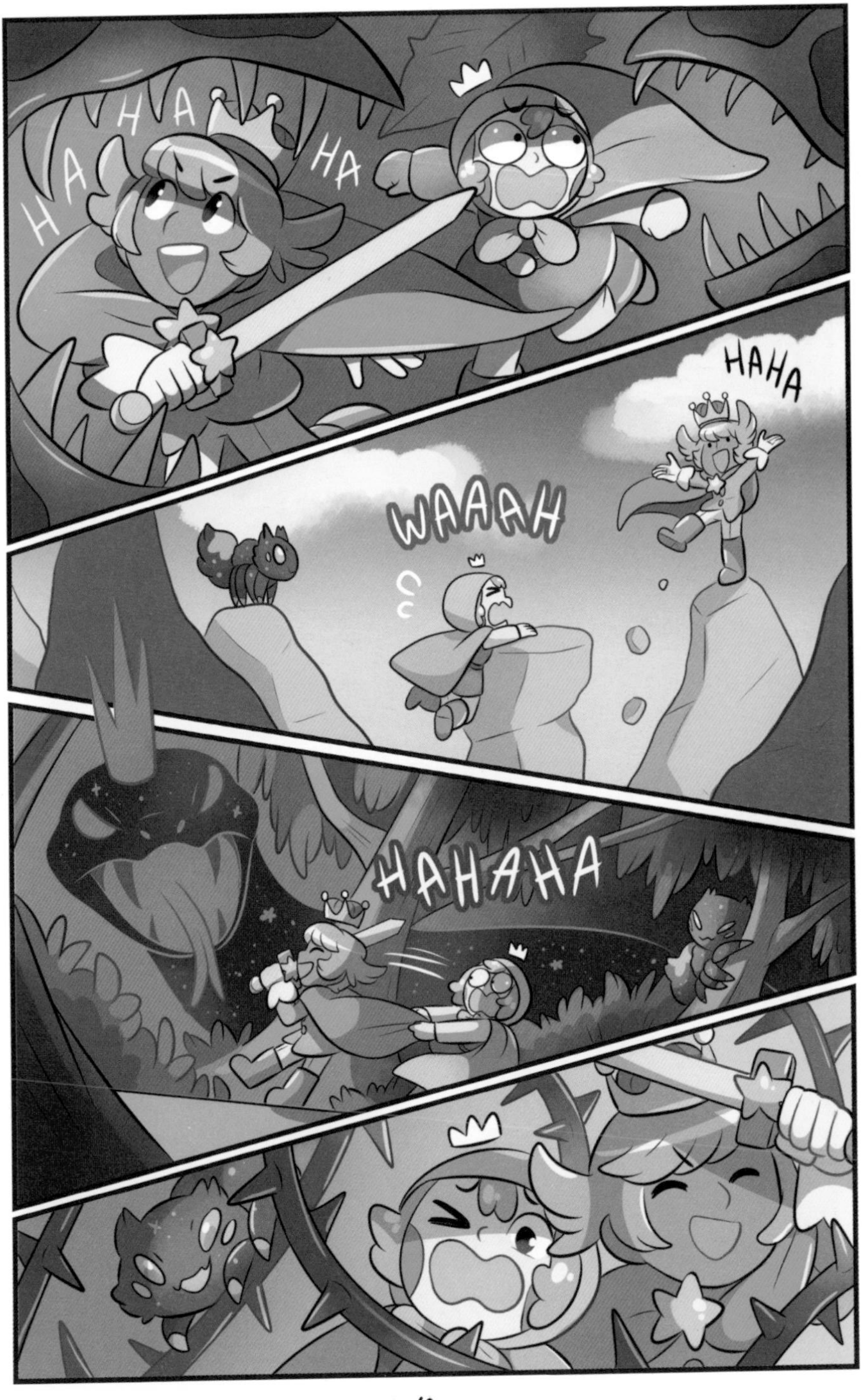
HA HA HA HA HA
HAHA
WAAAH
HAHAHA

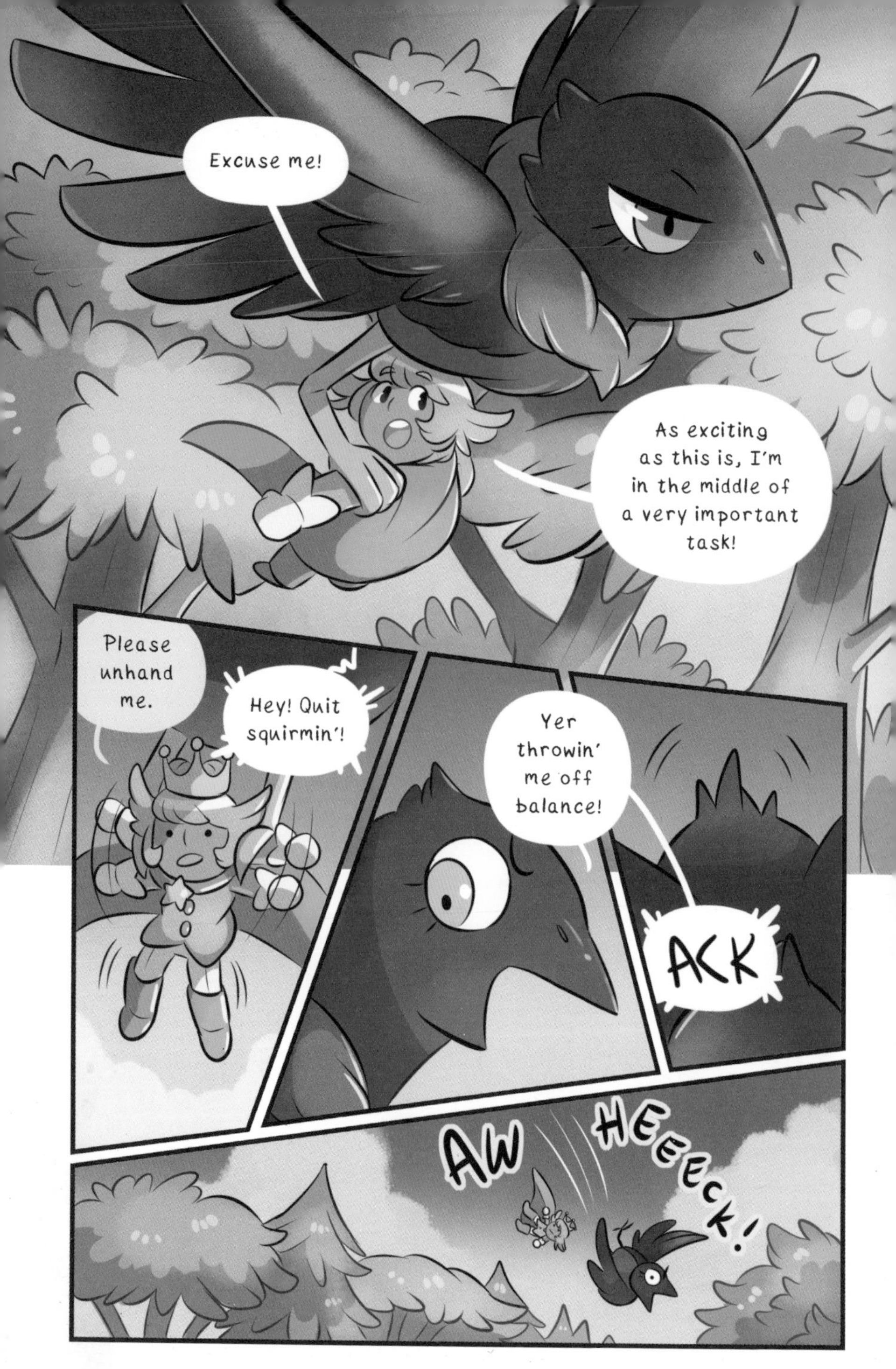
Excuse me!
As exciting as this is, I'm in the middle of a very important task!
Please unhand me.
Hey! Quit squirmin'!
Yer throwin' me off balance!
ACK
AW HEEECK!

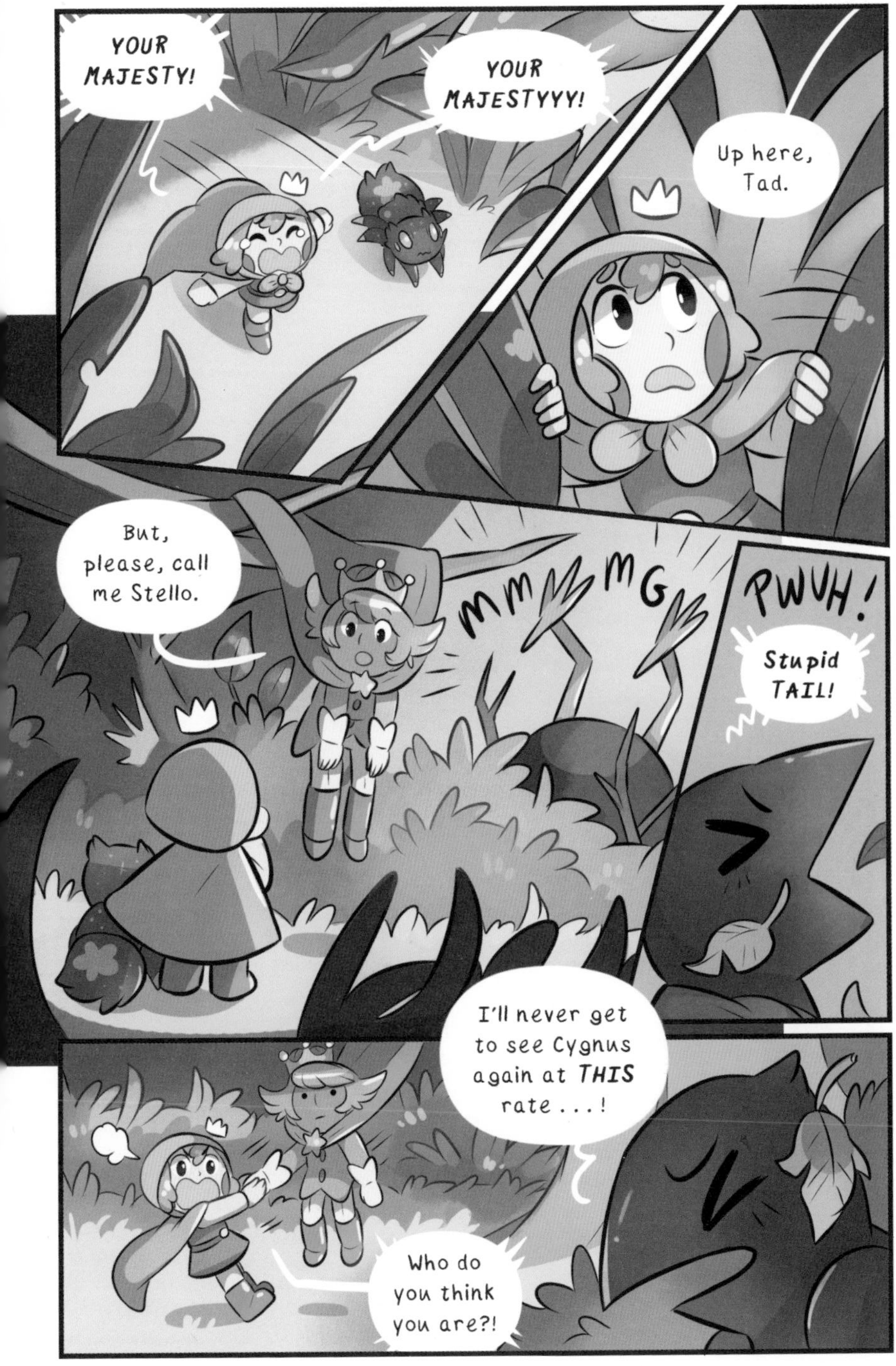

YOUR MAJESTY!
YOUR MAJESTYYY!
Up here, Tad.
But, please, call me Stello.
MMMMG
PWUH!
Stupid TAIL!
I'll never get to see Cygnus again at THIS rate . . . !
Who do you think you are?!

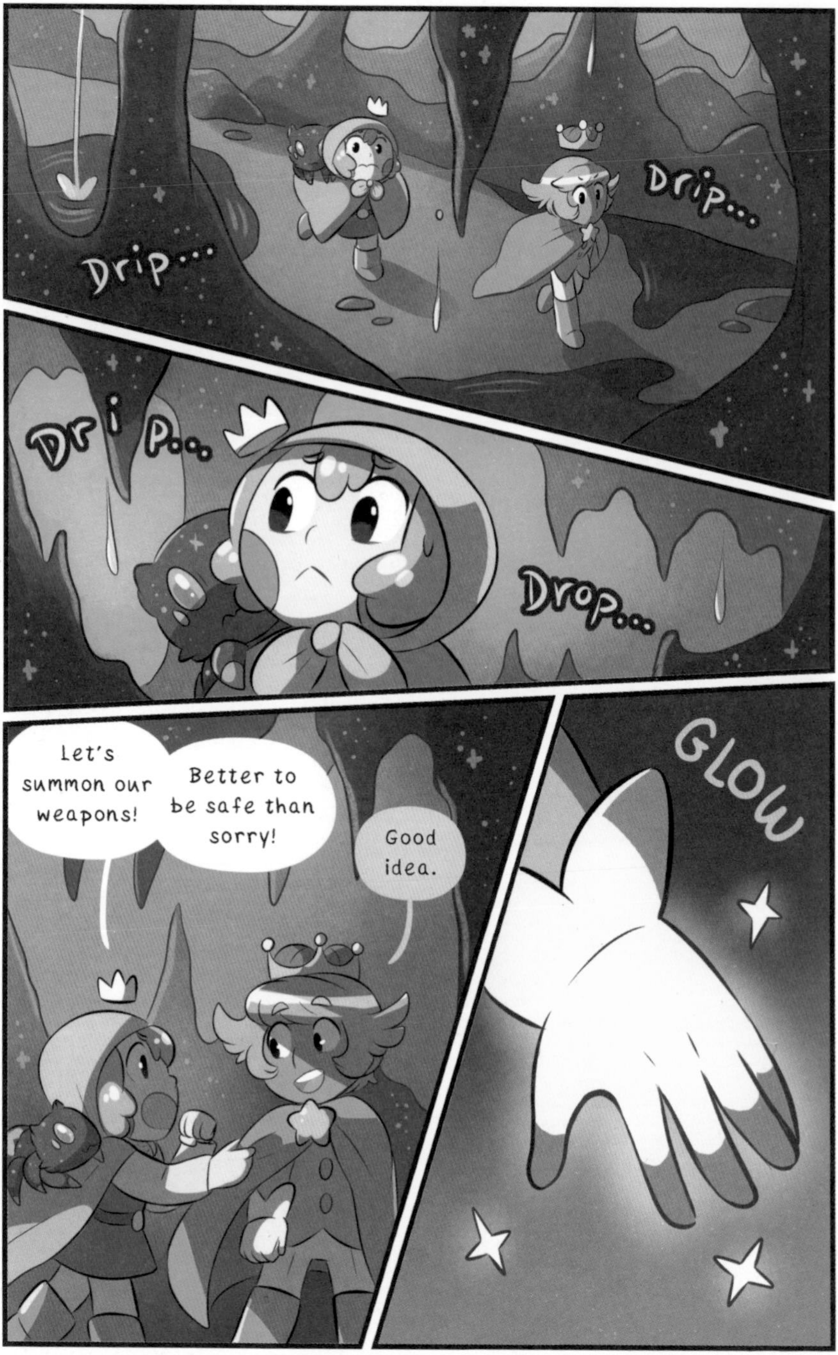
Drip...
Drip...
Drip...
Drop...
Let's summon our weapons!
Better to be safe than sorry!
Good idea.
GLOW

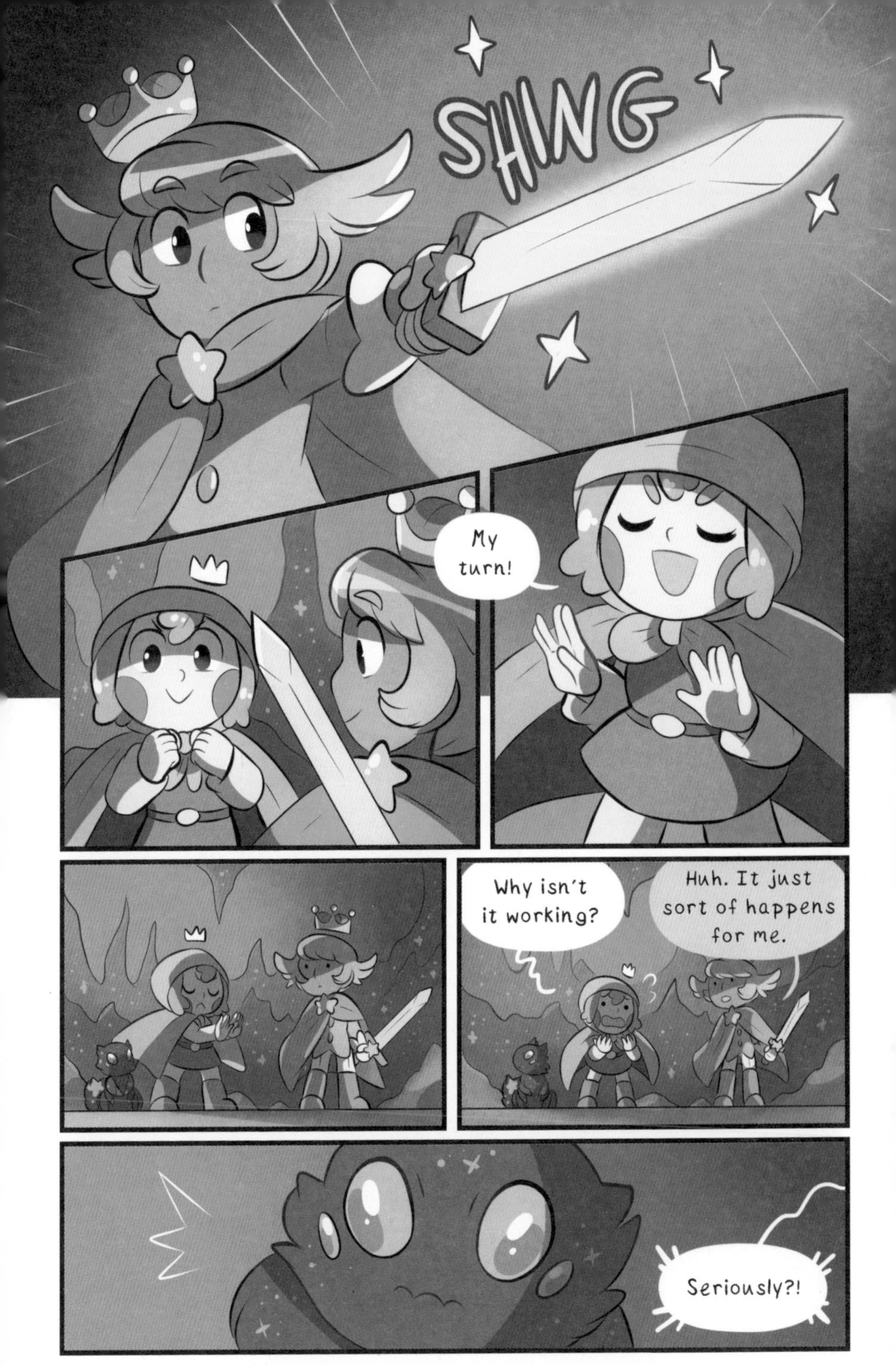
SHING
My turn!
Why isn't it working?
Huh. It just sort of happens for me.
Seriously?!

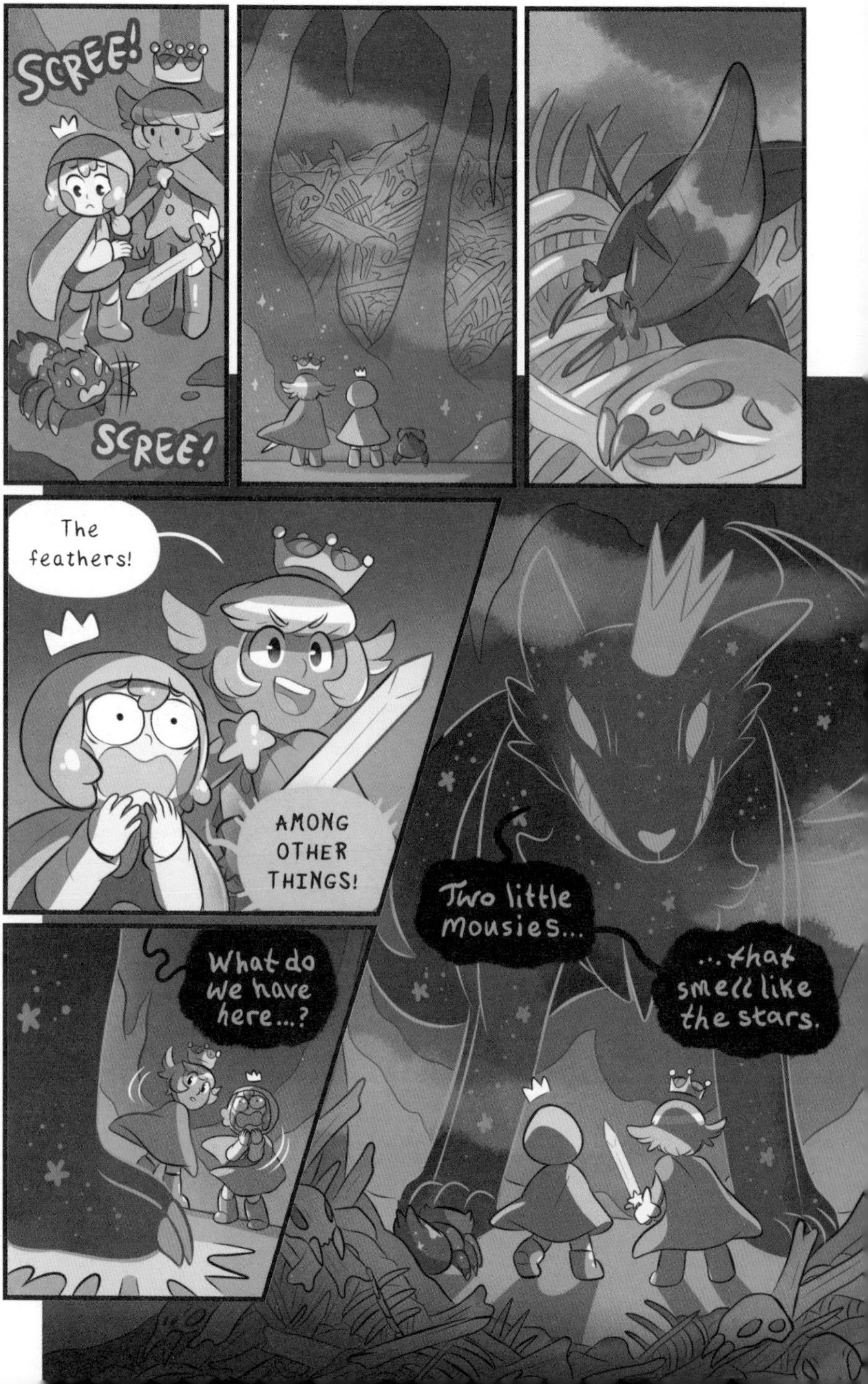
SCREE!
SCREE!
The feathers!
AMONG OTHER THINGS!
What do we have here...?
Two little mousies...
...that smell like the stars.

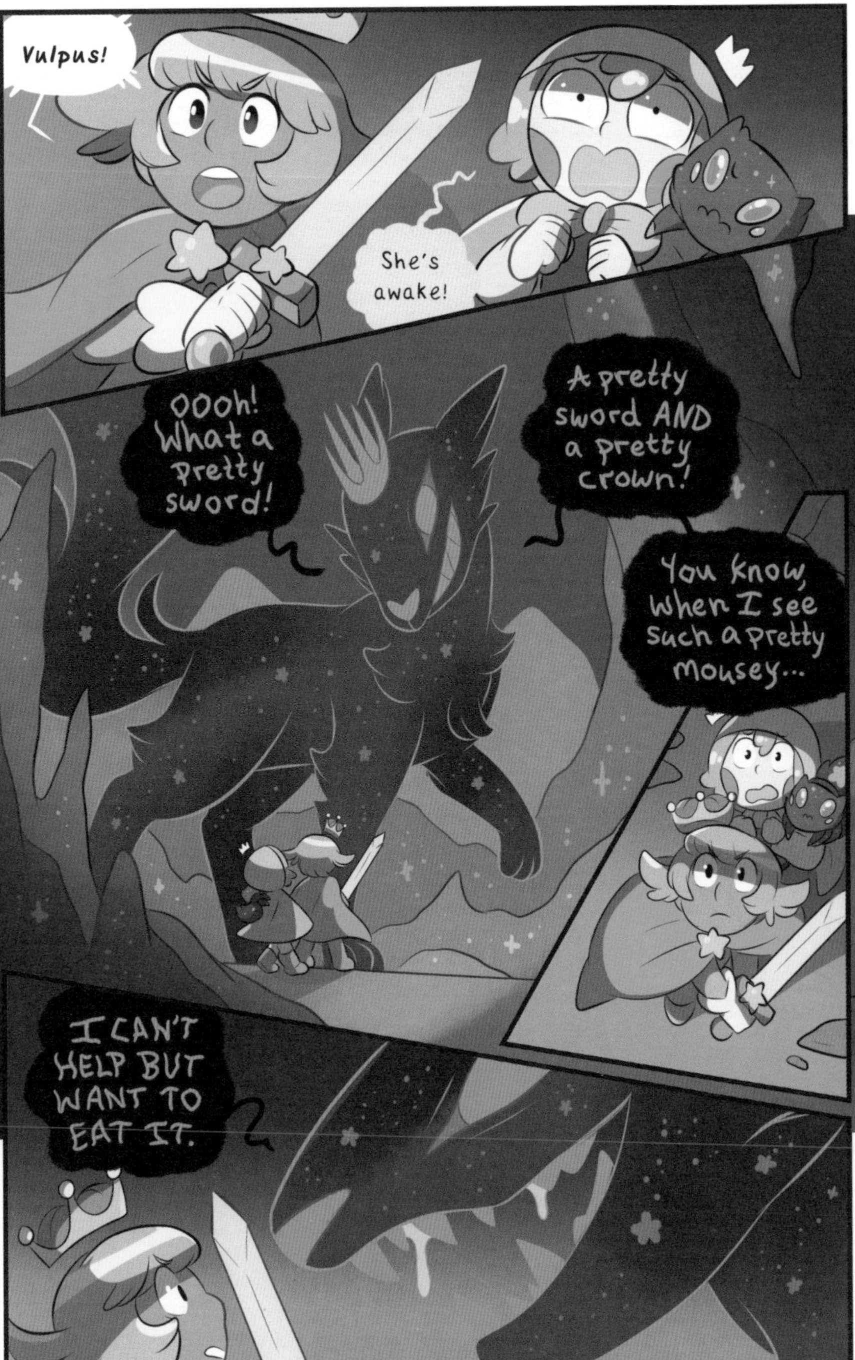

Vulpus!
She's awake!
OOOh! What a pretty sword!
A pretty sword AND a pretty crown!
You know, when I see such a pretty mousey...
I CAN'T HELP BUT WANT TO EAT IT.

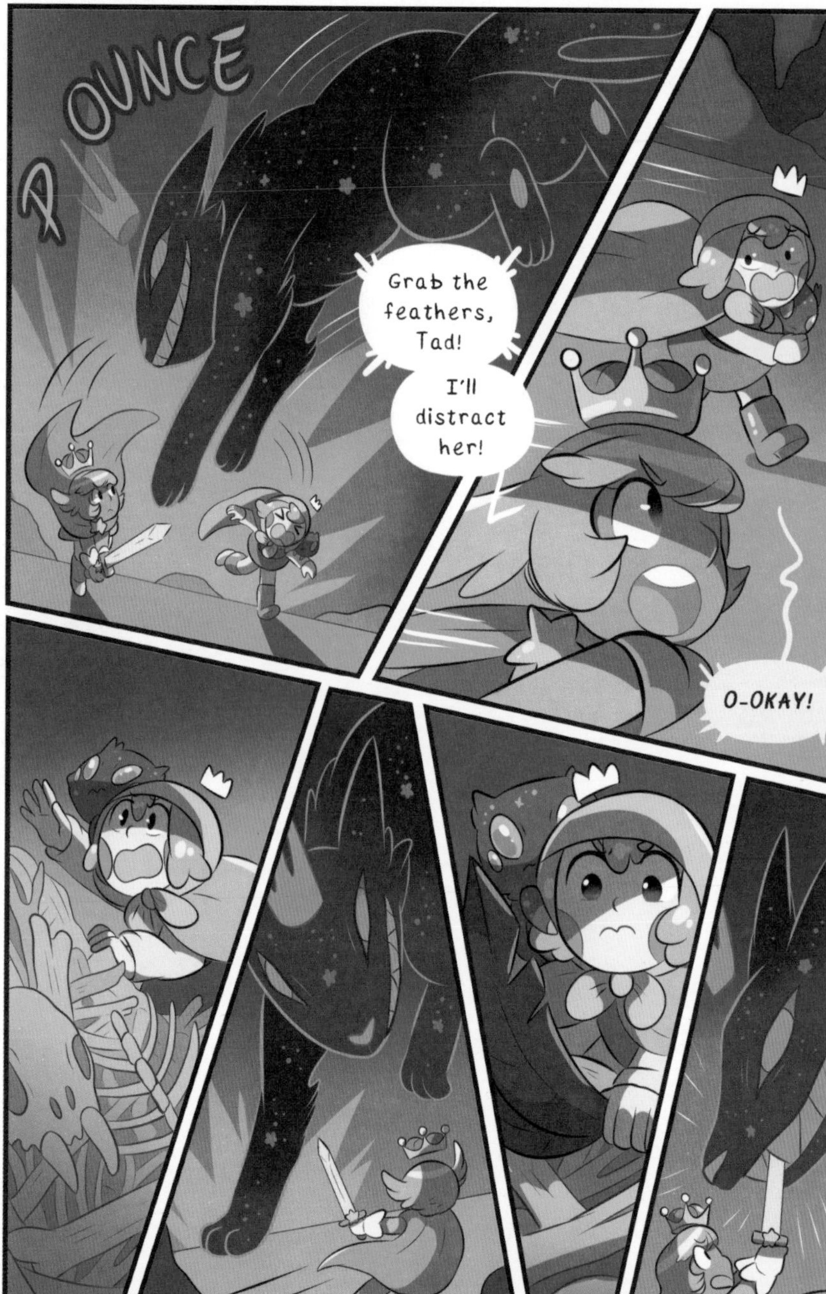
POUNCE
Grab the feathers, Tad!
I'll distract her!
O-OKAY!

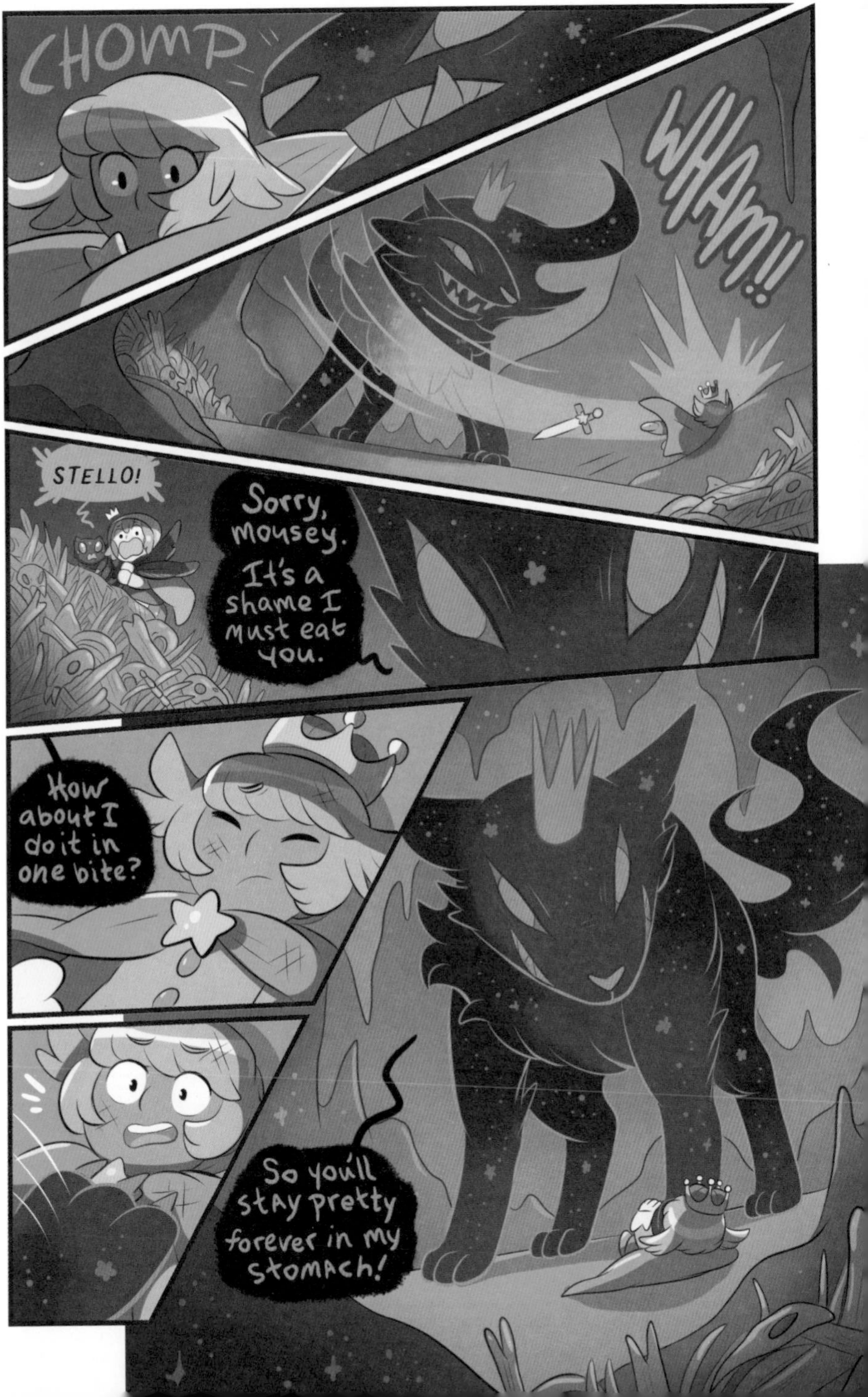
CHOMP
WHAM!!
STELLO!
Sorry, mousey.
It's a shame I must eat you.
How about I do it in one bite?
So you'll stay pretty forever in my stomach!

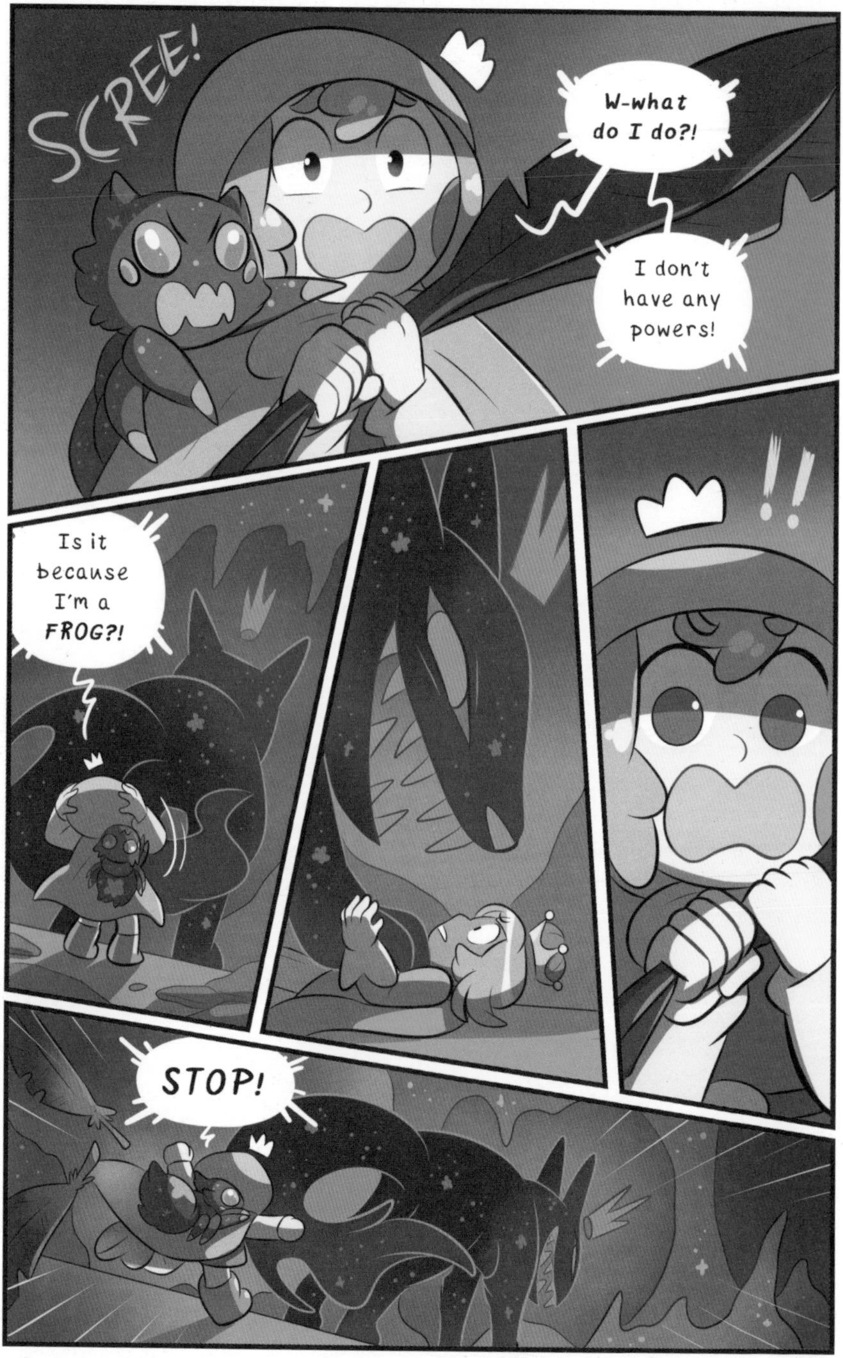
SCREE!
W-what do I do?!
I don't have any powers!
Is it because I'm a FROG?!
!!
STOP!

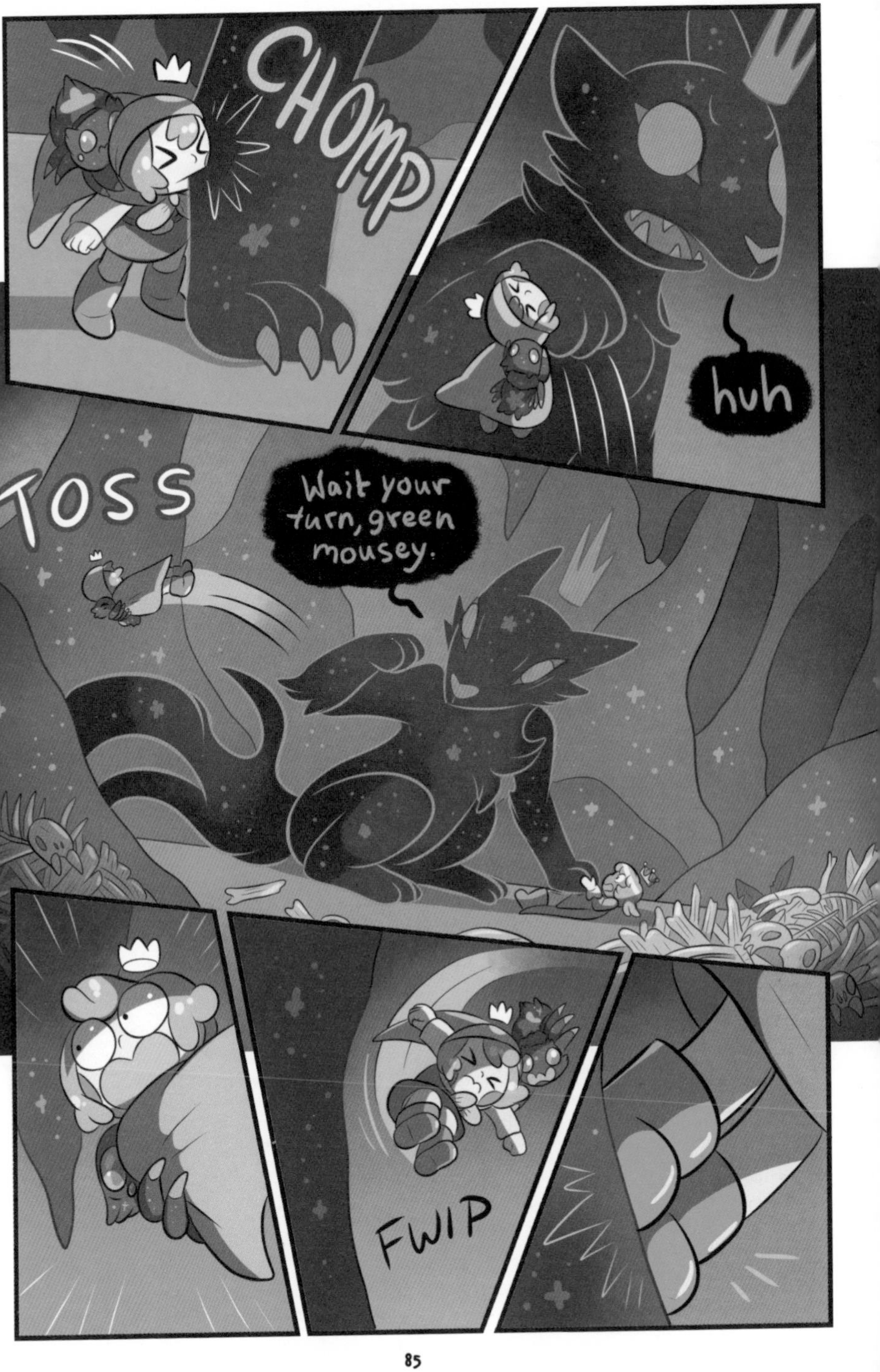
CHOMP
huh
TOSS
Wait your turn, green mousey.
FWIP

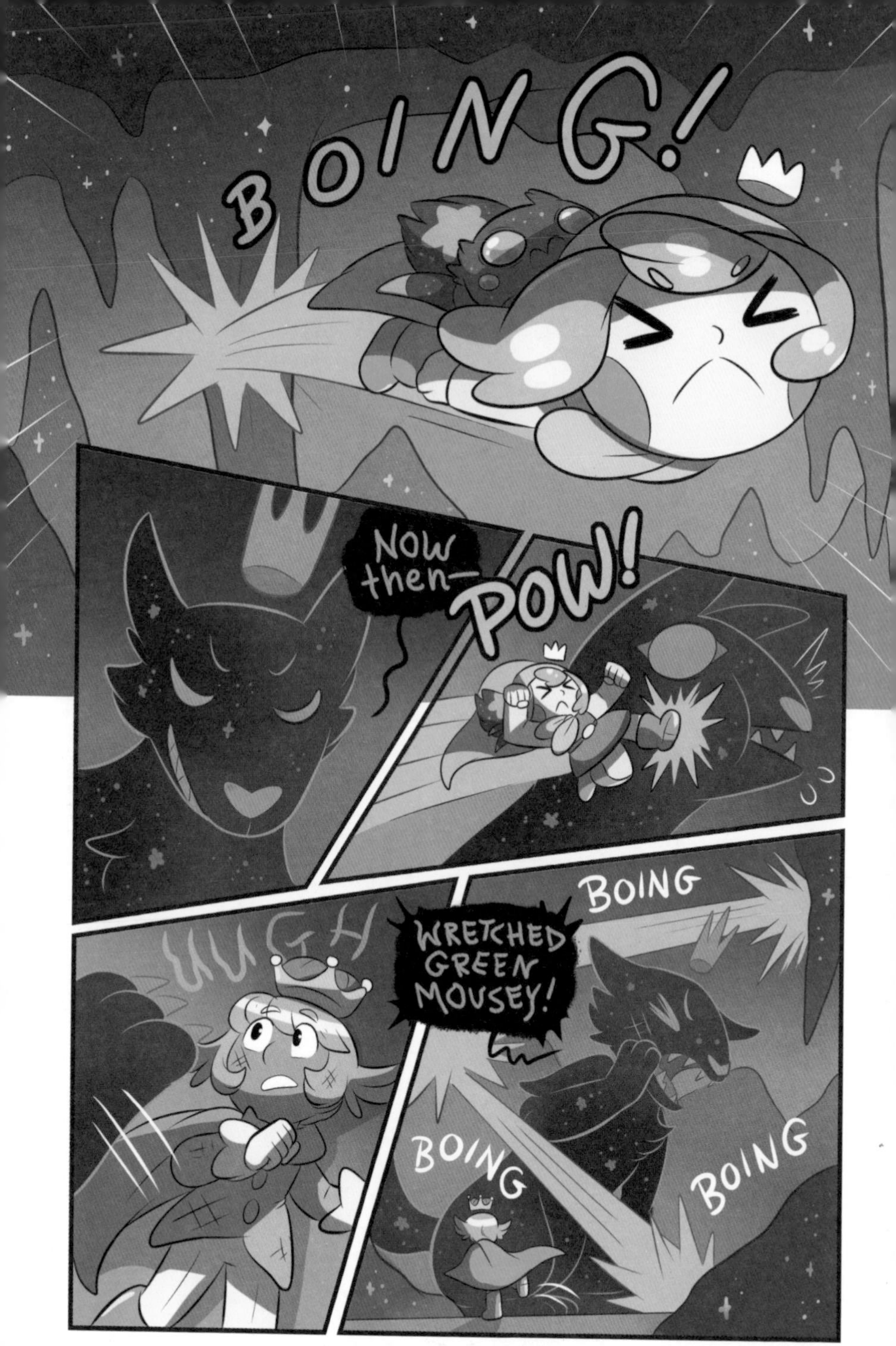
BOING!
Now then—
POW!
BOING
UUGH
WRETCHED GREEN MOUSEY!
BOING
BOING

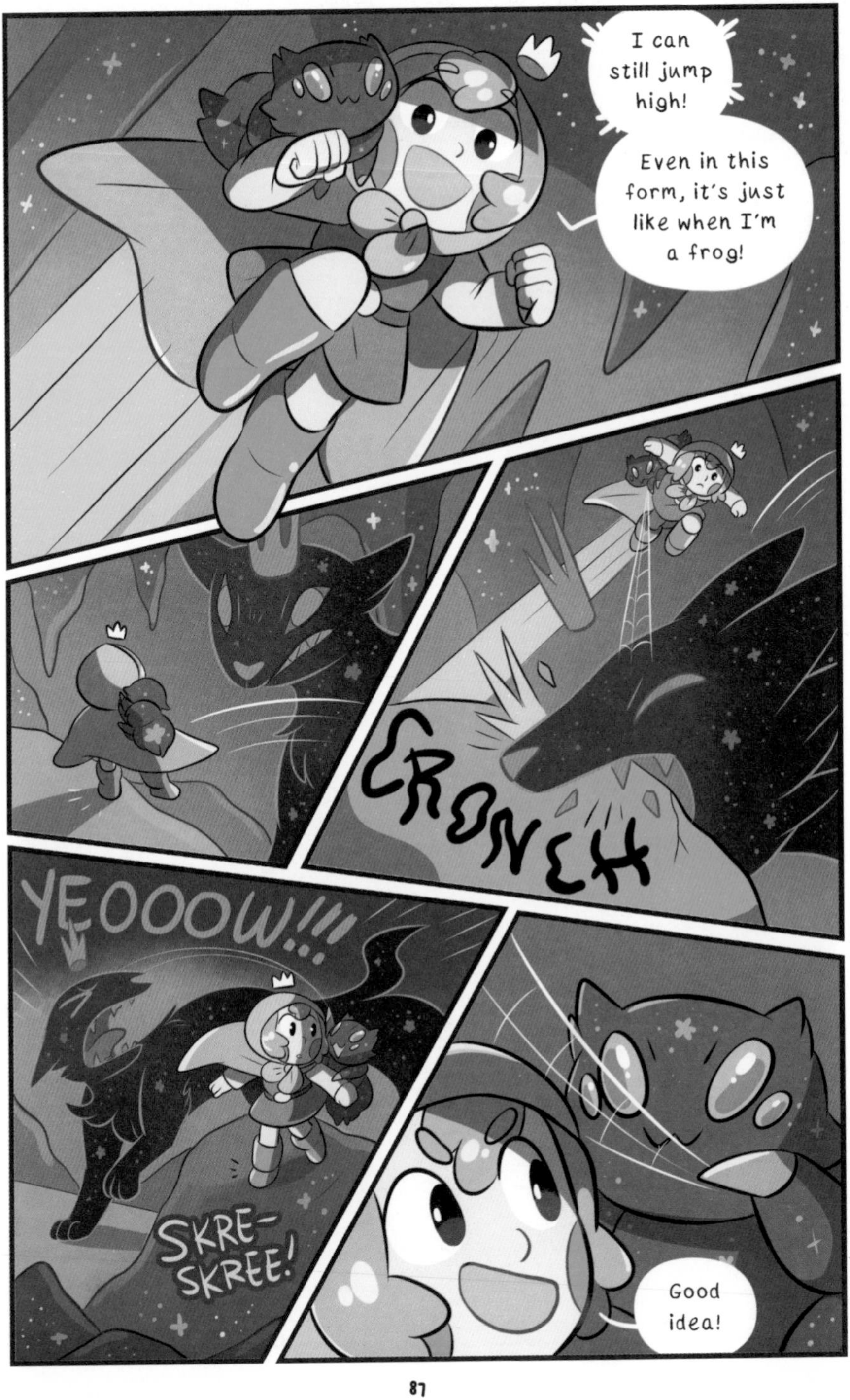
I can still jump high!
Even in this form, it's just like when I'm a frog!
CRONCH
YEOOOW!!!
SKRE-SKREE!
Good idea!

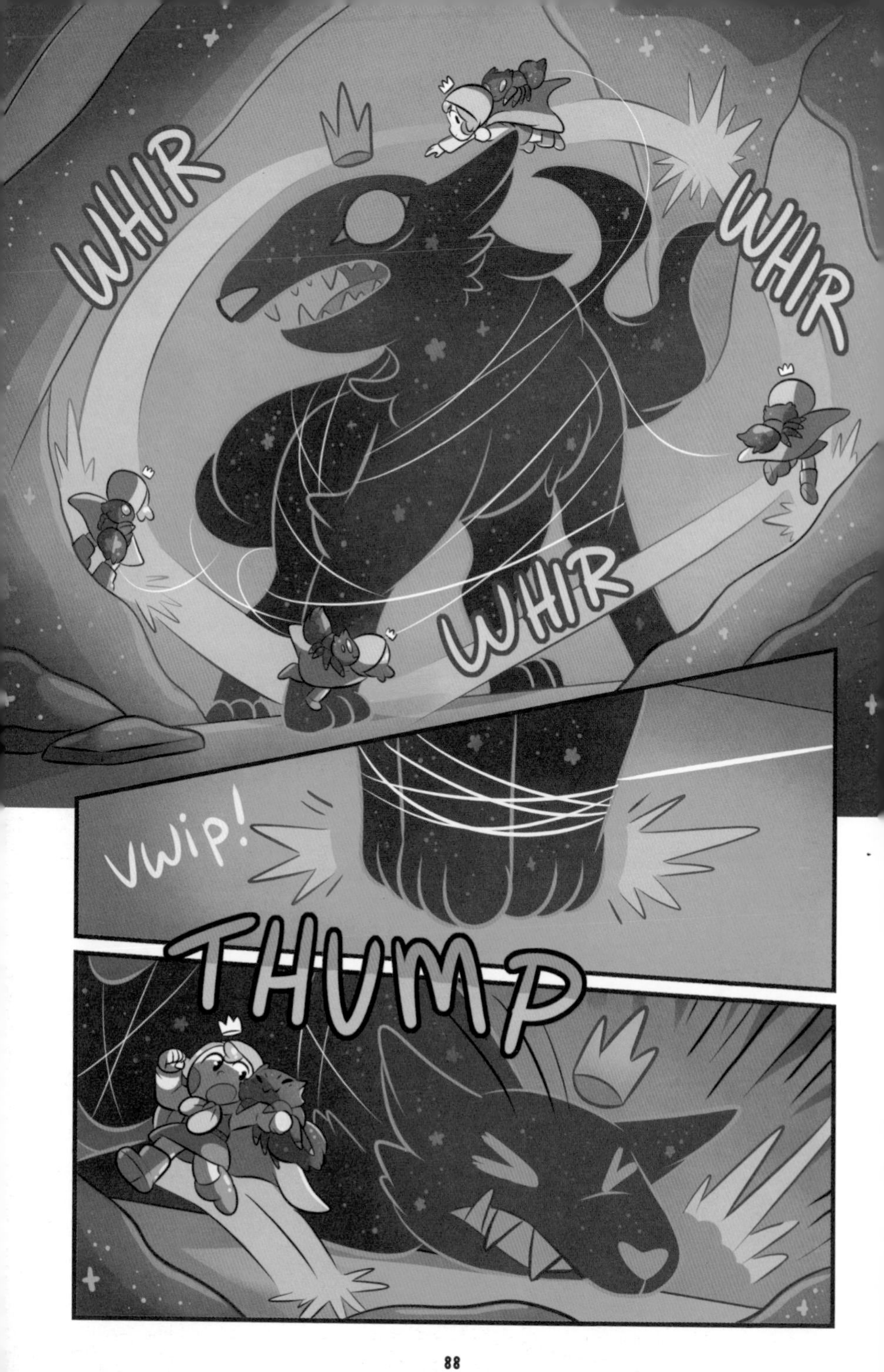
WHIR
WHIR
WHIR
VWIP!
THUMP

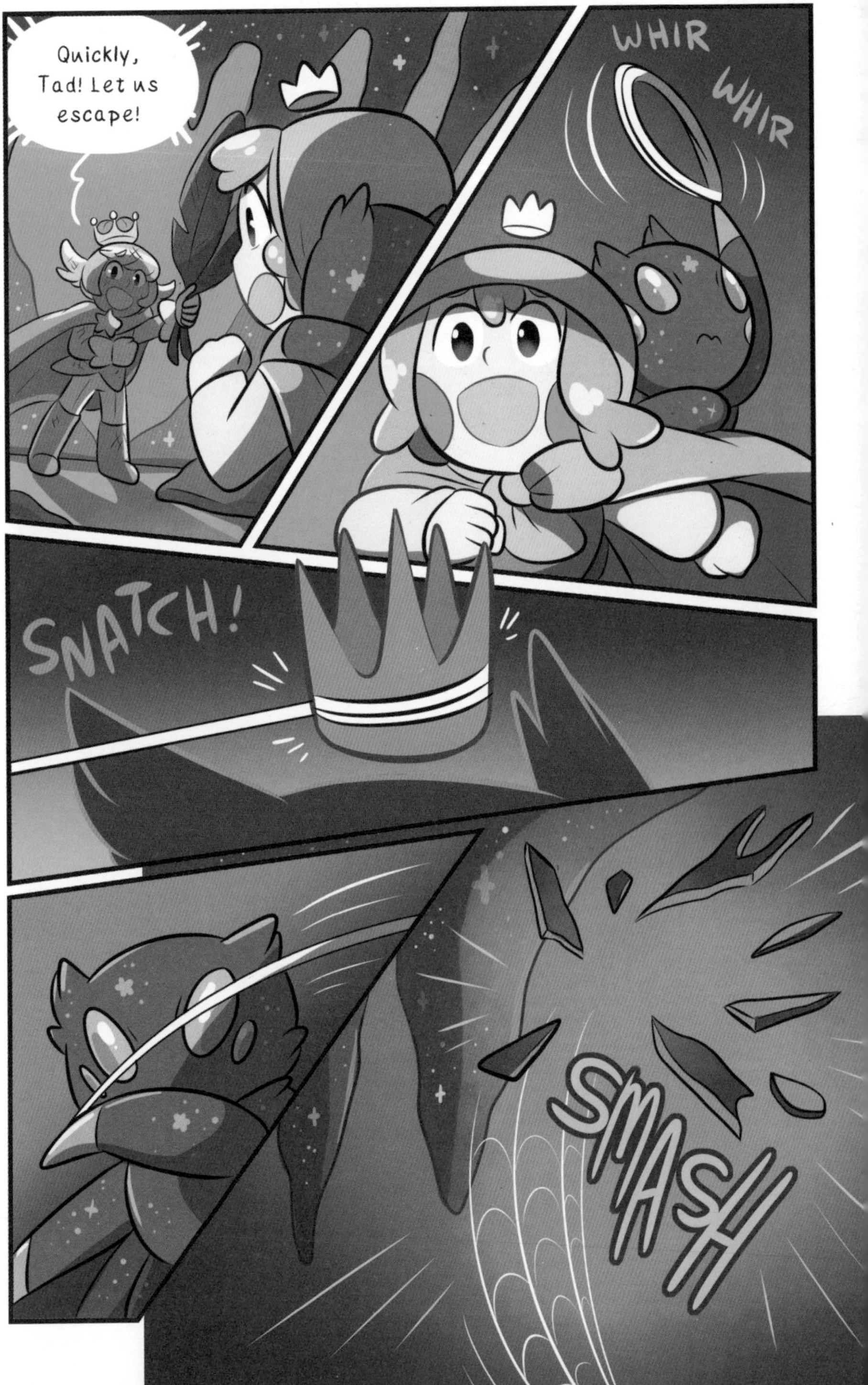
Quickly, Tad! Let us escape!
WHIR
WHIR
WHIR
SNATCH!
SMASH

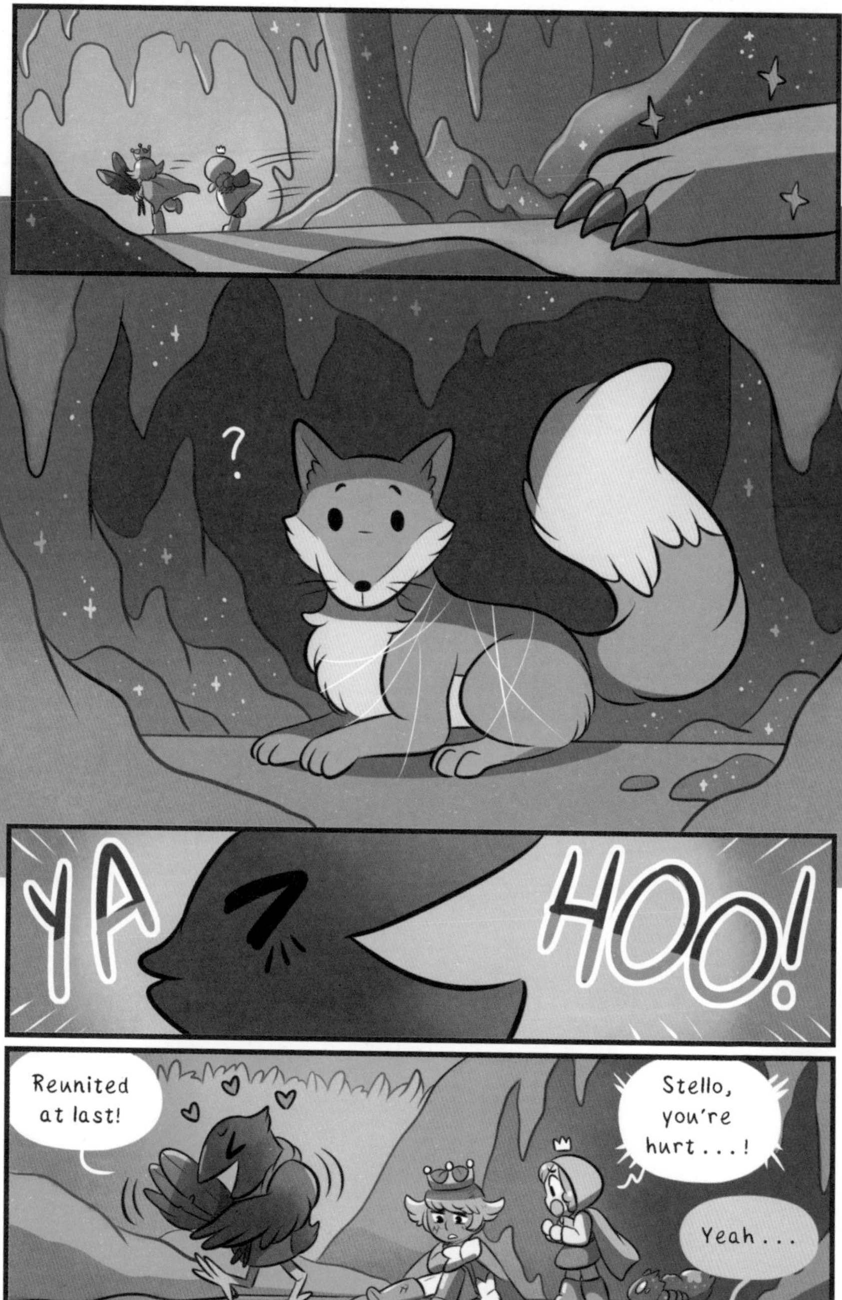
?
YA HOO!
Reunited at last!
Stello, you're hurt...!
Yeah...

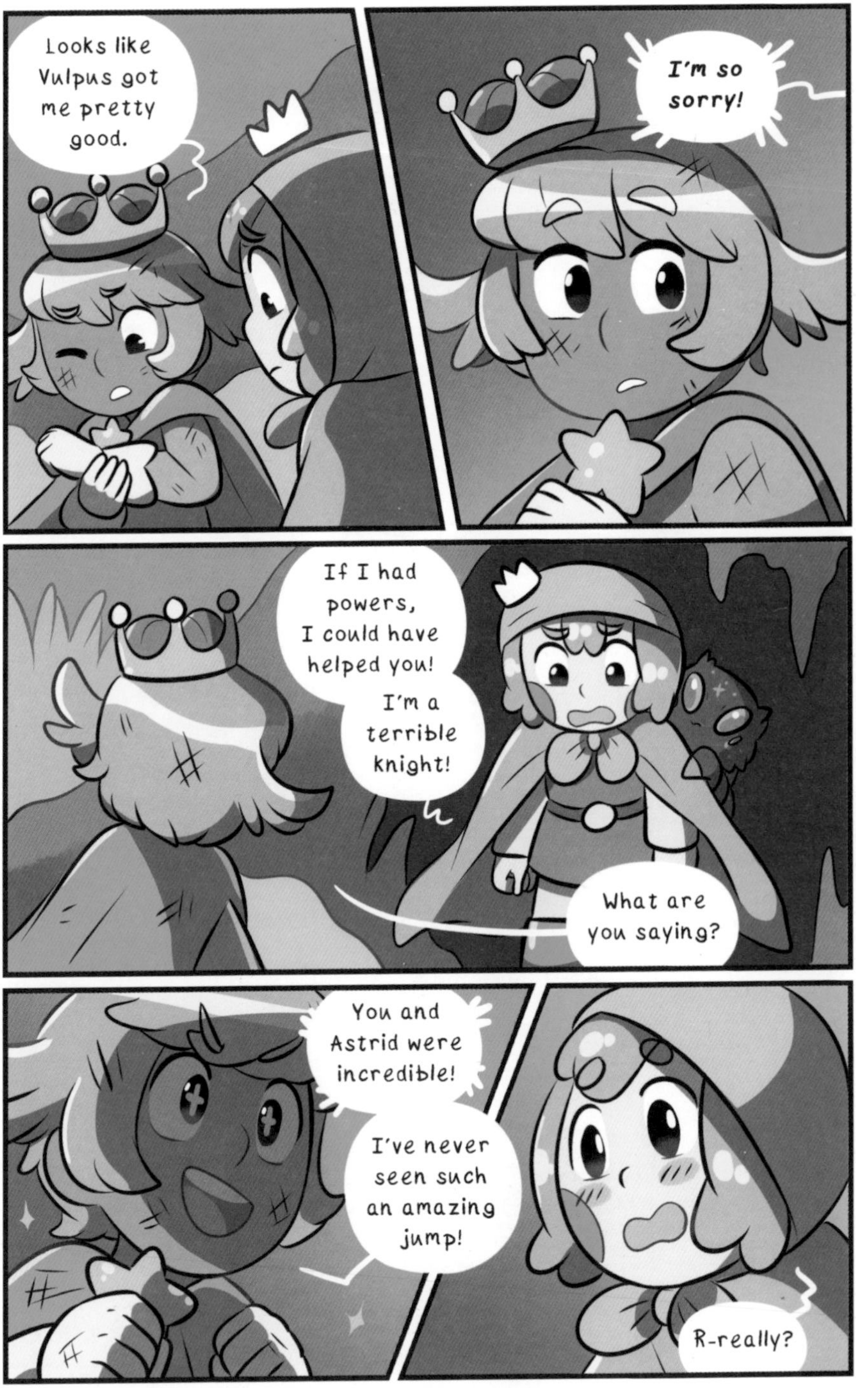
Looks like Vulpus got me pretty good.
I'm so sorry!
If I had powers, I could have helped you!
I'm a terrible knight!
What are you saying?
You and Astrid were incredible!
I've never seen such an amazing jump!
R-really?

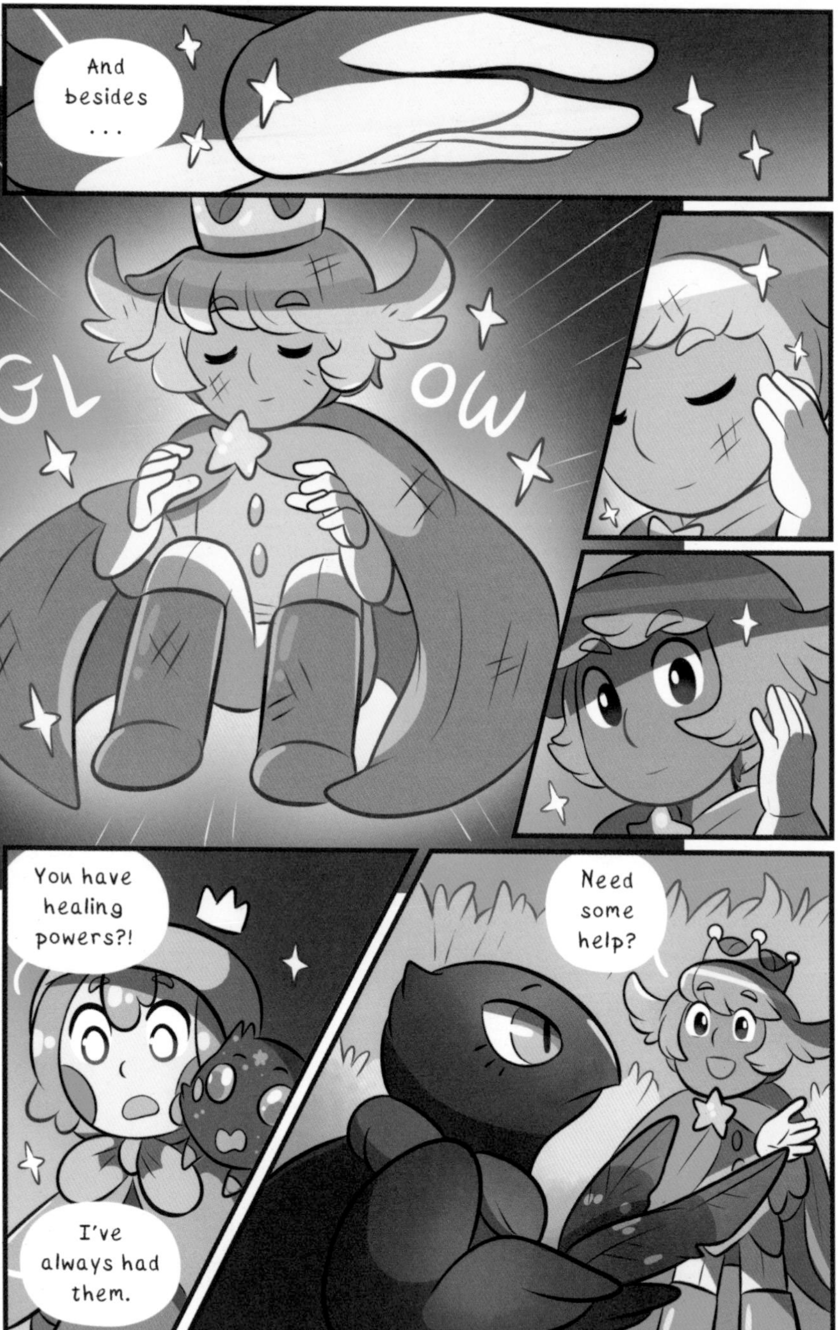
And besides . . .
GL OW
You have healing powers?!
I've always had them.
Need some help?

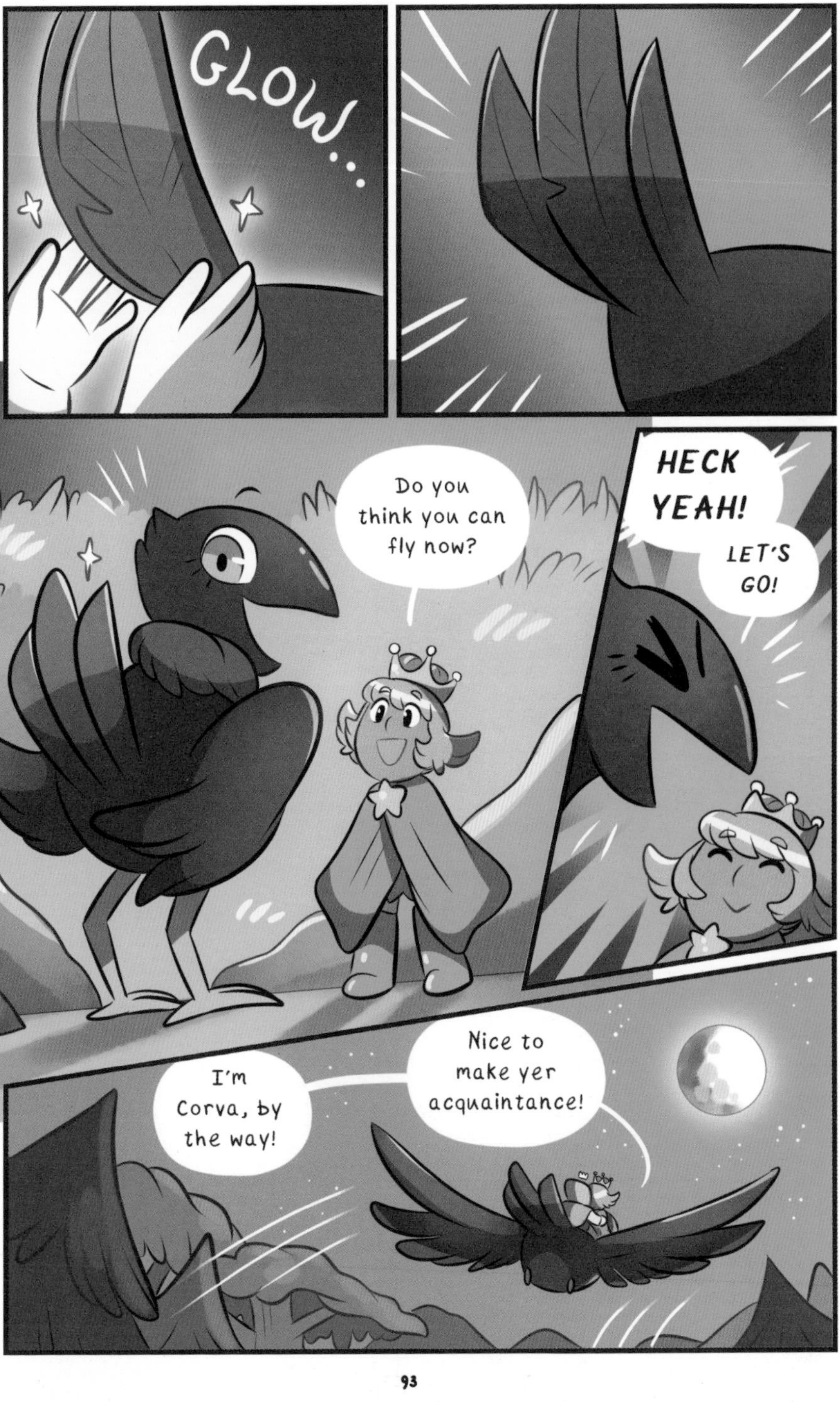
GLOW...
Do you think you can fly now?
HECK YEAH!
LET'S GO!
I'm Corva, by the way!
Nice to make yer acquaintance!

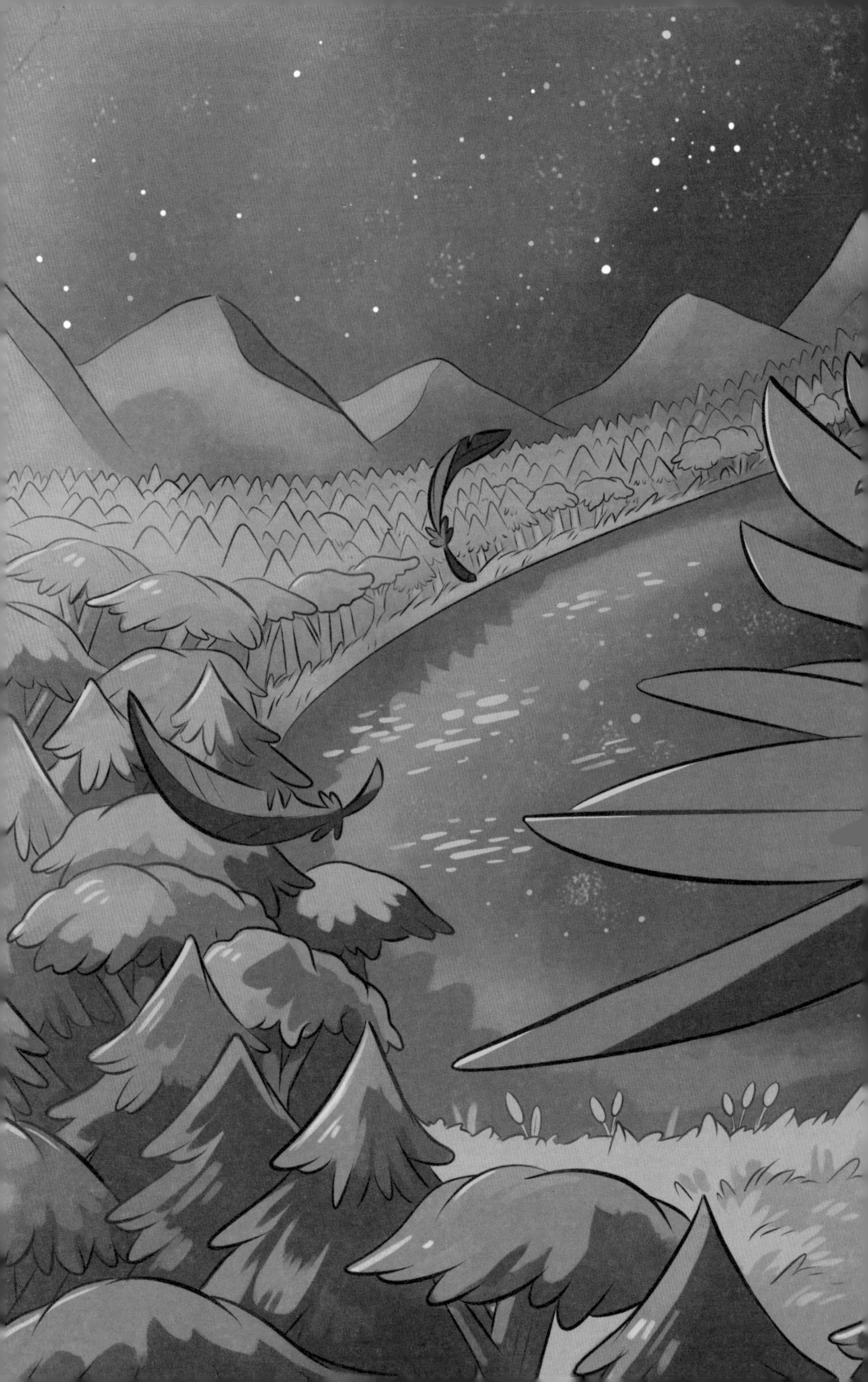

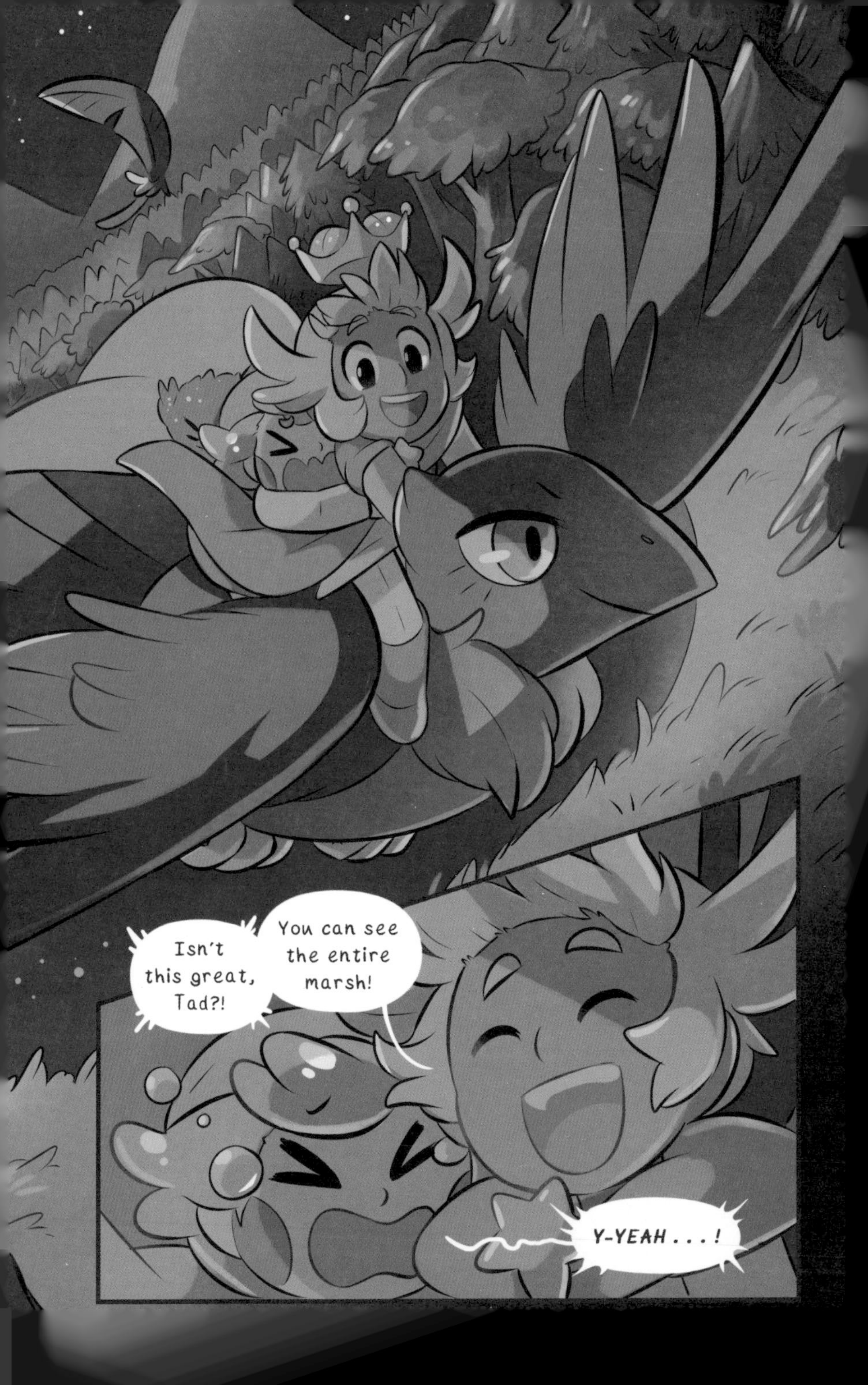
Isn't this great, Tad?!
You can see the entire marsh!
Y-YEAH . . . !

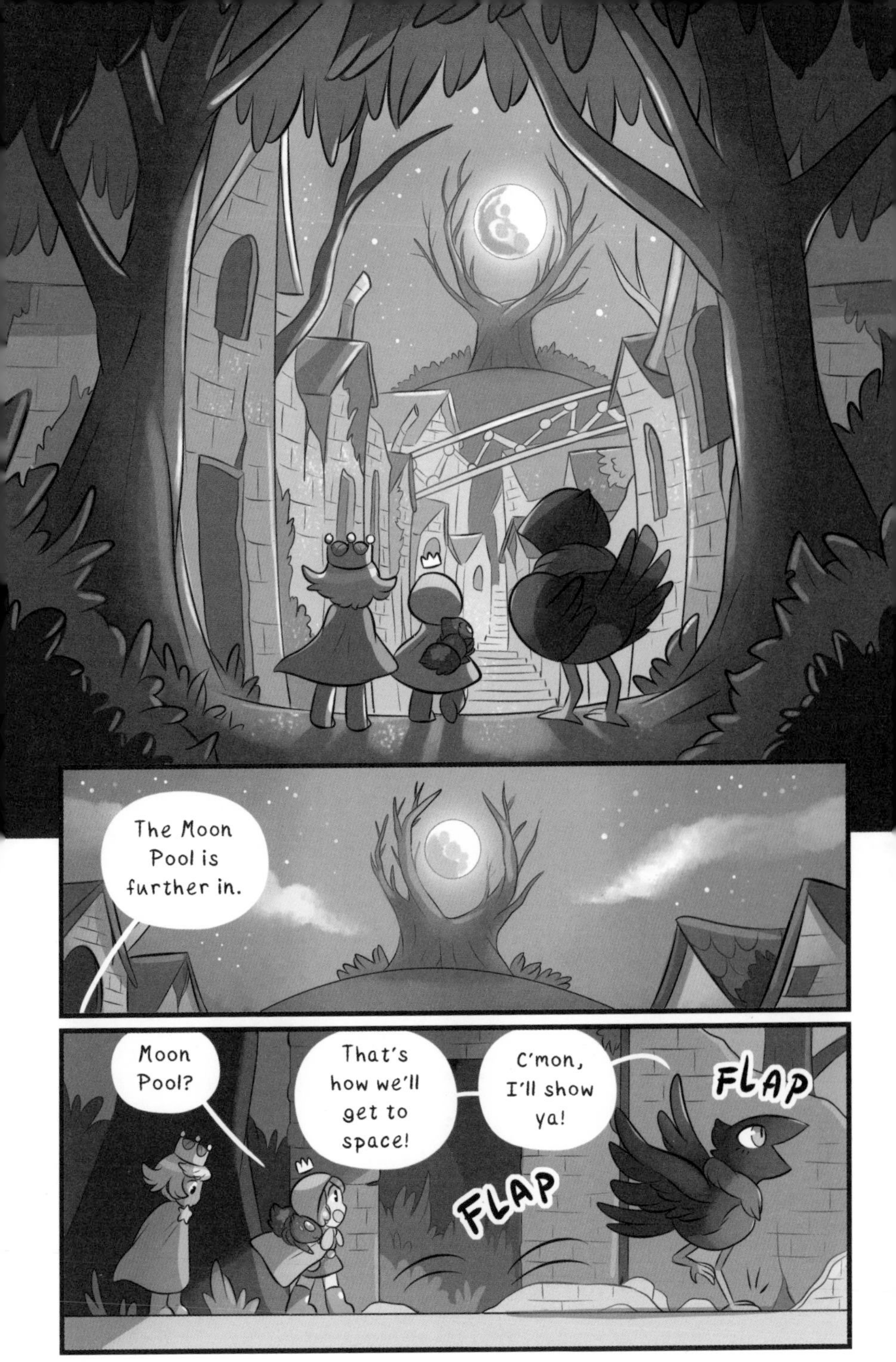
The Moon Pool is further in.
Moon Pool?
That's how we'll get to space!
C'mon, I'll show ya!
FLAP
FLAP

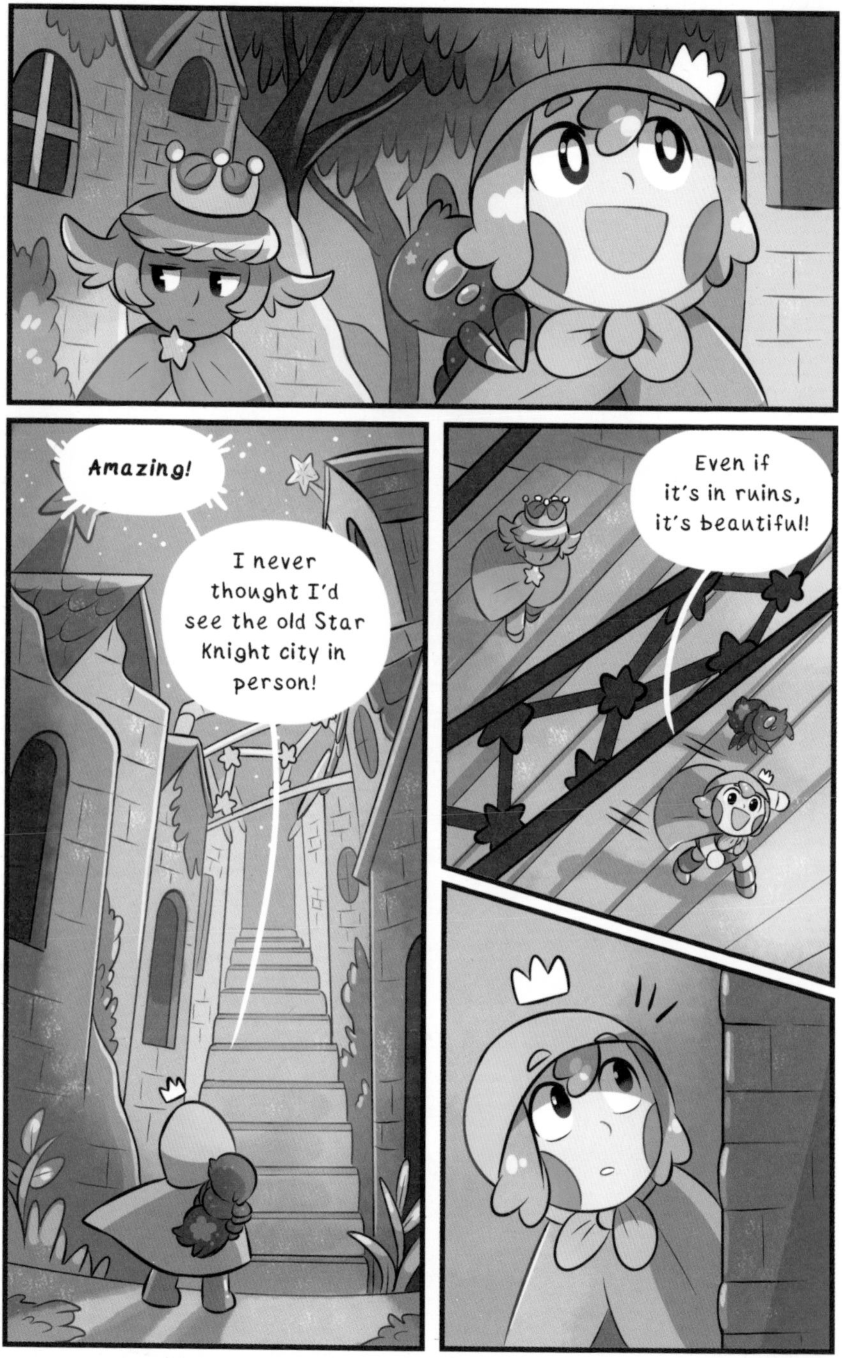
Amazing!
I never thought I'd see the old Star Knight city in person!
Even if it's in ruins, it's beautiful!

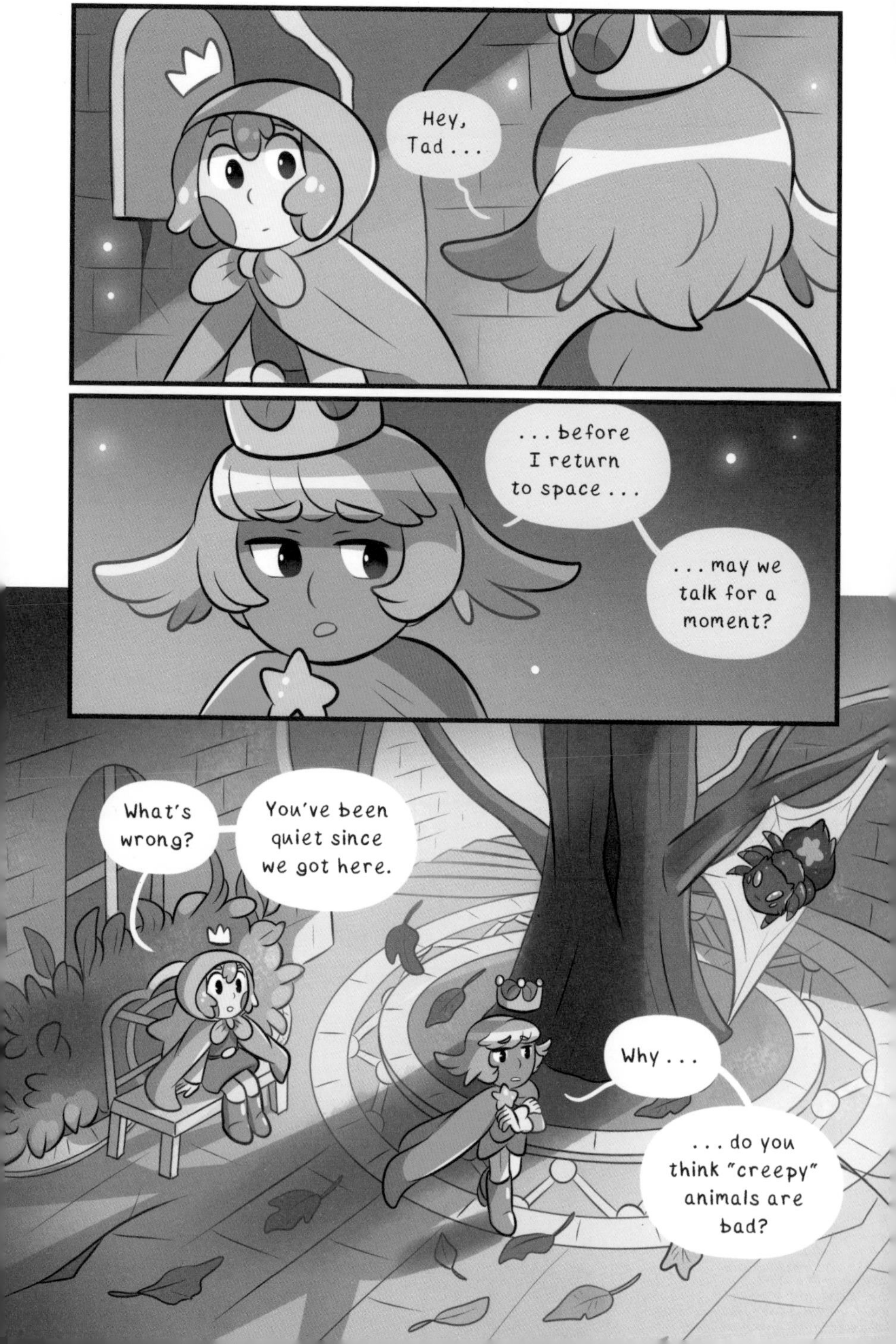
Hey, Tad . . .
. . . before I return to space . . .
. . . may we talk for a moment?
What's wrong?
You've been quiet since we got here.
Why . . .
. . . do you think "creepy" animals are bad?

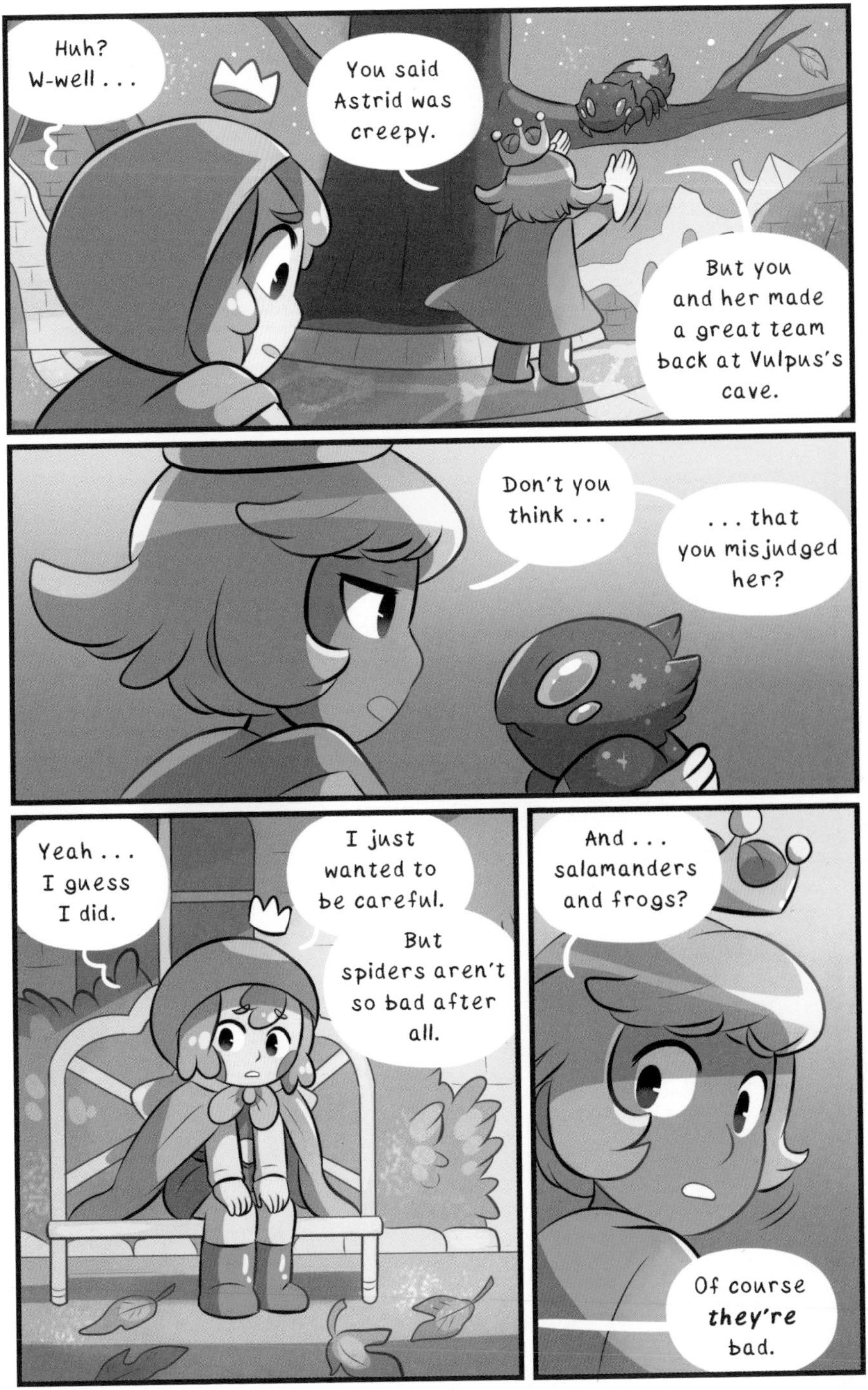
Huh? W-well . . .
You said Astrid was creepy.
But you and her made a great team back at Vulpus's cave.
Don't you think . . .
. . . that you misjudged her?
Yeah . . . I guess I did.
I just wanted to be careful.
But spiders aren't so bad after all.
And . . . salamanders and frogs?
Of course *they're* bad.

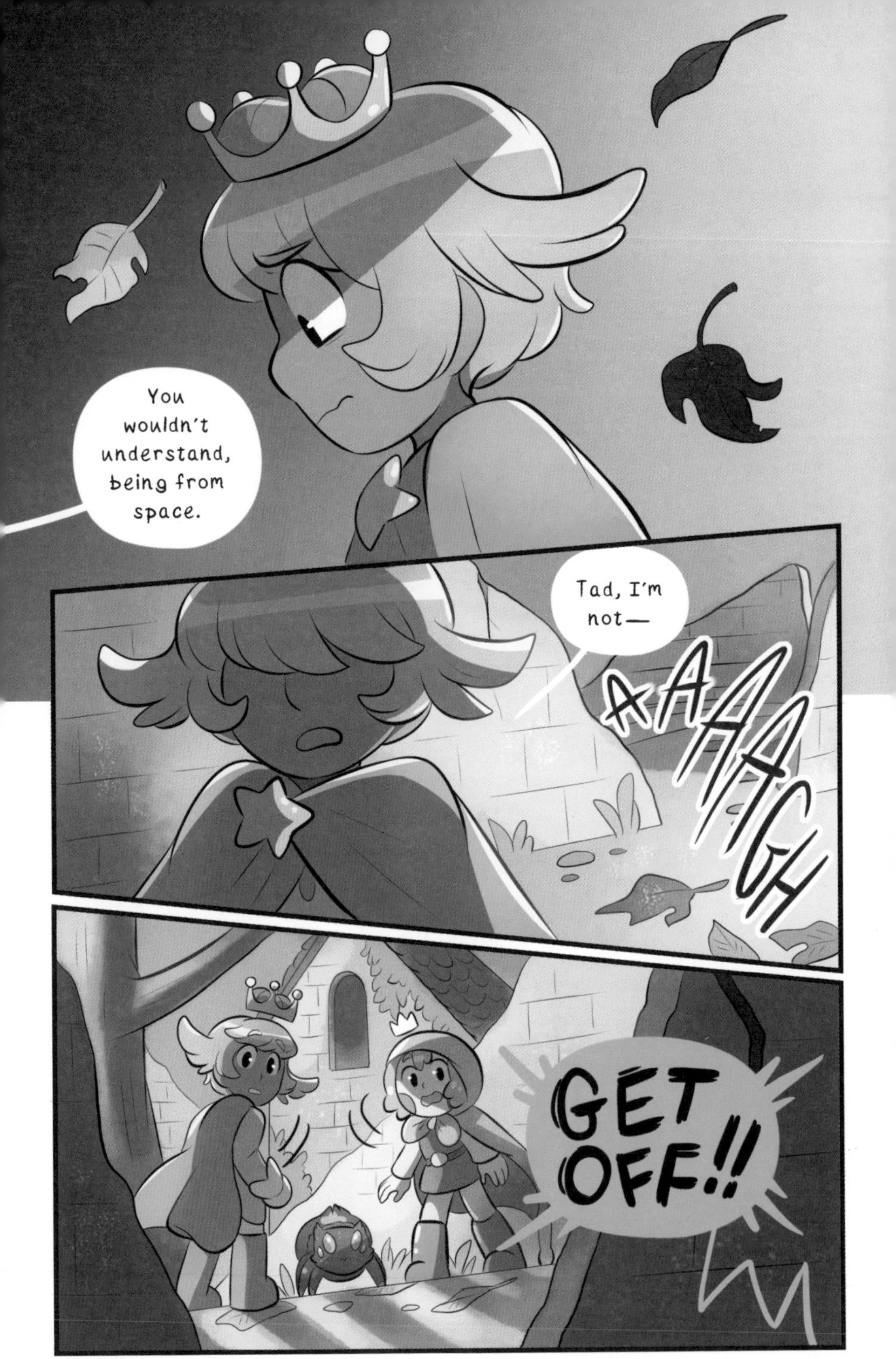
You wouldn't understand, being from space.
Tad, I'm not—
AAAAAGH
GET OFF!!

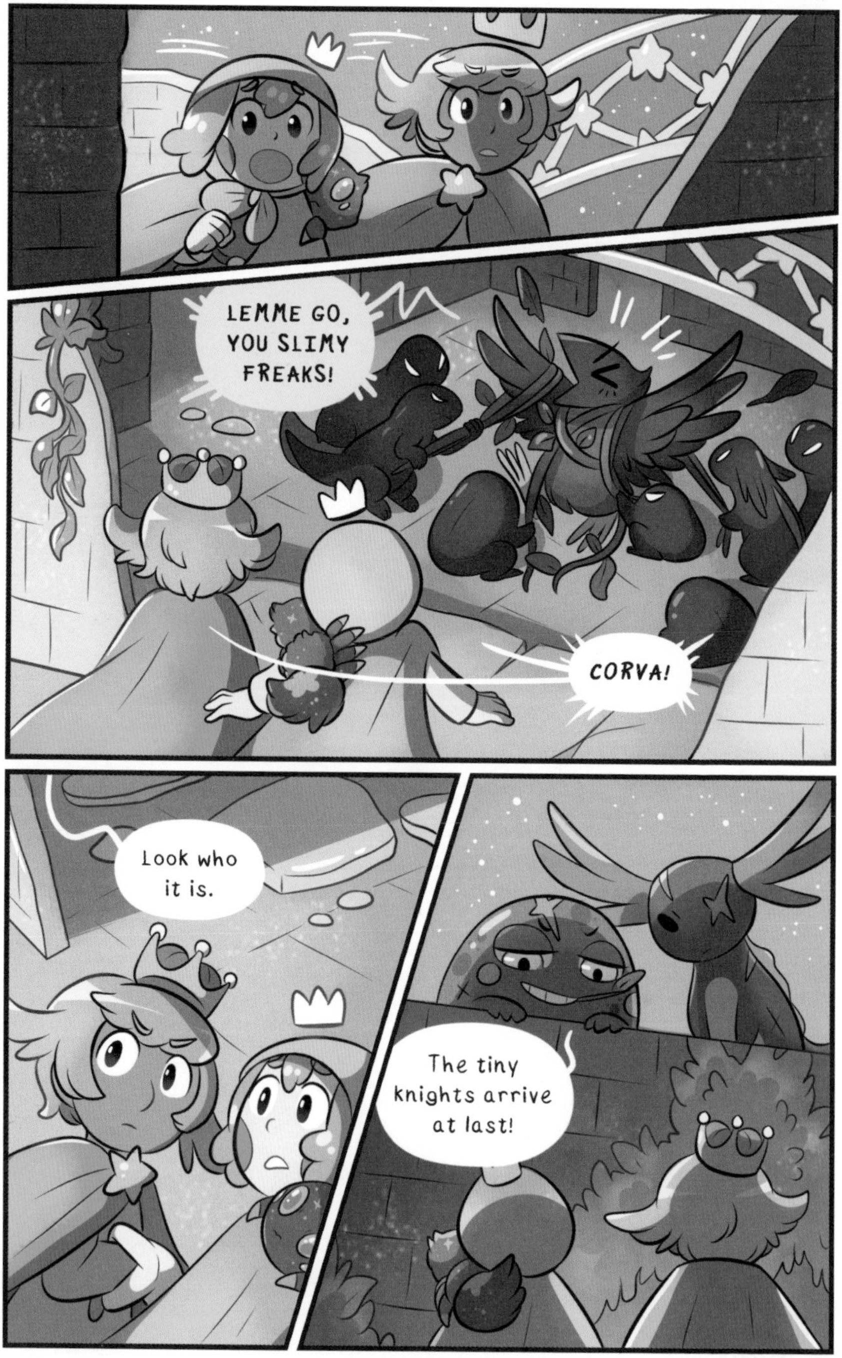

LEMME GO, YOU SLIMY FREAKS!
CORVA!
Look who it is.
The tiny knights arrive at last!

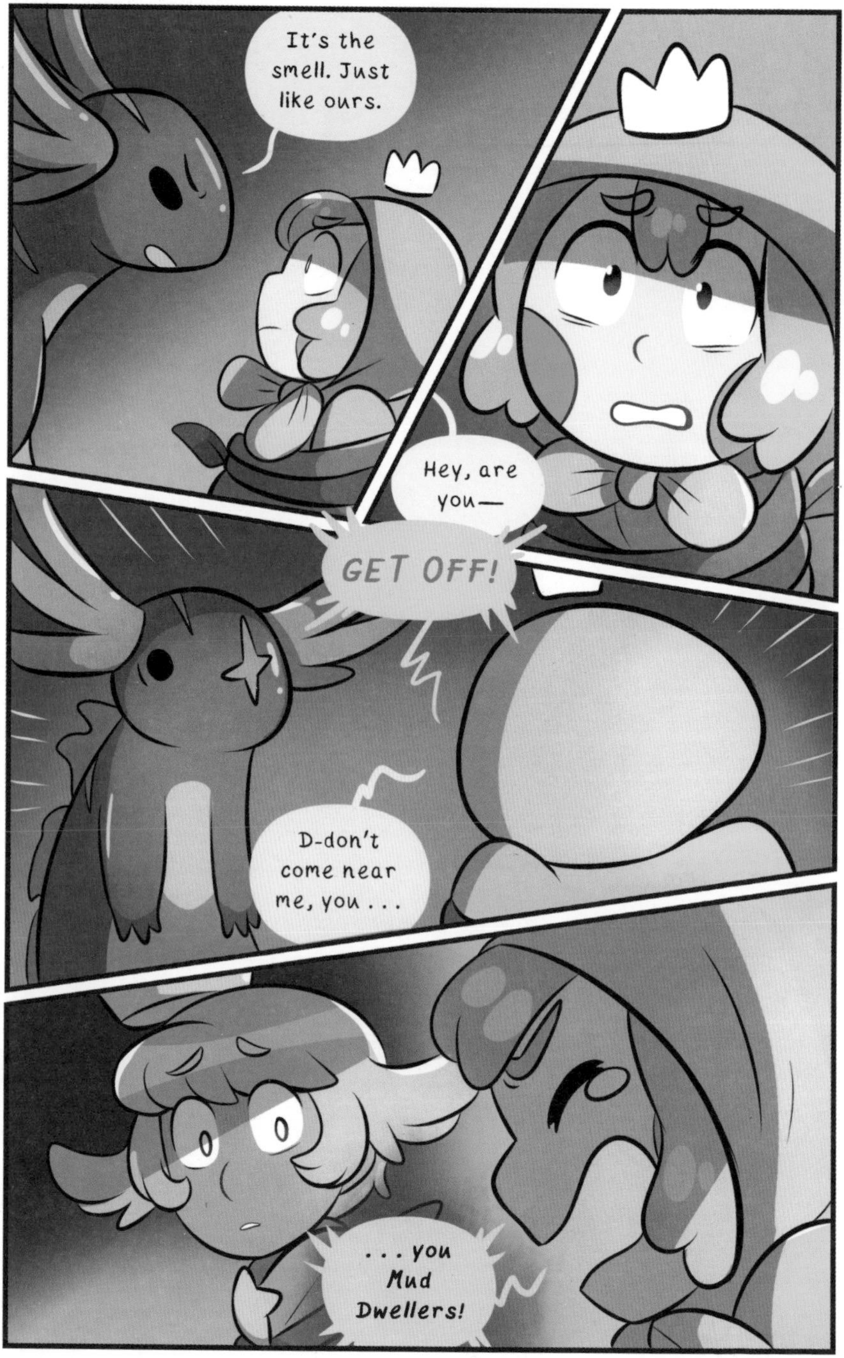
It's the smell. Just like ours.
Hey, are you—
GET OFF!
D-don't come near me, you . . .
. . . you Mud Dwellers!

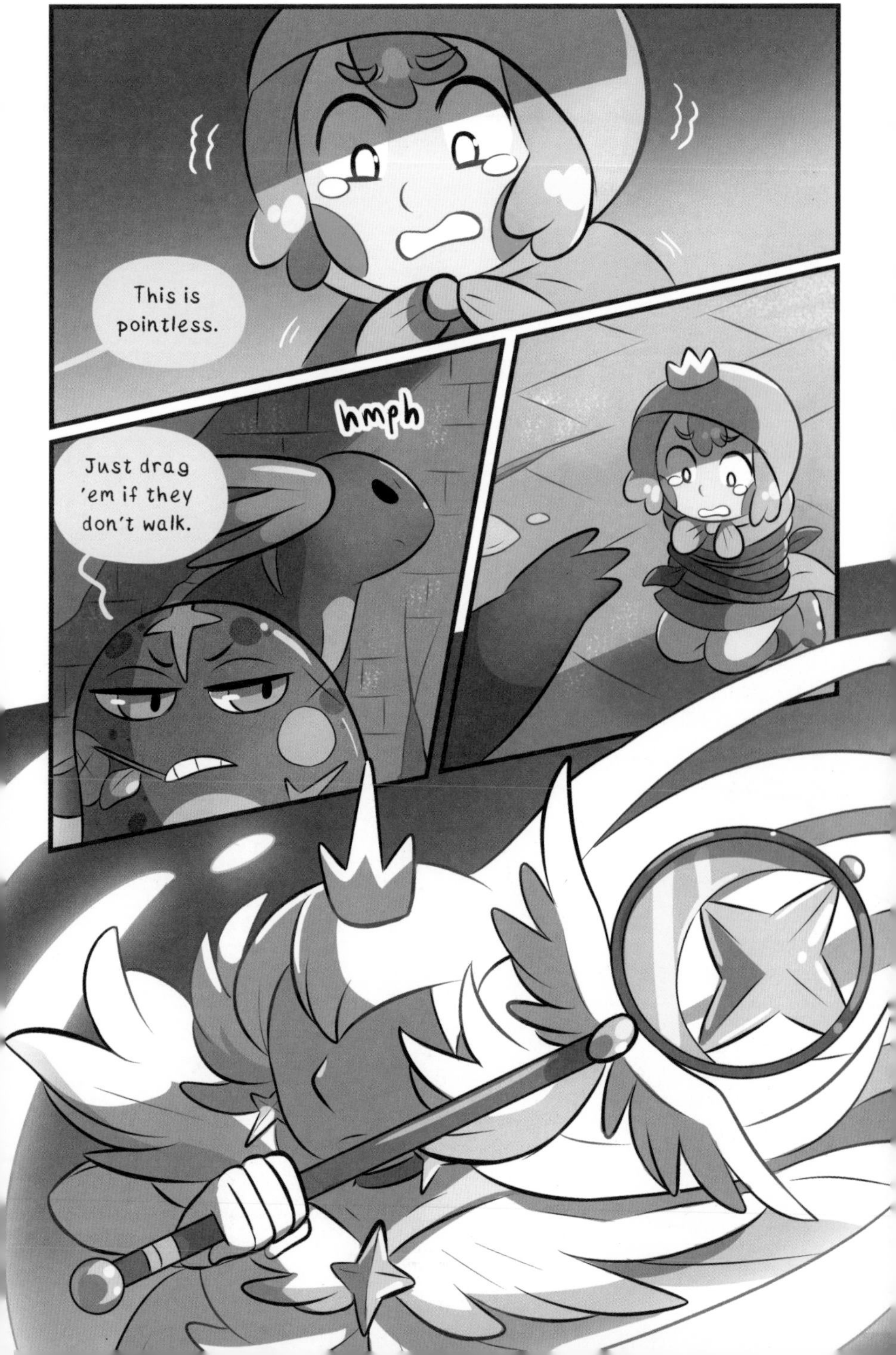
This is pointless.
hmph
Just drag 'em if they don't walk.

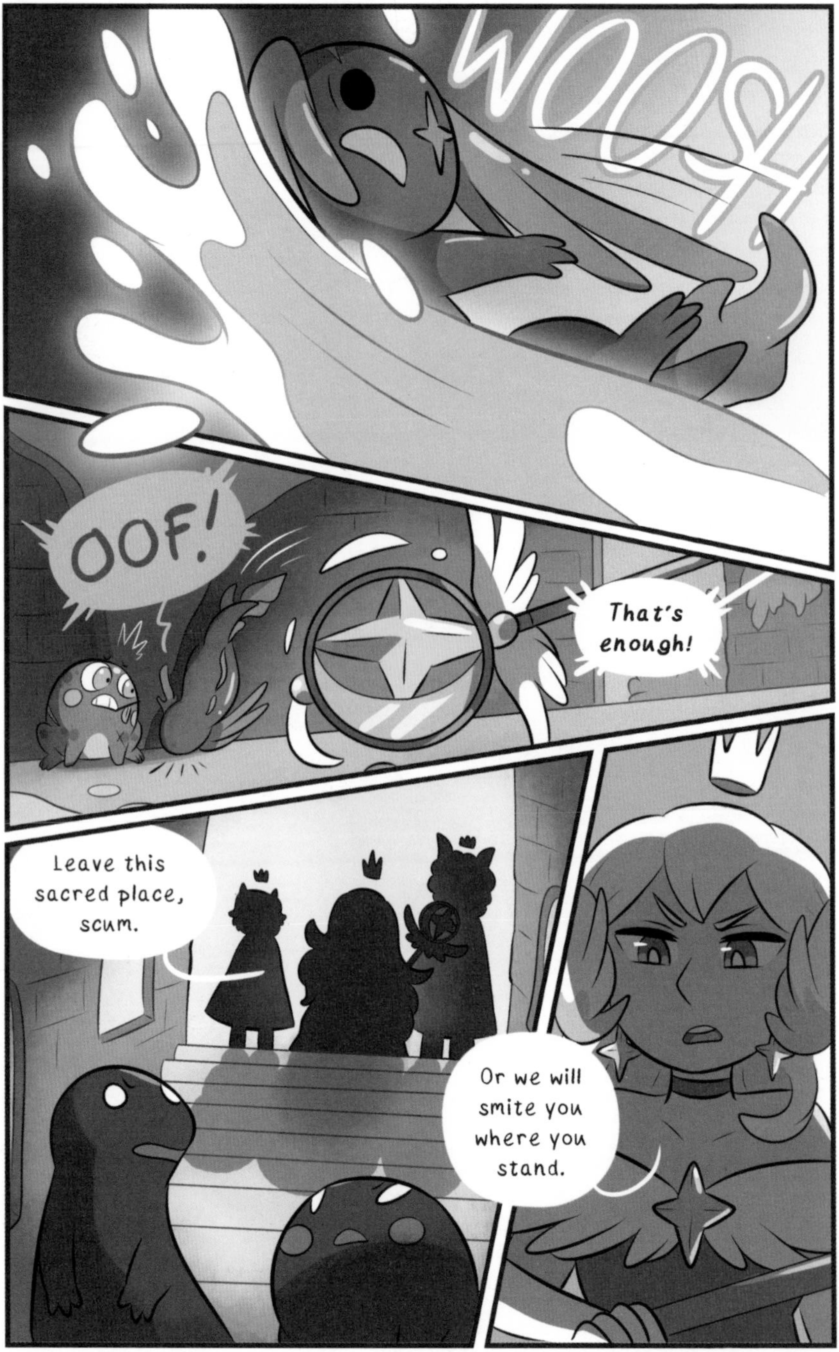
WOOSH
OOF!
That's enough!
Leave this sacred place, scum.
Or we will smite you where you stand.

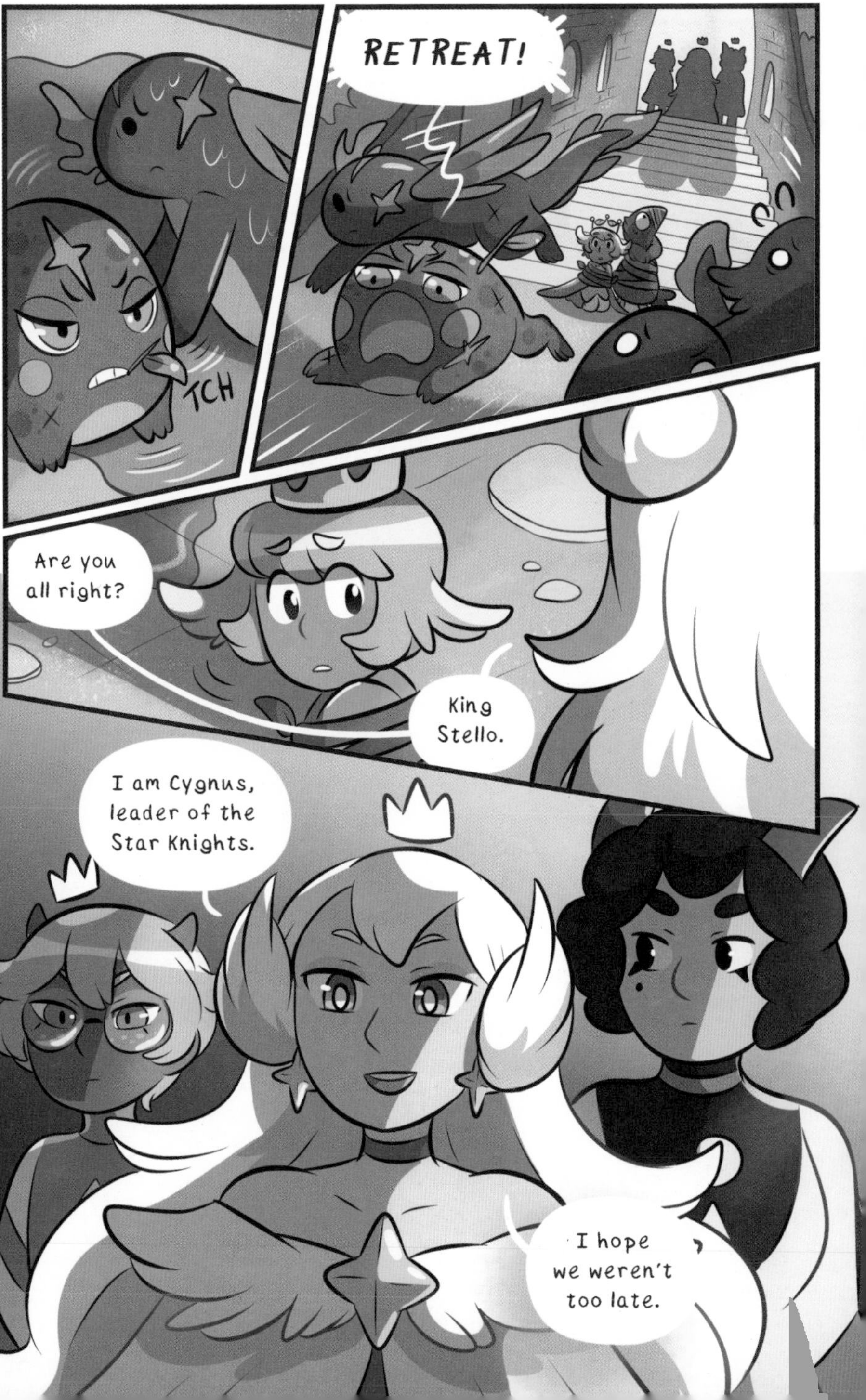
TCH
RETREAT!
Are you all right?
King Stello.
I am Cygnus, leader of the Star Knights.
I hope we weren't too late.

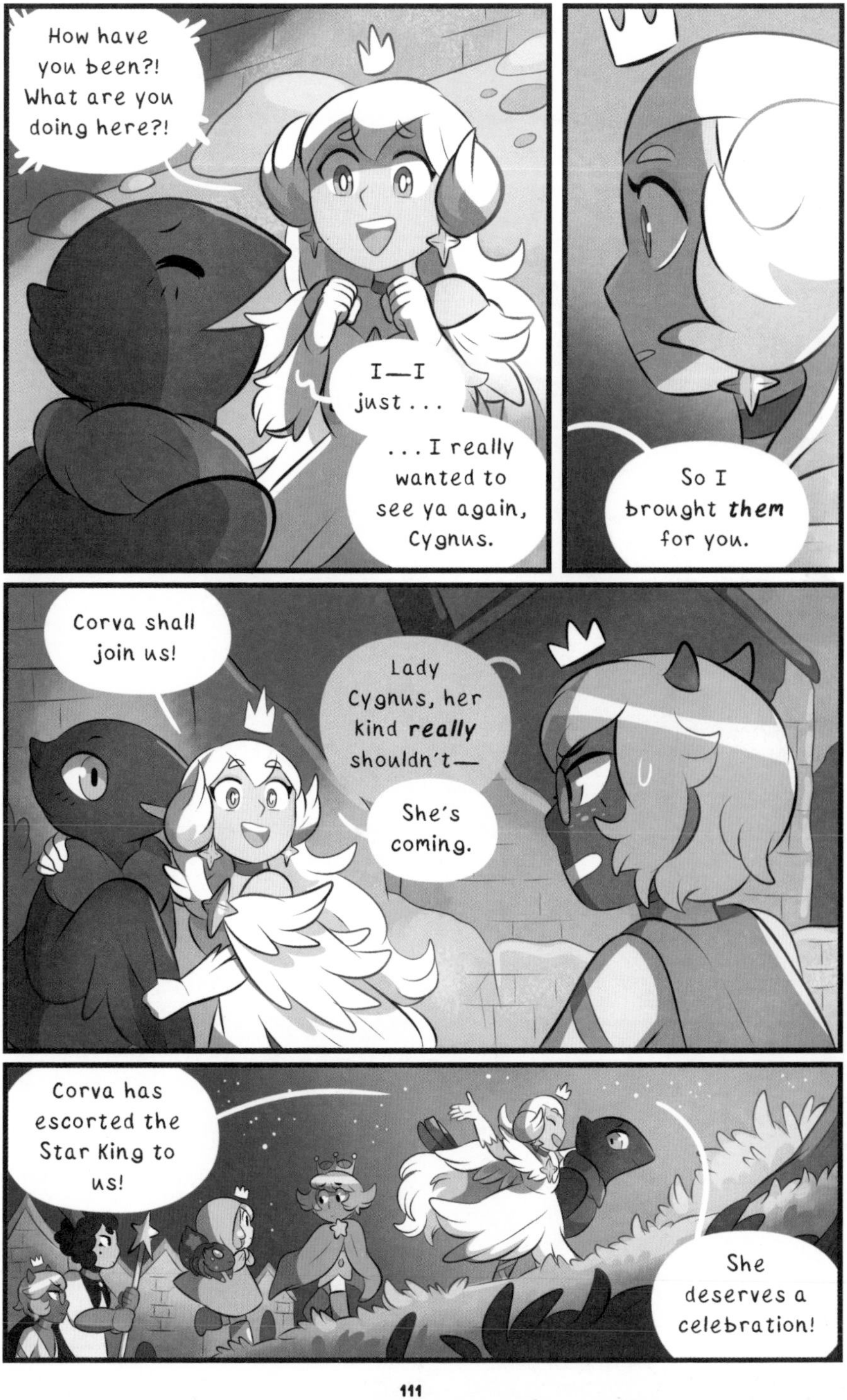
How have you been?! What are you doing here?!
I—I just . . .
. . . I really wanted to see ya again, Cygnus.
So I brought *them* for you.
Corva shall join us!
Lady Cygnus, her kind *really* shouldn't—
She's coming.
Corva has escorted the Star King to us!
She deserves a celebration!

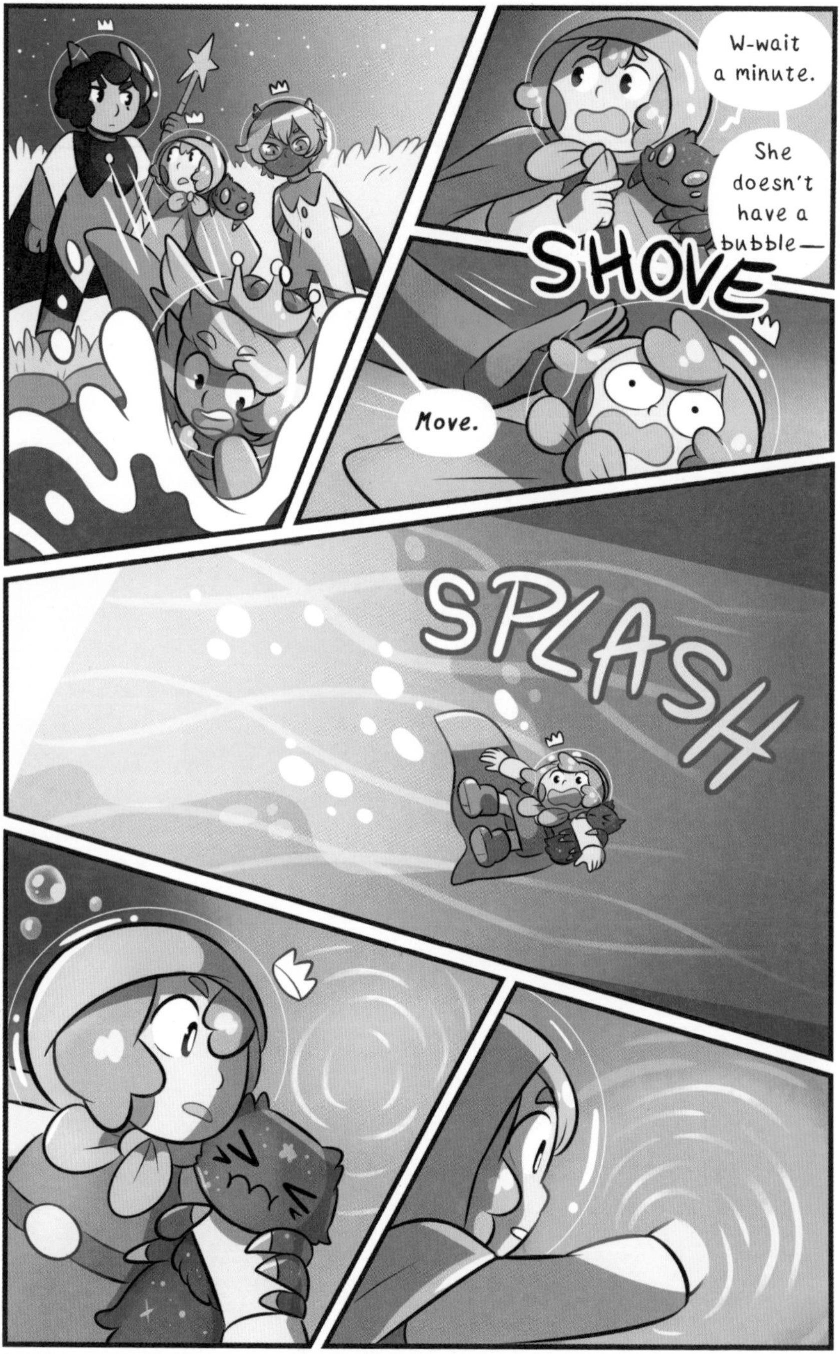
W-wait a minute.
She doesn't have a bubble—
SHOVE
Move.
SPLASH

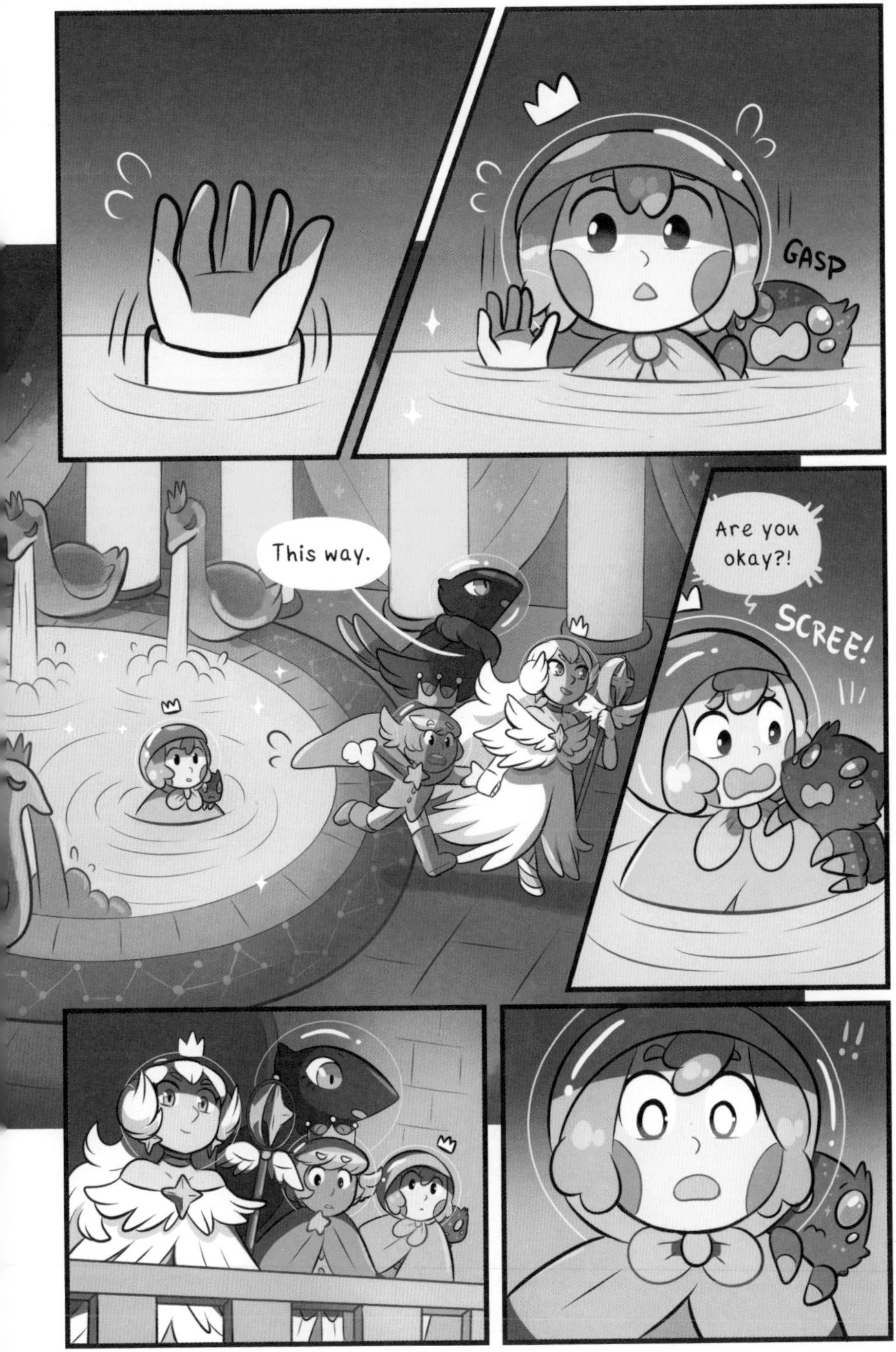
GASP
This way.
Are you okay?!
SCREE!
!!

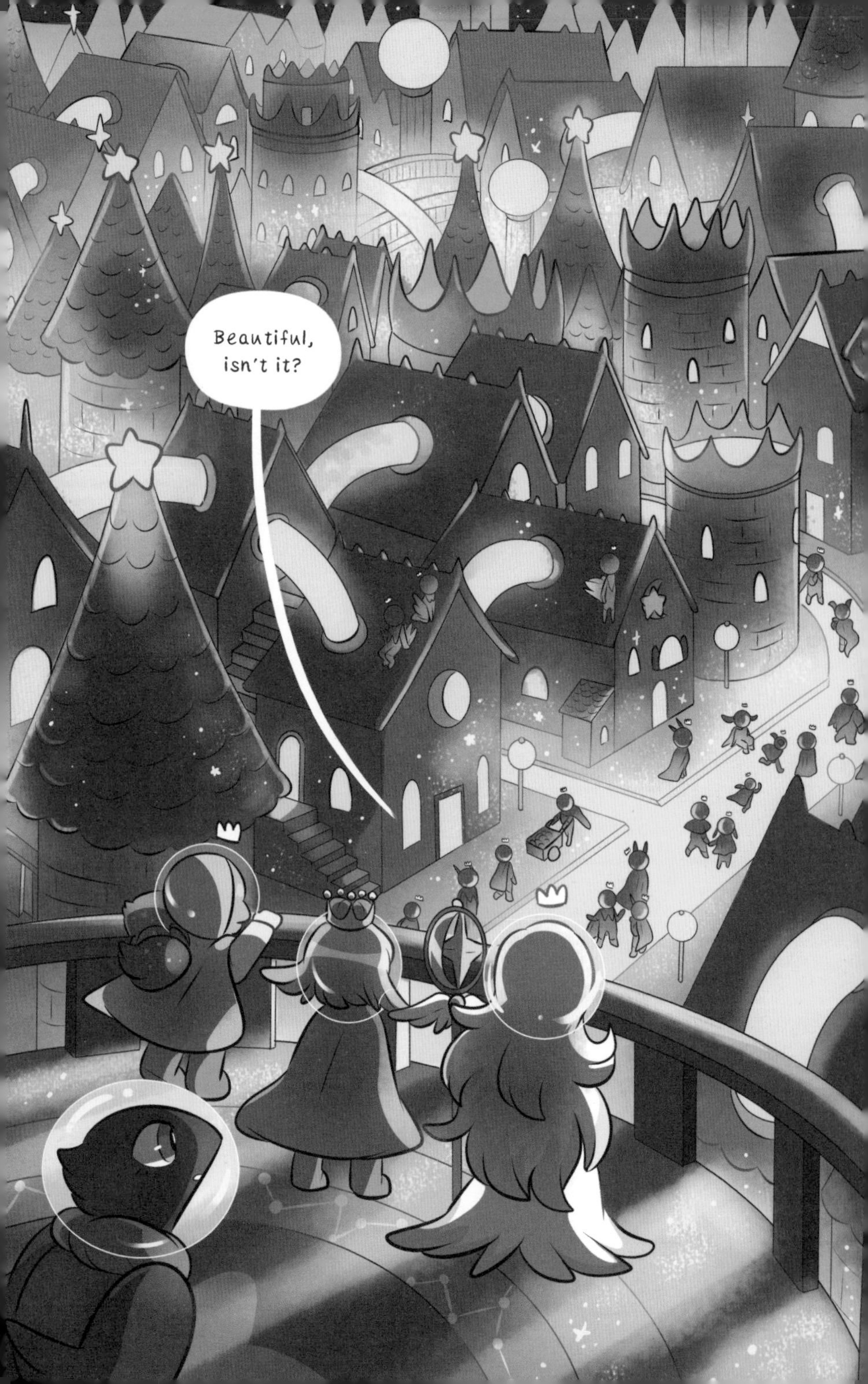
Beautiful, isn't it?

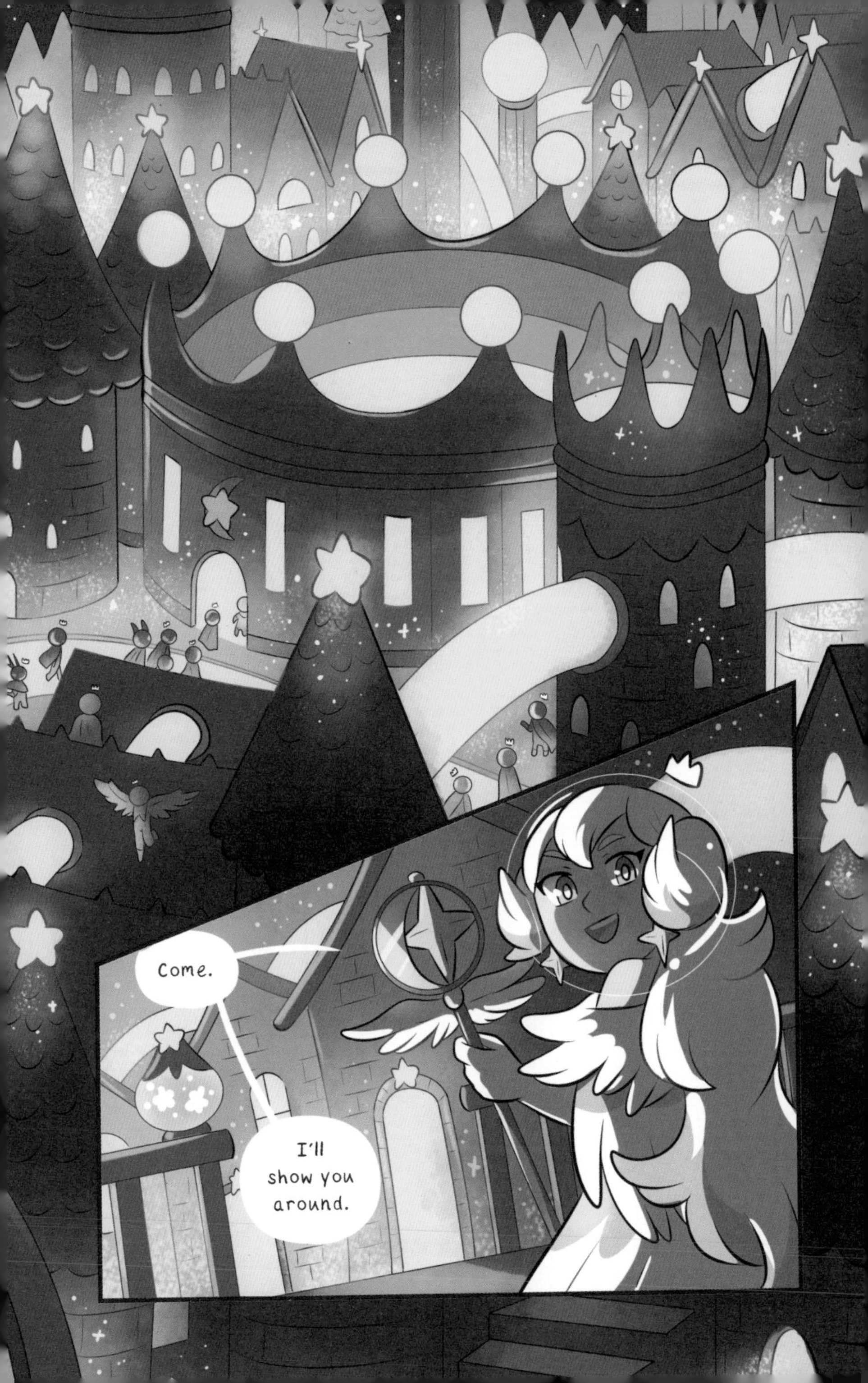
Come.
I'll show you around.

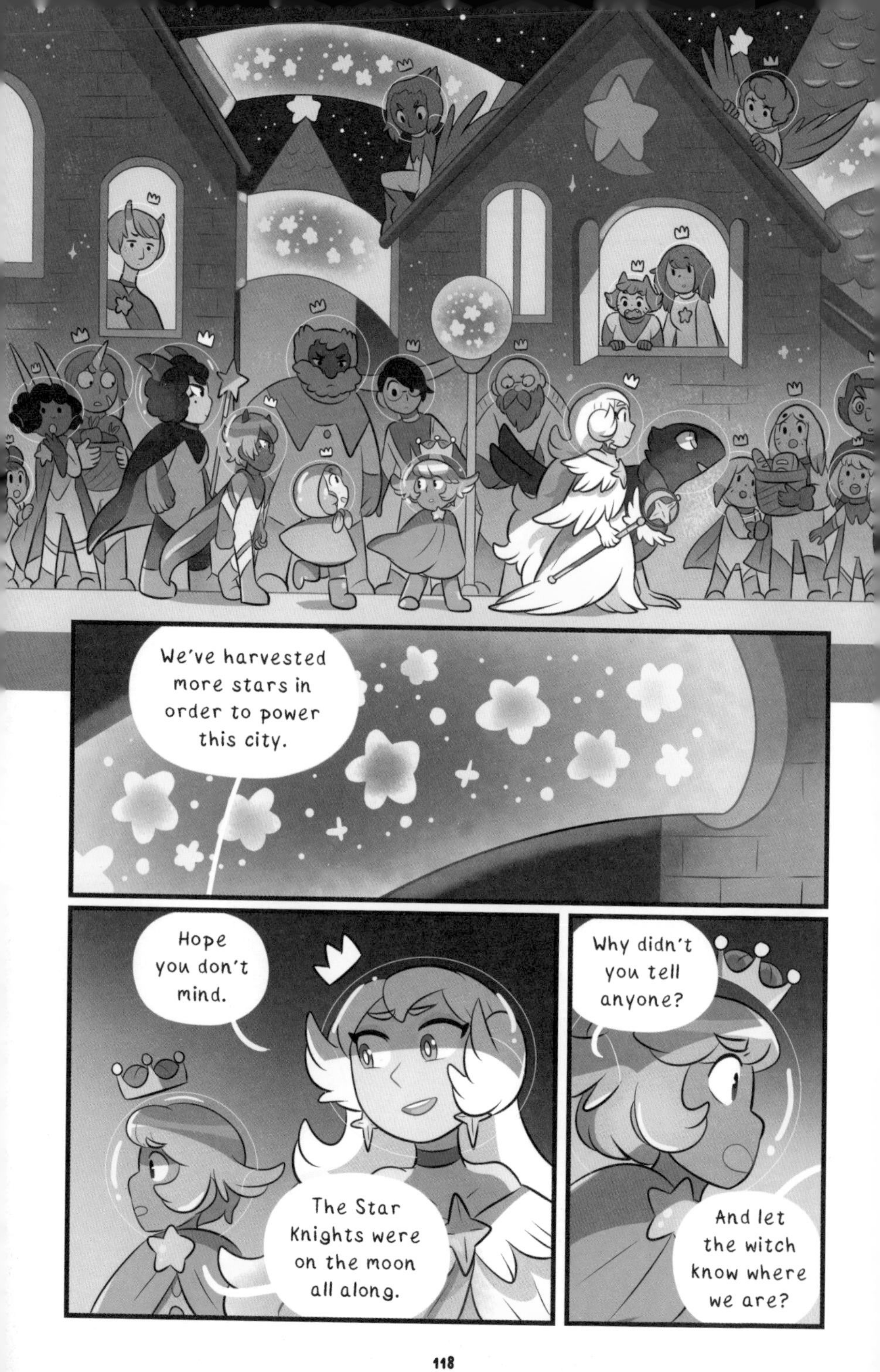
We've harvested more stars in order to power this city.
Hope you don't mind.
The Star Knights were on the moon all along.
Why didn't you tell anyone?
And let the witch know where we are?

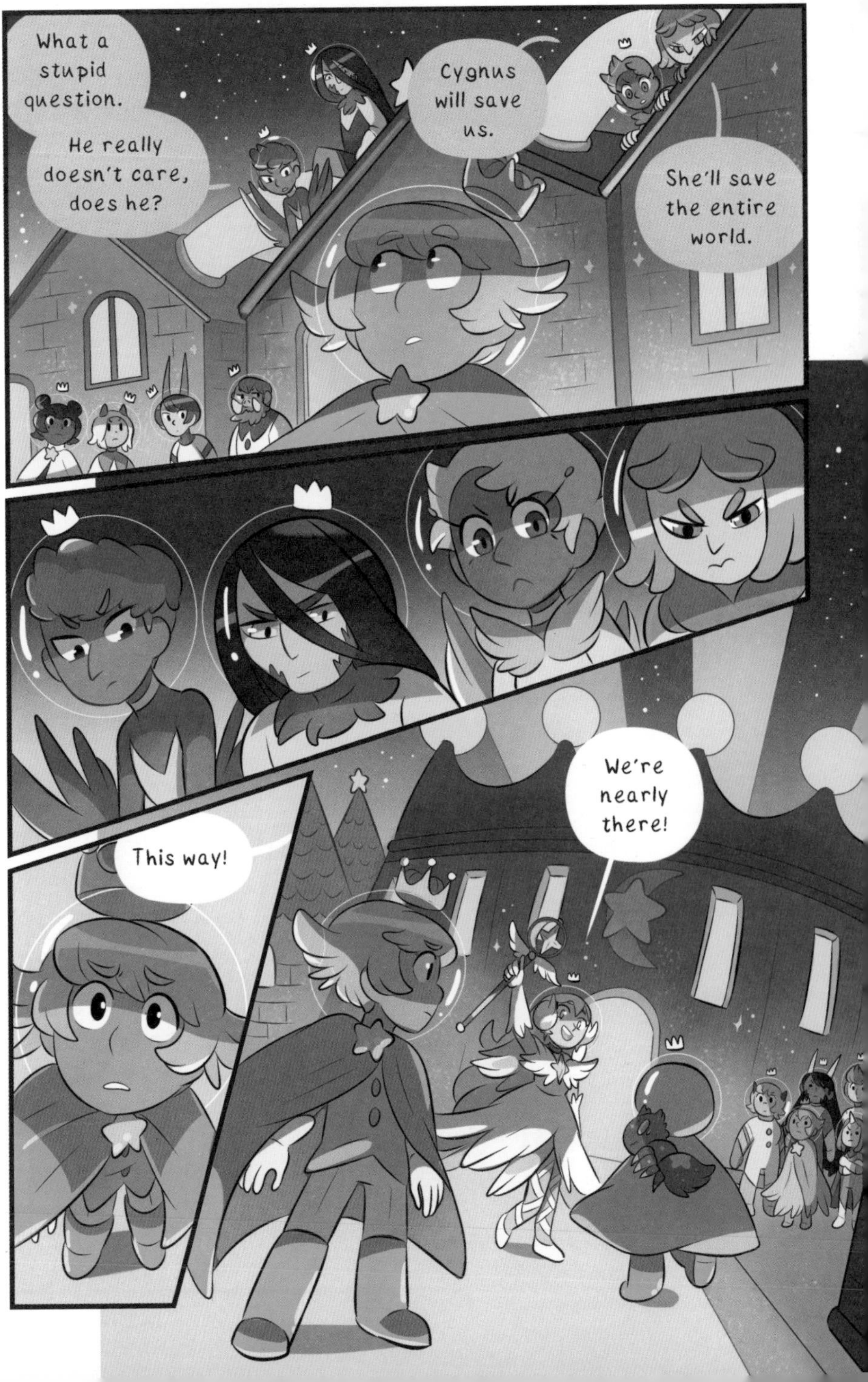
What a stupid question.
He really doesn't care, does he?
Cygnus will save us.
She'll save the entire world.
This way!
We're nearly there!

...

Thank you, my esteemed knights, for coming on such short notice!

I'm pleased to announce the Star King has finally been found!

RA A A A

Our ancestors believed the King would save us from the witch.

But centuries passed, and we were left in the dark.

A A A A

Meanwhile, our brethren in the marsh remain cursed as Fallen Fauna.

CYGNUS! ♡

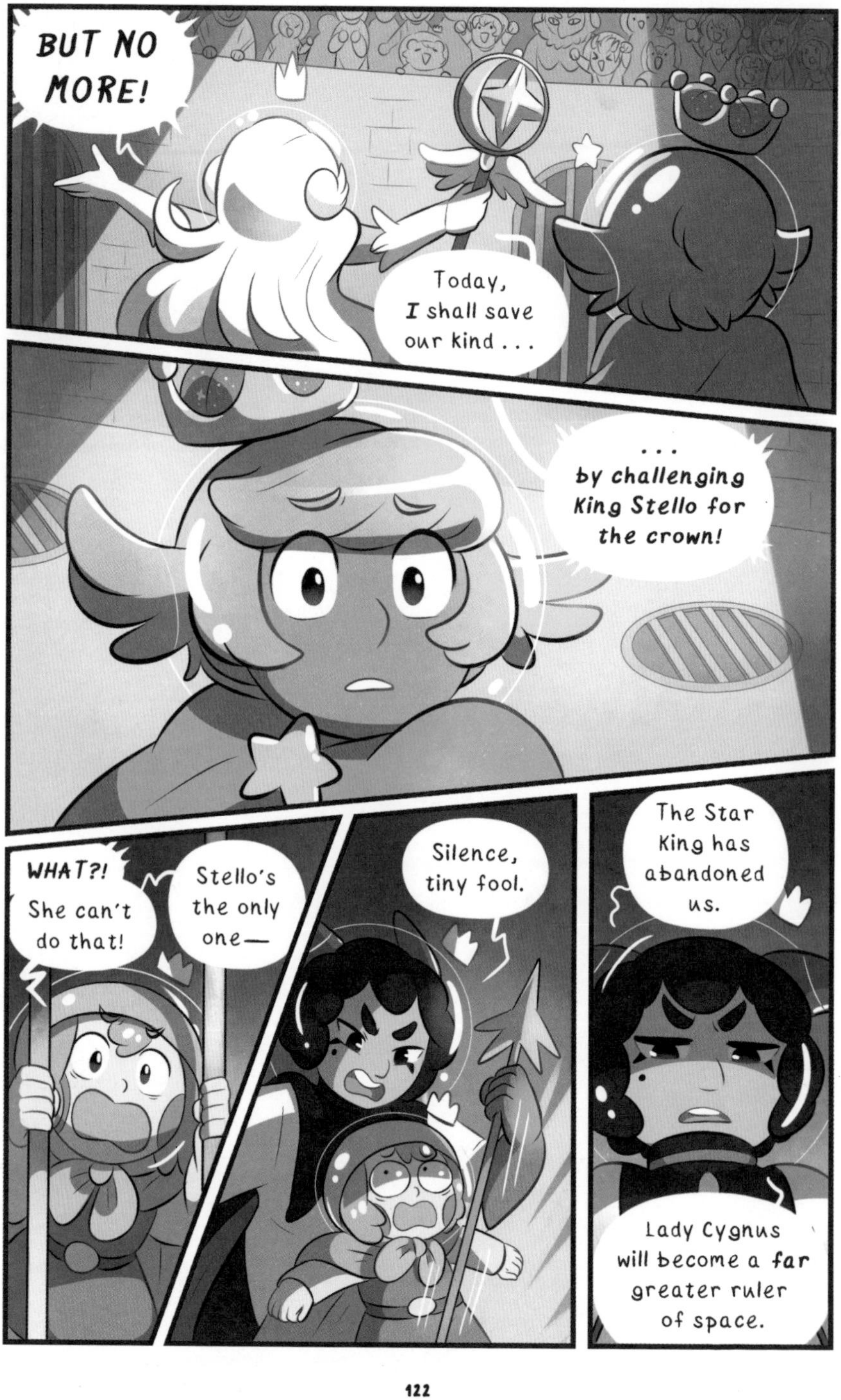
BUT NO MORE!
Today, I shall save our kind . . .
. . . by challenging King Stello for the crown!
WHAT?! She can't do that!
Stello's the only one—
Silence, tiny fool.
The Star King has abandoned us.
Lady Cygnus will become a far greater ruler of space.

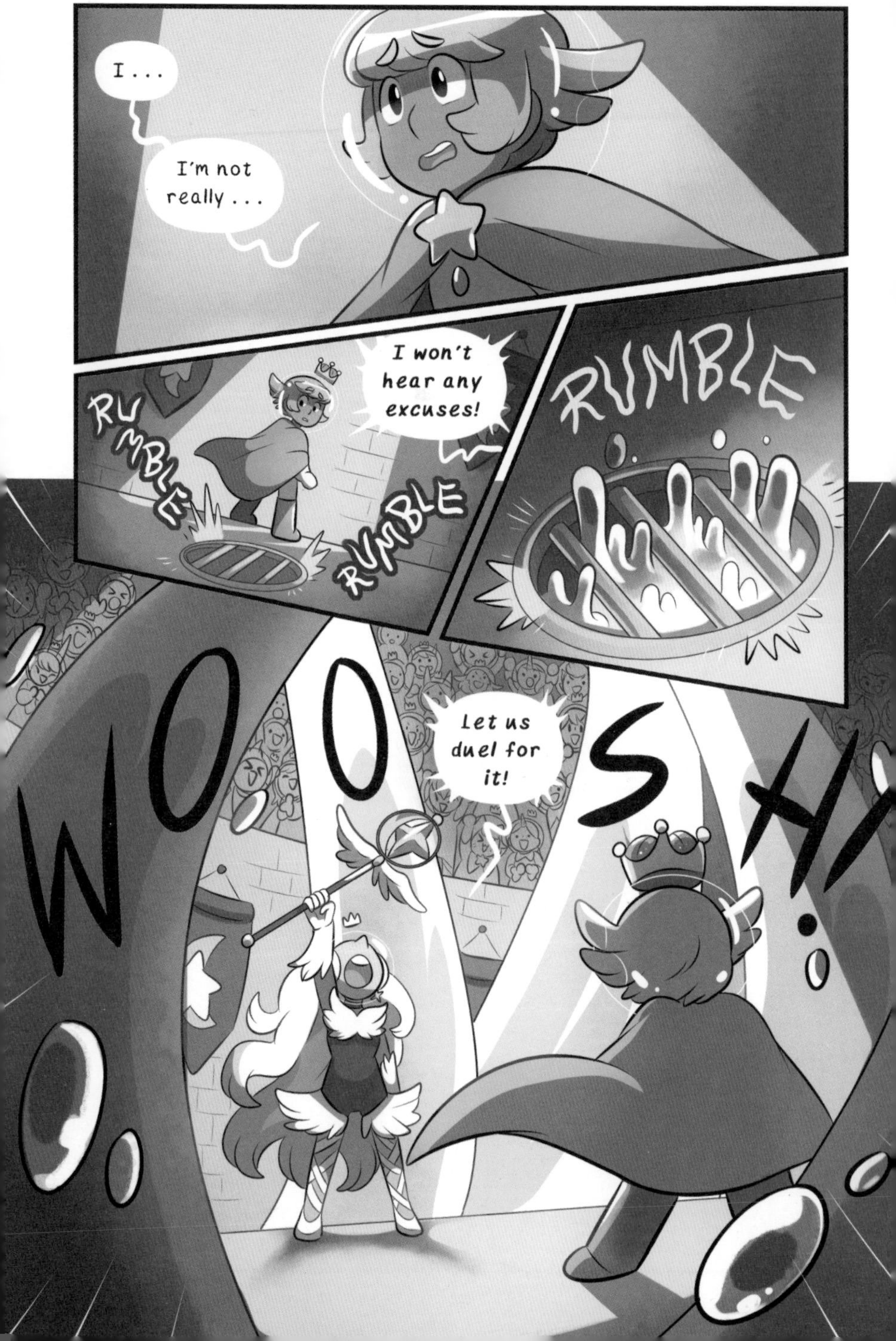
I . . .
I'm not really . . .
I won't hear any excuses!
RUMBLE
RUMBLE
RUMBLE
Let us duel for it!
WOOOSH!

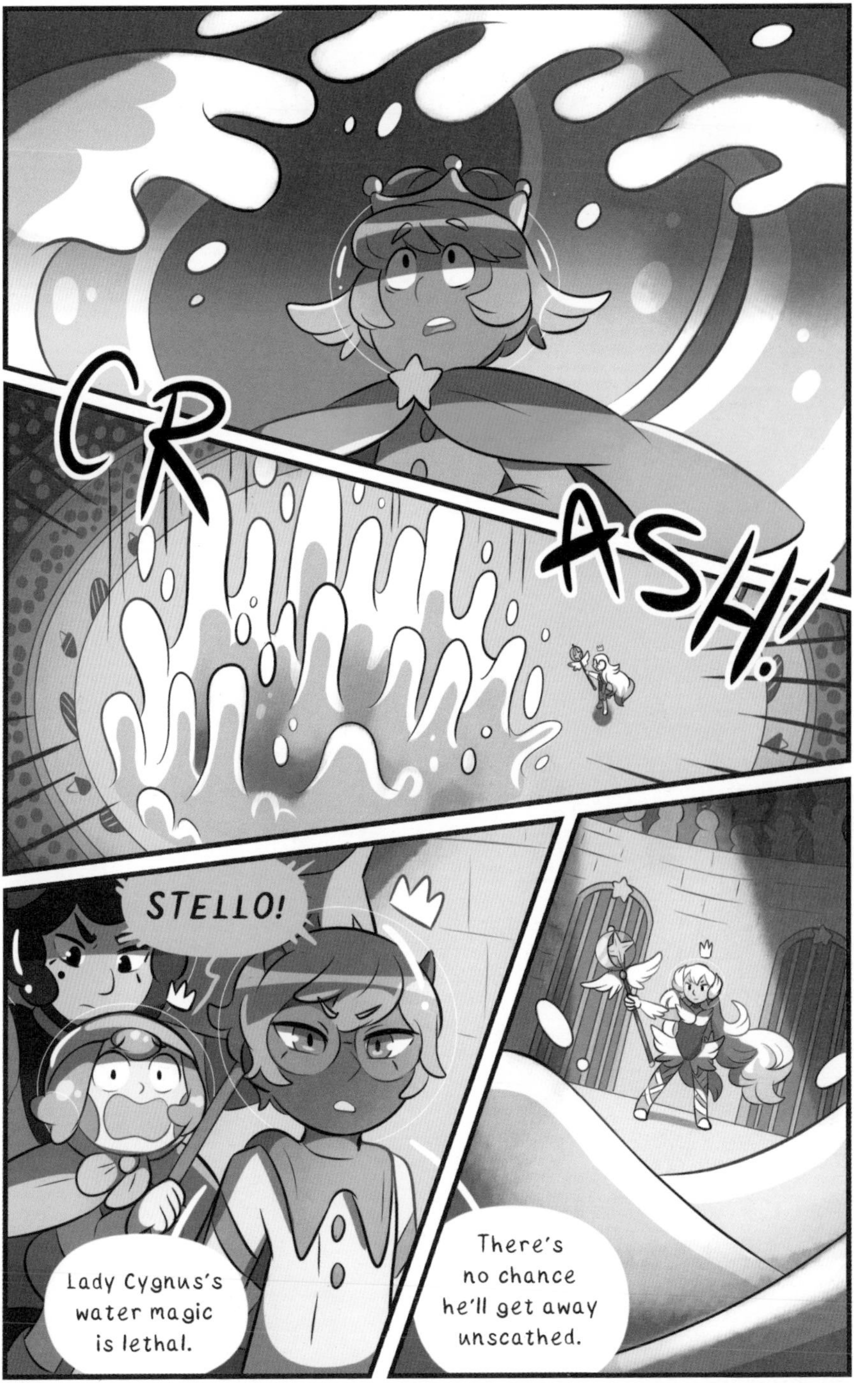
CRASH!
STELLO!
Lady Cygnus's water magic is lethal.
There's no chance he'll get away unscathed.

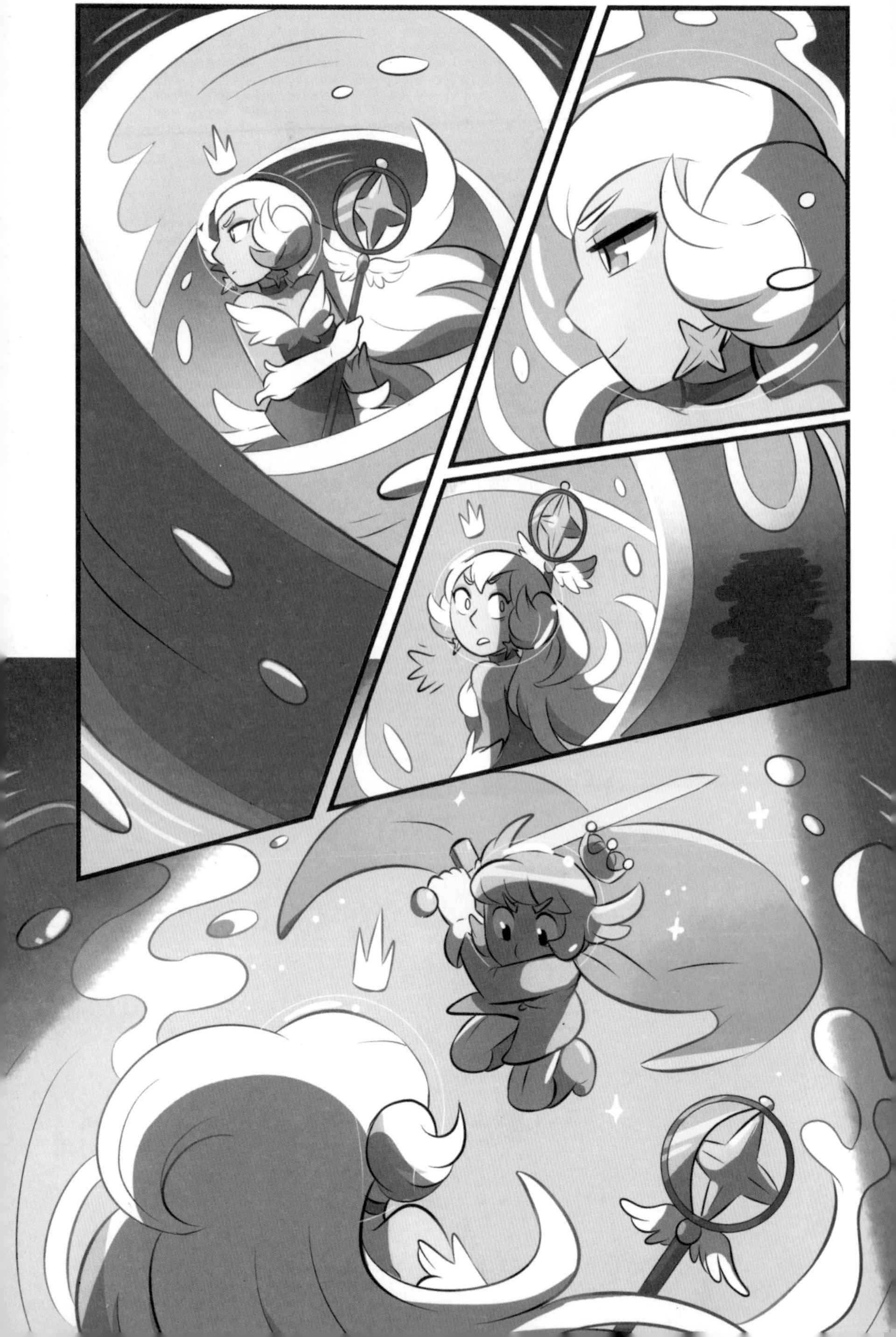

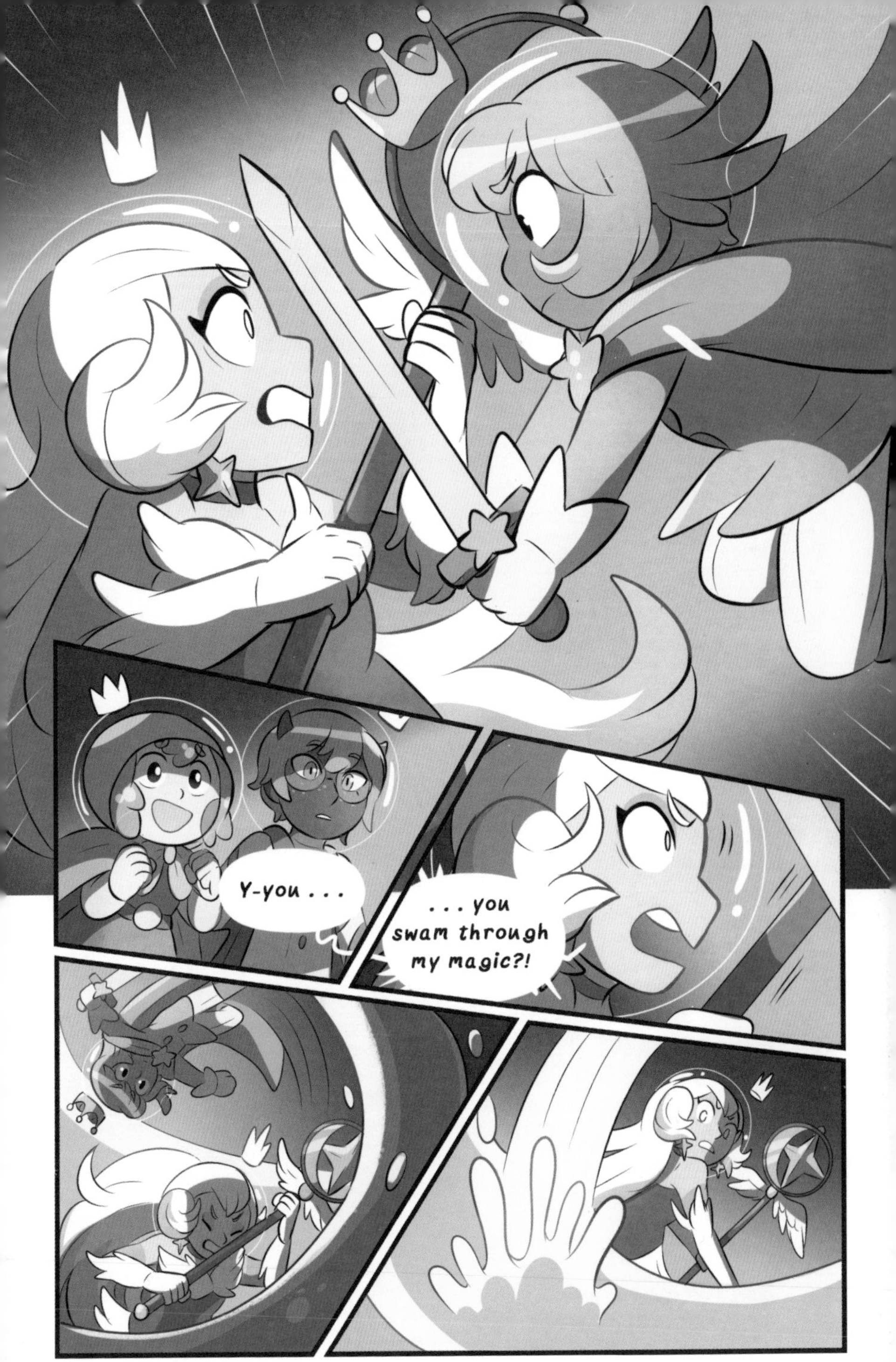
Y-you . . .
. . . you swam through my magic?!

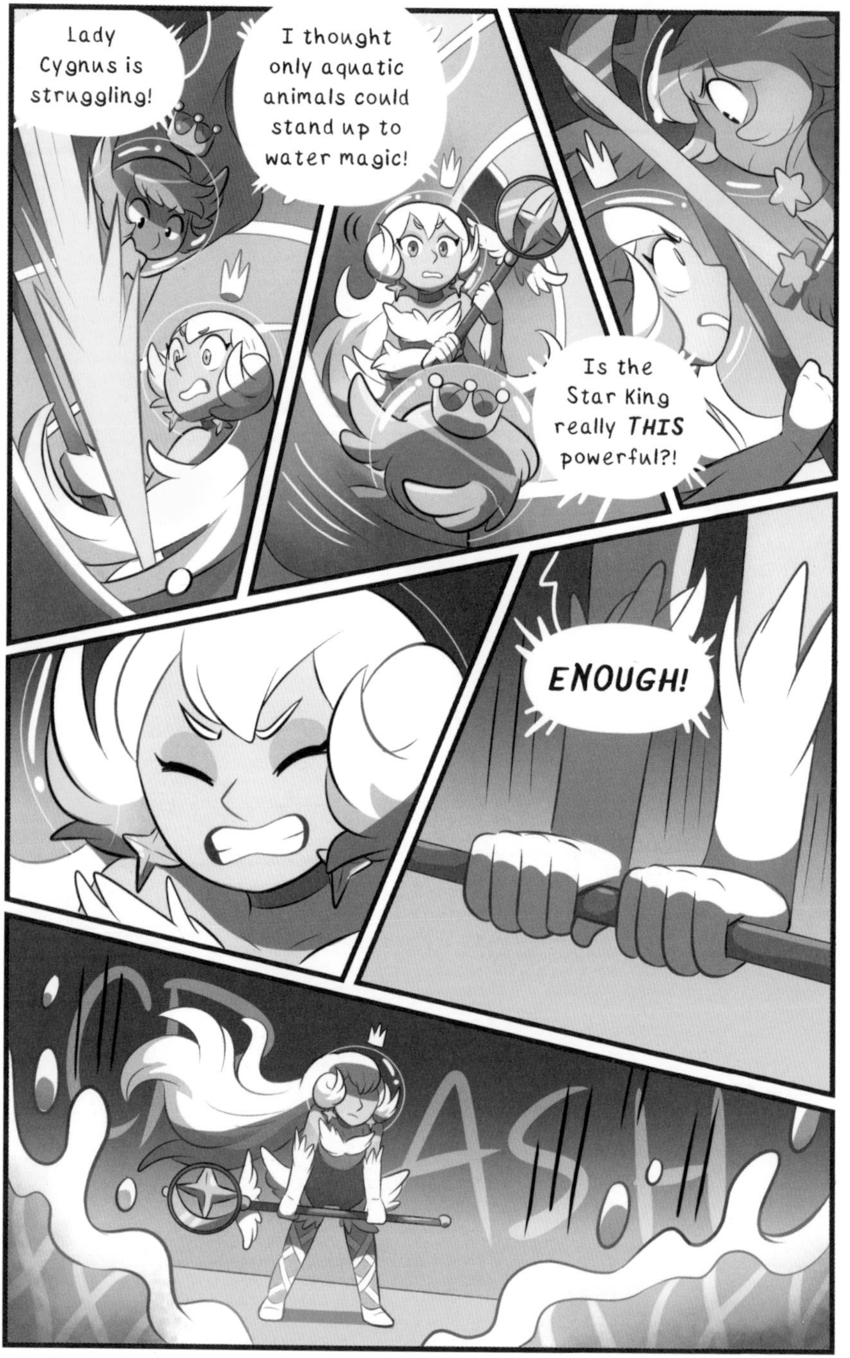
Lady Cygnus is struggling!
I thought only aquatic animals could stand up to water magic!
Is the Star King really THIS powerful?!
ENOUGH!
CRASH!

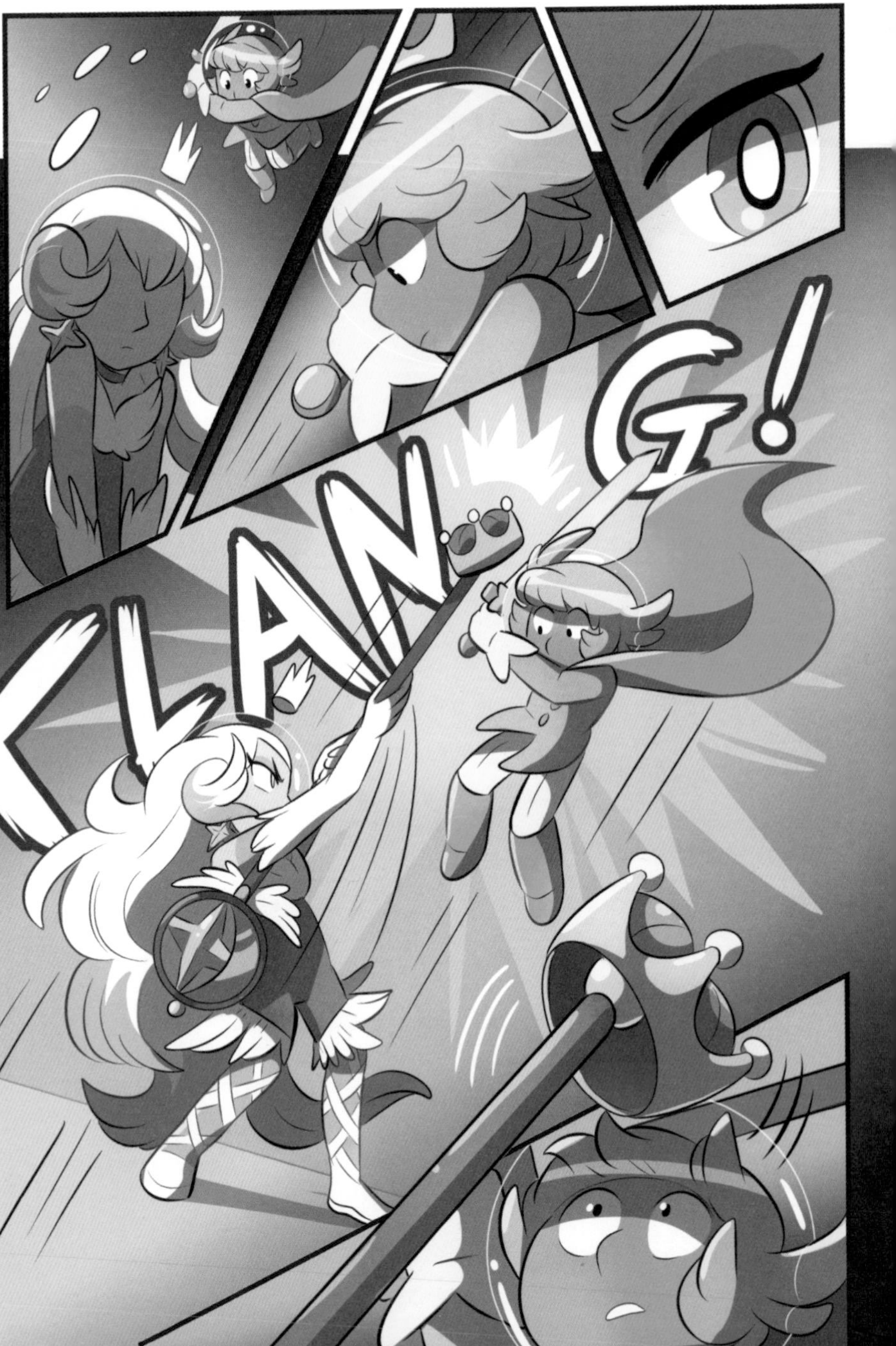
CLANG!

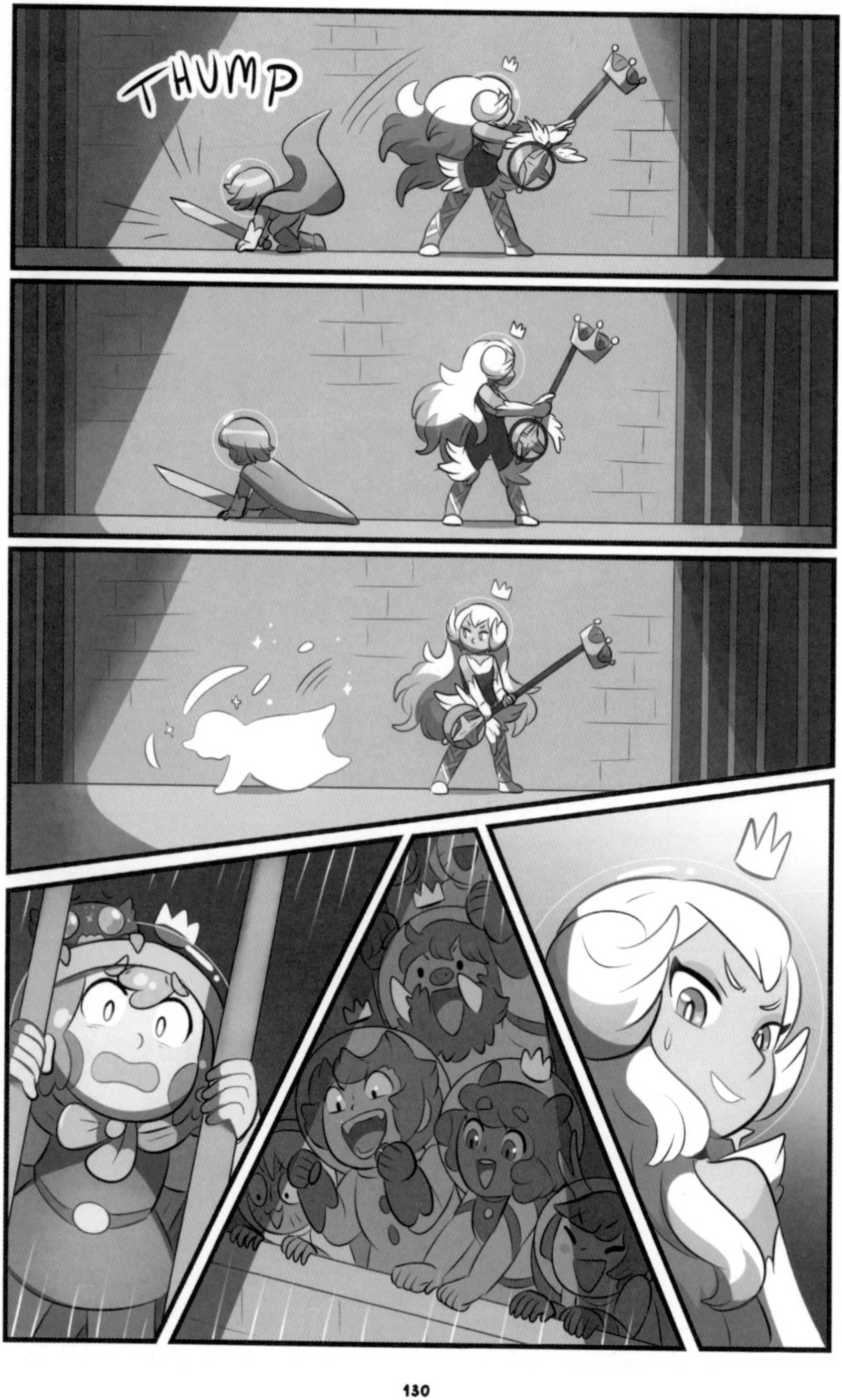
THUMP

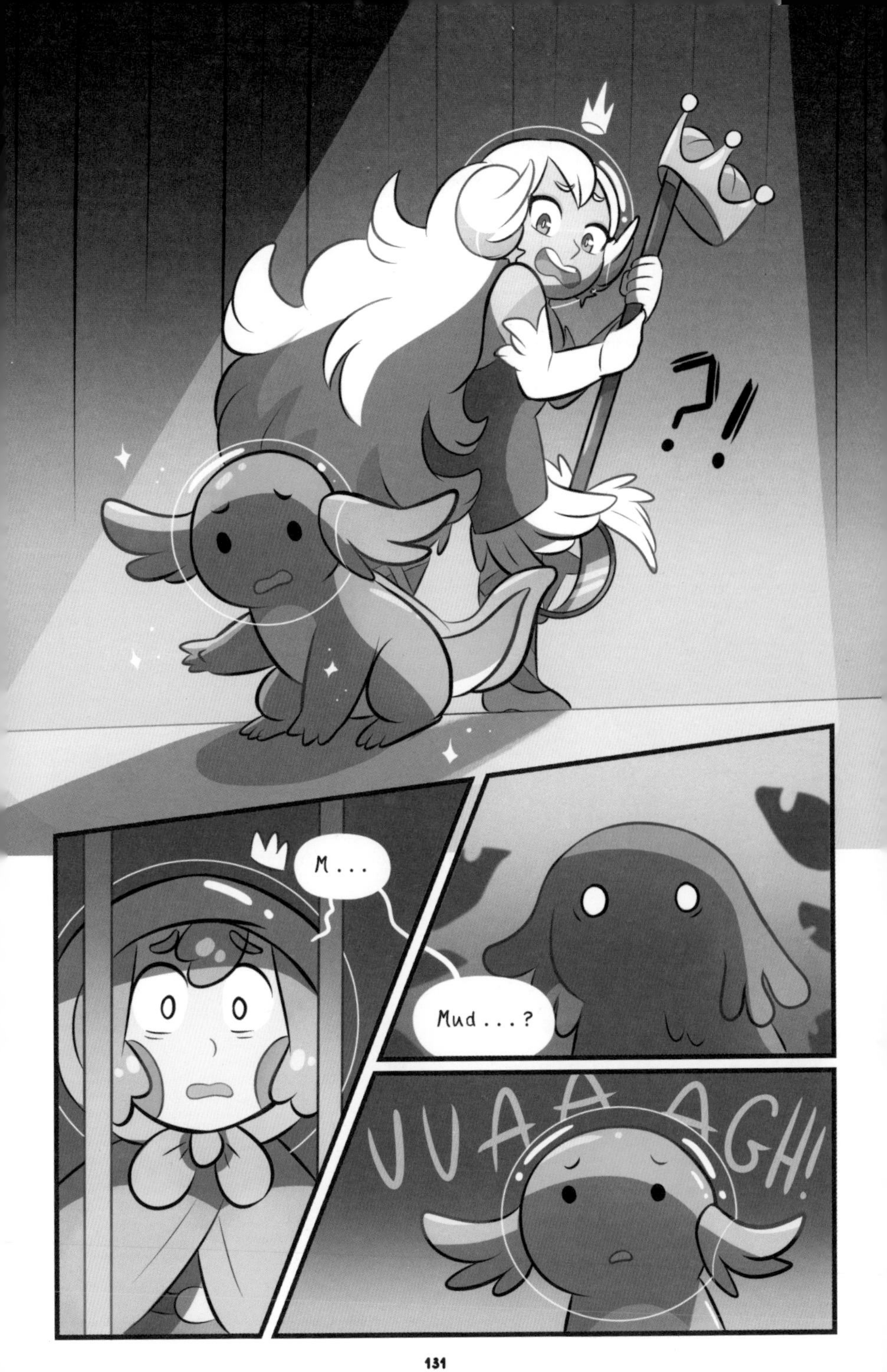
?!
M...
Mud...?
UUAAAGH!

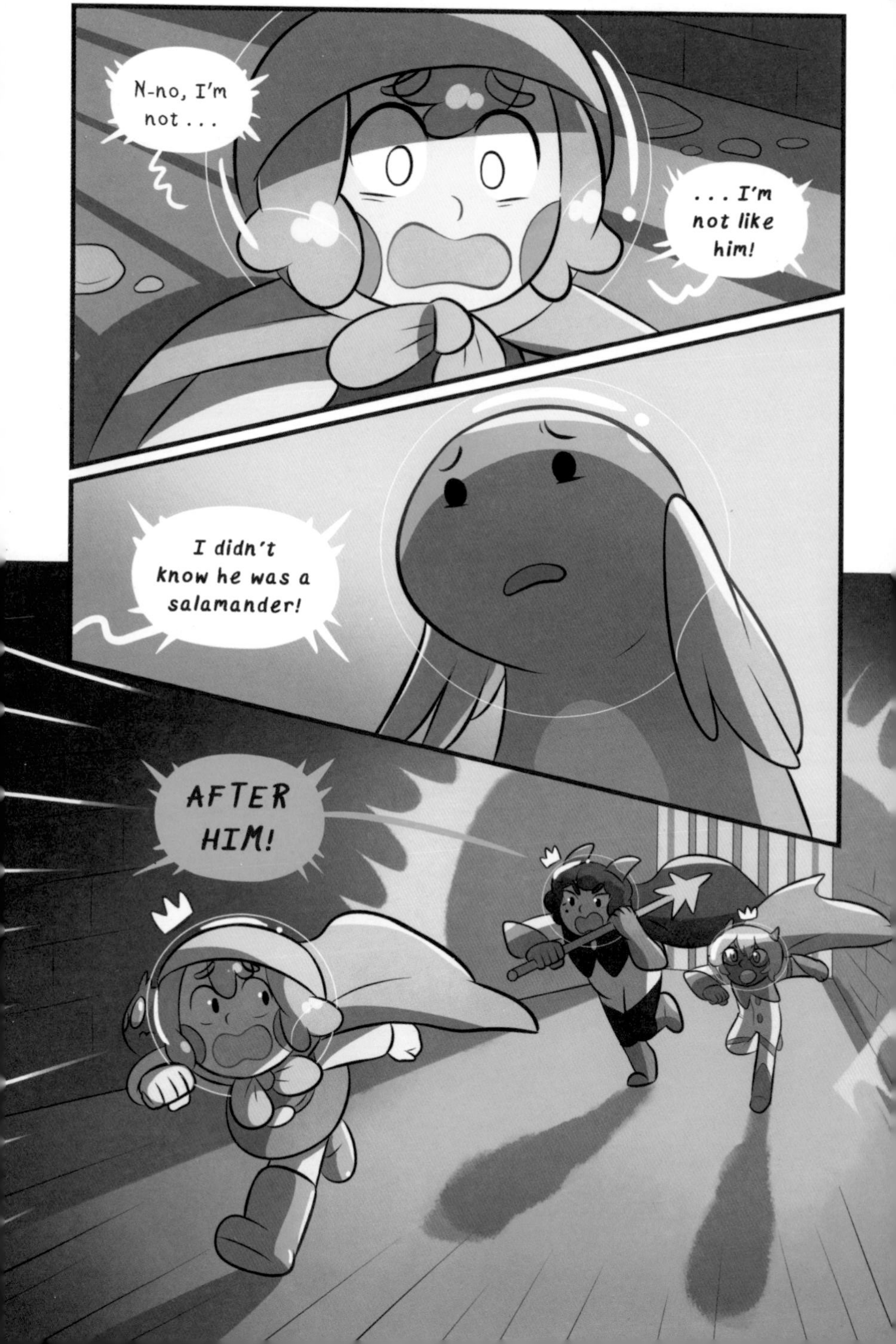
N-no, I'm not . . .
. . . I'm not like him!
I didn't know he was a salamander!
AFTER HIM!

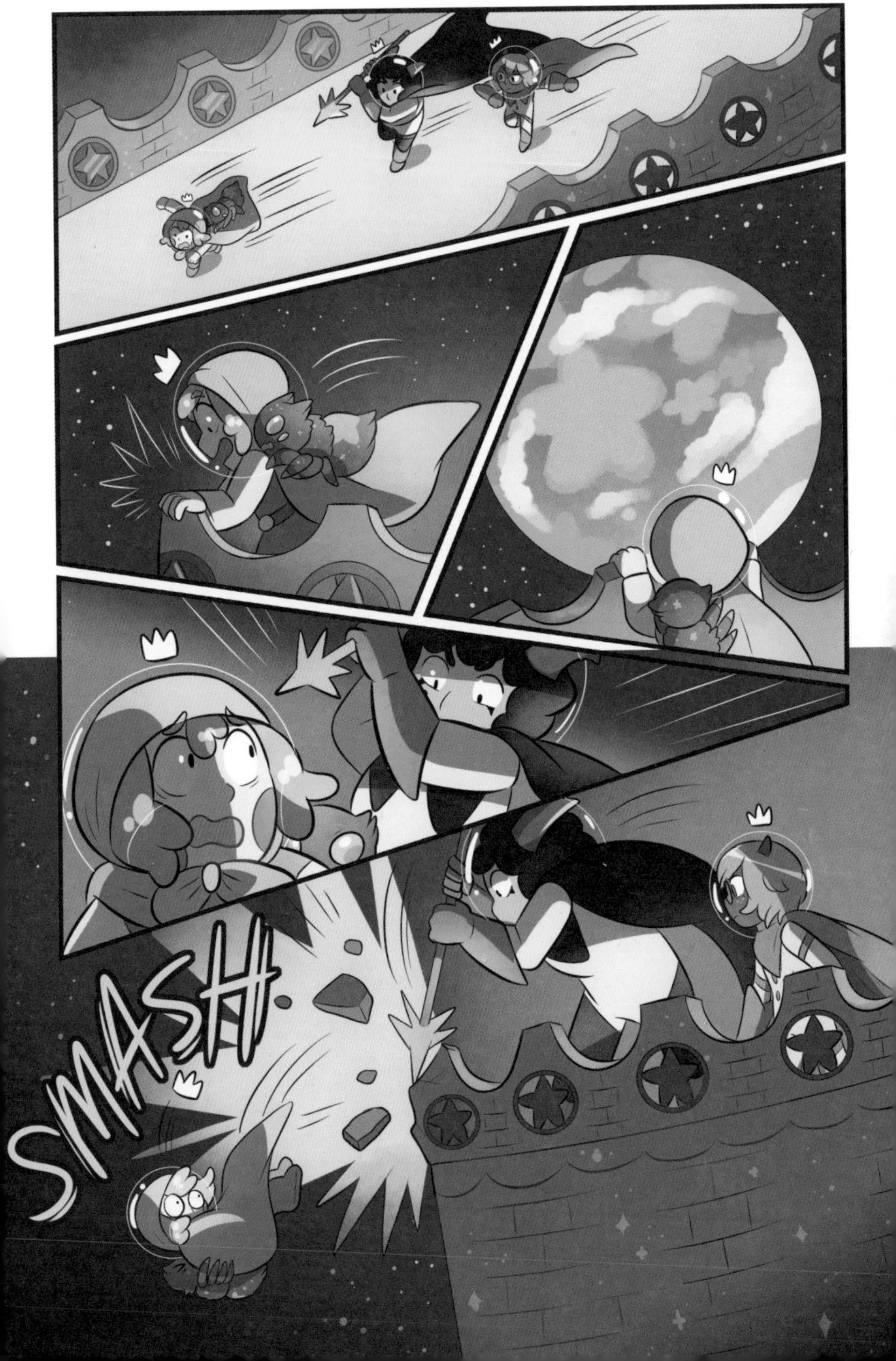
SMASH

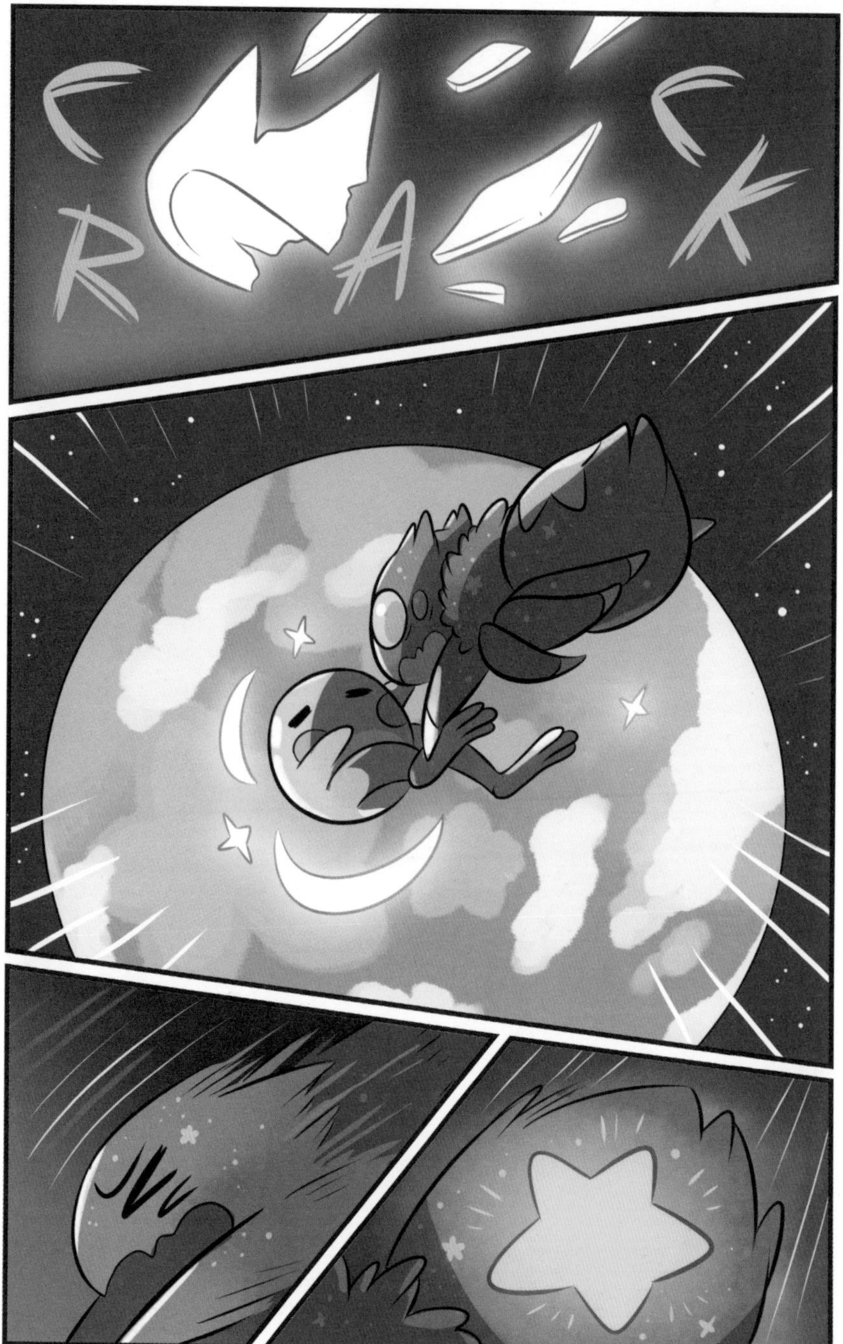
CRACK

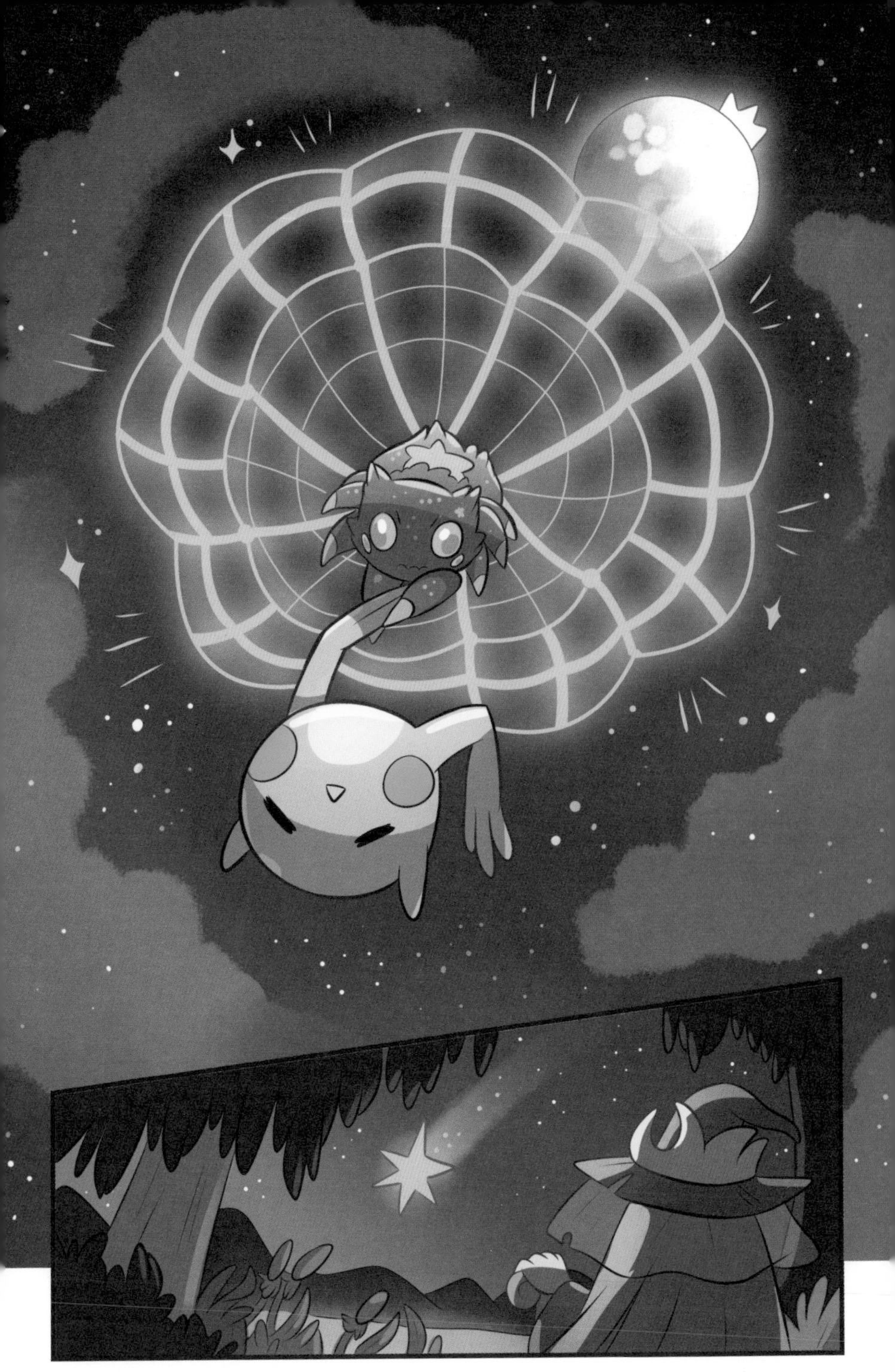

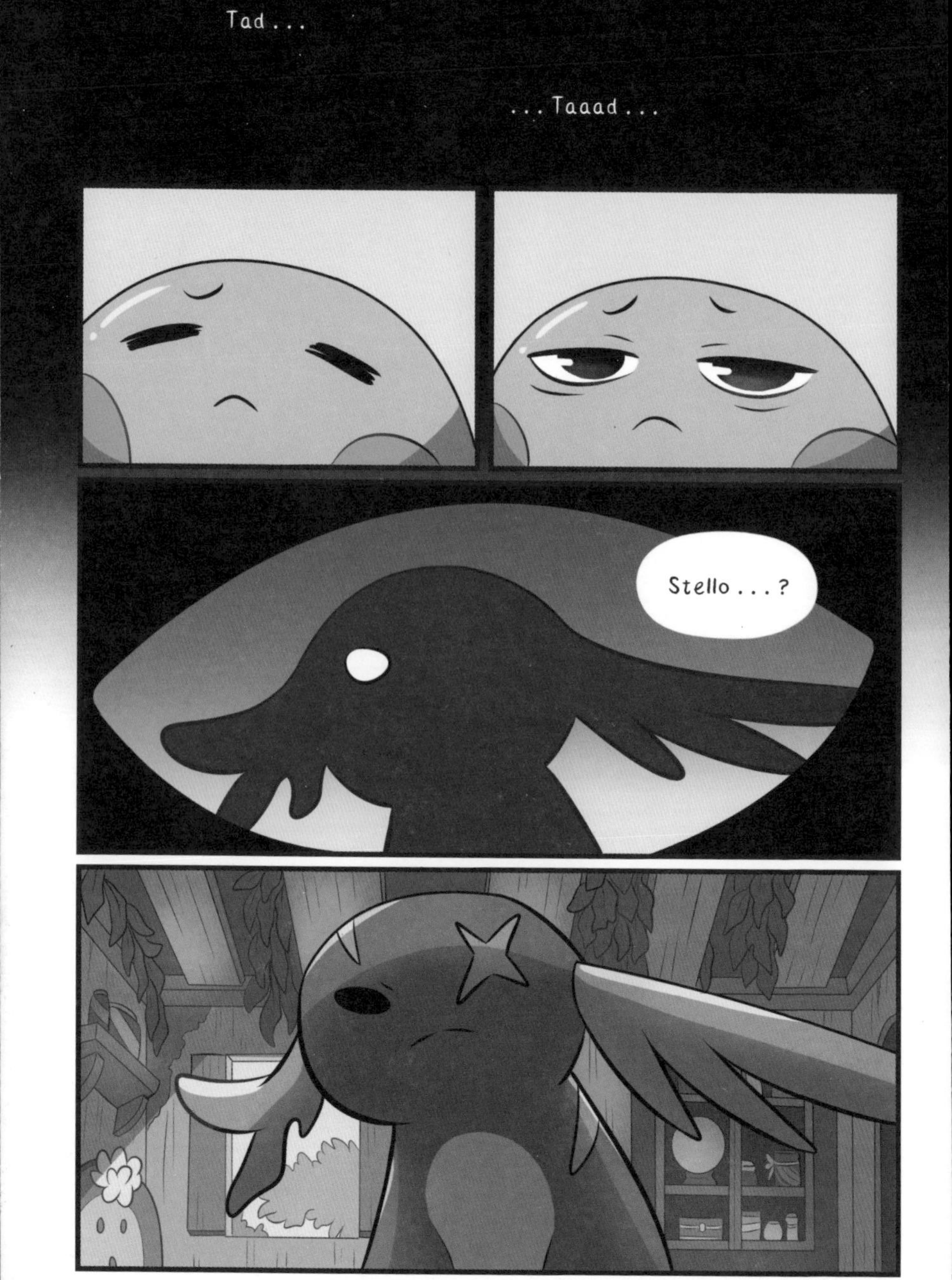
Tad . . .
. . . Taaad . . .
Stello . . . ?

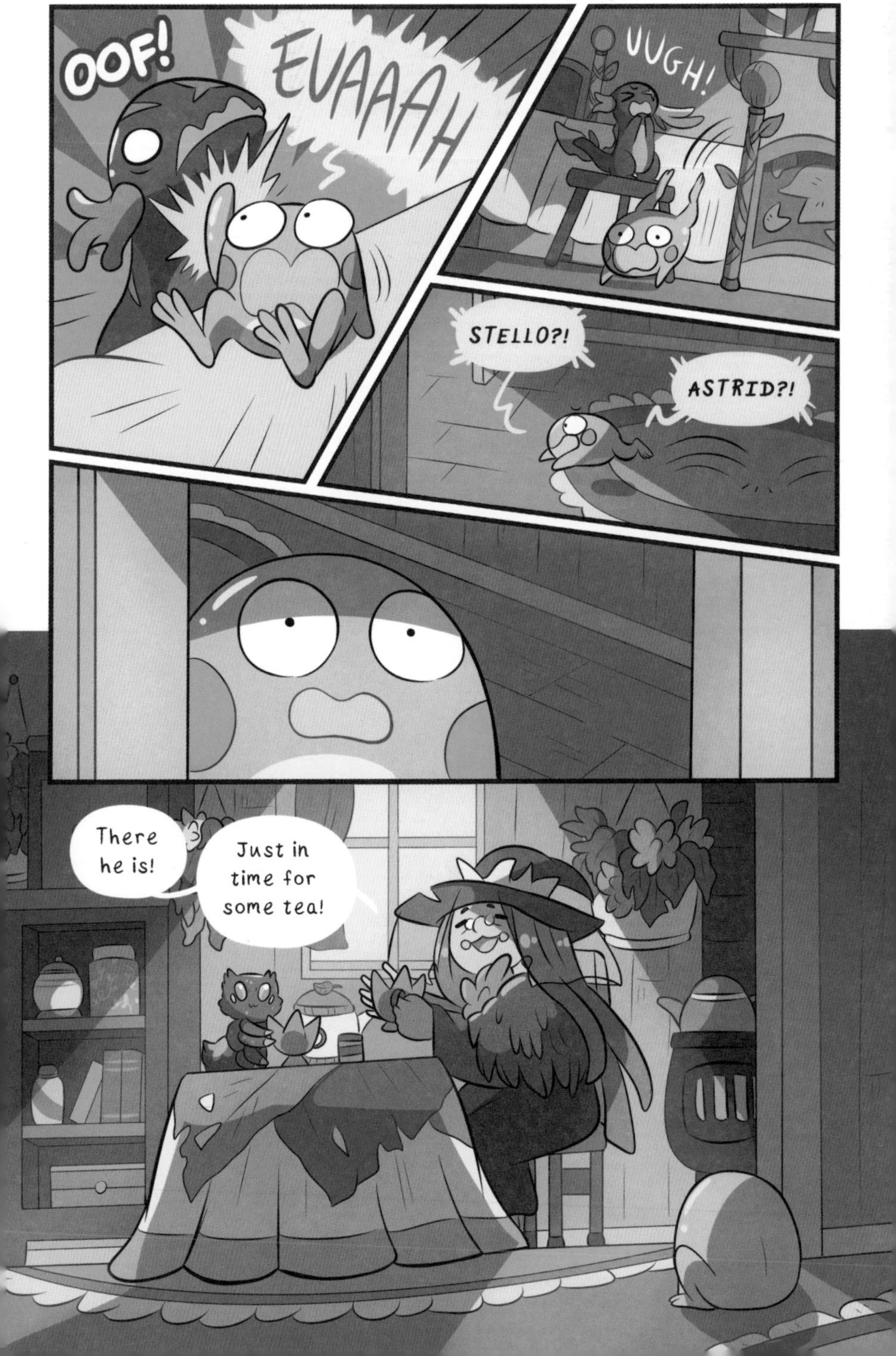
OOF!
EVAAAAH
UUGH!
STELLO?!
ASTRID?!
There he is!
Just in time for some tea!

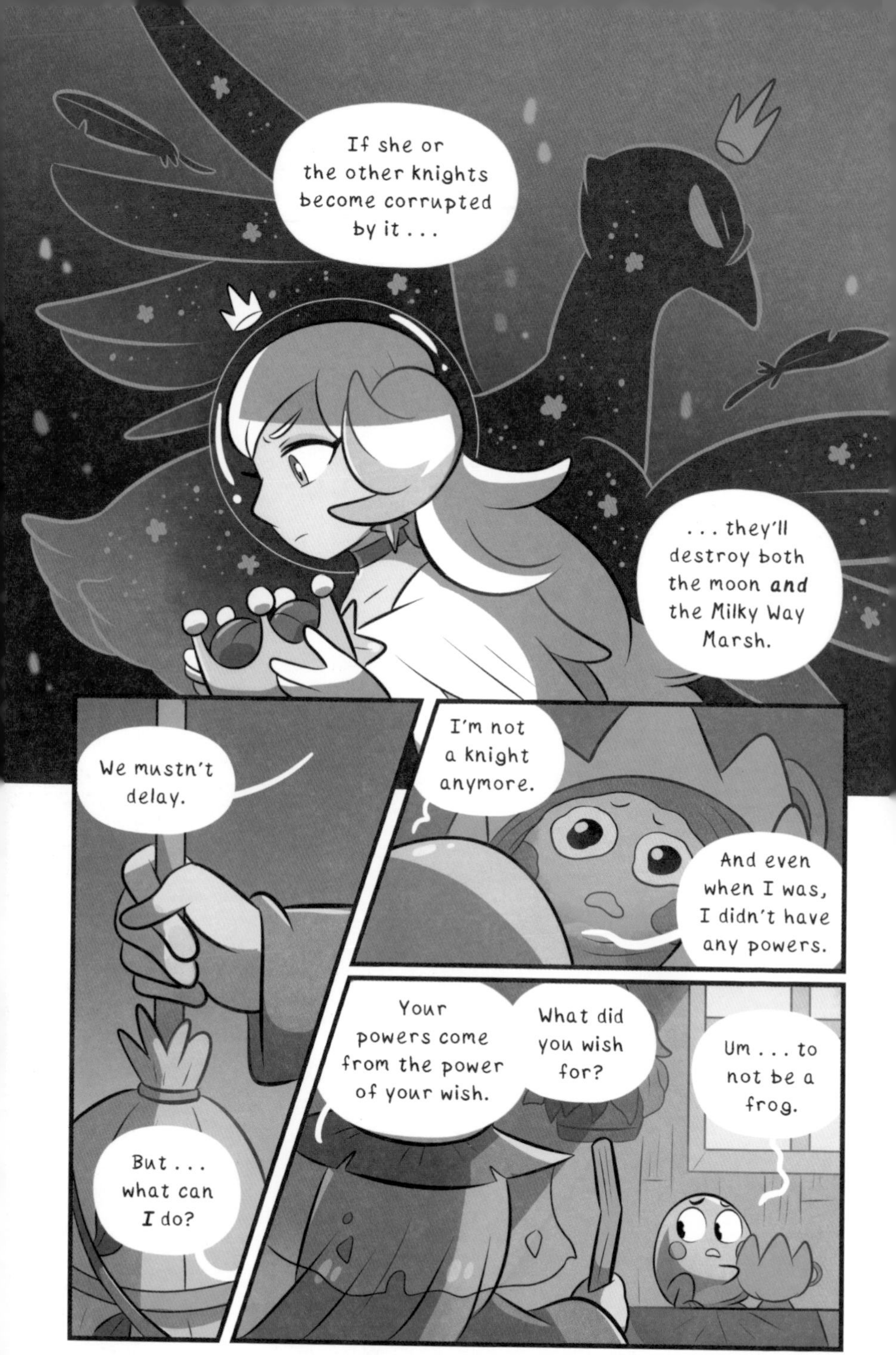
If she or the other knights become corrupted by it . . .
. . . they'll destroy both the moon **and** the Milky Way Marsh.
We mustn't delay.
I'm not a knight anymore.
And even when I was, I didn't have any powers.
But . . . what can *I* do?
Your powers come from the power of your wish.
What did you wish for?
Um . . . to not be a frog.

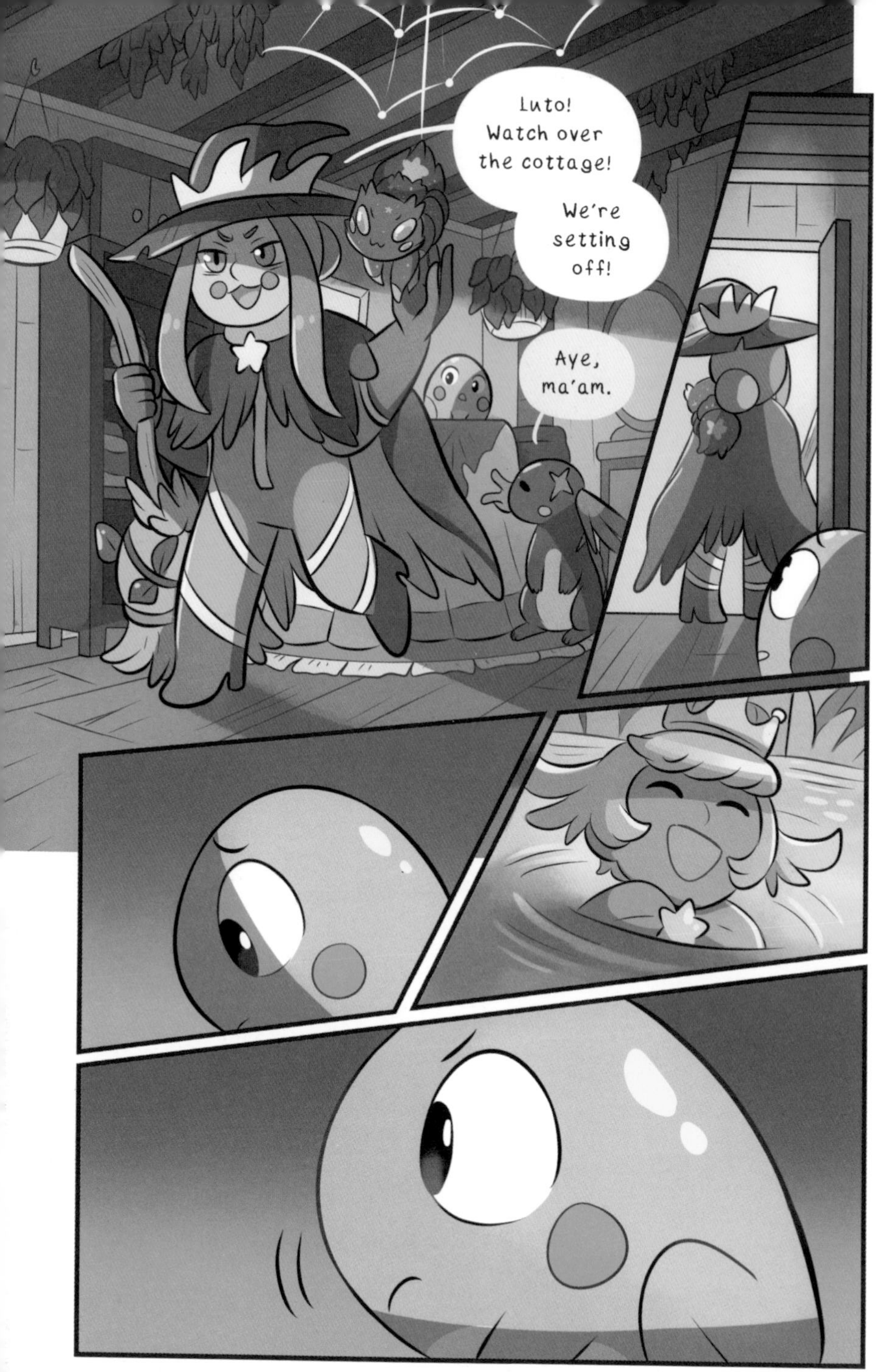
Luto!
Watch over
the cottage!
We're
setting
off!
Aye,
ma'am.

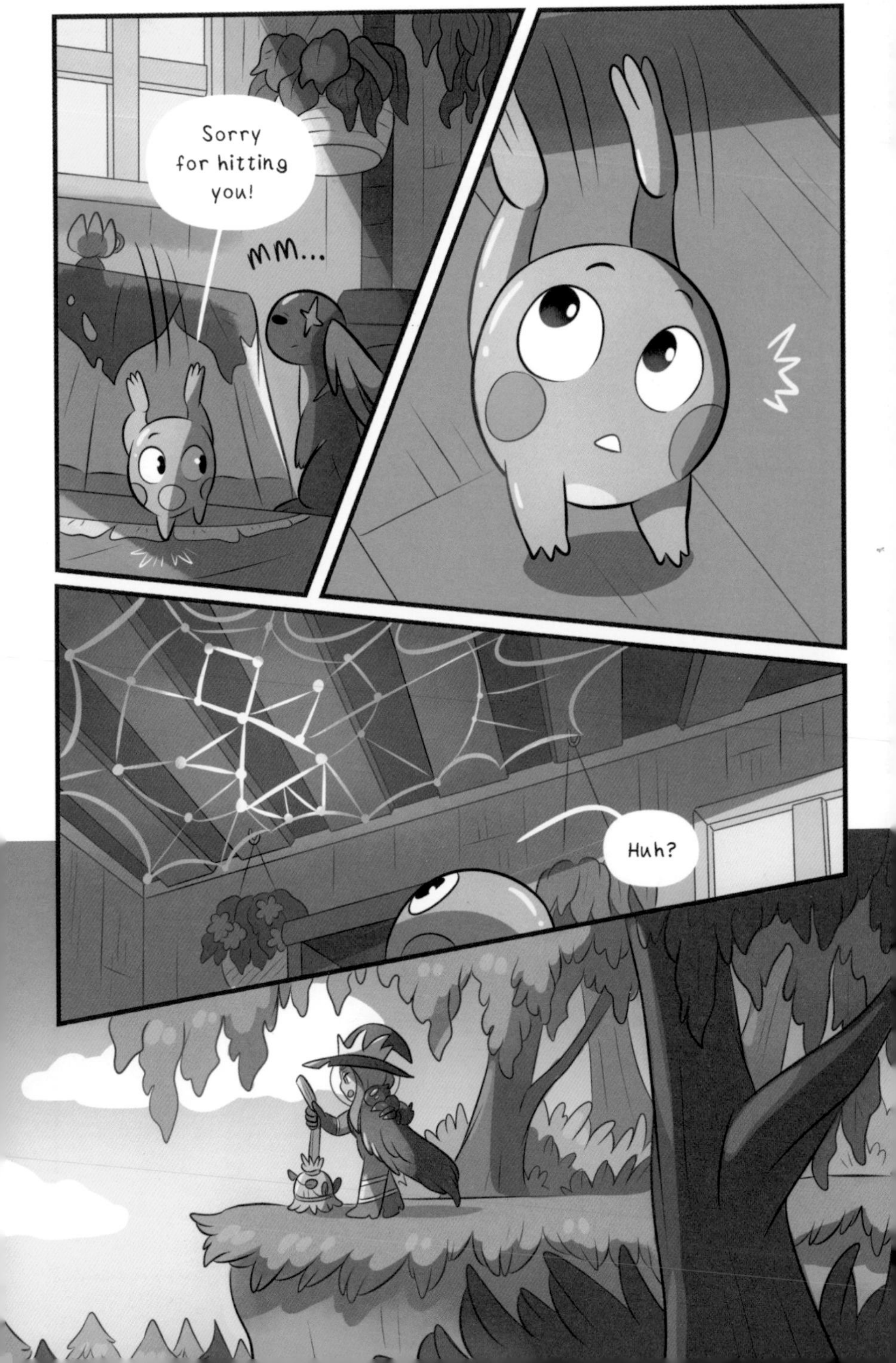
Sorry for hitting you!
MM...
Huh?

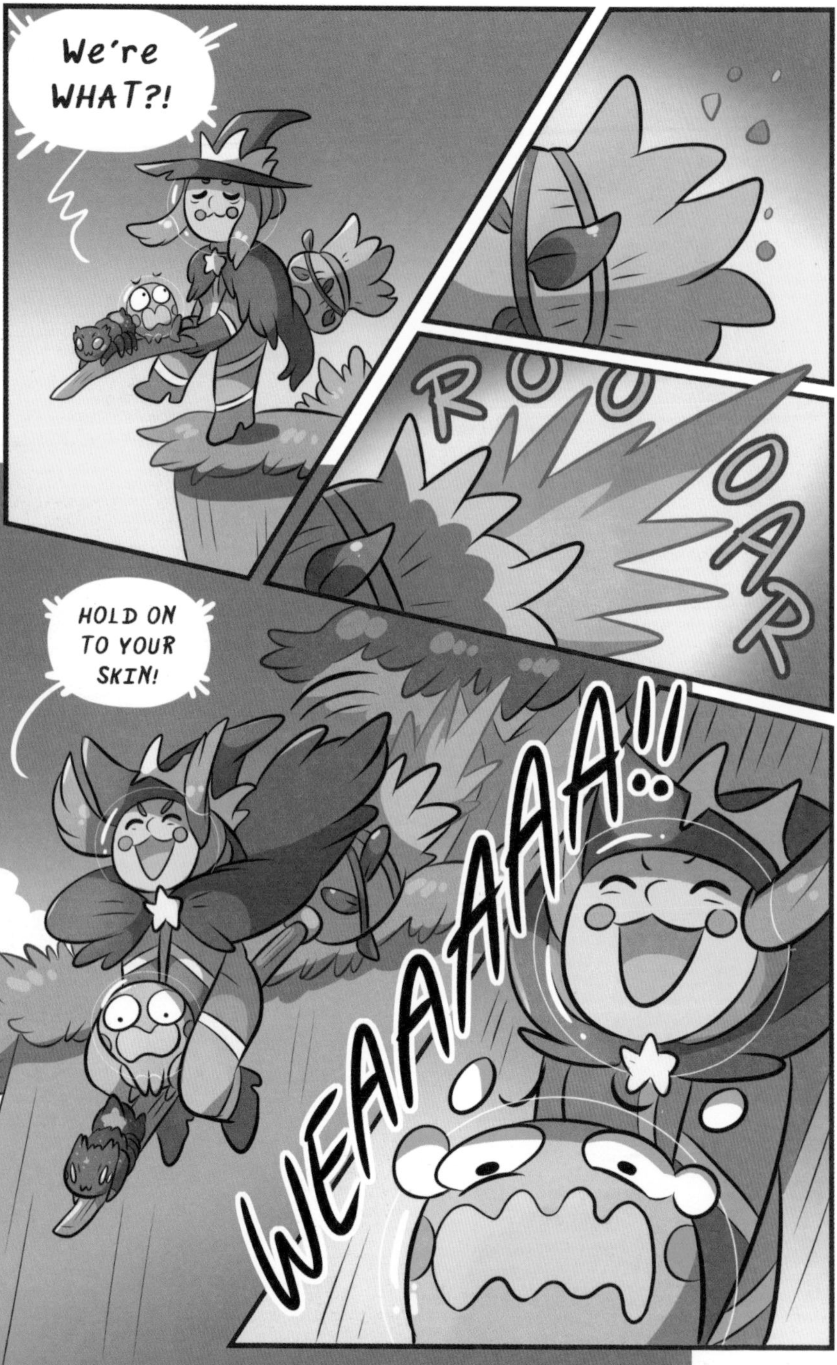
We're WHAT?!
ROOOOAR
HOLD ON TO YOUR SKIN!
WEAAAAAA!!

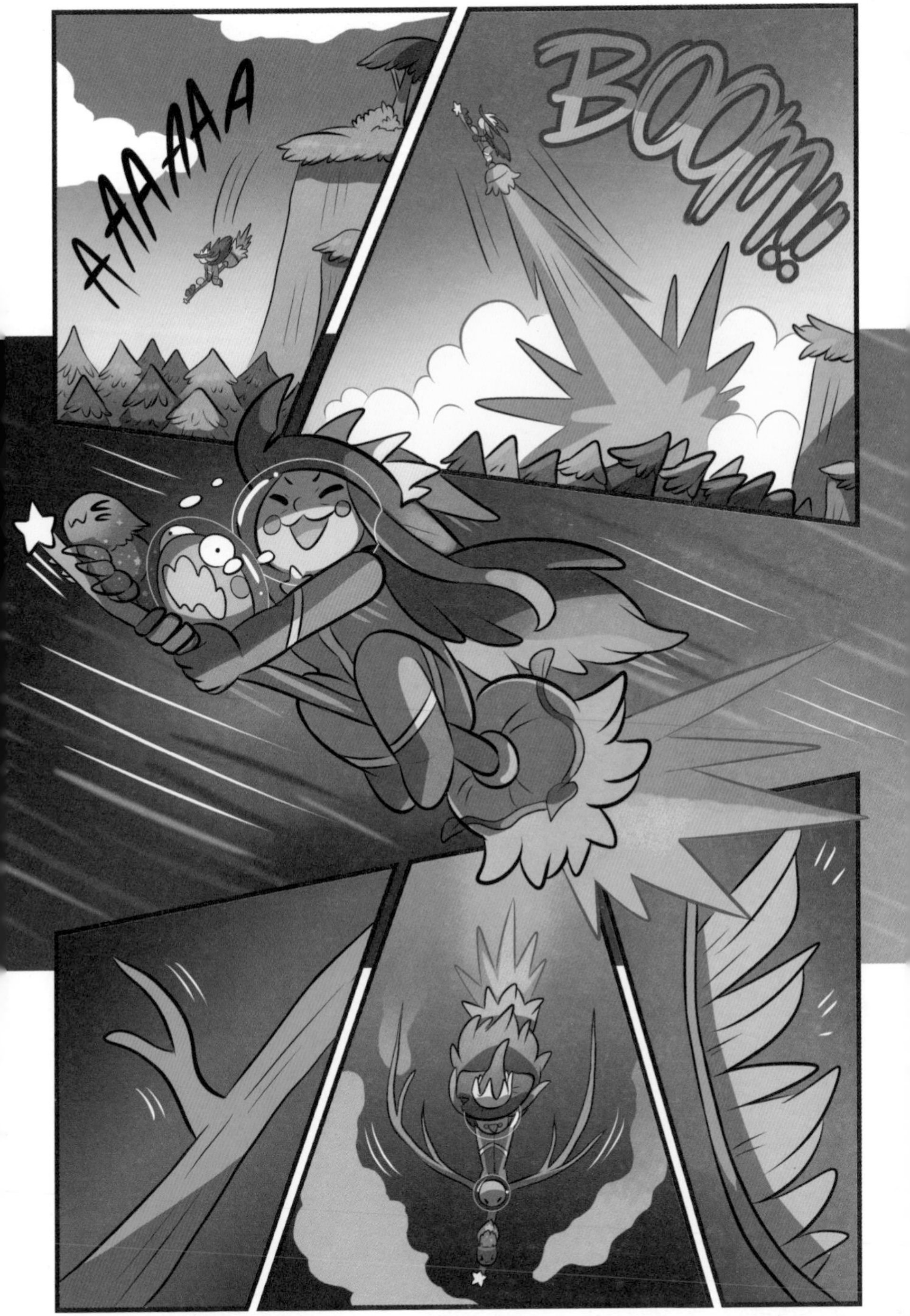
AAAAAA
BOOM!!

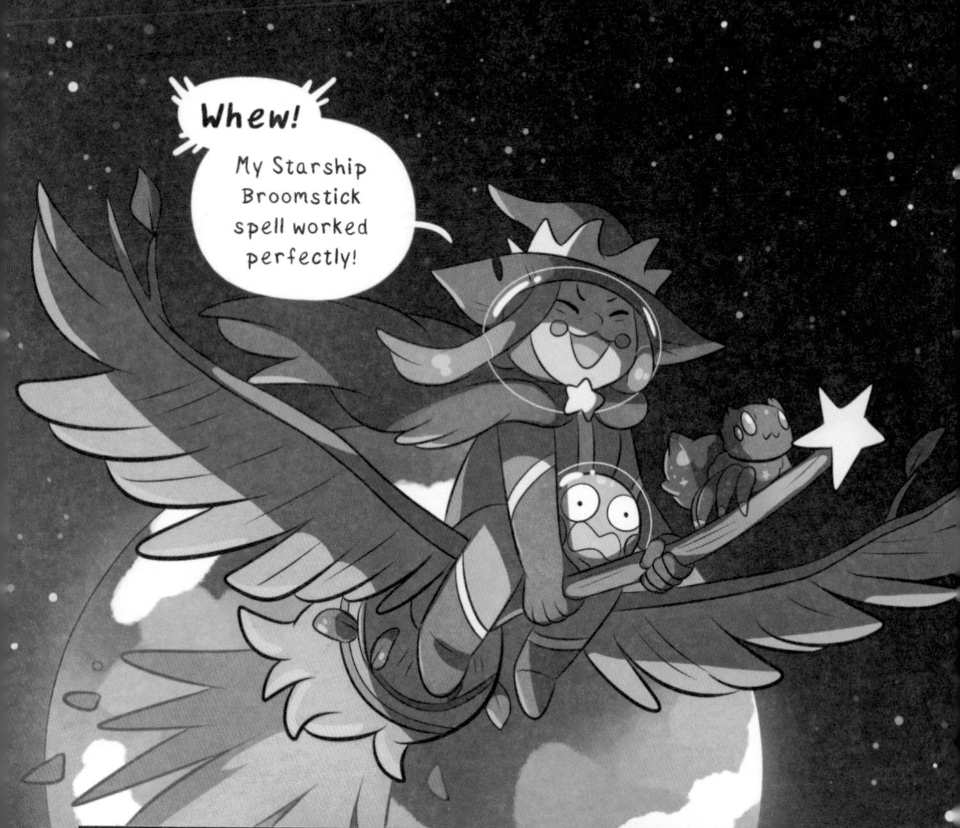
Whew!
My Starship Broomstick spell worked perfectly!

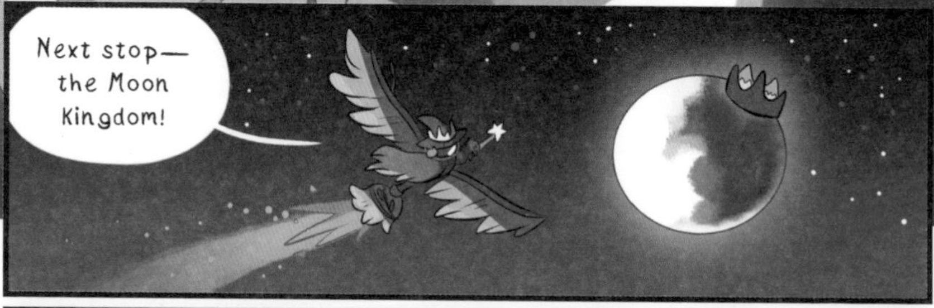
Next stop— the Moon Kingdom!

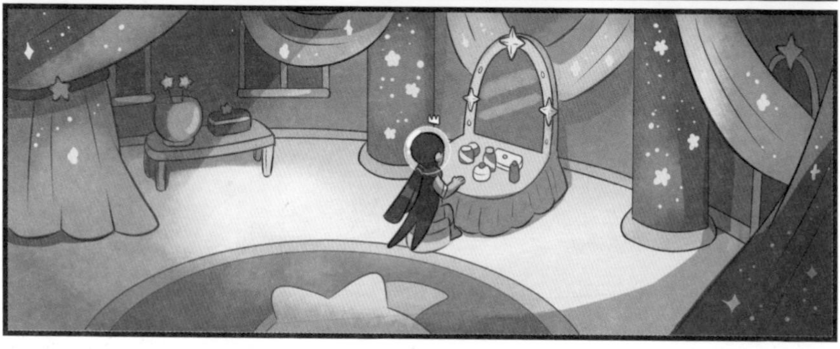

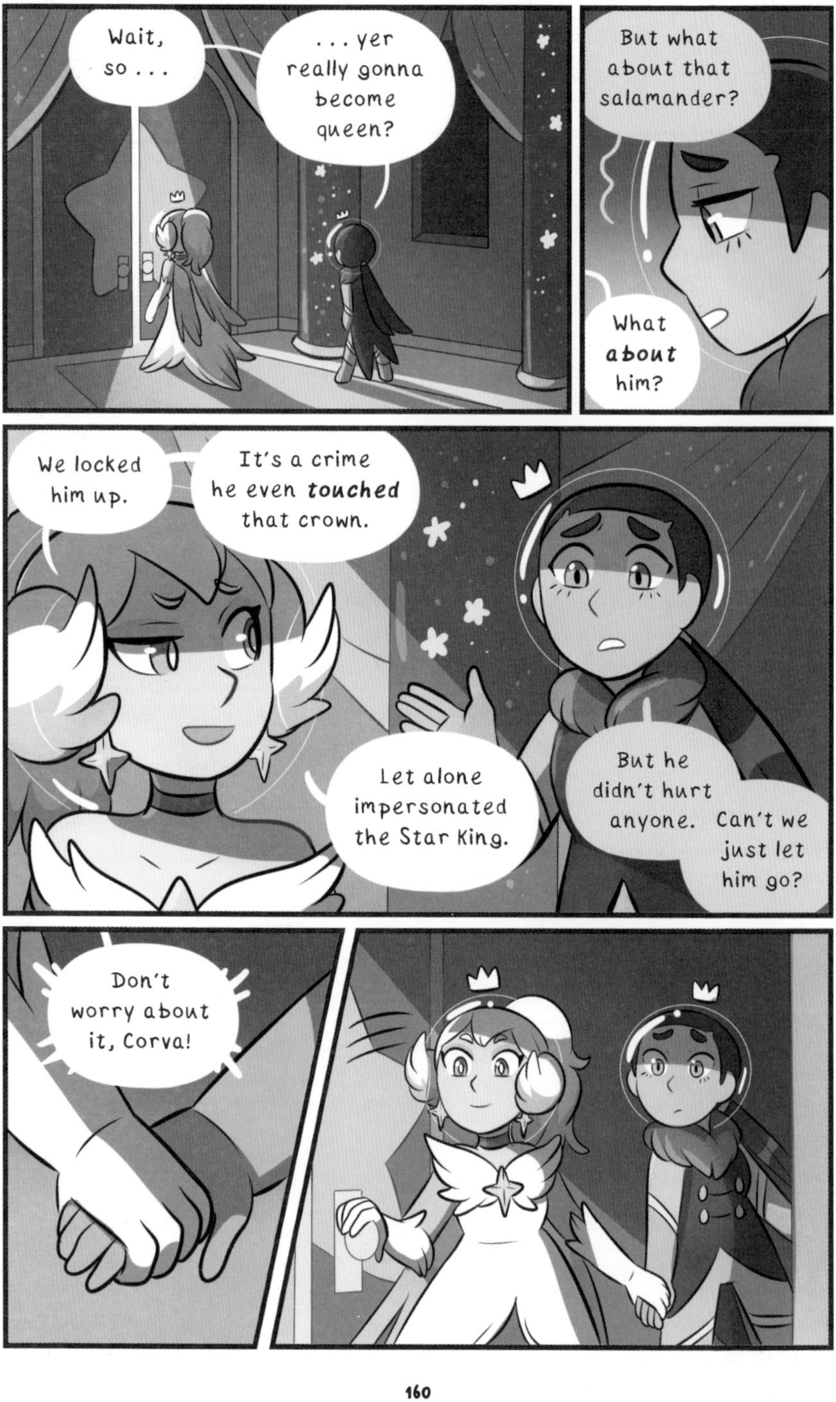
Wait, so . . .
. . . yer really gonna become queen?
But what about that salamander?
What **about** him?
We locked him up.
It's a crime he even **touched** that crown.
Let alone impersonated the Star King.
But he didn't hurt anyone.
Can't we just let him go?
Don't worry about it, Corva!

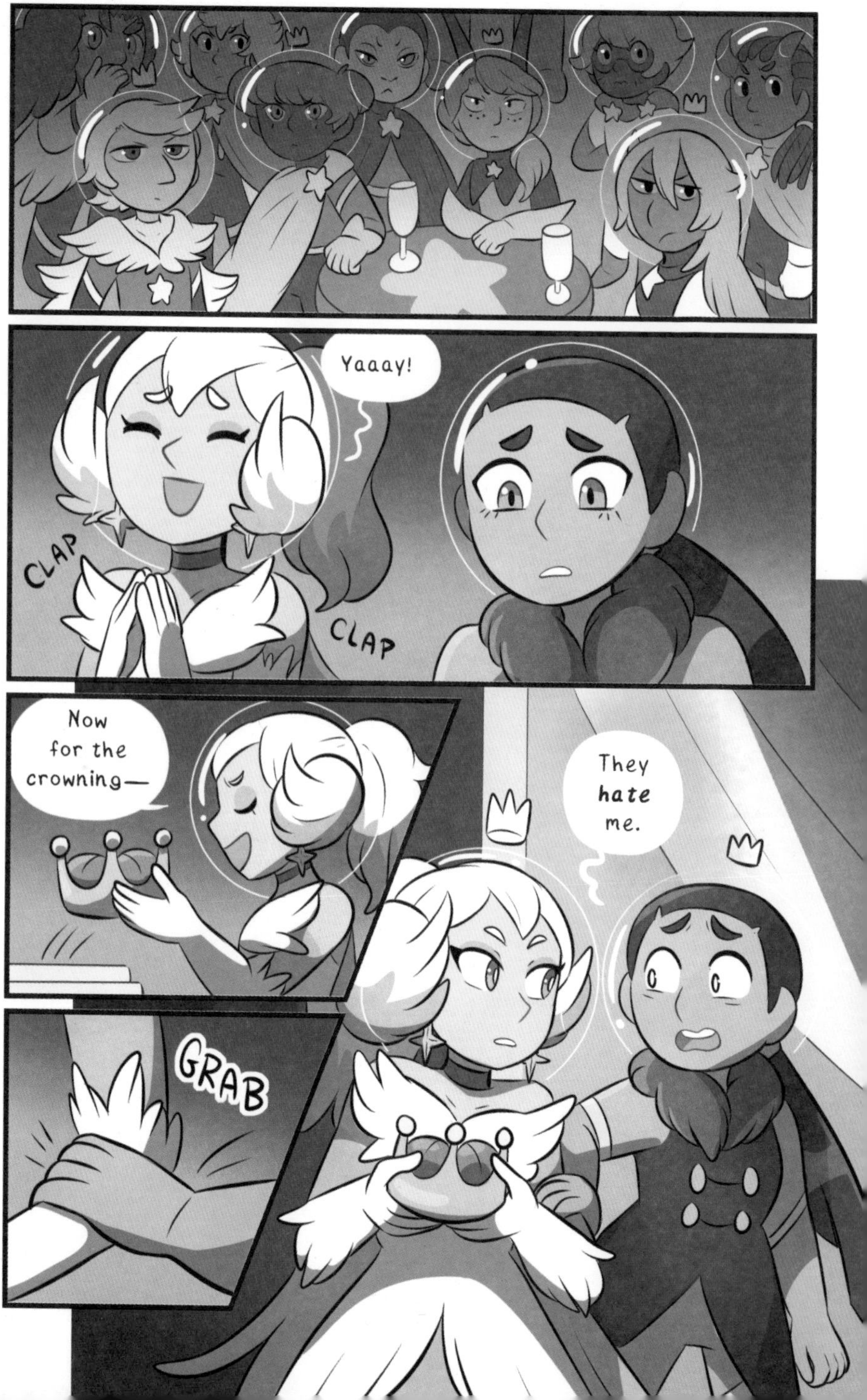
Yaaay!
CLAP
CLAP
Now for the crowning—
They **hate** me.
GRAB

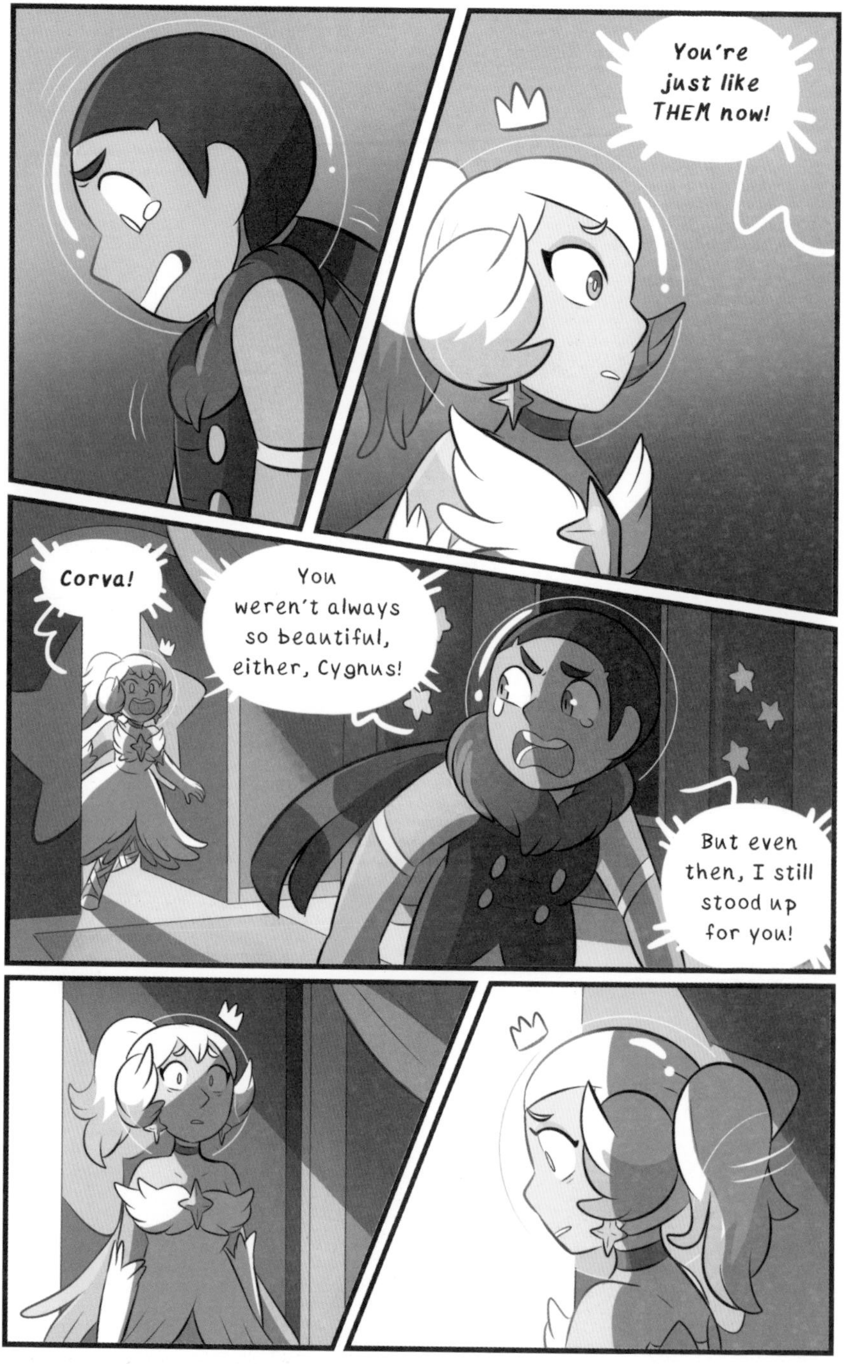
You're just like THEM now!
Corva!
You weren't always so beautiful, either, Cygnus!
But even then, I still stood up for you!

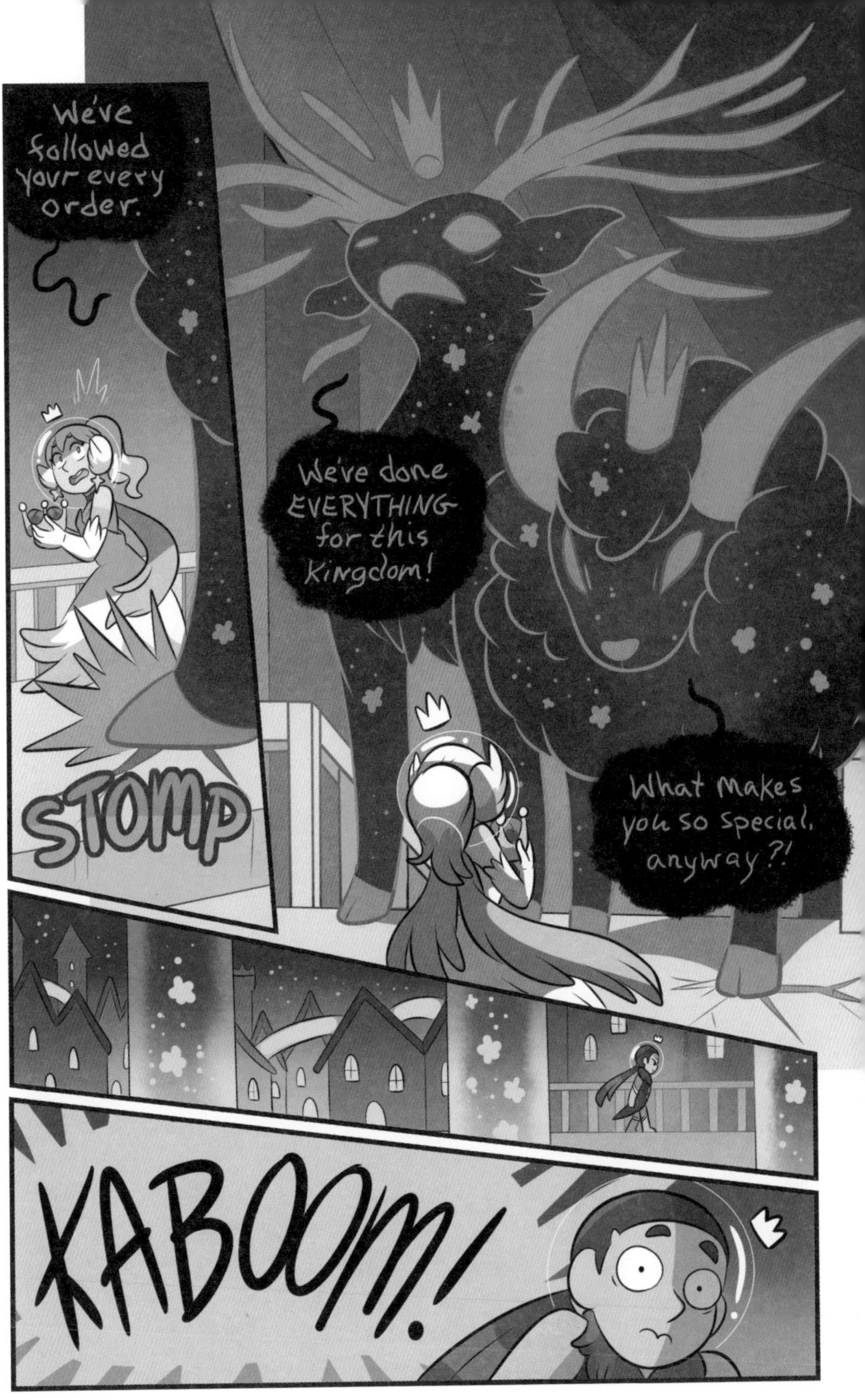
We've followed your every order.
We've done EVERYTHING for this kingdom!
STOMP
What makes you so special, anyway?!
KABOOM!

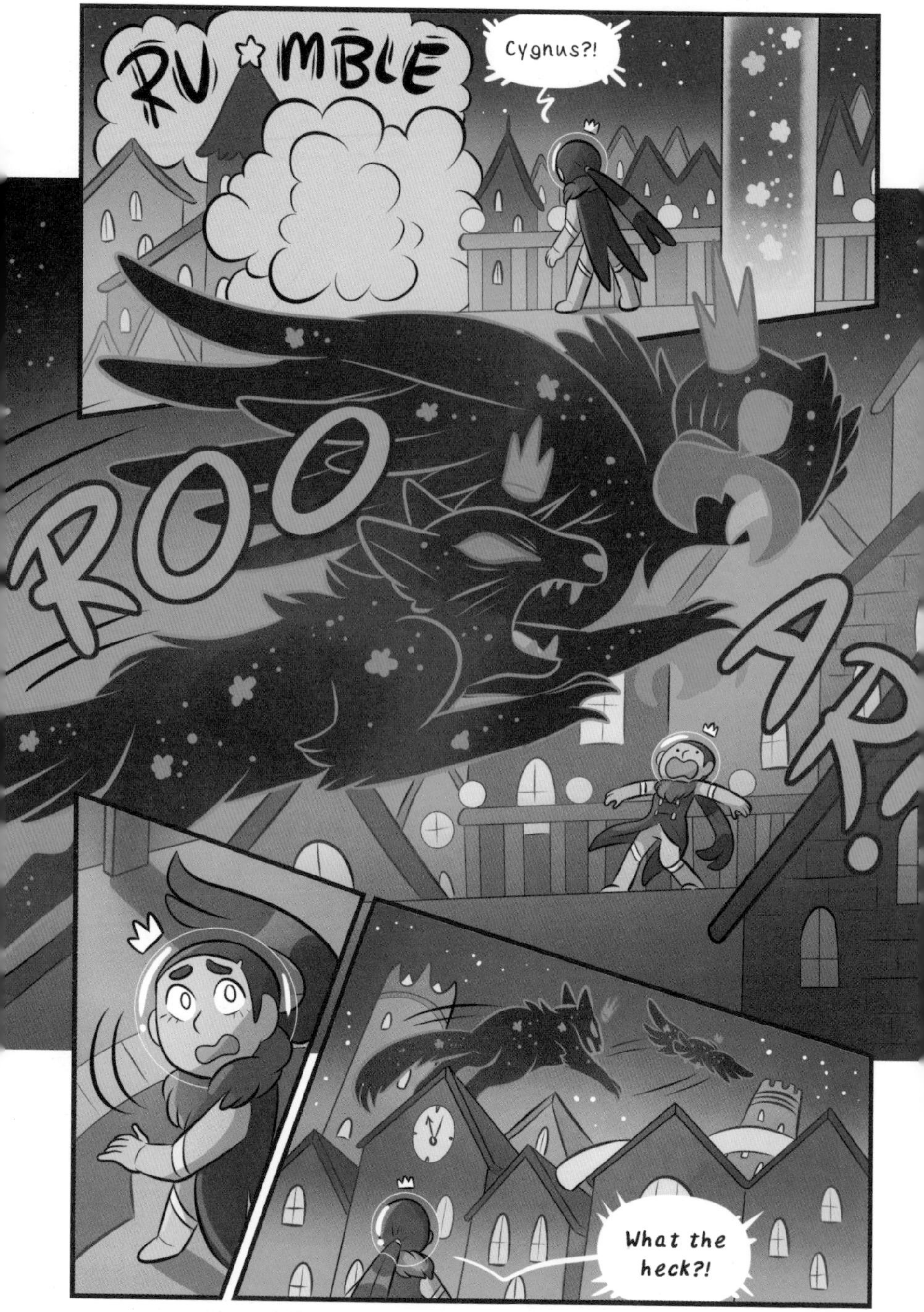
RUMBLE
Cygnus?!
ROOAR!
What the heck?!

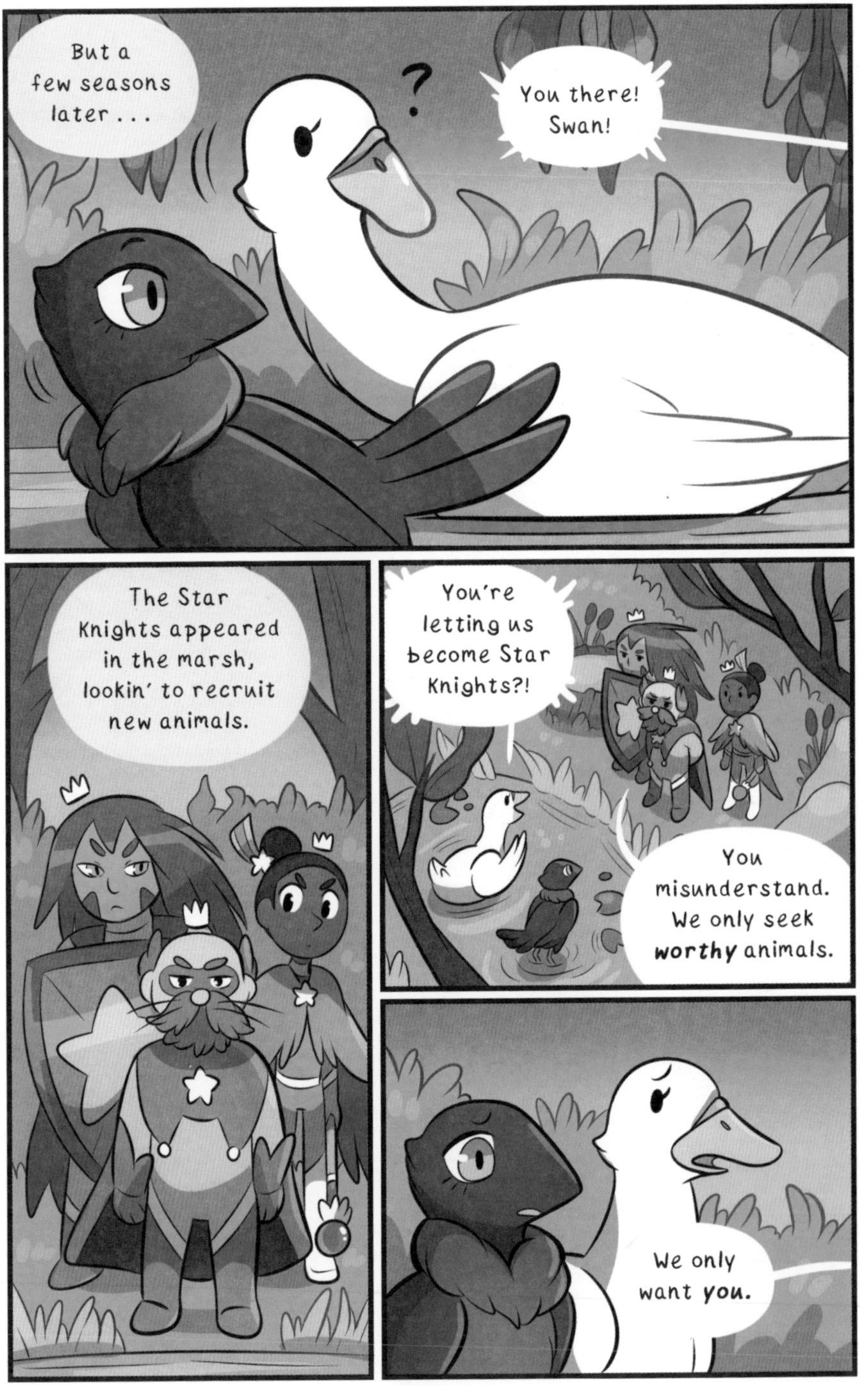
But a few seasons later . . .
?
You there! Swan!
The Star Knights appeared in the marsh, lookin' to recruit new animals.
You're letting us become Star Knights?!
You misunderstand. We only seek **worthy** animals.
We only want **you**.

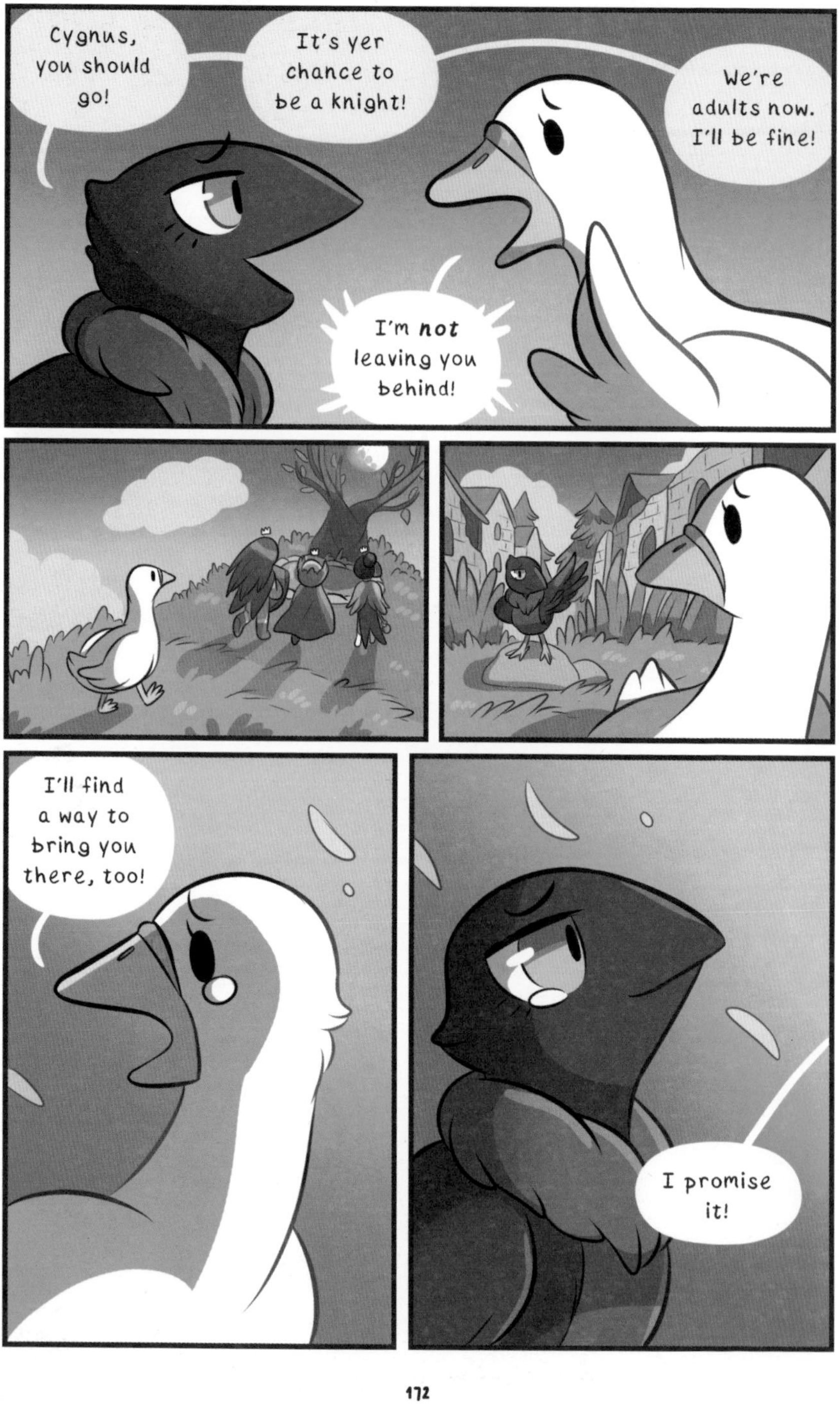
Cygnus, you should go!
It's yer chance to be a knight!
We're adults now. I'll be fine!
I'm **not** leaving you behind!
I'll find a way to bring you there, too!
I promise it!

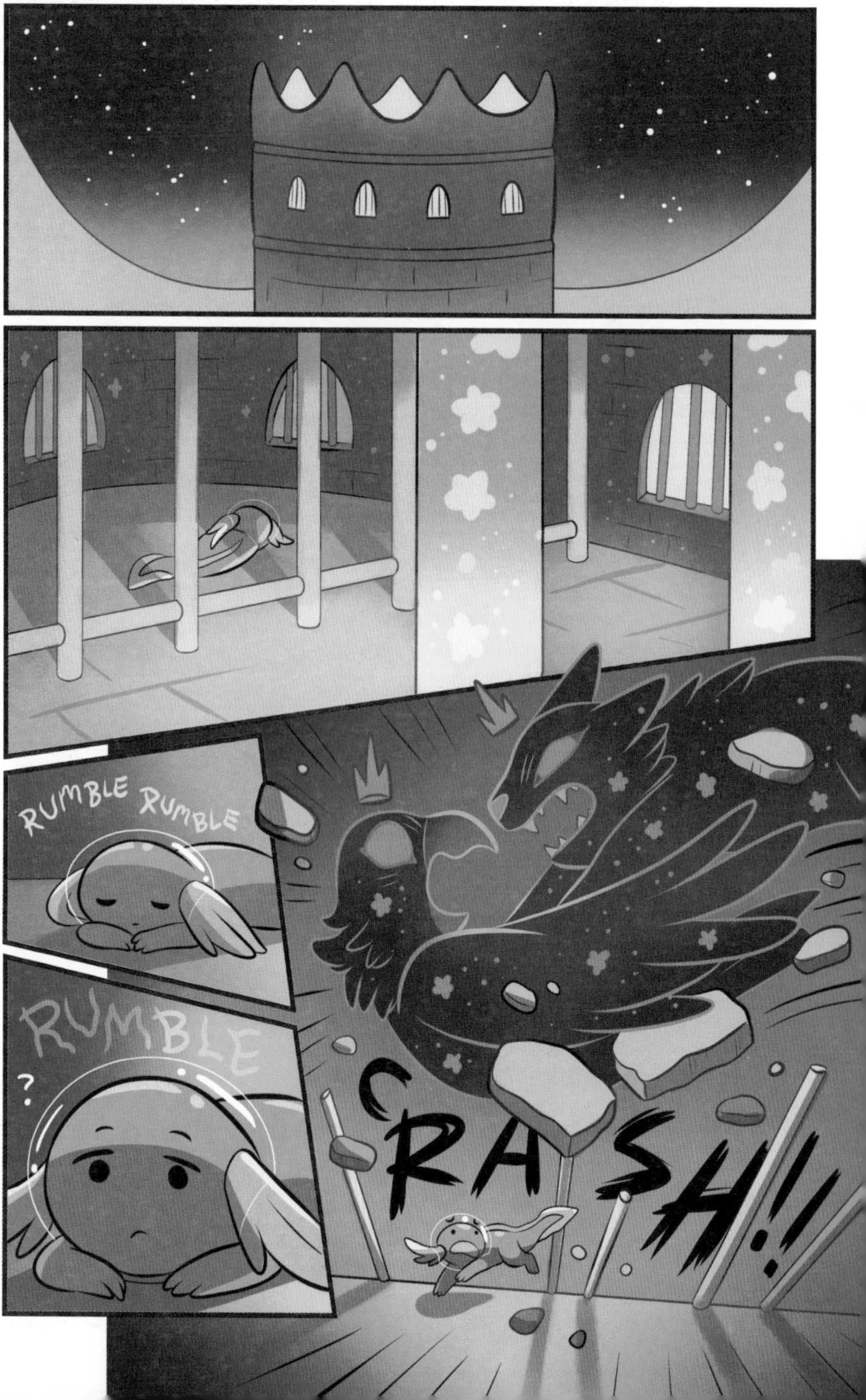
RUMBLE RUMBLE
RUMBLE
?
CRASH!!

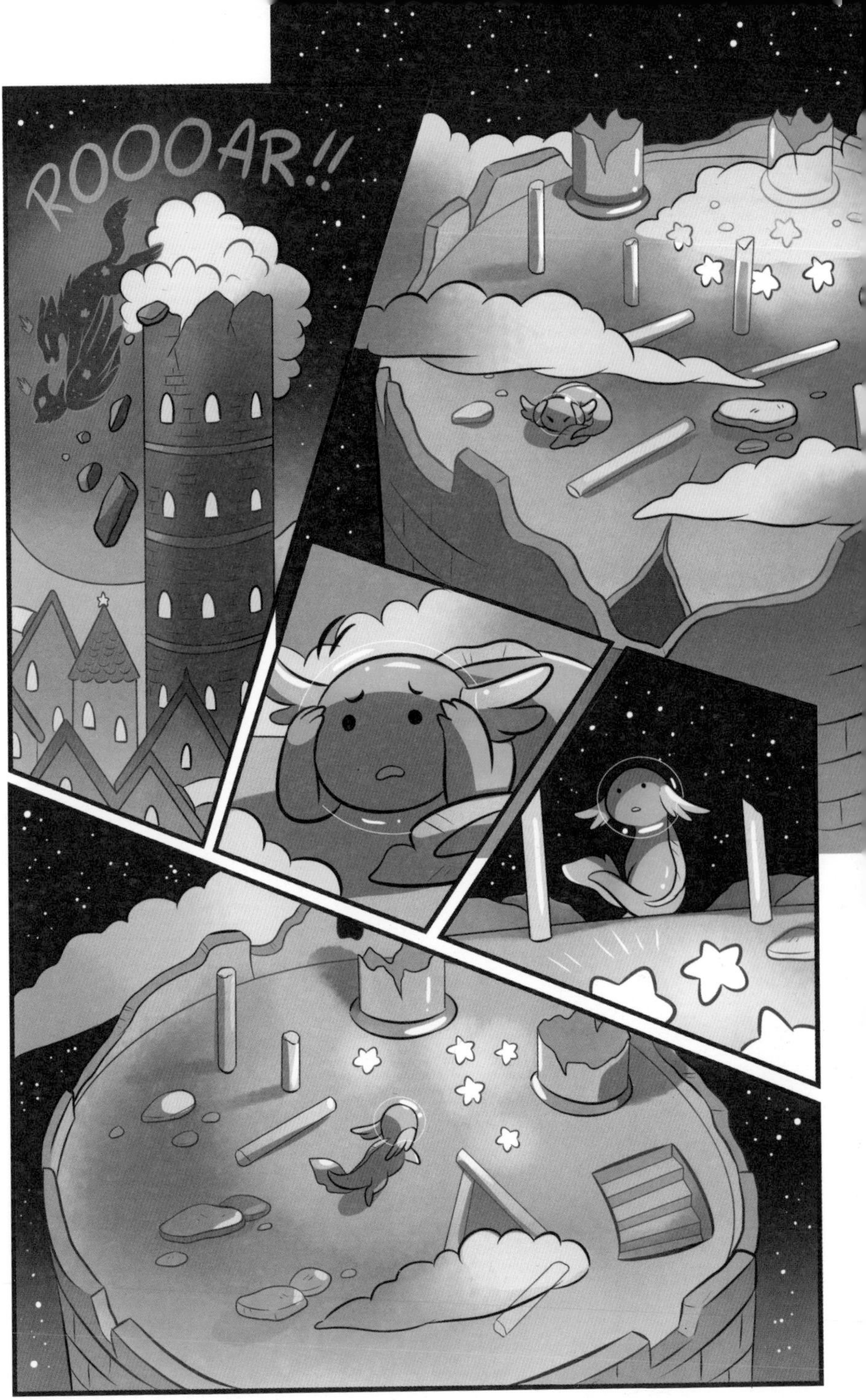
ROOOAR!!

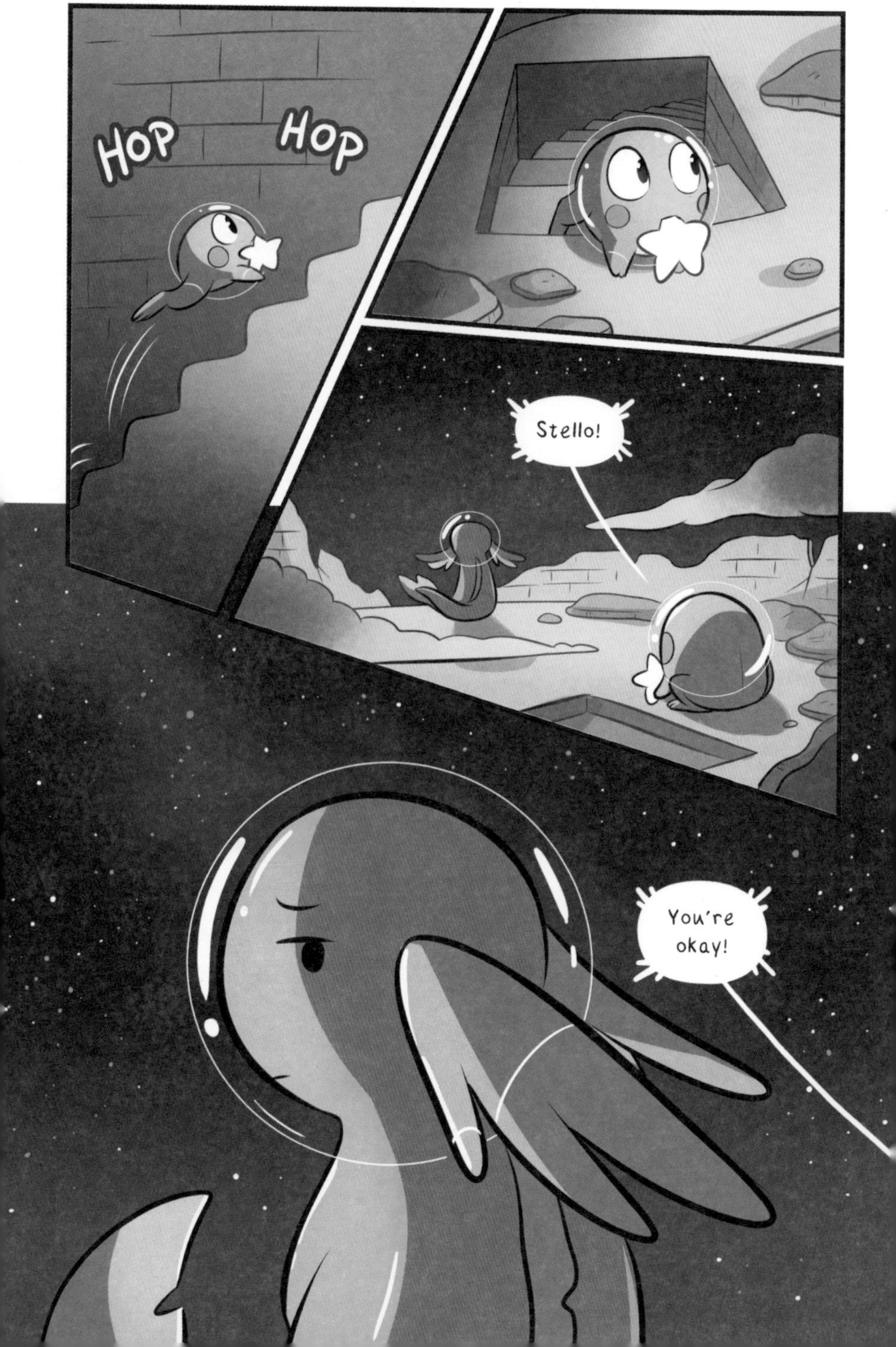
HOP
HOP
Stello!
You're okay!

Even if we return to the marsh, the animals will still hate us!
They'll still say those things about us!
About me.
Stello—
If the stars didn't exist, we would have normal lives!

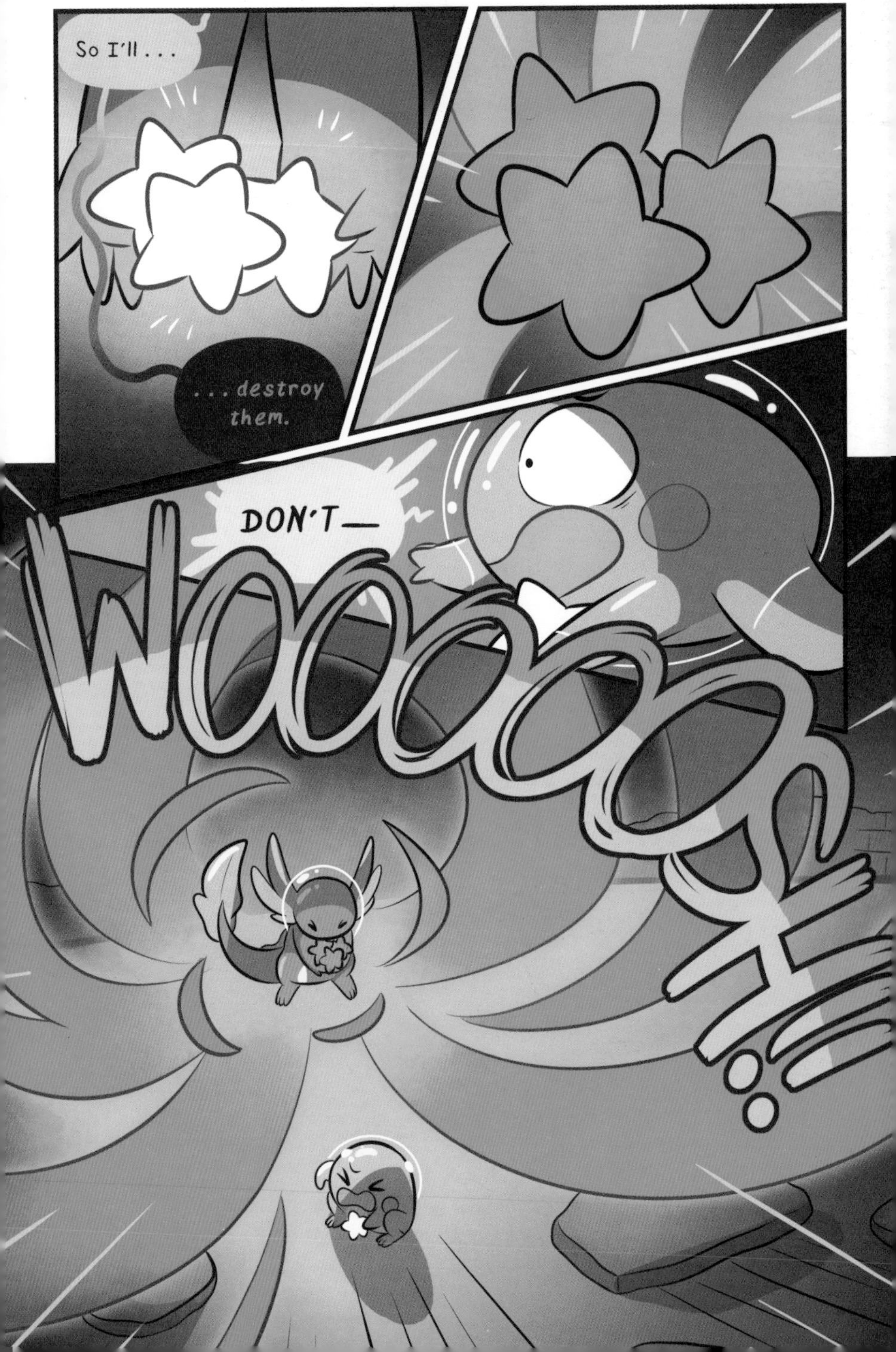
So I'll . . .
. . . destroy them.
DON'T—
WOOOOOOSH!!

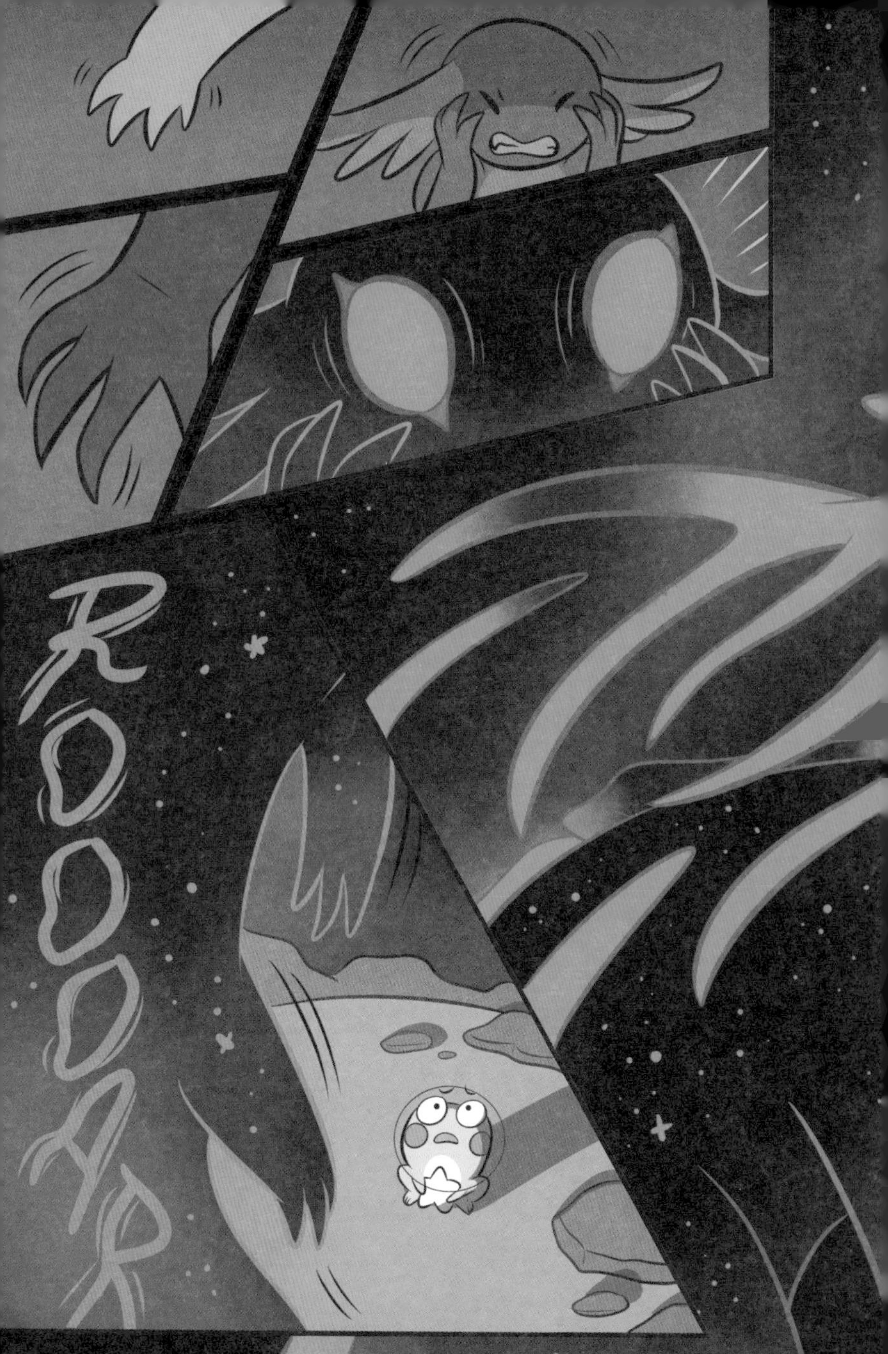
ROOOAR

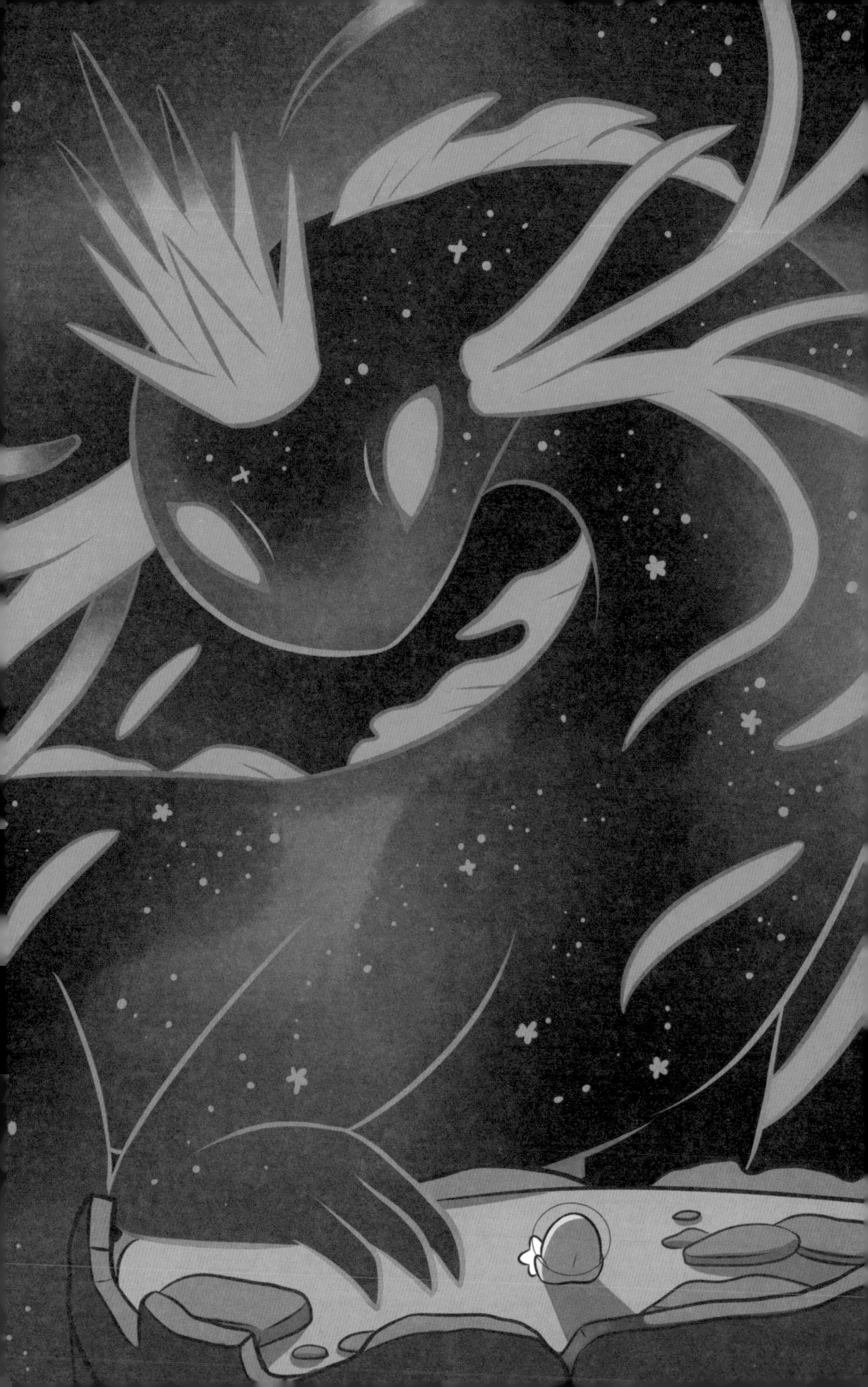

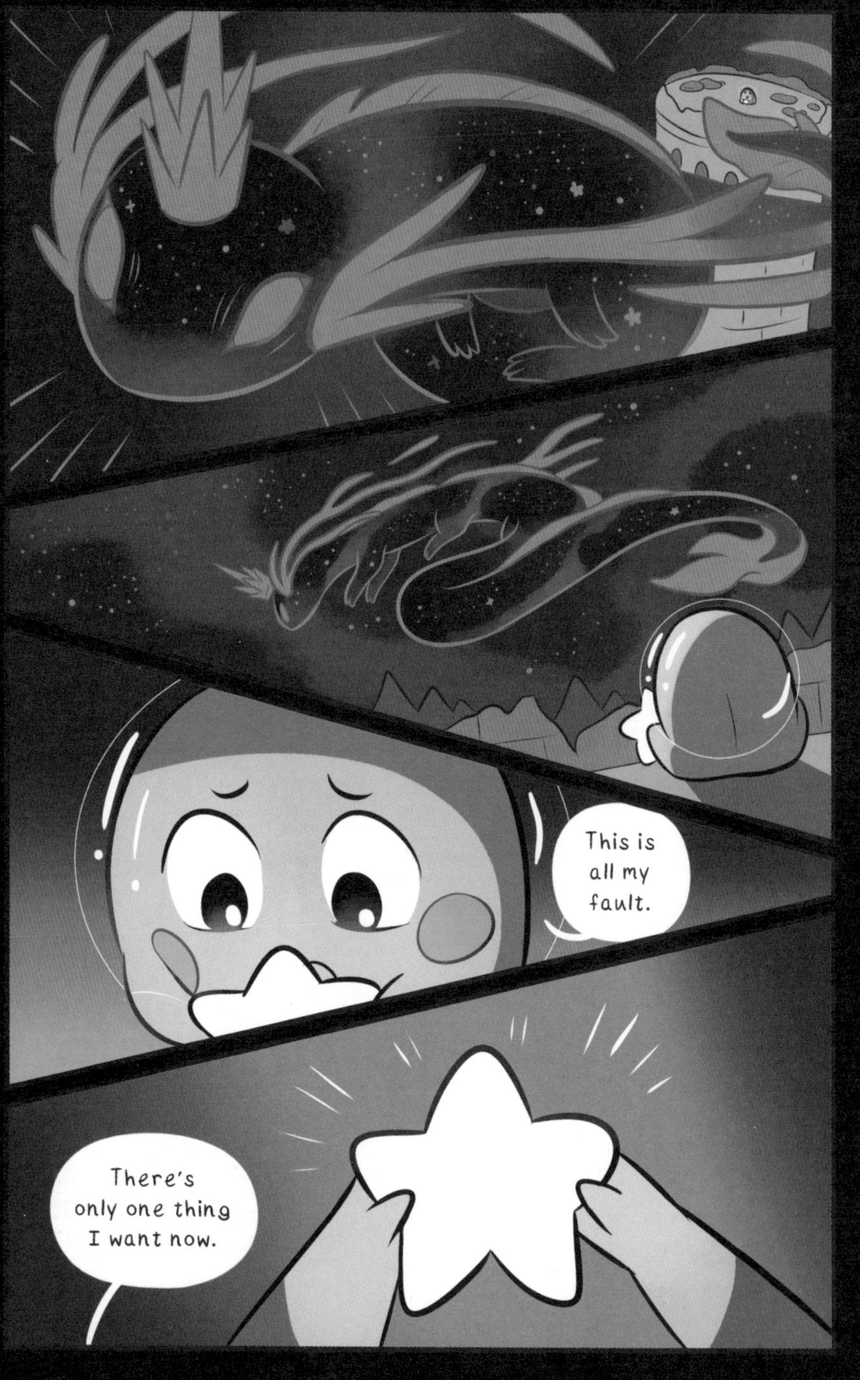
This is all my fault.
There's only one thing I want now.

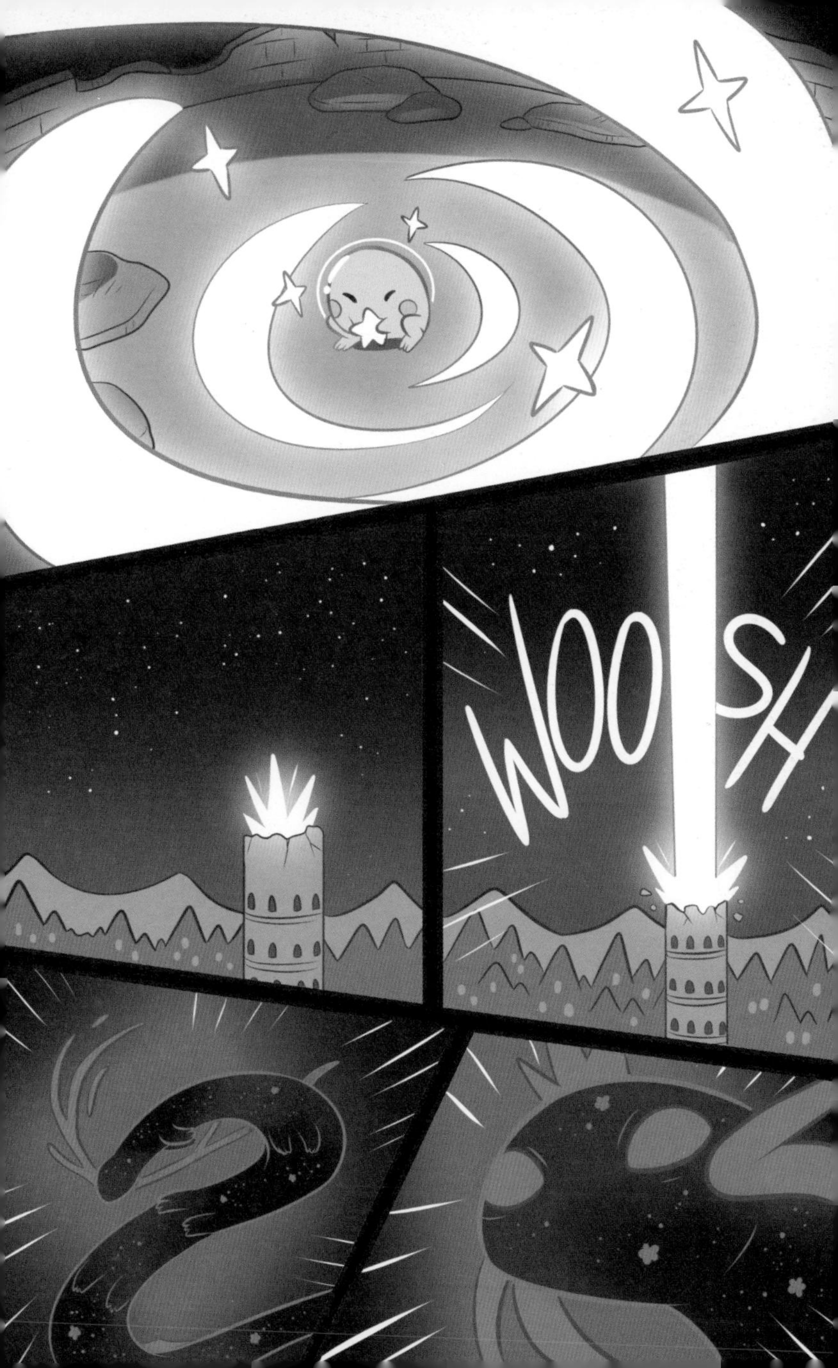
WOOSH

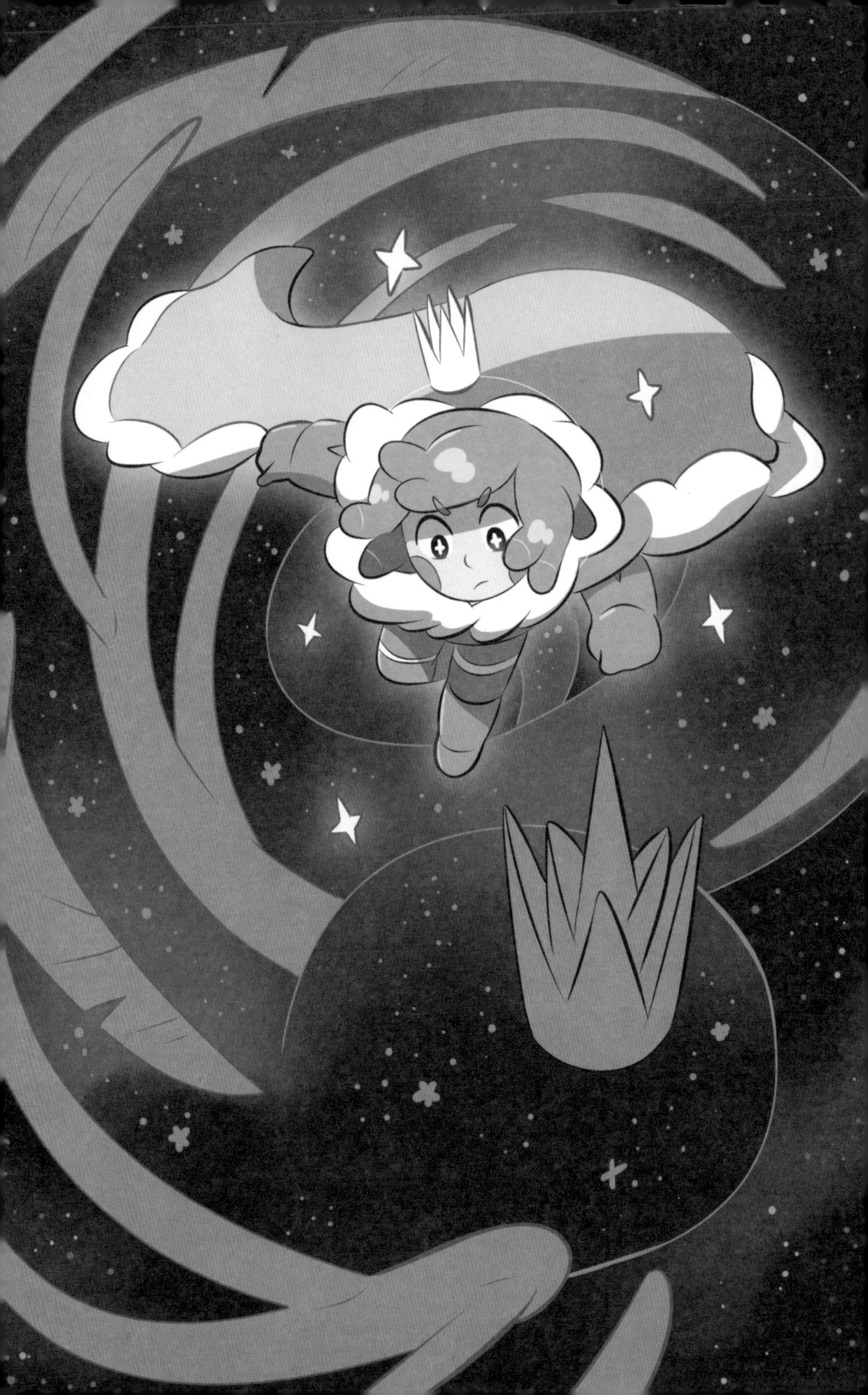

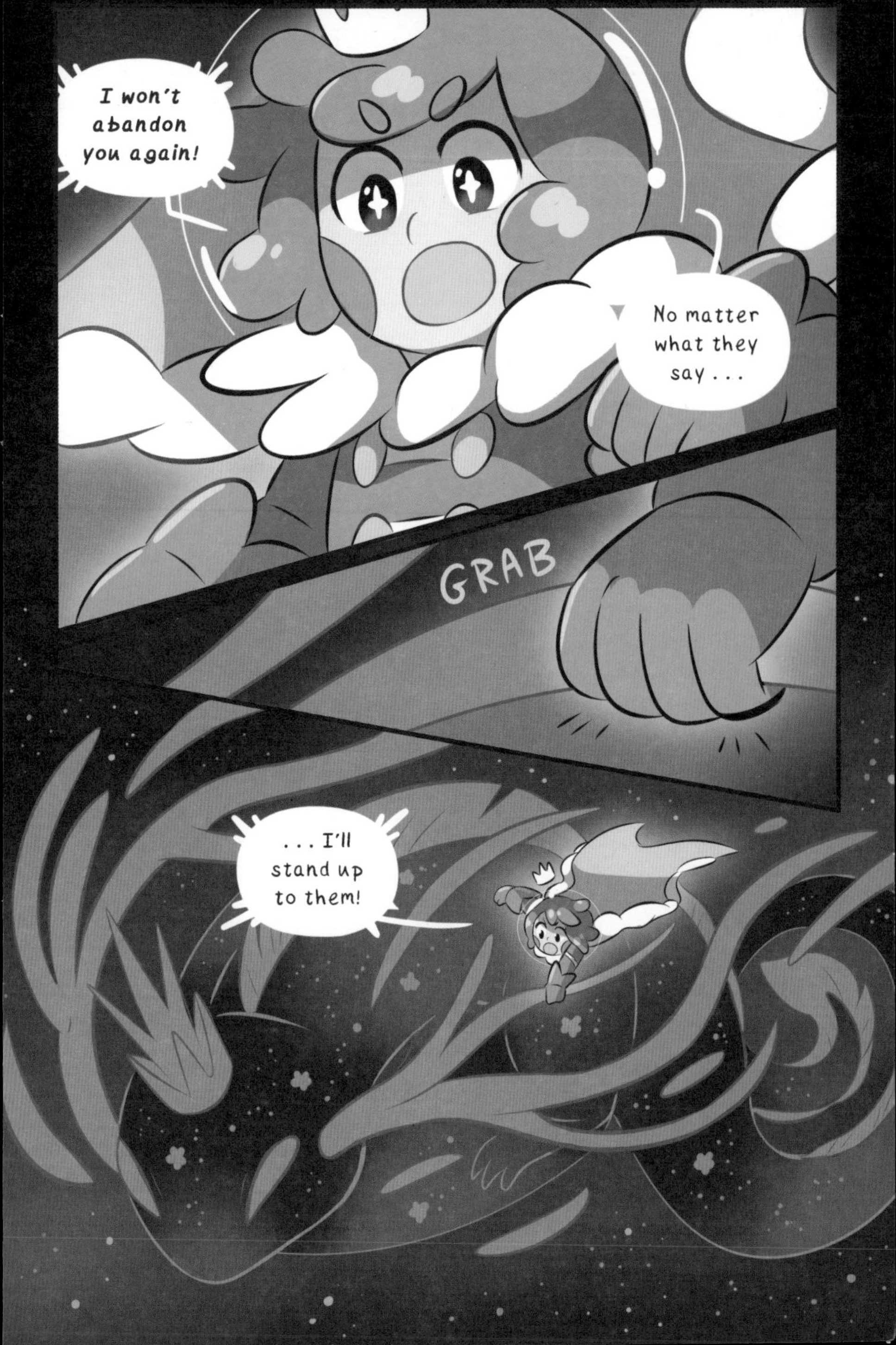
I won't abandon you again!
No matter what they say . . .
GRAB
. . . I'll stand up to them!

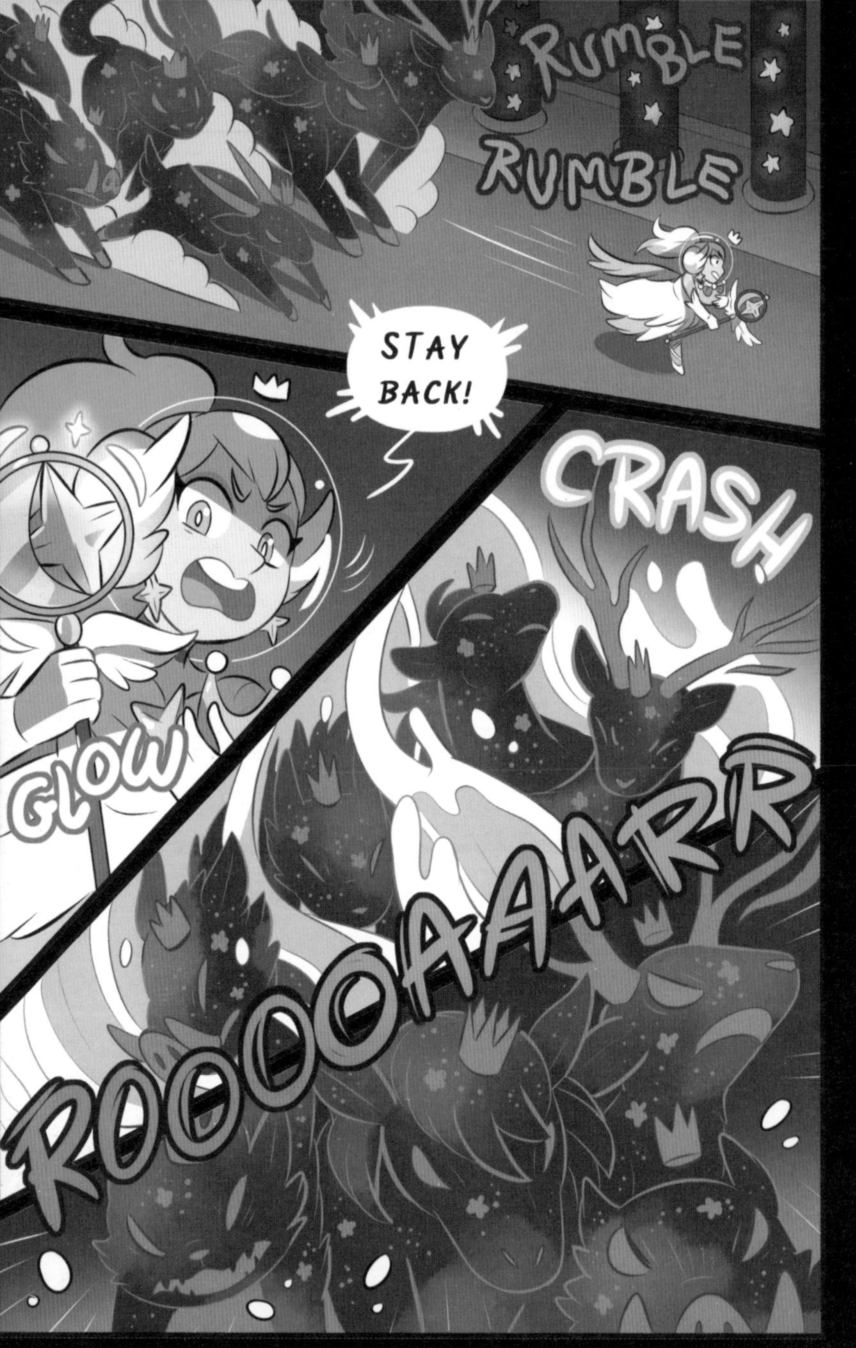
RUMBLE
RUMBLE
STAY BACK!
GLOW
CRASH
ROOOOAAARR

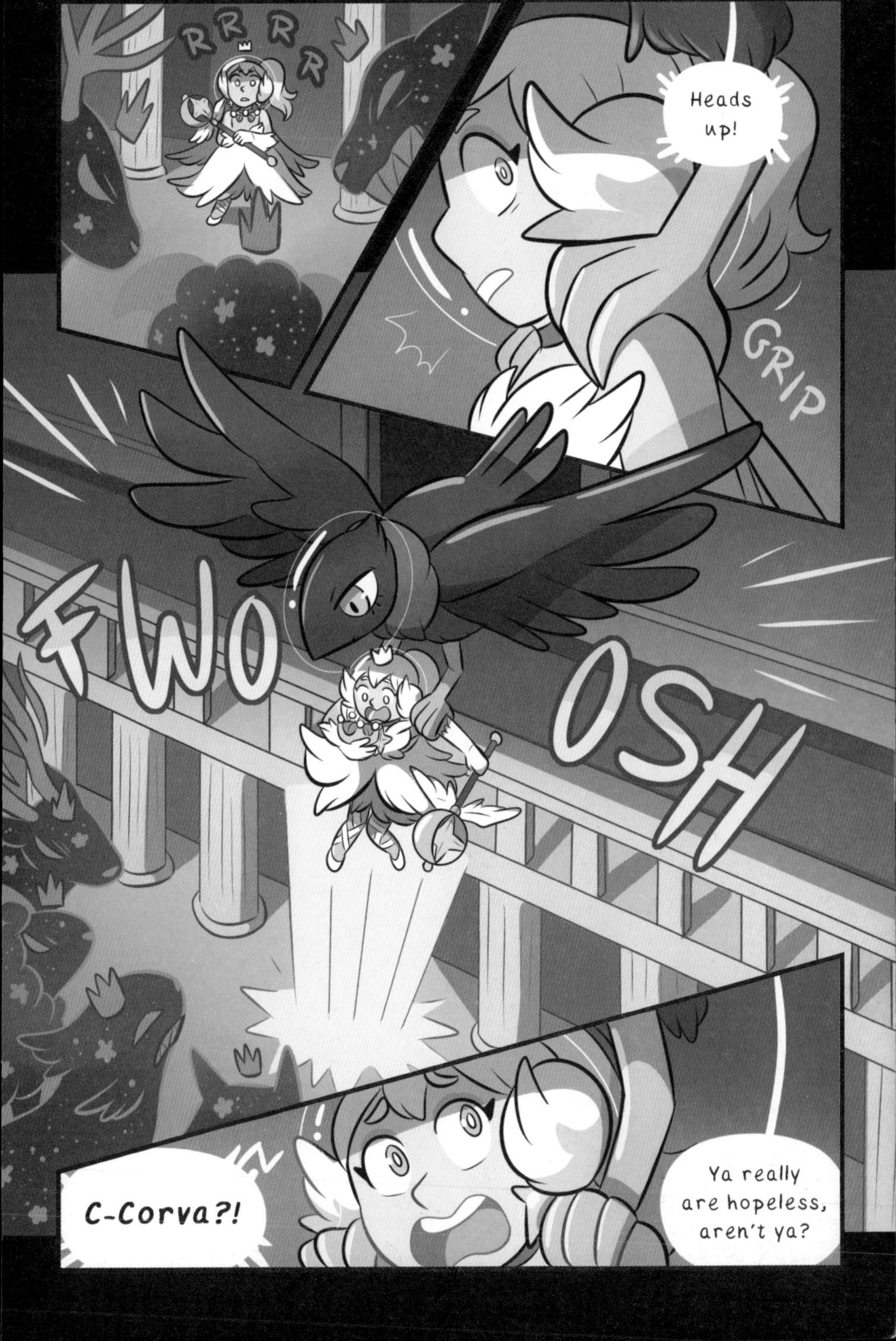
RRRRR
Heads up!
GRIP
FWOOSH
C-Corva?!
Ya really are hopeless, aren't ya?

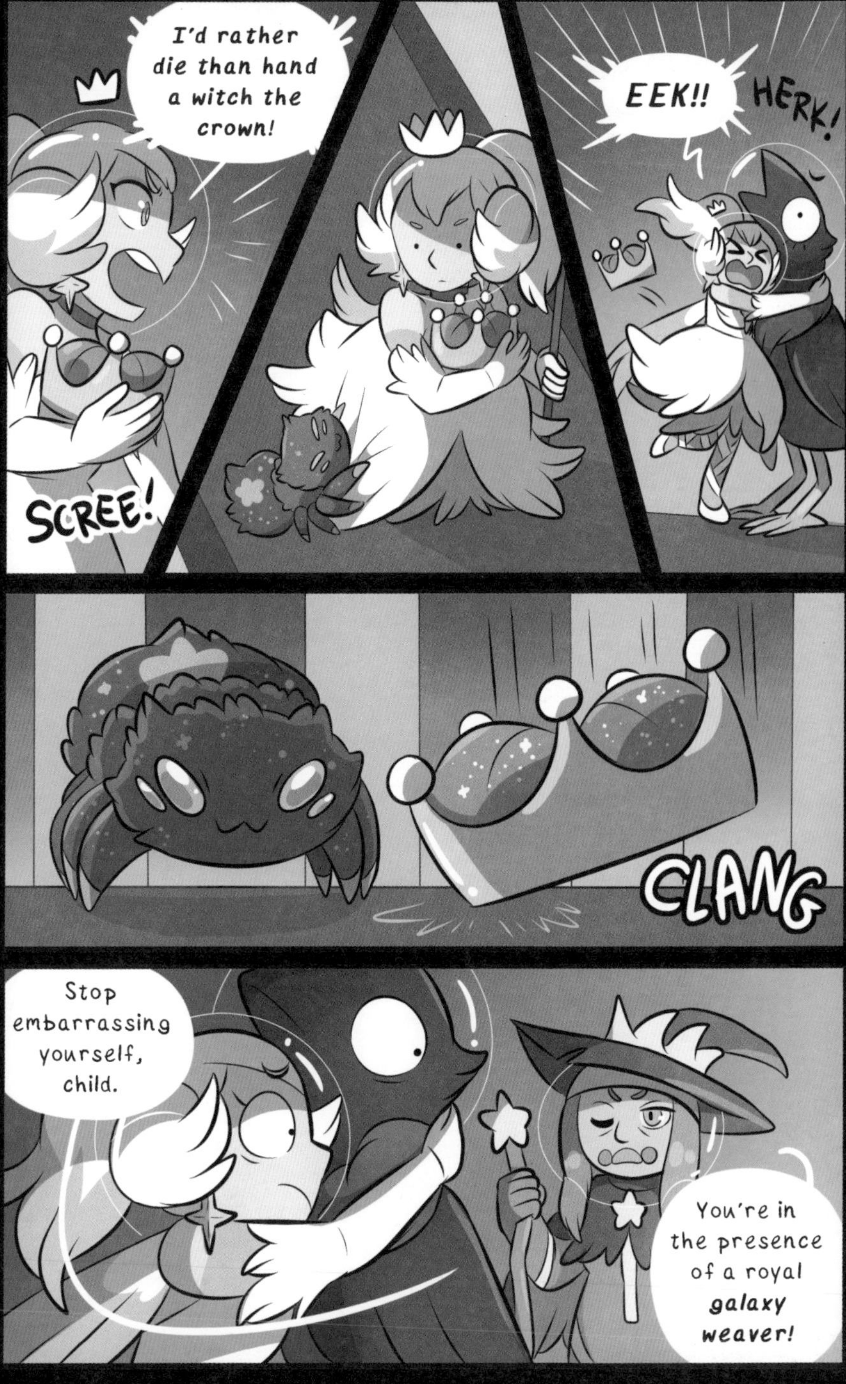
I'd rather die than hand a witch the crown!
SCREE!
EEK!!
HERK!
CLANG
Stop embarrassing yourself, child.
You're in the presence of a royal galaxy weaver!

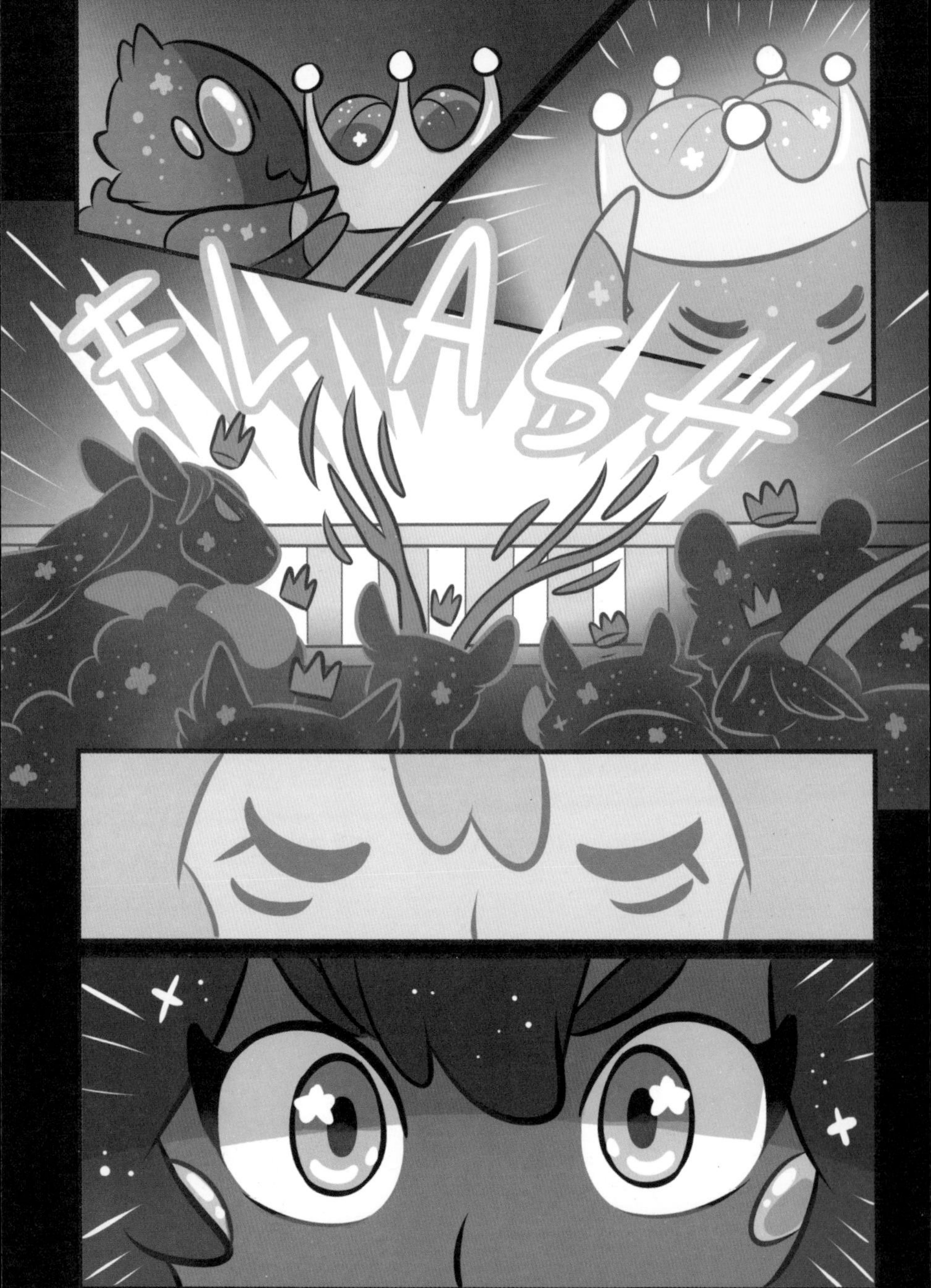
FLASH

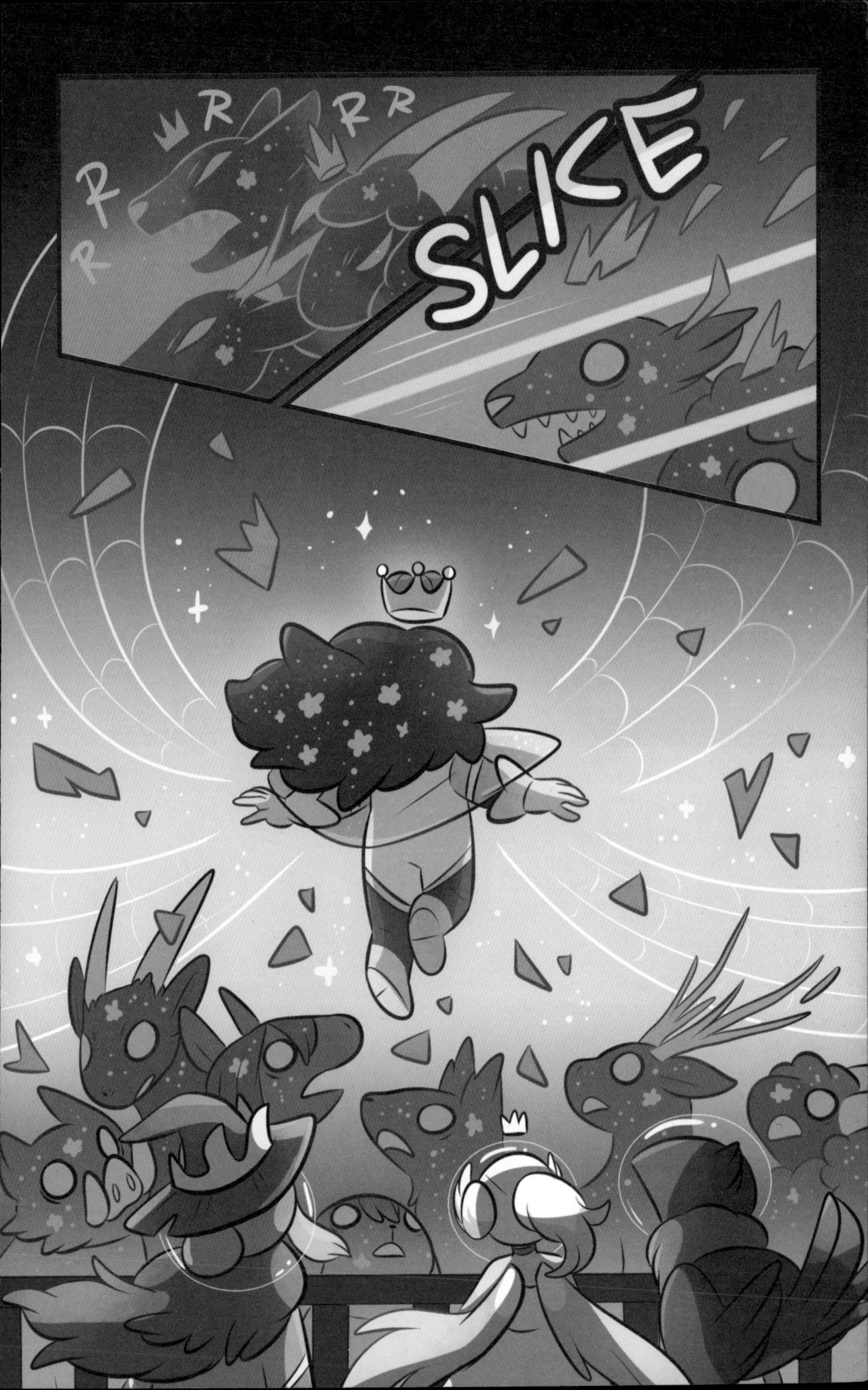
RRRRRRR
SLICE

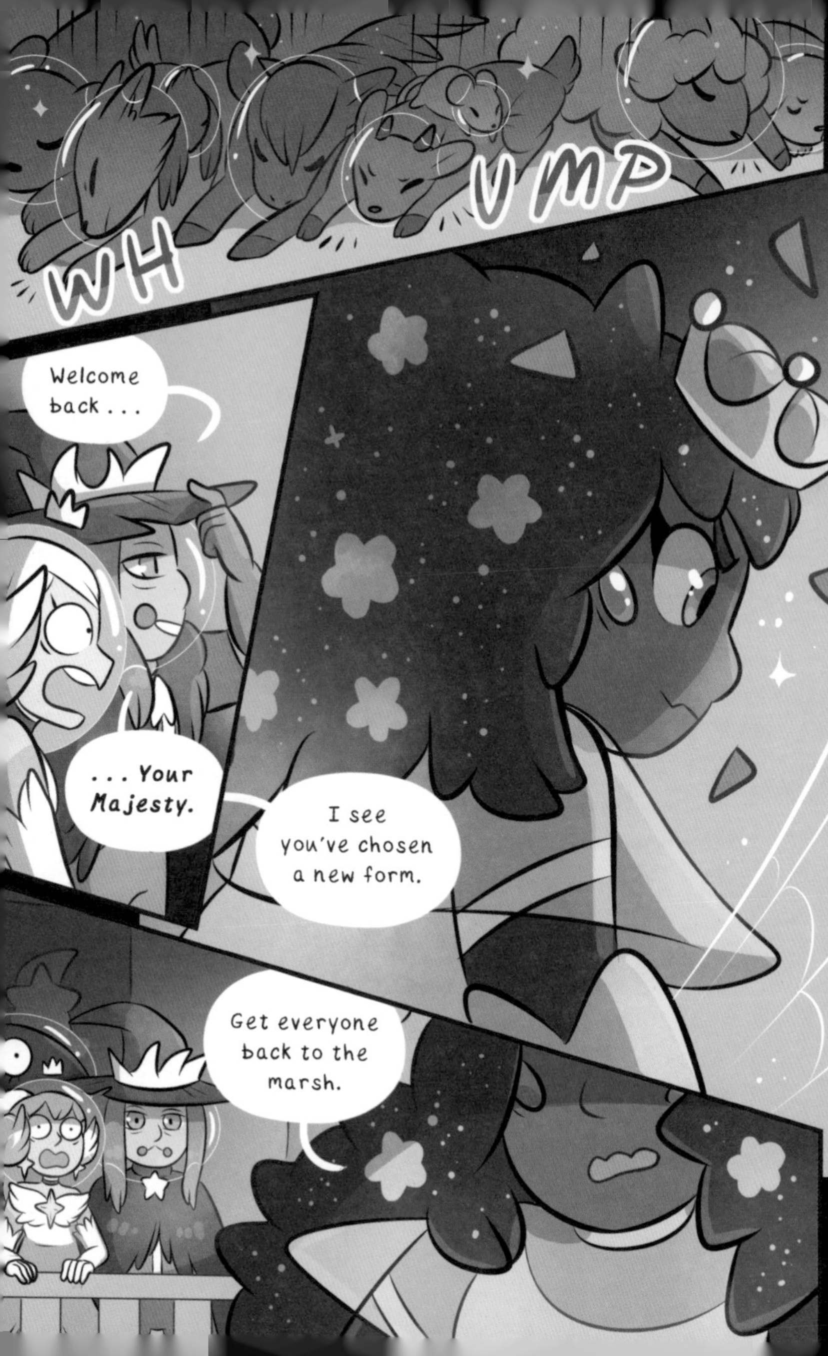
WH
UMP
Welcome back . . .
. . . Your Majesty.
I see you've chosen a new form.
Get everyone back to the marsh.

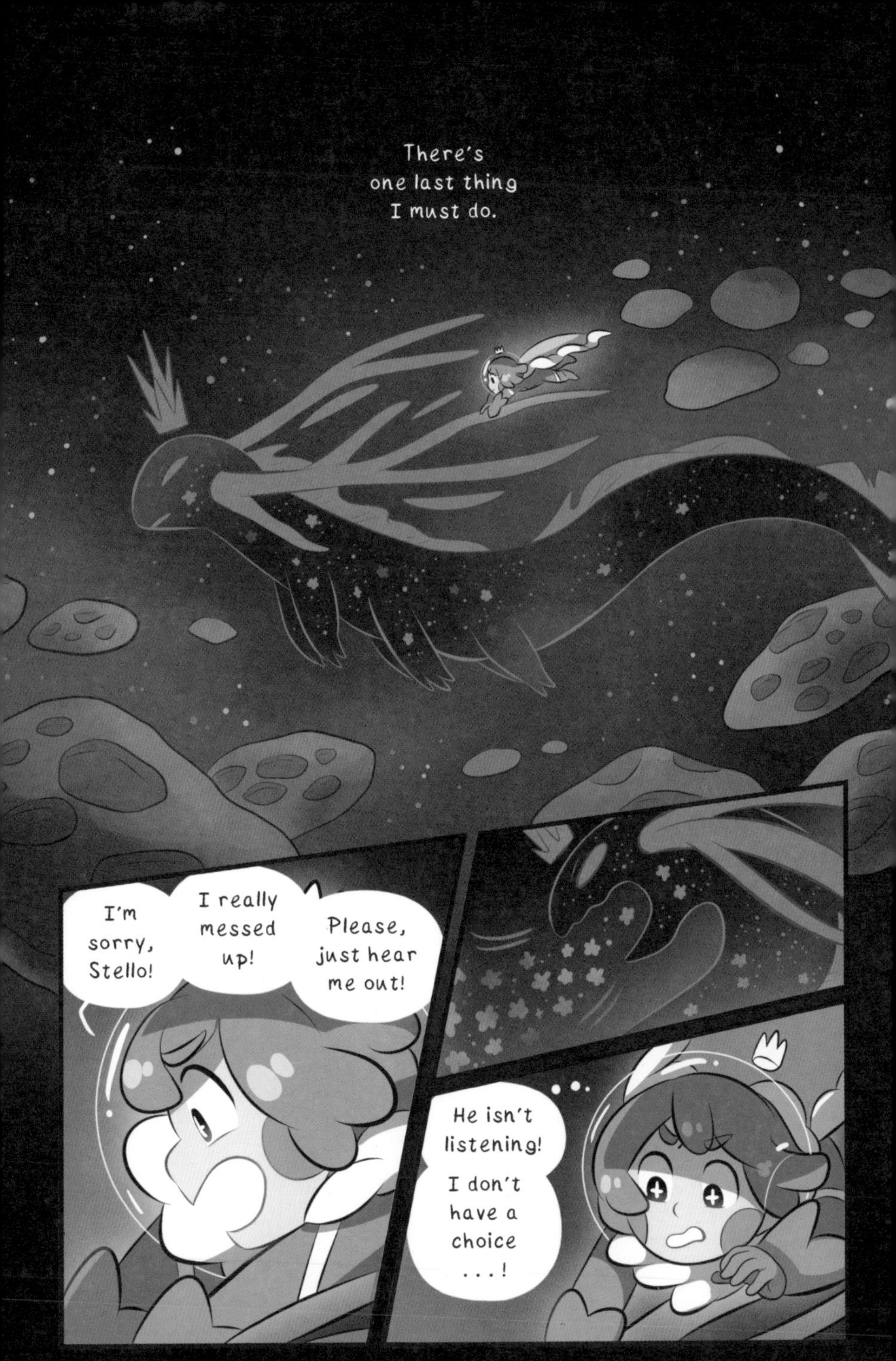
There's one last thing I must do.
I'm sorry, Stello!
I really messed up!
Please, just hear me out!
He isn't listening!
I don't have a choice . . . !

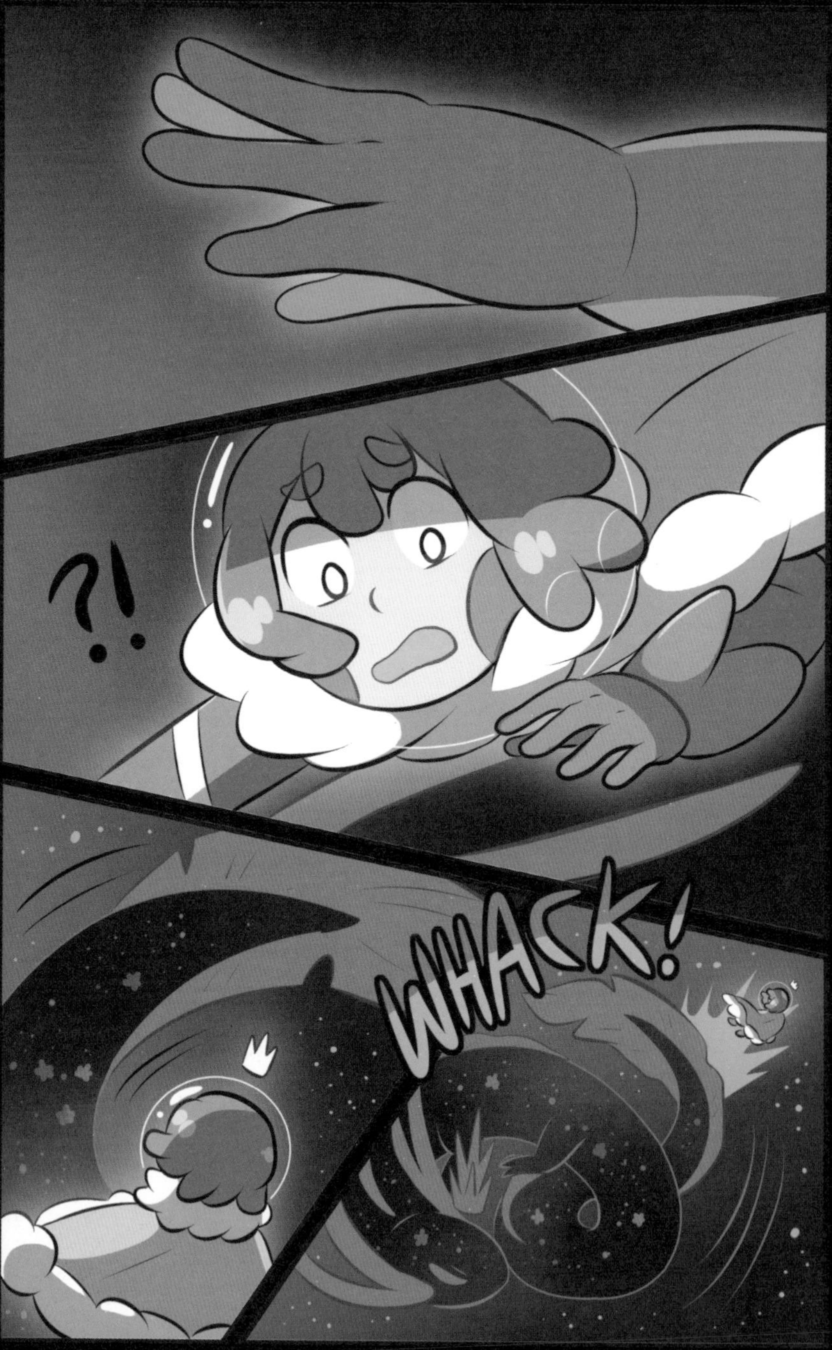
?!
WHACK!

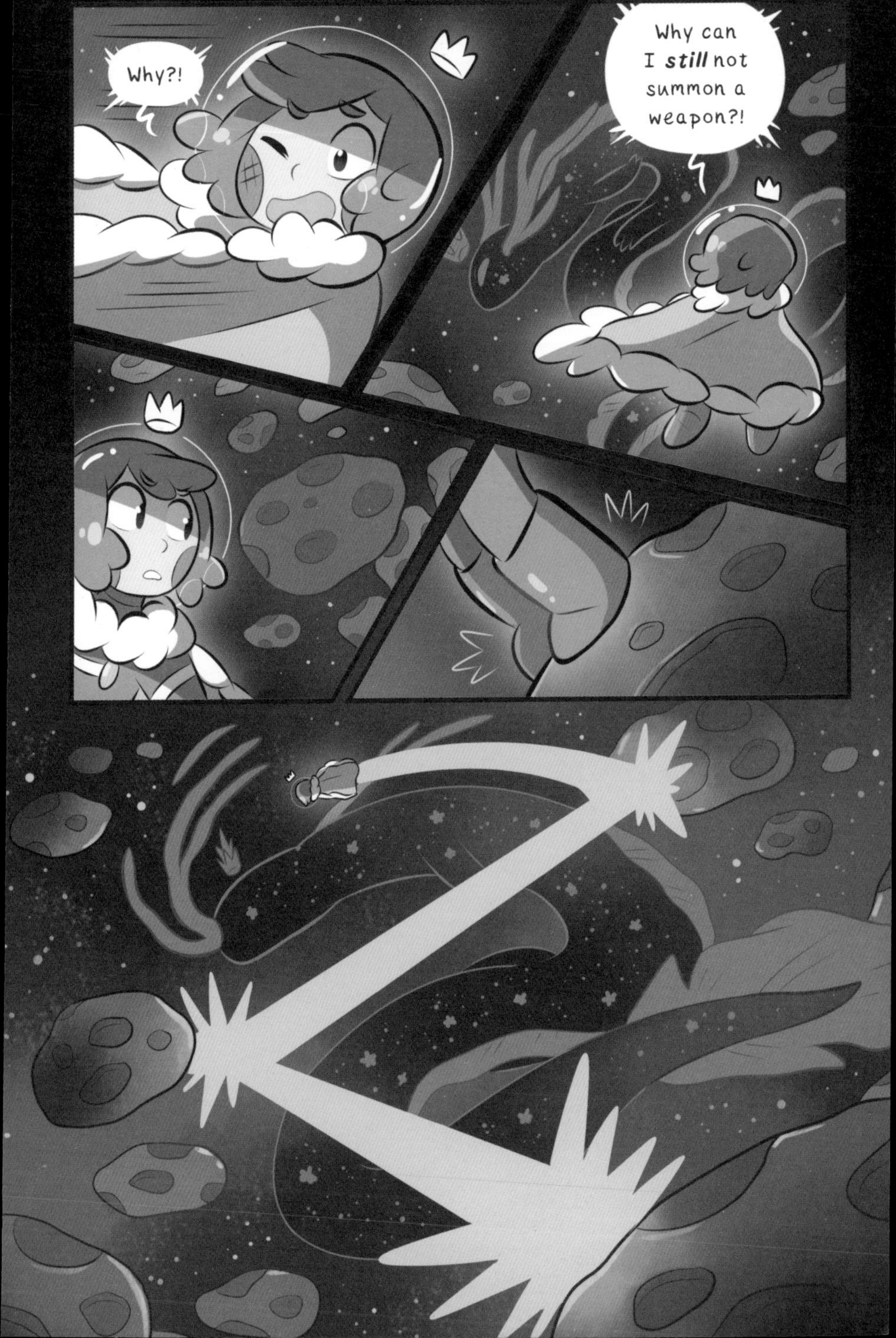
Why?!
Why can I ***still*** not summon a weapon?!

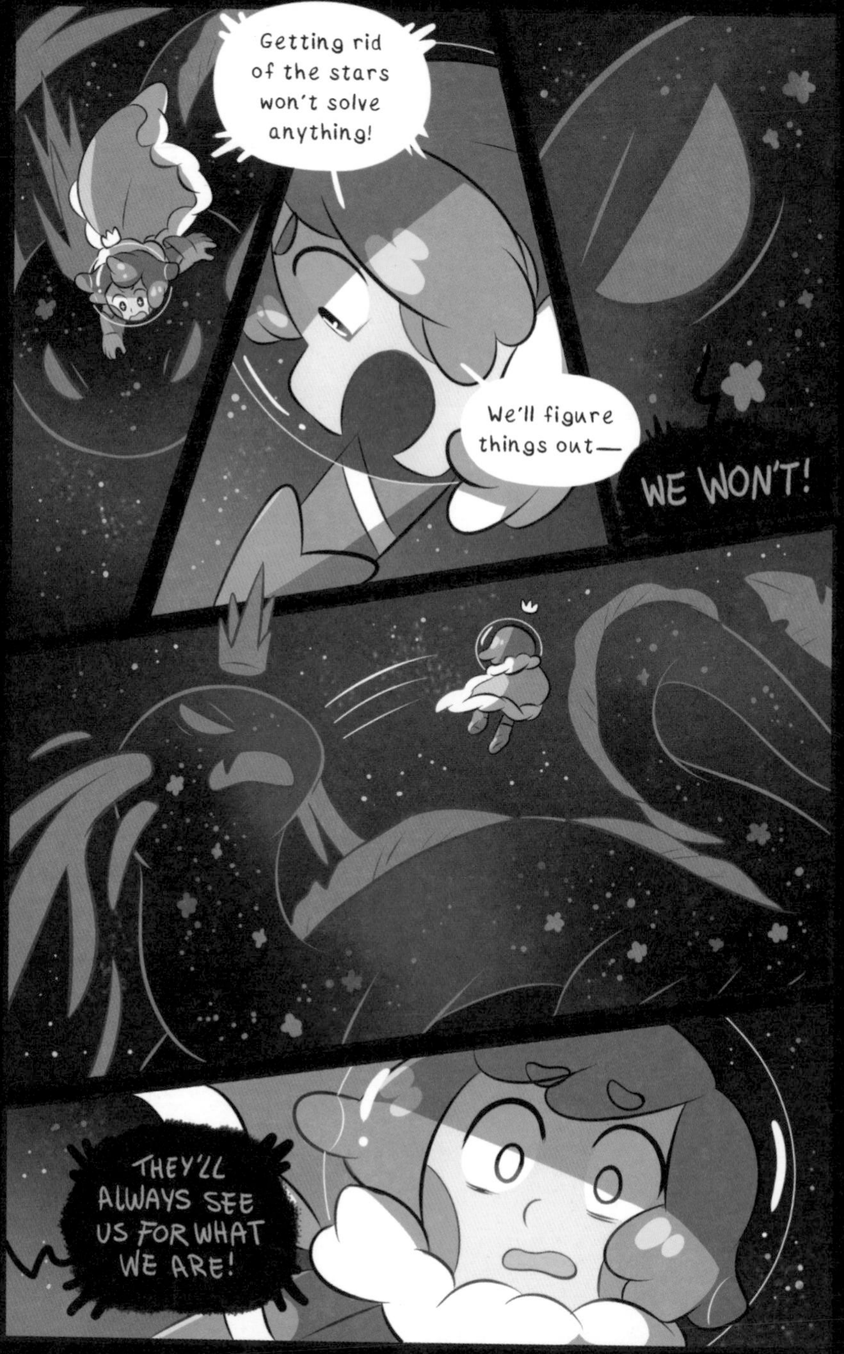
Getting rid of the stars won't solve anything!
We'll figure things out—
WE WON'T!
THEY'LL ALWAYS SEE US FOR WHAT WE ARE!

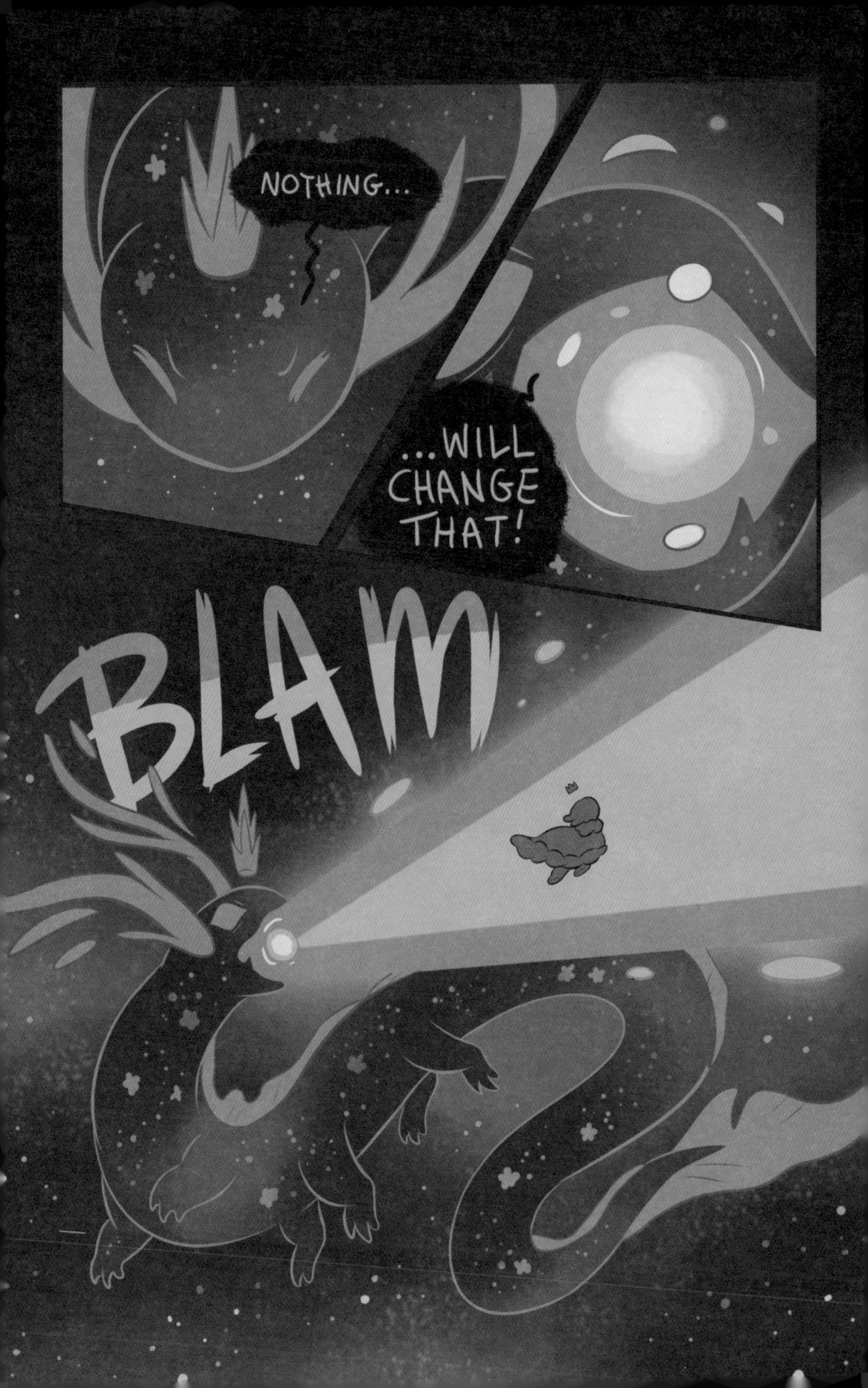
NOTHING...
...WILL CHANGE THAT!
BLAM

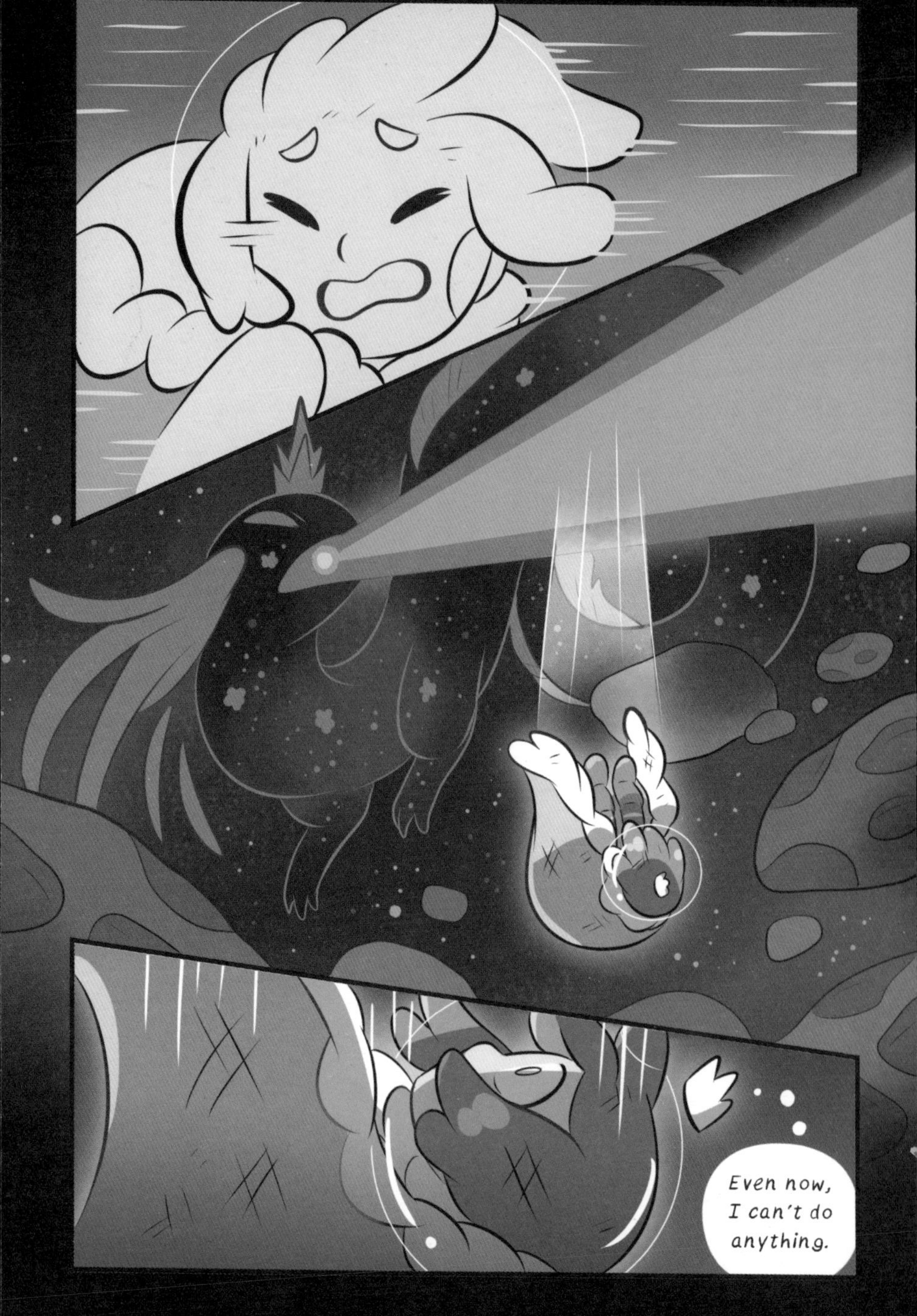
Even now,
I can't do
anything.

Am I really not worthy of the stars . . . ?
What are you doing, Tad?!
Aren't you supposed to be his knight?!

WHUMP
W-web?!
The creepy spider and the vile frog.
Looks like I have to help you out again.
Who knew **WE'D** be the ones to save the universe?

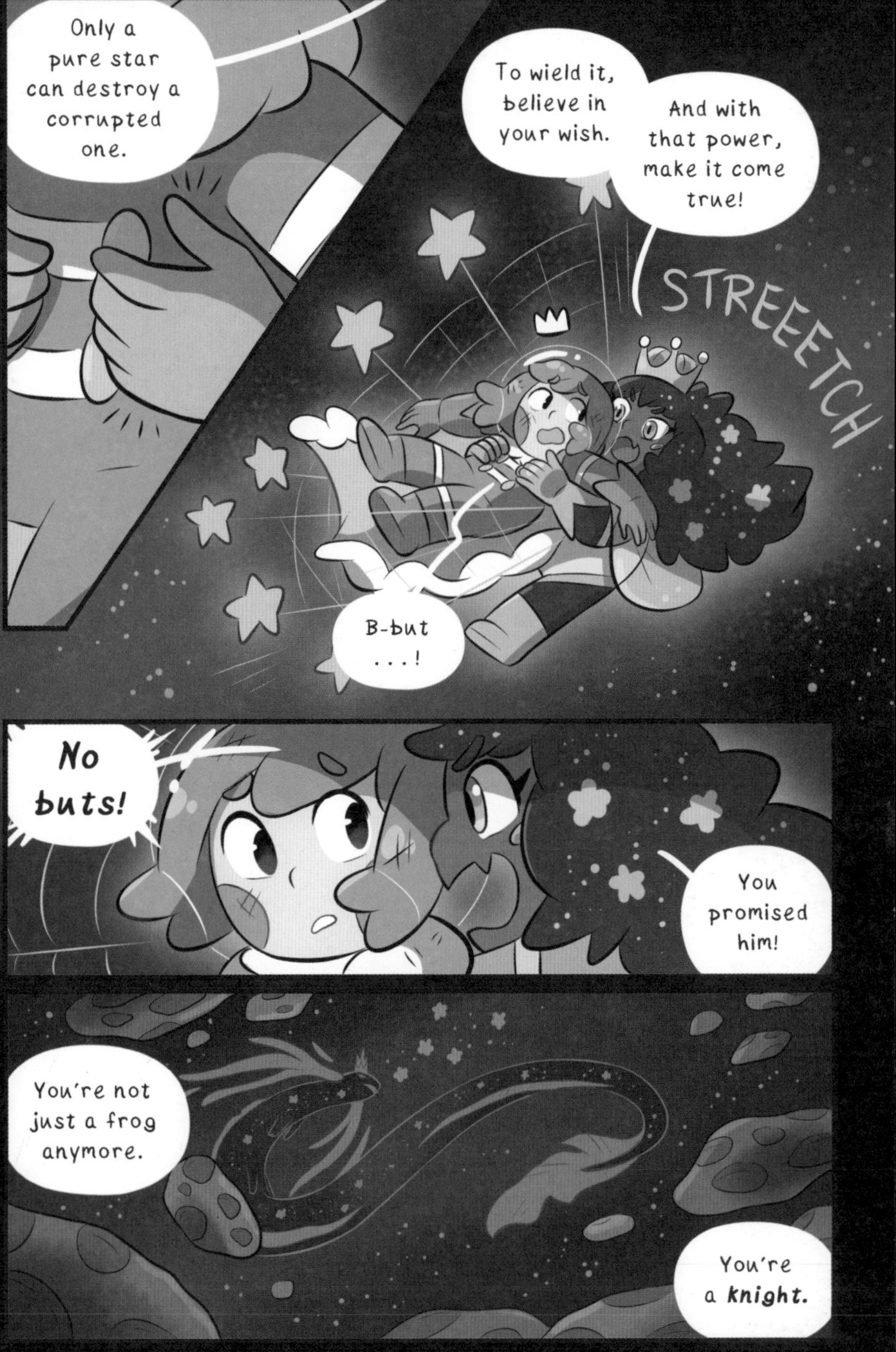
Only a pure star can destroy a corrupted one.
To wield it, believe in your wish.
And with that power, make it come true!
STREEETCH
B-but . . . !
No buts!
You promised him!
You're not just a frog anymore.
You're a knight.

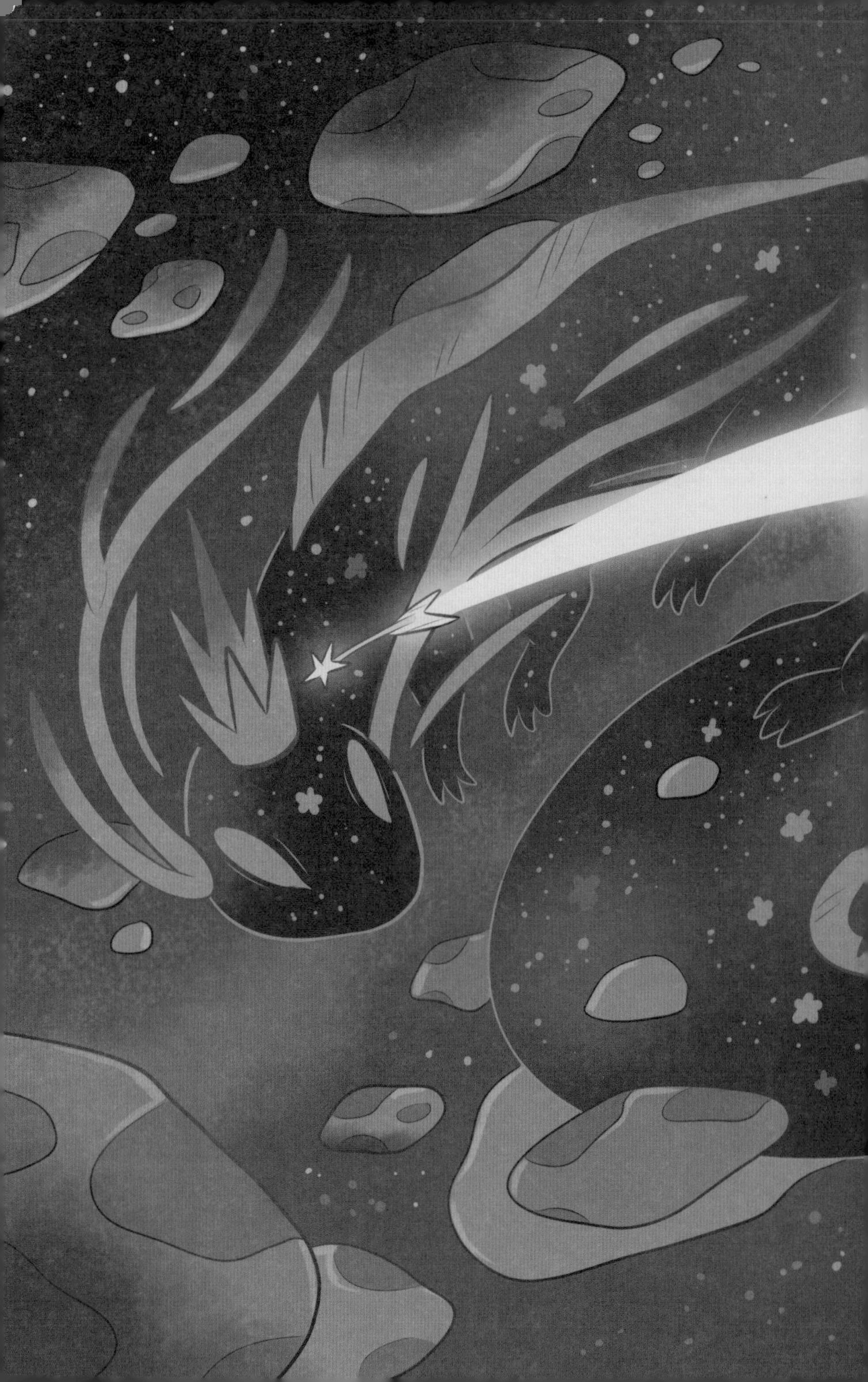

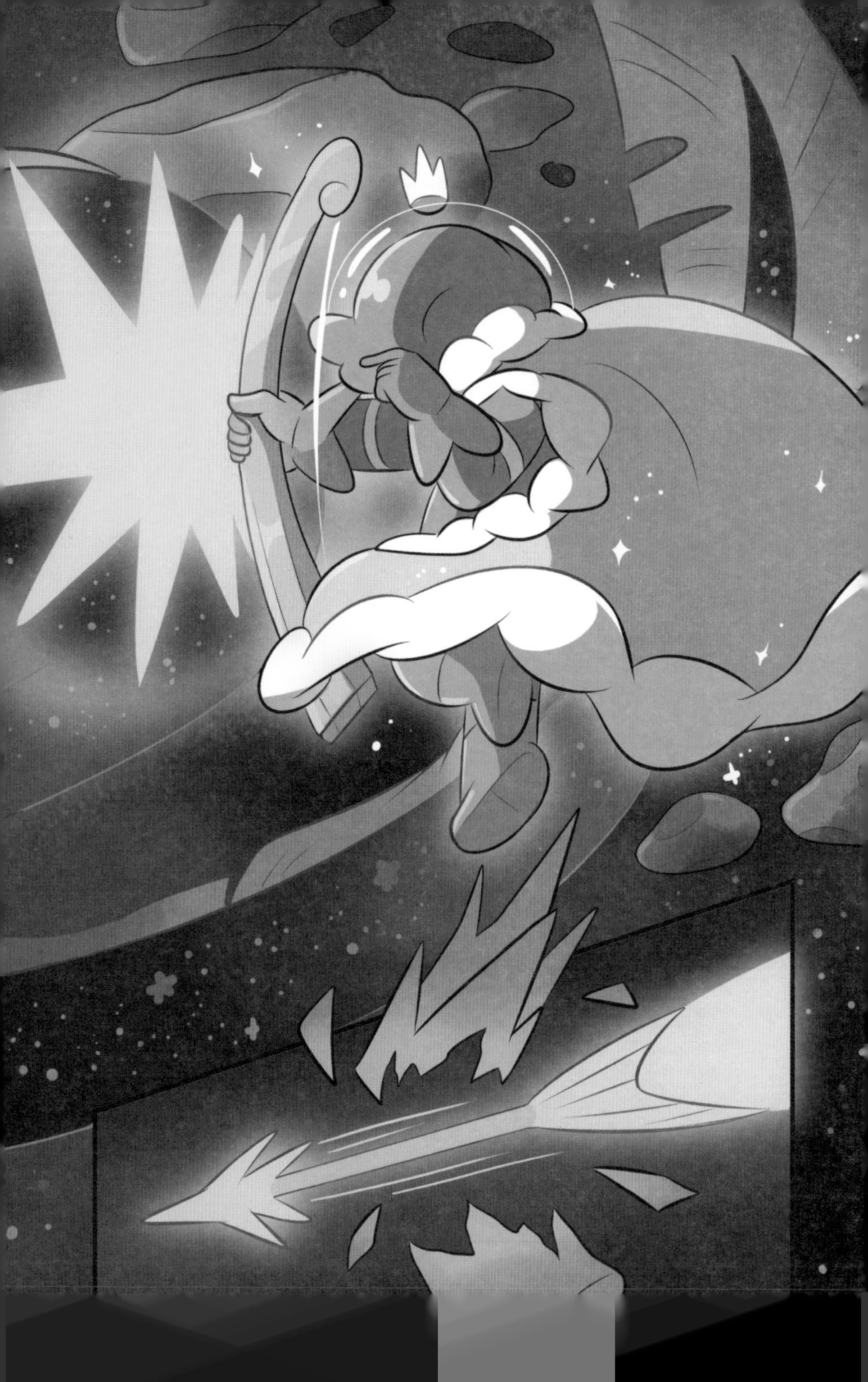

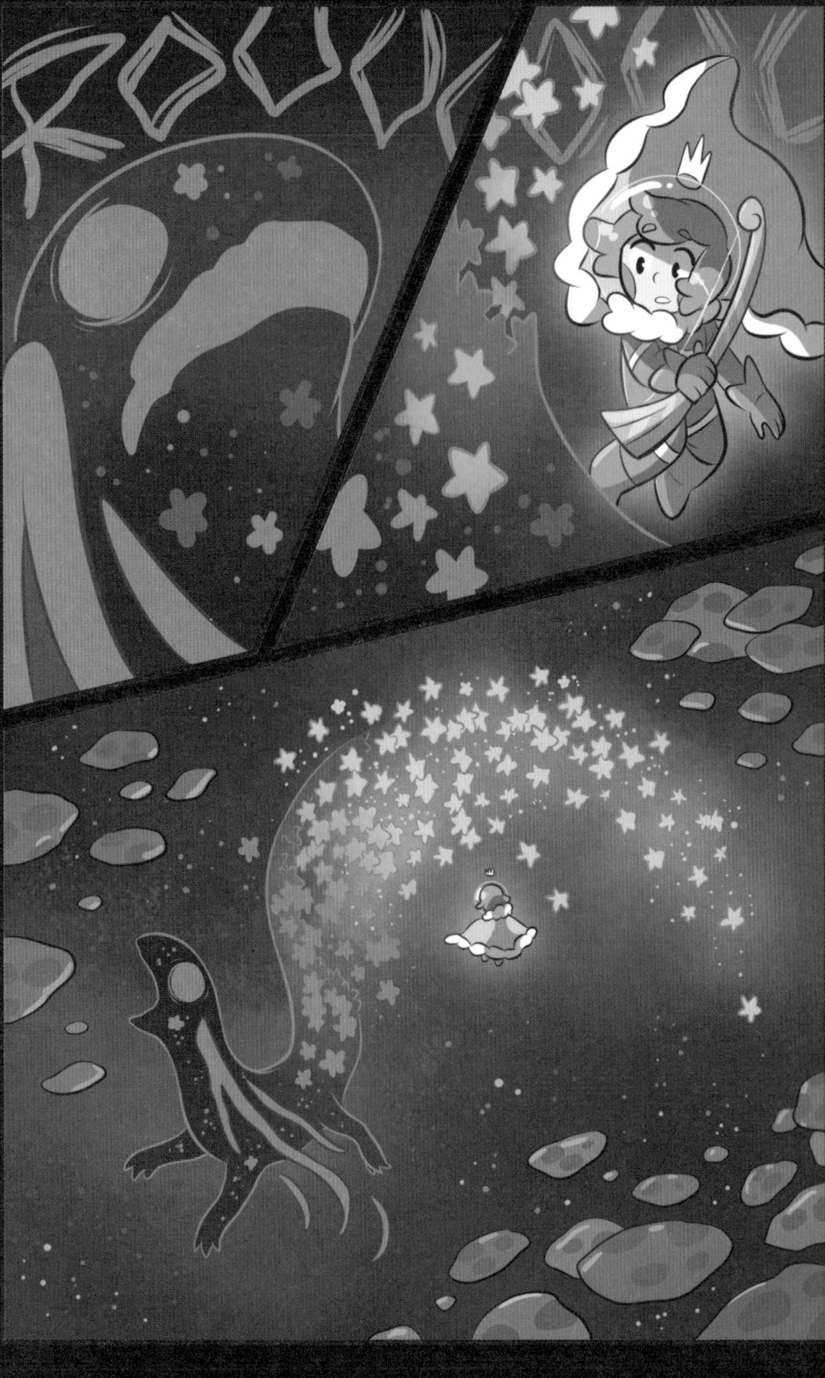
ROOOOOOO

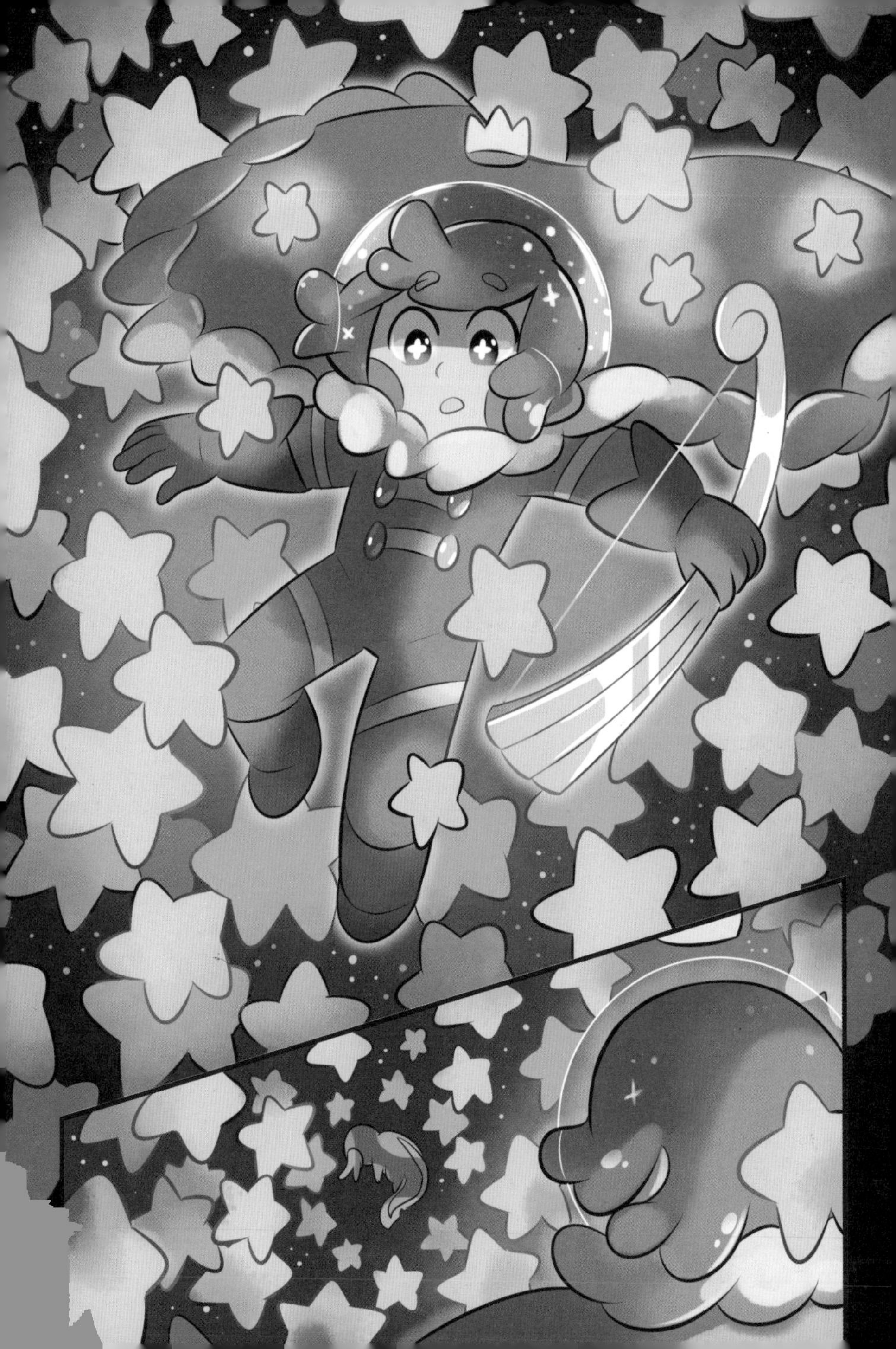

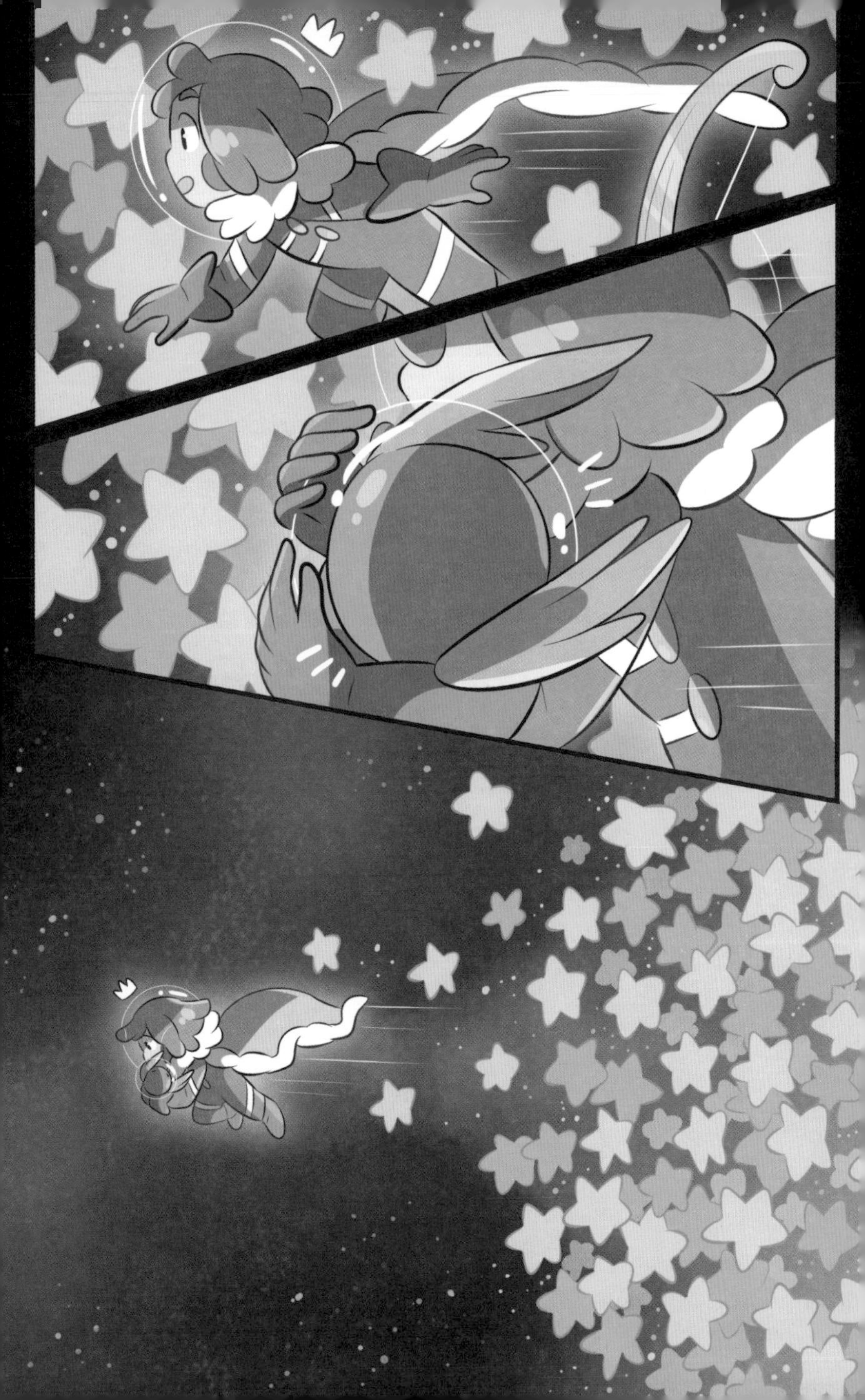

Tad . . .
. . . you were the first one to talk to me.
Since I was born, the animals have been afraid of me.
I buried myself in the mud just to avoid them.
I was afraid you'd hate me, too . . .
. . . if you found out I wasn't really the Star King.
But I only got you hurt.

Guess I should thank you, too.
Without your help, I would have never regained my place in the sky!
You're . . . Astrid, aren't you?
This entire time, **you** were the Star King?
I dunno about "king."
But if you're talking about the one who sent down the stars, yeah, that's me.

When Cygnus blasted me from the sky, I lost my crown AND my powers.
I was able to land safely in the marsh, thanks to my web.
?!
But her magic was so strong, I was turned into a normal spider.
All I knew was, I had to get that crown.
So I followed you two goofballs!
I'm so sorry, Astrid!
I had no idea . . .
It's fine!
I got to go on a grand adventure!
I never get to do anything like that here in space.
KEKE

The witch mentioned it earlier, but I'm actually a **galaxy weaver.**
We exist in every universe, weaving our webs and keeping everything in place.
Like the magic thread from the legends . . . !
I loved the animals of the marsh so much, I wanted to share my magic.
But after what I saw, I know now that the animals aren't ready for this power.
I've taken back the stars from the Star Knights.
You're the last of them, Tad . . .
and the only one I'll allow to remain.

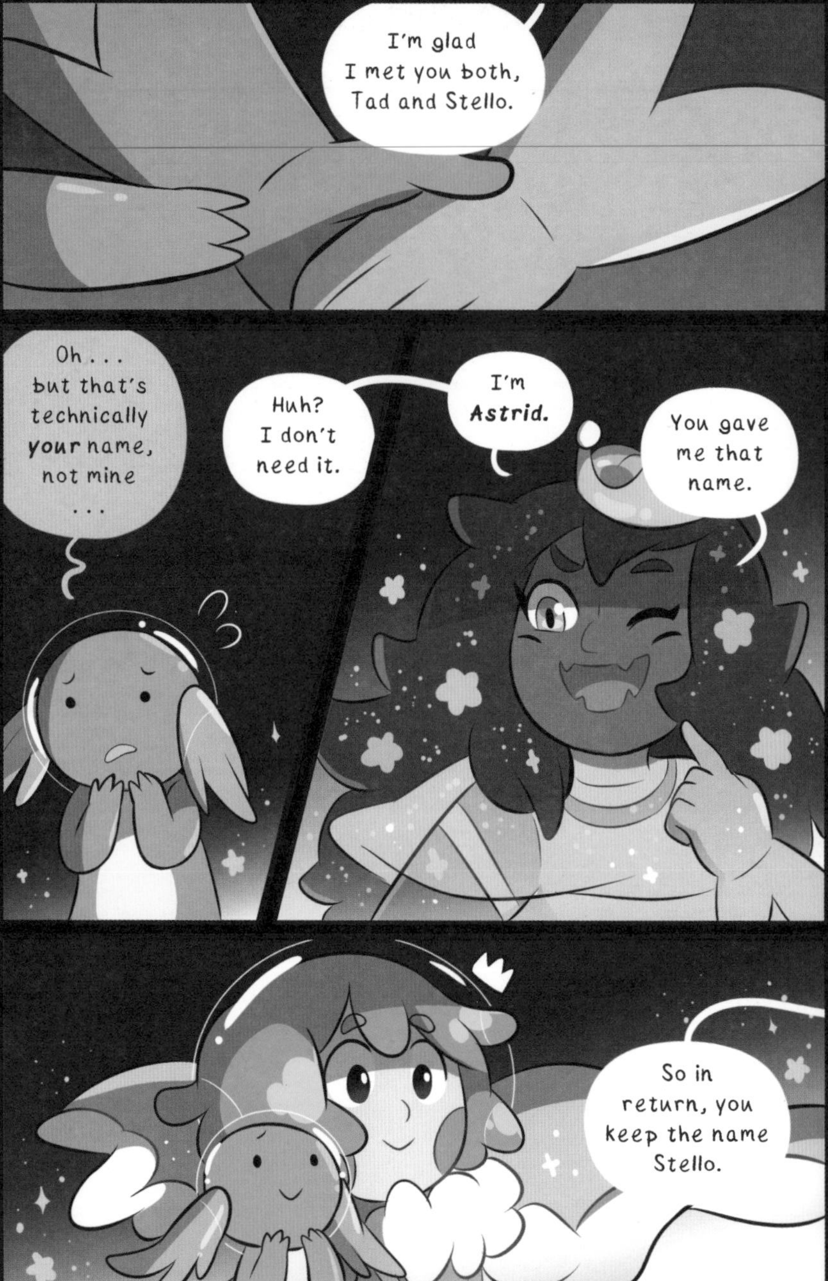
I'm glad I met you both, Tad and Stello.
Oh . . . but that's technically **your** name, not mine . . .
Huh? I don't need it.
I'm **Astrid.**
You gave me that name.
So in return, you keep the name Stello.

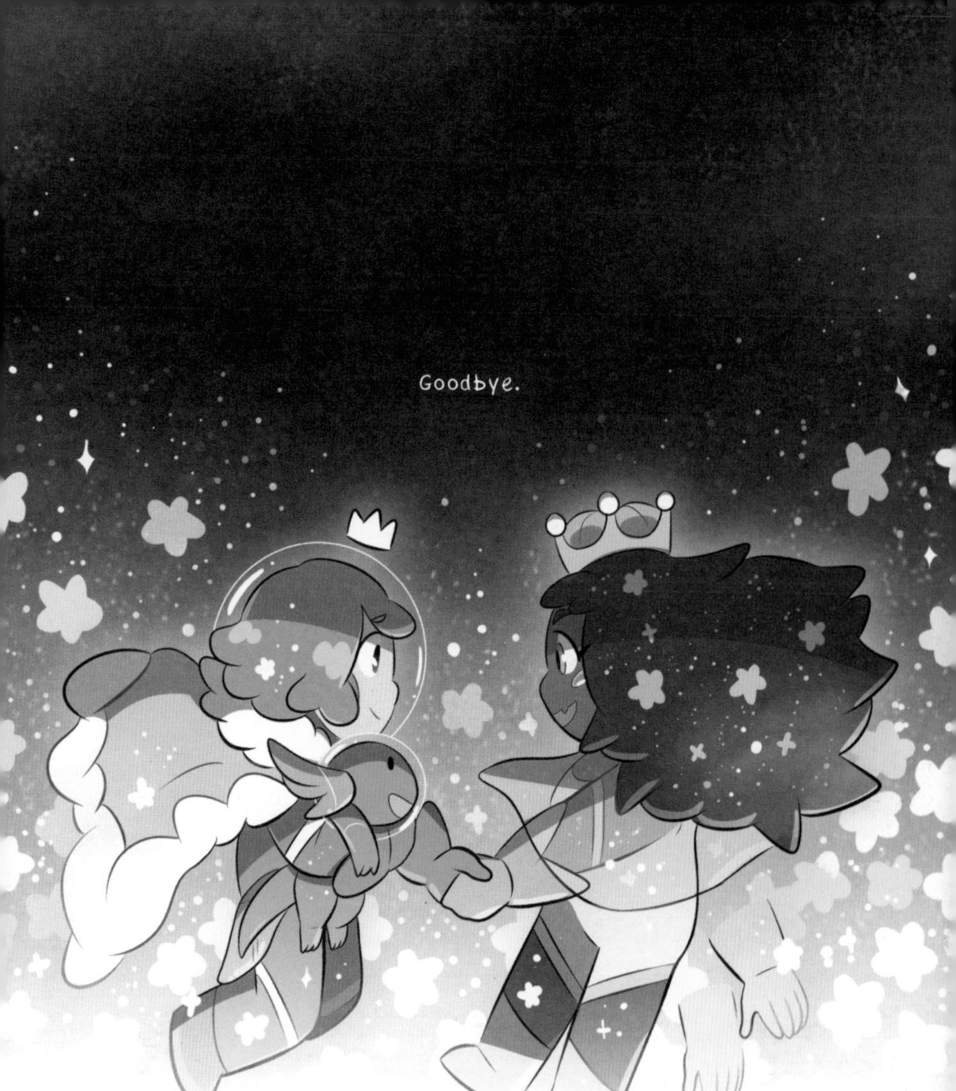
Goodbye.

For now.

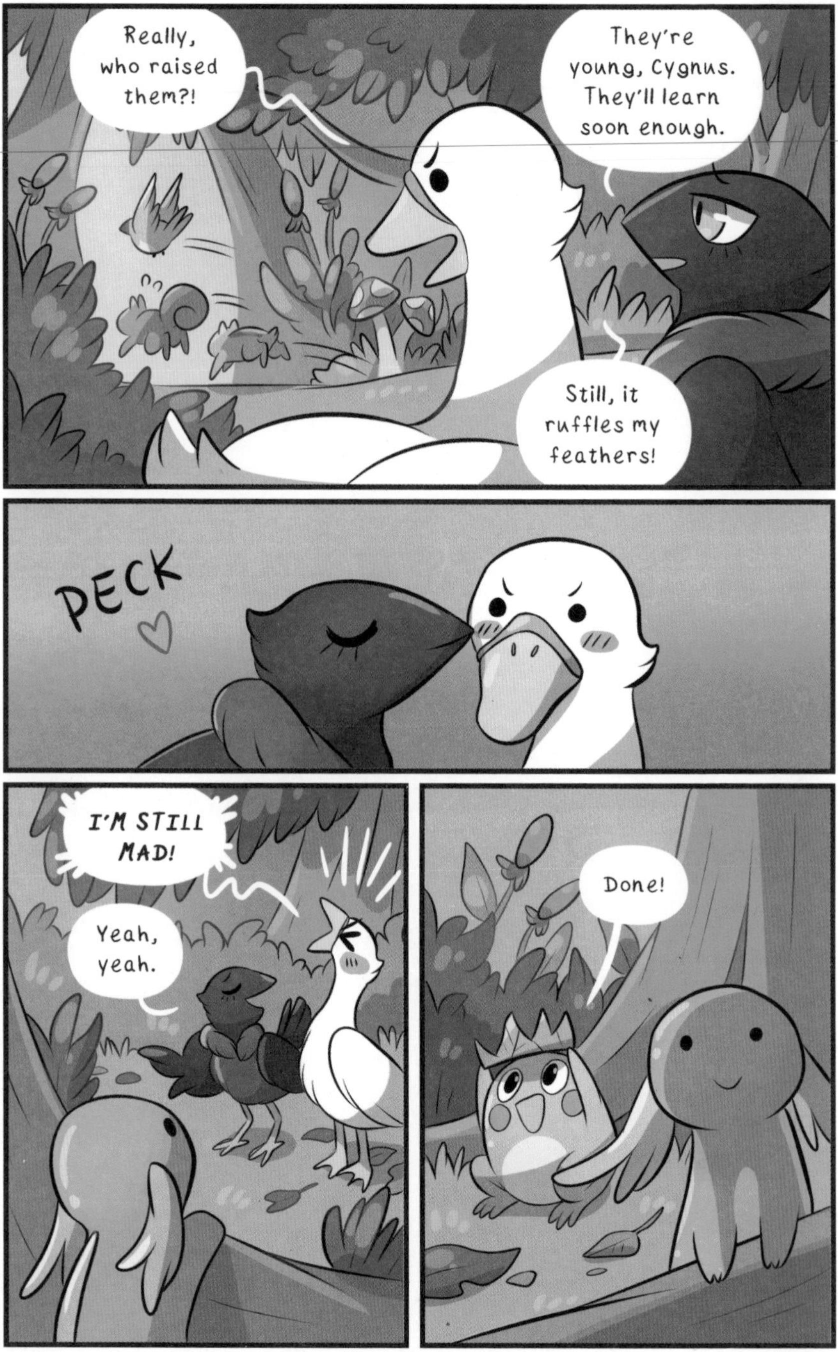
Really, who raised them?!
They're young, Cygnus. They'll learn soon enough.
Still, it ruffles my feathers!
PECK
I'M STILL MAD!
Yeah, yeah.
Done!

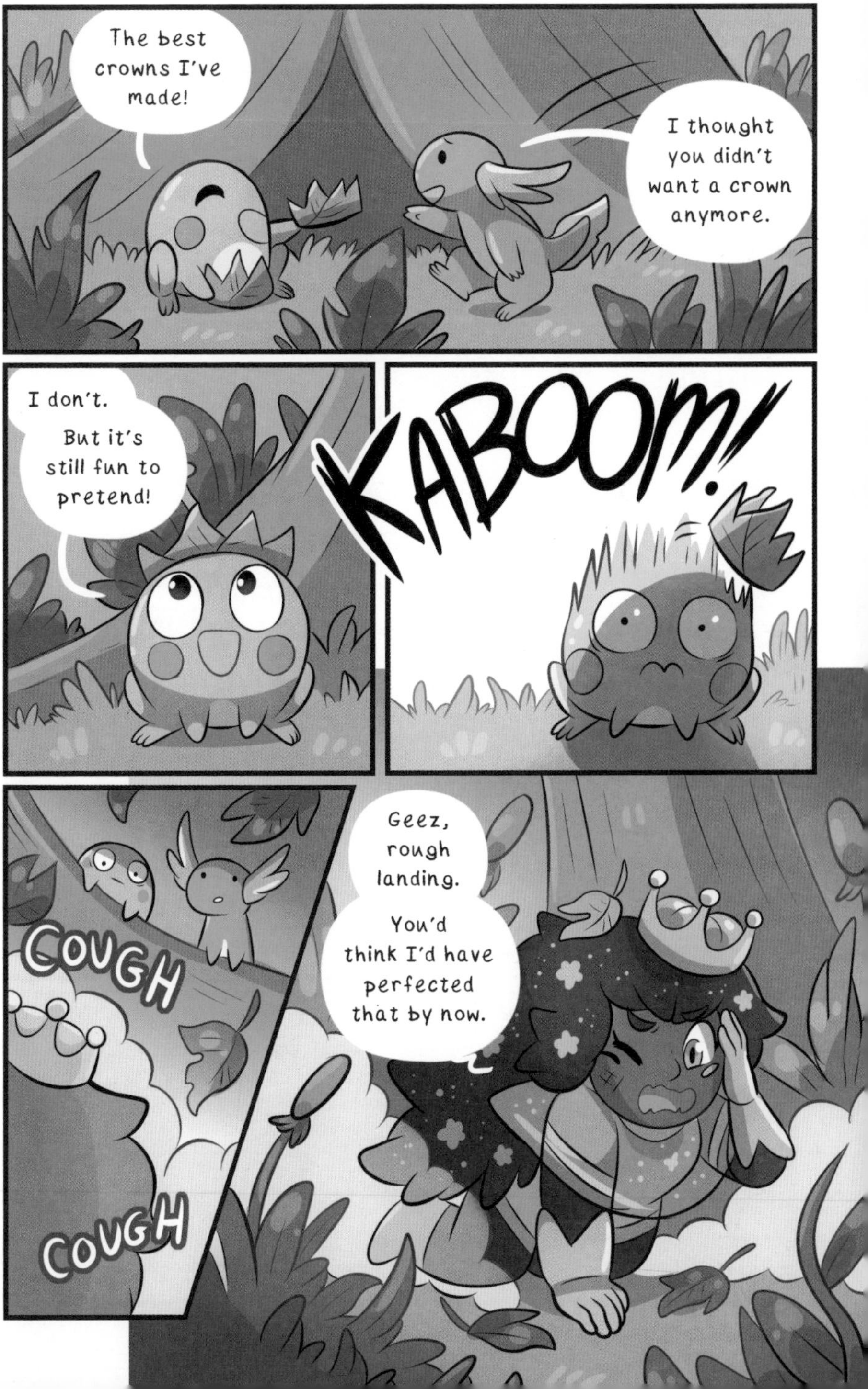
The best crowns I've made!
I thought you didn't want a crown anymore.
I don't.
But it's still fun to pretend!
KABOOM!
COUGH
COUGH
Geez, rough landing.
You'd think I'd have perfected that by now.

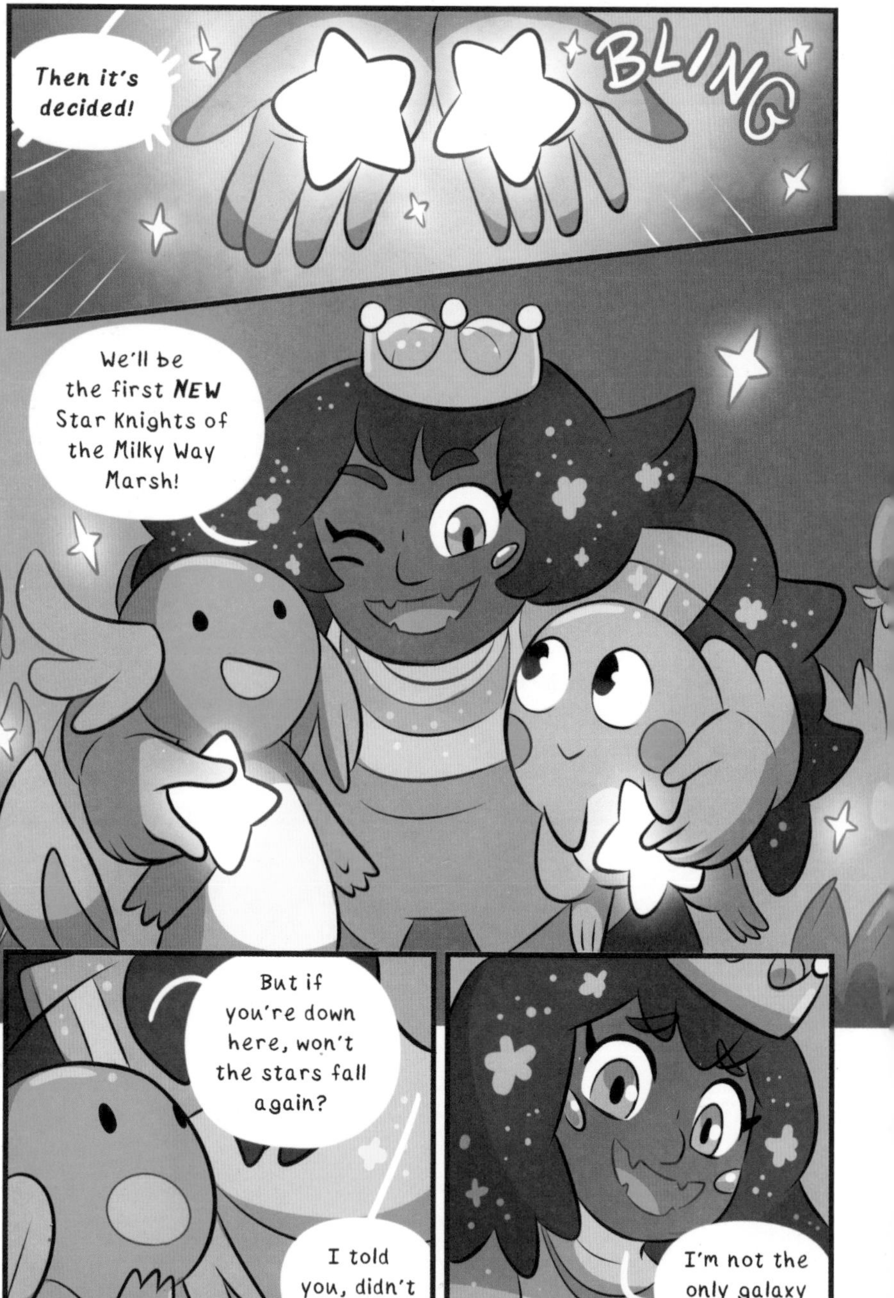
Then it's decided!
BLING
We'll be the first NEW Star Knights of the Milky Way Marsh!
But if you're down here, won't the stars fall again?
I told you, didn't I?
I'm not the only galaxy weaver.

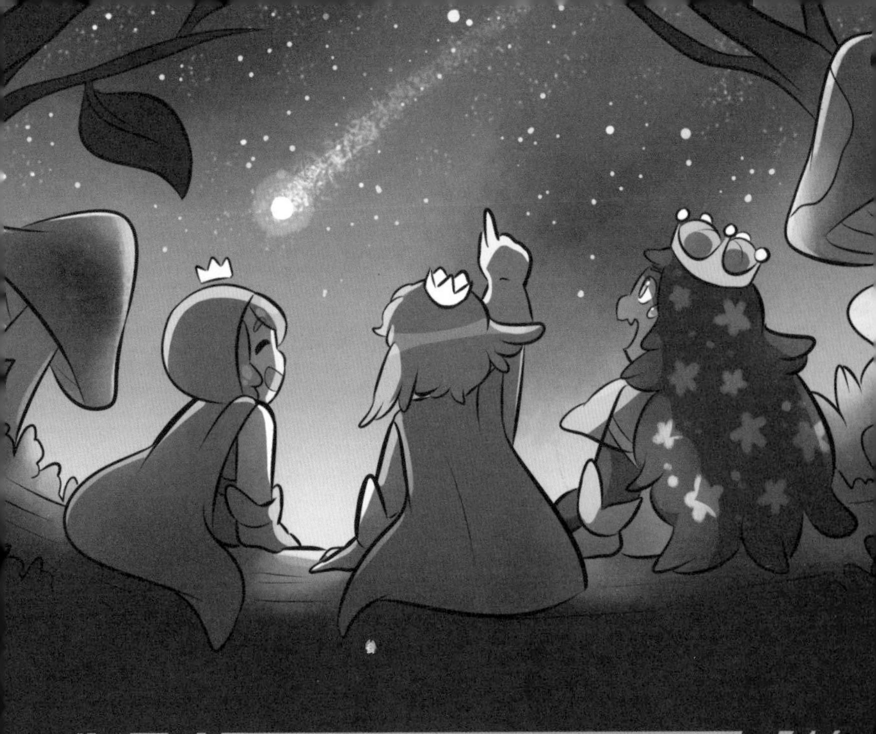

Acknowledgments

To everyone who has supported me on this journey—thank you! It has meant the world, and whether big or small, I could not have completed this journey without you.

To my friends Natalie, Alicea, Vyvy, Lea, Pat, Jenny, Abi, and Lena, for the many fun drawing sessions and games, and for providing company during an otherwise secluded time.

My mentors Blake, Shane, and Michele, for their guidance and encouragement over the years.

My amazing agent, Britt, and everyone on the Random House Graphic team for helping me create this story, as well as giving me the opportunity to tell it.

And of course, my family for their support, and my mom, who always believed in me, even when I could not.
Thank you so much.

Kay Davault is a comic artist from Nashville,
Tennessee, who enjoys drawing cute characters and
scary monsters and combining the two together.
Her first major work was the all-ages mystery
series Oddity Woods, which kickstarted her obsession
with drawing hundreds of pages of comics.

Star Knights is Kay's first published work.
She hopes you enjoyed Tad's story as much as
she enjoyed telling it.

@kaydavault

kaydavault.com

"Journey to Stars"

In 2017, I created a small comic about a frog prince's adventure to find the stars. Here's a look at the tiny story that eventually became the inspiration for *Star Knights*!

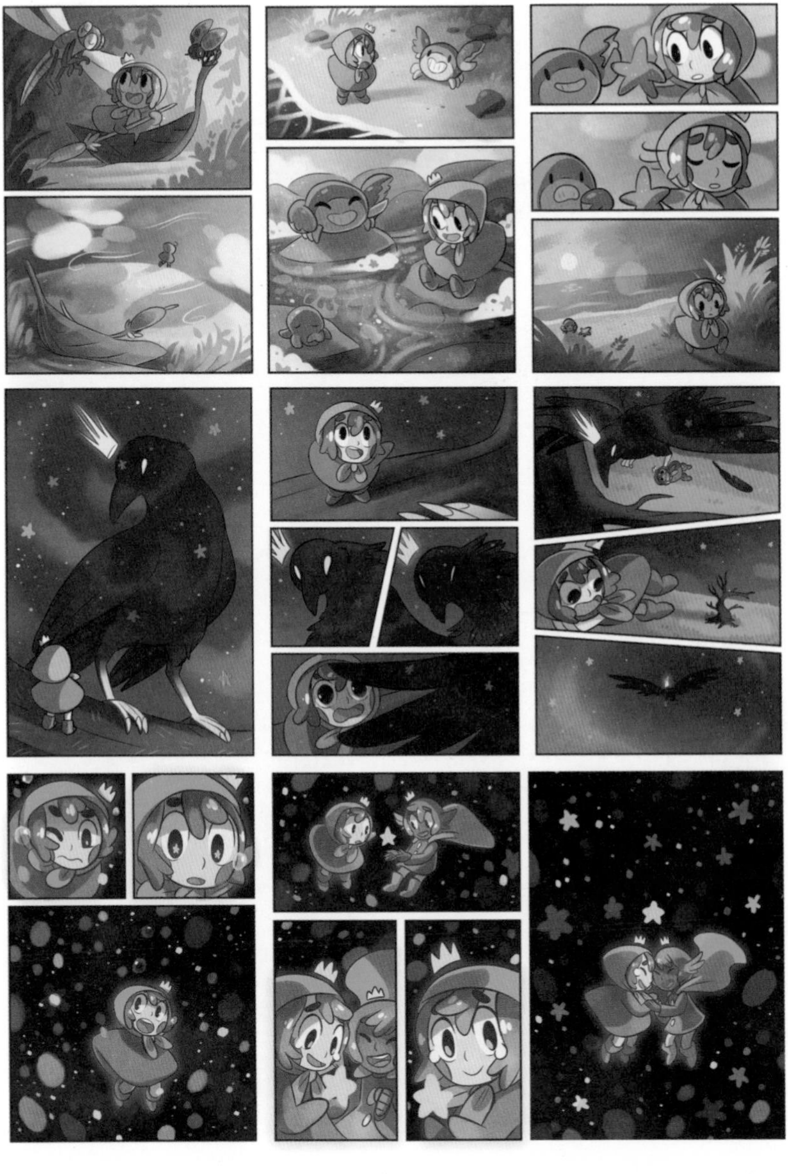

Concept Art

Tad

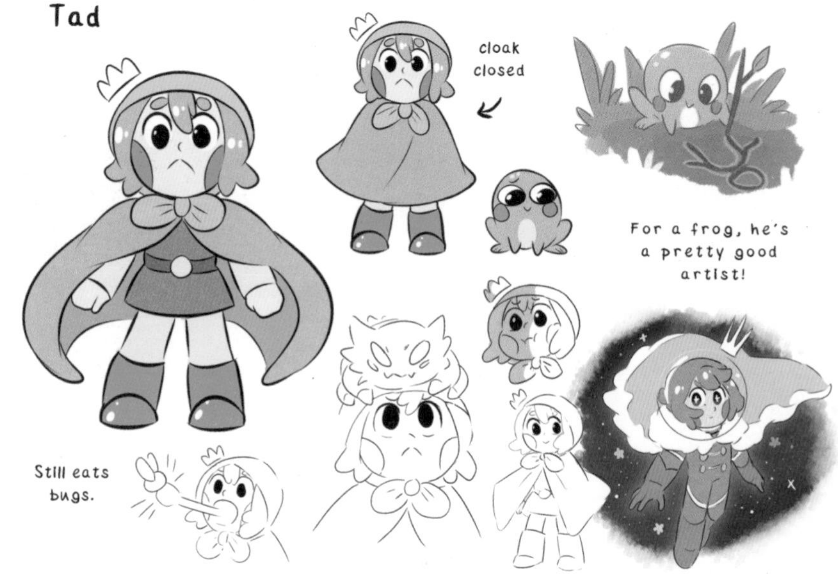
cloak
closed
For a frog, he's
a pretty good
artist!
Still eats
bugs.

Stello

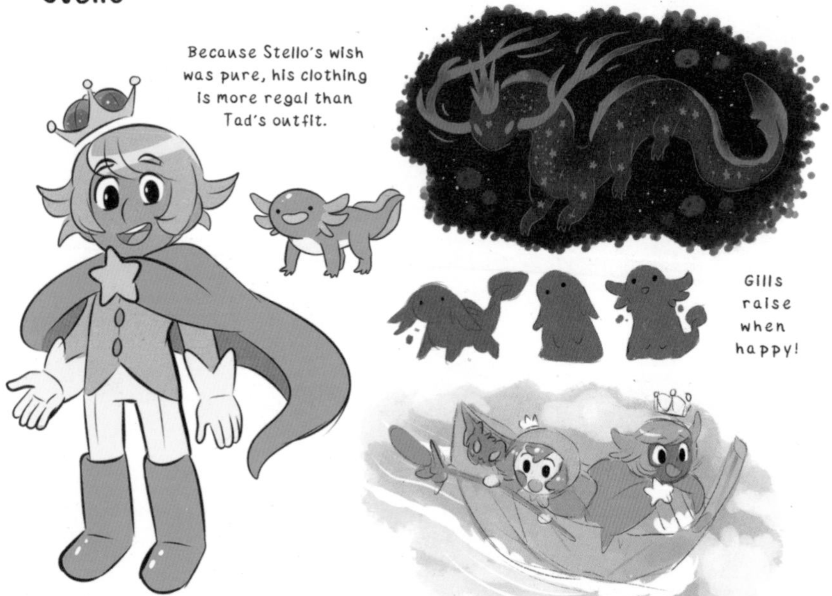
Because Stello's wish
was pure, his clothing
is more regal than
Tad's outfit.
Gills
raise
when
happy!

Astrid

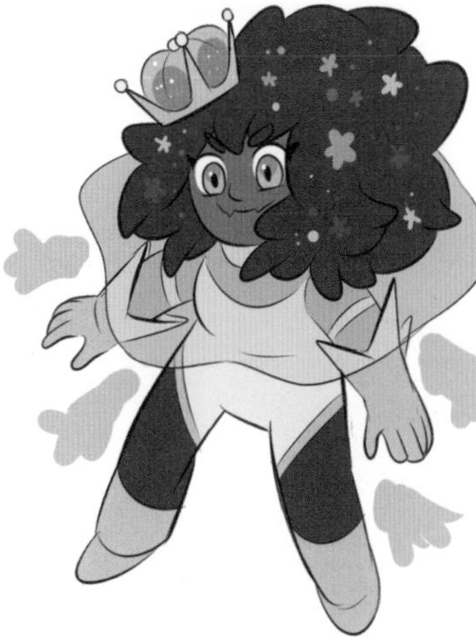

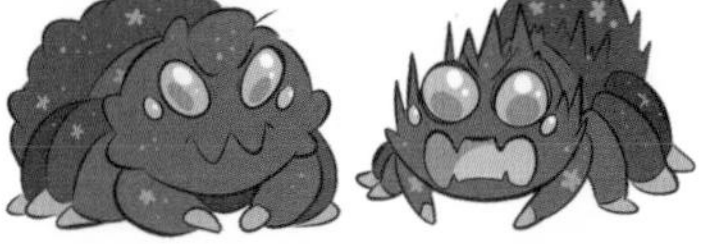

In her human form, she creates four extra arms with starlight.

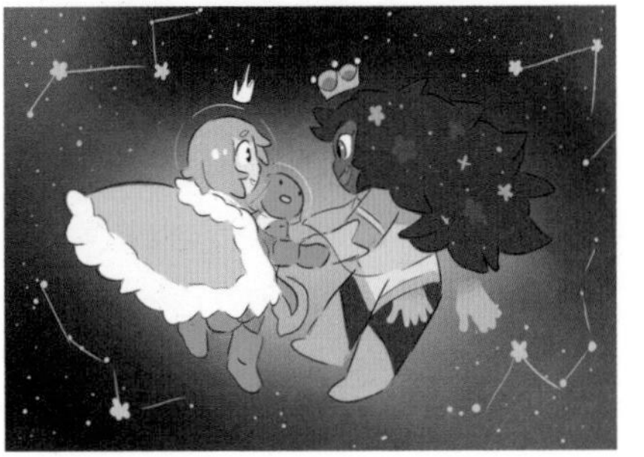

Star Knights

Their human designs are inspired by their animal forms, as well as their own idea of what they'd look like. All knights have special powers depending on their species!

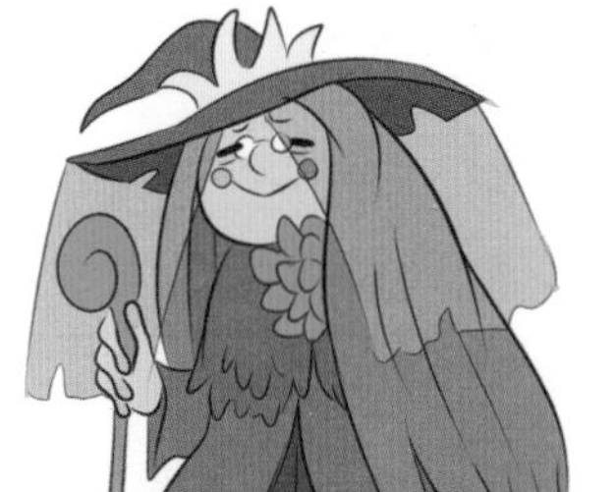

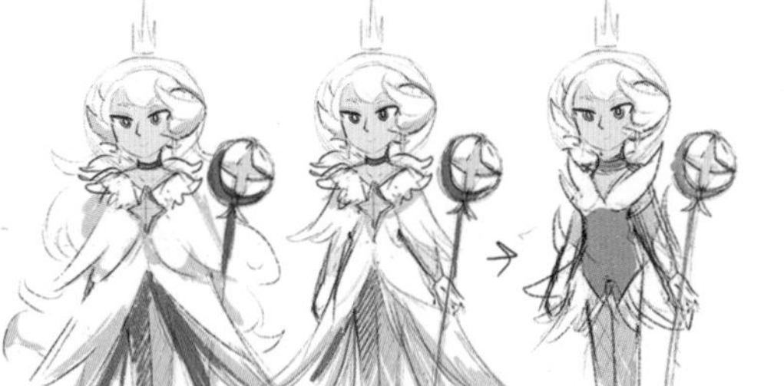

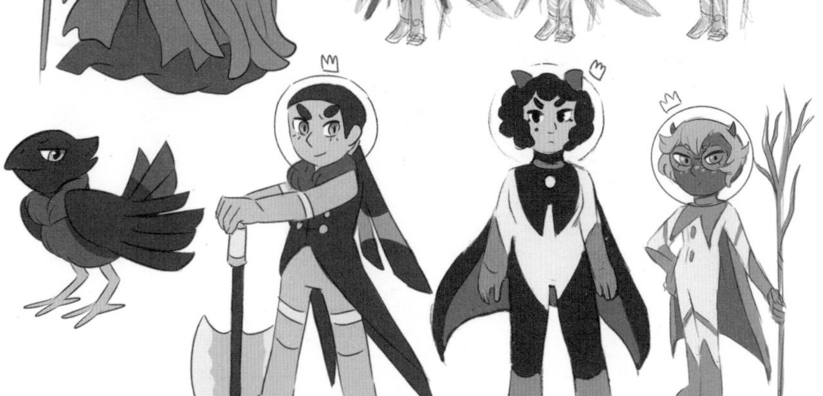

MAGIC AND ADVENTURE AWAIT

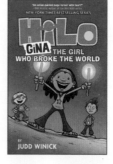